John Torrey Morse

The Life of Alexander Hamilton

Vol. 2

John Torrey Morse

The Life of Alexander Hamilton
Vol. 2

ISBN/EAN: 9783337415396

Printed in Europe, USA, Canada, Australia, Japan

Cover: Foto ©Raphael Reischuk / pixelio.de

More available books at **www.hansebooks.com**

THE LIFE

OF

ALEXANDER HAMILTON.

BY

JOHN T. MORSE, JR.

IN TWO VOLUMES.

VOL. II.

BOSTON:
LITTLE, BROWN, AND COMPANY.
1876.

CONTENTS OF VOLUME II.

LIFE OF

ALEXANDER HAMILTON.

CHAPTER I.

DISSENSIONS IN THE CABINET.

THE conductors of newspapers in the latter half of the eighteenth century were wont to make up for any lack of ability by the uncompromising vehemence with which they entered into partisan warfare. They poured abuse upon their political enemies and panegyrics upon their political friends, with the same reckless disregard of facts and contempt for proof. Ingenuity in the perversion of truth, inventiveness in the suggestion of evil motives, were the chief qualifications of an able editor, while to admit the possibility of any virtue in an opponent was a fatal weakness. Great magnificence of language was affected, and the grossest invectives were couched in language which would have highly gratified Dr. Johnson. A fine gift of moralizing was sedulously cultivated; a victim was destroyed in superb generalizations and in a series of high-flown criticisms upon human nature. Men would not now-a-days read such articles as fell in with the taste of that age.

But however inferior were the journals of that day to those of our own, it must be acknowledged that the former enjoyed one great advantage in the custom which prevailed for men of the highest distinction in public life to use them as vehicles for disseminating opinions among the people. Many instances of this occur at once to memory, notably the numerous papers constituting the "Federalist," which appeared at first as newspaper letters under the signature of "Publius." While John Adams was vice-president of the United States he engaged in enterprises of this kind, contributing a series of articles concerning French politics, known as the "Discourses on Davila." Indeed, so universal was the practice that Mr. Hildreth says that, " of all the men of the Revolution capable of producing a newspaper essay, Jefferson was, perhaps, the only one who never touched pen to paper for the political enlightenment of the contemporaneous public." His preference was for correspondence. He practised political letter-writing as an art, making it so efficient and manifesting in it so much skill as would have called forth the sincere admiration of Machiavelli. If one could give him the benefit of honorable motives, it would be necessary to praise his behavior in this respect; for anonymous political writing in the newspapers by prominent or responsible members of the government is a custom much to be deprecated. All that can be said is that the rules of that era permitted it; and when Vice-President Adams and Mr. Secretary Hamilton furnished anonymous columns to editor Fenno, they did only what they had ample precedent for doing, and what the faulty taste of the times permitted.

The " Gazette of the United States " was at this period the leading Federalist sheet. Especially was it devoted to the praises of Hamilton and all his measures, lauding the one as the greatest statesman, the others as the wisest policy, that the world had ever seen. For a time, being unprovoked by any hostile publication, personalities were few and not severe. But it was not to be supposed that the anti-federalists would long remain without an organ of their own. Politically it was necessary; as a commercial venture it might not improbably be remunerative. Accordingly on October 31, 1791, appeared the first number of the " National Gazette." Its *raison d'être* was the vilification of the secretary of the treasury, and the reprobation of all his schemes; and with such merciless vigor did it fulfil this its chief function, that from this time forth there was an end not only of all amenities, but even of all decency, in the newspaper war. The articles in the new sheet were often as clever as they were always scurrilous; and the champions of the galled sufferers returned the same kind of missiles which were hurled so effectively against them.

Though such a birth seemed a natural event enough, yet certain occurrences caused it to be supposed that the operations of nature had been materially accelerated by the kindly industry of a member of the cabinet. Only five days prior to the publication of the first number, Freneau, the editor, had received an appointment from Jefferson as translating clerk in the department of state. The salary was insignificant, to be sure, being only two hundred and fifty dollars per annum; but it was the sole position which the secretary of state had power to dispose of; for his patronage was vexatiously small. Investigation led to the discovery of certain other corroborative circumstances, so that Hamilton and the Federalists quickly became convinced that Jefferson had been mainly instrumental in establishing a newspaper intended to assail the administration of which he himself was a member. Ere long certain misrepresentations in the new sheet tempted Hamilton to take up his pen in reply; and in a communication sent to the rival "Gazette," over the signature of "An American," he plainly charged that the "National Gazette" was the organ of the secretary of state, and forcibly attacked the indelicacy of holding office in a government and using the patronage of that office to further systematic assaults upon that government.

Forthwith Freneau came out with an affidavit, to the effect that he had had no negotiations with Jefferson concerning the establishment of his paper; that Jefferson had never controlled or influenced him, and had never contributed a line to the paper. Hamilton replied, and a lively newspaper war ensued in which many writers volunteered to break a lance.

Washington's retirement at Mount Vernon was invaded by the newspapers containing these criminations and recriminations. Such an unhappy strife, breaking out almost actually in his cabinet, caused him much disquietude and sorrow. He addressed letters of expostulation to Hamilton and to Jefferson. The latter replied that, whether the appointment of Freneau had preceded or succeeded his first knowledge of that gentleman's intention to establish a newspaper, his memory, after the lapse of nearly a year, could not now inform him. He acknowledged that he had heard with pleasure of a publication which promised to administer an antidote to the aristocratical and monarchical doses lately given by the unknown writer of the "Discourses on Davila," and which also would probably reproduce, at his request, certain extracts from the "Leyden Gazette" concerning French politics. Such extracts he had furnished; but was innocent of any other contributions. Subscriptions he admitted to have solicited, from a charitable desire to aid his clerk, whom he thought to be a man of good parts. He protested "in the presence of Heaven" that he had made no effort to control the conduct or sentiments of the paper. The denial of complicity in the management of the paper was distinct, indeed was put with even too much strength of protestation. But the denial of being concerned in its establishment was not so plainly declared, and remained a mere matter of vague inference. But however ingeniously the debate was carried on, there has never been any substantial doubt that Jefferson was intimately connected with the anti-federal sheet. Such connections cannot always be proved clearly, or even described accurately; since that day we have learned to use the word "inspire," for the purpose of expressing the function fulfilled by the gentleman in concealment.

The letters of "An American" did not constitute the full share which Hamilton took in the newspaper controversy inaugurated by them. His blood was warmed by the giving and taking hard blows; he considered that having descended into the arena he was fairly committed to the strife, and not even at the solicitation of Washington could he promise to refrain under certain possible circumstances. Those circumstances unfortunately occurred, and he continued the contest as he had begun it. His assault was upon Jefferson, and so in his second communication he explicitly avowed, saying that his reproaches and accusations were aimed not at the editor, but at the secretary of state. He did not spare his adversary, nor overlook a vulnerable point. The charge of impropriety in the alleged connection with the opposition newspaper was succeeded by an accusation of much more heinous conduct. It was declared that when the prospect of our repaying our debt to France was very gloomy, Jefferson had advised that a good face should be put upon matters for the purpose of effecting a transfer of the indebtedness from that nation to certain individuals in Holland; the acknowledged reason being that it would be less injurious to the United States to be in default to private parties, though it should ruin them, than to fail to pay its dues to a powerful and friendly country. The baseness of such a step was dwelt upon with much animation. Of course the charge was replied to and denied. The language of Jefferson was said to have been misconstrued, misrepresented, garbled. At the close each side claimed to be victorious; but any one who will be at the pains to study the documents must admit that Jefferson can be acquitted only through receiving the benefit of as narrow and meagre a doubt as ever served the turn of a criminal with a tender-hearted and scrupulous jury.

Washington, it has been said, so soon as he became aware of the grievous condition of affairs which has been depicted, wrote to his two secretaries exhorting them to greater forbearance, and to "temporizing yieldings," and expressing his dread that by such dissensions the "fairest prospect of happiness and prosperity that ever was presented to man would be lost perhaps for ever." But not even the influence of Washington could bring together opponents separated by such hostility as had opened between Hamilton and Jefferson. A wide discordance in political opinion had established a breach which personal antipathy had of late opened to a greater extent.

If, however, the president's letter failed of its immediate purpose and in no degree assuaged the wrath of the warring secretaries, it at least was of service to the historian in drawing from them respectively very noteworthy and characteristic replies, both bearing date as it happened upon the same day, September 9, 1792. Hamilton's letter was short and frank. If there should be any prospect of healing or terminating existing differences he professed himself ready to embrace it, though considering himself to be the "deeply injured party." If Washington's praiseworthy endeavors to this end should prove unsuccessful, then Hamilton was of opinion that the period was not remote when the public good would require substitutes for the differing members of the administration. "The continuance of a division there must destroy the energy of government, which will be little enough with the strictest union. On my part there will be a most cheerful acquiescence in such a result." He refused to conceal that he had had some instrumentality of late in the retaliations which have fallen upon certain public characters, nor was he able at once to withdraw from the prosecution of them. To this course he had been compelled by reasons " public as well as personal, of the most cogent nature." From evidence in his possession he could not doubt that the " National Gazette " had been instituted by Jefferson for political purposes, and that one of its leading objects had been to render him and all the measures connected with his department as odious as possible. Nevertheless, except in communications to confidential friends, Hamilton denied that he had ever directly or indirectly retaliated or countenanced retaliation till very lately. So long as he had seen no danger to the government he had resolved to bear assaults upon himself in silence, wishing not to manifest to the world the existence of dissensions in the cabinet. But he had at last felt that a public discussion of certain matters was necessary. Pledging his honor to a faithful concurrence in any future plan which Washington might devise for re-uniting the members of the cabinet, Hamilton closed his reply.

This letter has been often mentioned and compared with the contemporaneous effusion from Jefferson with no small degree of pride upon the part of Hamilton's admirers. Certainly their satisfaction is based upon some substantial grounds. The moment of writing happened to fall in the midst of a time of much excitement. It was no small measure of indignation which had at last brought Hamilton to the point of assailing Jefferson in the public prints. Yet his correspondence shows no letter more fair and temperate in tone than this. He accused Mr. Jefferson of laboring to accomplish his political destruction, and of employing "unkind whispers and insinuations" to this end. This was a moderate description of the conduct of Jefferson. The president himself well knew that Jefferson had not hesitated to assail Hamilton's personal character as freely as his statesmanship, both in private correspondence and in private conversation. For upon the files of Washington's letters was one from Jefferson, written in the preceding winter and composed with even more than that gentleman's wonted art, in which the "corrupt squadron" of the treasury department was assailed, and the Federalists who were making the new government a mere "stepping stone" to monarchy were denounced. The writer had not mentioned Hamilton's name, but the mark was none the less certainly aimed at because the arrow was winged from a covert. Shortly afterward, in an interview, Jefferson had charged that the most mischievous consequences had ensued upon Hamilton's measures, which had been conducted to success through the corrupt connivance of an interested majority in Congress.

That until the initiation of the newspaper controversy Hamilton had refrained from retaliation may be believed, if not because he says so, yet at least because no evidence to the contrary exists. Perhaps his own assertion is none the less worthy of credit because it was not accompanied by any formal attestation of the Almighty or address to the "God who made me," by which impressive remarks both in his epistles and in his conversation Jefferson was wont to usher in any tale, particularly if it related to Hamilton, which he feared his readers or hearers might find too incredible if put forth solely upon his own mortal authority. The general statement that the measures of the opposite party seemed to him to endanger the government, which Hamilton had already openly made in print, and which at best was and purported to be nothing else than his individual opinion upon questions of policy and statesmanship, it was surely proper for Hamilton to express.

Such were the contents of Hamilton's letter. Jefferson himself, though repudiating its sentiments, could hardly have objected to its tone. Unfortunately a different criticism must be passed upon his epistle. It was a long, elaborate document which would have cost most writers and perhaps cost him, in spite of all his readiness in such matters, no small amount of labor and time in the preparation. Whatever may be thought of the political views which it embodies, even a Jeffersonian disciple could not but regret that the animosity of the secretary of state, smarting from the fresh wounds inflicted by his adversary, should have led him into such a composition.

He had entered upon the duties of his present position in the cabinet, he said, with the determination to "intermeddle not at all with the legislative and as little as possible with the co-departments." His earliest grievance was that he had been "*duped*" by the secretary of the treasury into neglecting the former of these good resolutions, and had so been "made a tool for forwarding his schemes." That he had ever "intrigued among members of the legislature to defeat the plans of the secretary of the treasury" Jefferson asserted to be "contrary to truth." But that he had "utterly, in his private conversations, disapproved of the system" of that secretary, and that "this was not merely a speculative difference," he acknowledged. Hamilton's policy "flowed from principles adverse to liberty, and was calculated to undermine and demolish the republic, by creating an influence of his department over the members of the legislature." This nefarious influence Jefferson had seen "actually produced, and its first fruits" were the establishment of the great outlines of Hamilton's project by the interested votes of those who had "swallowed his bait" and were "laying themselves out to profit by his plans;" men who did not vote as "representatives of the people," but simply "to enrich themselves."

Shocking as those "who wished for virtuous government" must consider what had been "actually done," there was worse behind. The report on manufactures recommended nothing else than an arrogation of all governmental powers to the central government. The object of all "these plans taken together is to draw all the powers of government into the hands of the general legislature; to establish means for corrupting a sufficient corps in that legislature to divide the honest votes and preponderate by their own the scale which suited; and to have that corps under the command of the secretary of the treasury for the purpose of subverting, step by step, the principles of the Constitution which he has so often declared a thing of nothing which must be changed."

Jefferson and Hamilton each doubtless honestly thought that the policy of the other, if it should prevail, would destroy the government established by the Constitution. Each was free, nay, bound, to say so and to give his reasons. But it was hardly fair in Jefferson to write a private letter to the president charging his opponent with having already indulged in actual corruption of members of the legislature, with intending to extend and systematize this process, and with entertaining the deliberate design of subverting the Constitution. This was no charge of error in judgment or mistaken statesmanship, but of deeply conceived treason and intentional villany.

Jefferson then complained that Hamilton had interfered with the administration of the department of state, to the detriment of certain plans there maturing for the good of the country. The " style, manner, and venom " of " An American " assured him that the writer must be Hamilton, and he reprobated the charges of that writer. Especially he defended his original position towards the Constitution. He had objected to it because he wished to see a bill of rights : Hamilton had objected to it, because he wanted a king and a house of lords.

A statement was made, which must be regarded as amusing in view of the obstinacy with which not far from this time Jefferson's followers in the legislature opposed Hamilton's various schemes for the redemption of the public debt. For his own part, the writer said, he " would wish it paid to-morrow ; " but Hamilton " wishes it never to be paid, but always to remain a thing wherewith to corrupt and manage the legislature."

Then came the protests in the presence of Heaven already mentioned, concerning Freneau and the " National Gazette."

In closing, Jefferson professed his intention to retire at the end of the present presidential term, to which period he looked forward "with the longing of a wave-worn mariner." This touch of pathos in his own behalf was followed by a slur flung against Hamilton, which was certainly an undignified and unnecessary outburst and, whatever may be said of the rest of his letter, altogether indefensible. Conscious as he was of his own "title to esteem from his integrity and an enthusiastic devotion to the rights and liberty of his countrymen, he would not suffer his retirement to be clouded by the slanders of a man whose history, from the moment at which history can stoop to notice him, is a tissue of machinations against the liberty of the country which has not only received and given him bread, but heaped its honors on his head." Verily as the two men stand side by side for comparison in these two letters, apart from all questions of statesmanship, to be judged as to their manliness, candor, and spirit, Hamilton has nothing to fear in the decision.

The endeavors made by Jefferson in this letter and previously to excite in Washington's mind alarm and distrust towards Hamilton were sedulously followed up by him. Nor does he appear to have seen any impropriety in his conduct, for he records it for publication in his "Ana." For example, he records a conversation which occurred a few weeks later betwixt himself and the president, in which he asserted, contrary to Washington's expressed opinion, that there was a numerous sect having monarchy in contemplation, and that the secretary of the treasury was one of these; that he had often heard the secretary say that the

Constitution was a " shilly-shally thing, of mere milk and water, which could not last and was only good as a step to something better." Divine Providence was not vouched in to obtain credence for this assertion. Probably it was not thought to be worth while, for the gross improbability that Hamilton, if he entertained such sentiments, would be reckless enough to utter them in such language, especially in the presence of Jefferson, and that too not once alone but repeatedly, somewhat surpasses that measure of credulity which even sacred attestations can reach in the minds of men. Yet a little earlier in this same veracious post-mortuary chronicle we find that Hamilton had spoken on this subject with Jefferson, in terms more " lengthy " and " formal " than are " usual for a private conversation," and perhaps with the purpose of " qualifying some less guarded expressions which had been dropped on former occasions." In this interview Hamilton is related to have expressed a private opinion that it might " probably be found expedient to go into the British form. However," he said, " since we have undertaken the experiment, I am for giving it a fair course, whatever my expectations may be. The success, indeed, so far is greater than I had expected, and therefore at present success seems more possible than it has done heretofore ; and there are still other and further stages of improvement, which, if the present does not succeed, may be tried and ought to be tried before we give up the republican form altogether ; for that mind must be truly depraved which would not prefer the equality of political rights, which is the foundation of pure republicanism, if it can be obtained consistently with order."

It may be said that these contradictory reports simply leave Hamilton's true opinion in doubt, and it may be suggested that this "formal" conversation was intended to throw dust in Jefferson's eyes. Admitting the possibility of such an explanation, two questions will remain to be answered. First, if Hamilton had *previously* described, and frequently too, the Constitution as a shilly-shally thing, of milk and water, would Jefferson, cherishing enmity as he did towards Hamilton, have contented himself with simply intimating that Hamilton had previously used "less guarded expressions"? This is possible of course, but it is certainly unlikely. Secondly, after Hamilton had been at the pains to qualify "less guarded expressions," and after the breach betwixt himself and Jefferson had been opened much more widely, would he have used such language often in the presence of his arch-enemy? This it must be acknowledged is not reasonably possible. It is not possible to prove affirmatively that Hamilton never did say what Jefferson pretended to repeat to Washington; but it must be admitted that it is a tale, which, if true, is even more strange than true.

The other grand charge against Hamilton — that of corrupt practices — was also reiterated by Jefferson in the ear of Washington. The president said that it was impossible to prevent individuals personally interested in public measures from gaining admittance to the legislature, unless particular descriptions of men, such as fund-holders, were to be excluded from all office. "I told him," says Jefferson, "there was great difference between the little accidental schemes of self-interest, which would take place in every body of men and influence their votes, and a regular system for forming a corps of interested persons who should be steadily at the orders of the treasury." Peculiar indeed was Jefferson's opinion of Hamilton, for he thought him at once an upright and a base man, a respecter of integrity and a systematic corruptionist! He was, says Jefferson, a man " of acute understanding, disinterested, honest, and honorable in all private transactions, amiable in society, and duly valuing virtue in private life; yet so bewitched and perverted by the British example as to be under thorough conviction that corruption was essential to the government of a nation." This sentence was written long after Hamilton's death, when, as the writer remarked, " the passions of the time " had " passed away and the reasons of the transactions act alone upon the judgment." Yet not a single act of corruption had been brought home to Hamilton, either in the heats of party controversy during his life, nor by subsequent historical research or reminiscence, which often brings to light so much truth that is kept carefully hidden till the grave has closed over the party most interested. Nay, more than this, not a *specific* charge had been brought, nothing more than the vague general hue-and-cry such as is repeated in this very sentence from the Jeffersoniana.

The occurrences which have been narrated, and the condition of affairs superinduced by them, furnished a needless proof of the truth of a great political axiom. It had been well understood in England long before the birth of the United States, that in a country governed in an important measure by a legislative body, elected by a people divided into two great and opposing political parties, it was impossible to form a cabinet by the process of amalgamation. One or other of the two great discordant bodies must for the time being prevail in the councils of the State, and the one which does prevail is entitled to exert and will exert control over the measures of administration. To seek to represent the minority in the *administration* is a problem as yet insoluble.

This vain effort was made by Washington, and in time it met its predestined end in utter failure. The experiment has never been renewed in this country, and is never likely to be, at least when any important questions of policy divide the people. But the attempt was highly honorable to Washington, and the exceptional circumstances justified it. At the inauguration of the government no parties had been organized ; it was matter of speculation and prediction only how soon such separations would take place and upon what questions. It was uncertain also upon which side of the dividing line, when it should be drawn, individuals would be found. Jefferson and Hamilton were not professed political opponents when the appointment of the former to the secretaryship of state brought them together in the first cabinet. It cannot therefore be fairly said that the formation of the cabinet was originally made with the purpose of uniting the prominent men of opposite political parties. The original design of Washington was to bring together the most distinguished men who could be expected to support the new Constitution with any certain friendship and faithfulness. It was hoped that each would influence a large circle of followers, and that unanimity might be maintained for an indefinite period. Upon this it was supposed that the success of the great experiment might depend. There must be a combination of all who wished to see the government succeed; they must reconcile or ignore discrepancies of opinion, and present an harmonious front to the people. Thus alone Washington hoped to be able to make the machine of government run so smoothly that its popularity would become assured. The theory was not wanting in wisdom; under the peculiar circumstances of the time it actually worked well for two years or more. But the mistake began with the effort to perpetuate the existence of this composite cabinet after party lines had been clearly drawn, party feelings strongly roused, party doctrines definitely announced; after dissensions in the administration had become evident to the people, and feuds between the two principal secretaries had reached the point where reconciliation could no longer be hoped for. It was preposterous to strive to keep the heads of two bitterly hostile factions as efficient coadjutors in the administration. So soon as Hamilton and Jefferson assumed these characters respectively, it was time, as the former suggested and the latter saw, that one or other of them should be superseded.

The nation suffered no grave detriment from this improper and abnormal condition of things so long as it continued to exist. The great influence of Washington warded off the grave mischiefs which under any less revered chieftain would have been likely to befall. Nor can he be blamed for seeking to avert to the last moment the breaking up of an able cabinet, powerful with the people, and with the individual members of which he was on kindly terms. But the result for Hamilton and Jefferson was much to be deplored. It put them in an entirely false position towards each other. It has been well said that if they had never been colleagues in a cabinet, but from the outset had been the avowed leaders of the opposing parties in the State, they might have preserved very different feelings and pursued a very different course of conduct towards each other. They were very unfortunately compelled to preserve an external aspect of concord, even to pretend and actually try to coöperate with each other, long after each had arrived at the settled conviction that the policy of the other must prove in its success destructive of the commonwealth. It was a grave evil that such a relationship should ever have come about; it was a gross blunder to seek to maintain it for so much as a day after it had become established. This ill-starred persistence it was which drove Hamilton to assail his co-secretary under a nominal disguise in the public newspapers, and led Jefferson to disseminate calumnies against his adversary in the privacy of conversation and of correspondence. Neither could appear to advantage in so forced and unnatural a position. The dignity and reputation of both must be admitted to have suffered some derogation in such a contest; and if Jefferson must bear vastly the weightier share of condemnation, it is not agreeable to think that a portion also must be laid upon his adversary. Even so qualified an admission may vex many of the admirers of Hamilton, yet it was hardly a possibility for him to escape quite scathless from a conflict of so unhappy a nature.

CHAPTER II.

THE SECRETARY'S VINDICATION.

On February 7, 1792, Hamilton sent in to the House of Representatives, in response to an order, a report concerning the subscriptions to the funded debt. The time limited by the act for subscribing for the new loan had elapsed, and the secretary fortunately had very gratifying results to narrate in justification of his scheme. The subscription on account of the national portion of the domestic debt had amounted to between thirty-one and thirty-two million dollars, and of this sum upwards of eleven hundred thousand dollars stood to the credit of the trustees of the sinking-fund in consequence of purchases of the public debt made under their direction. The unsubscribed residue amounted to $10,616,604.65. Two large items made up nearly the whole of this sum. The one consisted of $6,795,815.26, in the registered debt, principal and interest. This was chiefly owned by the citizens of foreign countries, who not unnaturally had been somewhat tardy in getting their subscriptions across the Atlantic. But extensive orders received from these distant creditors since the expiration of the limited period gave ample proof of their desire to adopt the alternative held out to them. Wherefore Hamilton recommended that the opportunity for subscription should be renewed, and the term extended until the last day of September of the current year.

The other large item of unsubscribed indebtedness consisted of outstanding or floating evidences of debt, the amount of which the secretary estimated at $3,697,466.14. Many holders of this species of debt had exchanged their old claims for the certificates of the new funded loan; but some had refrained from doing so, alleging dissatisfaction with the provisions made in their behalf. Hamilton did not conceal his opinion that the objections taken by these persons were colorable if not factious; the larger proportion had seen the wisdom of subscribing, and he thought the rest would have their eyes opened in good time. Yet there was an element of reasonableness in the criticisms of the malcontents; there was a certain aspect as of a feeble degree of compulsion exercised towards them, and Hamilton had firmly resolved and plainly announced in the outset that the consent of the creditors "ought to be voluntary in fact as well as in name." He now proposed therefore to deal tenderly with these discomforted ones, making a slight modification of his former plan in order to obviate their objections, and extending until the close of September the time in which they also might come in with their delayed subscriptions.

The total of subscriptions in the debt of the respective States had fallen short of the total of the sums assumed for them respectively by nearly $4,500,000. A strong desire had been expressed, in two instances even by acts of the State legislatures, for a renewal of the opportunity, and the secretary thought that this would be wisely granted. In this connection he renewed his original proposition for a general assumption. At present some of the States still had an unassumed balance, so that the plan so imperfectly carried into execution was producing only a portion of its promised benefits, and was not securing fundamental justice. The additional sum necessary to be assumed was less than $4,000,000. It was no great additional burden, and its prompt assumption would symmetrically complete an arrangement which had been very illogically divided, and would secure the full operation of all the beneficial influences embodied in the plan.

The indebtedness of the United States to foreign officers who had served in our army during the Revolutionary war had been allowed to lapse into a condition not very creditable to either the honesty or the gratitude of the country. In accordance with a resolution of the Congress of the Confederation, the interest periodically falling due to these gentlemen had been made payable "at the house of Monsieur le Grand, in Paris." This excellent resolution had unfortunately been acted upon only for a very short time, and since December 31, 1788, Monsieur le Grand had had no funds of the United States wherewith to honor the maturing instalments. Such arrears were felt to be singularly disgraceful, and the secretary was urgent that these creditors at least should be at once paid off in full.

Finally the secretary closed with the suggestion that a "systematic plan should be begun for the creation and establishment of a sinking-fund." He referred to certain measures of Congress which indicated their intention "as early and as fast as possible to provide for the extinguishment of the existing debt." Already the nucleus of a sinking-fund had been formed by the accumulation in the treasury of the interest on the certificates of debt which had been hitherto purchased on behalf of the United States; further purchases would continue to be made in the future and would steadily increase this amount. It might also be expected to be augmented from other sources; notably from a saving by the operations pending with regard to the foreign debt, and in a still greater degree from the sales of western lands. He suggested therefore that all interest on the purchased debt should hereafter be appropriated and set apart, "in the most firm and inviolable manner, as a fund for sinking the public debt by purchase or payment." So thoroughly in earnest was he in this matter, so anxious to cut off any possibility of a subsequent tampering with this fund or misdirection of its proceeds in any moment of economy or exigency, that he even proposed that it would "deserve the consideration of the legislature whether this fund ought not to be so vested as to acquire the nature and quality of a *proprietary trust*, incapable of being diverted without a violation of the principles and sanctions of *property*." This was indeed clinching the nail! But Hamilton heartily intended all that he advised in this matter, and was resolved to escape the possibility of candid misconstruction or honest doubt. There were reasons why he felt obliged to express himself so that only the disingenuous and malicious could misrepresent him in this regard.

When the report came before Congress, the portions of it which concerned the extension of time for subscription, the modification of terms for certain aggrieved holders, and the payment in full of the dues to foreign officers were very favorably received. But the proposition for the assumption of the balances of the State debts aroused a vehement opposition. Giles, a voluble and abusive declaimer, took the occasion to deliver a very vehement tirade, wherein Hamilton and pretty much all that Hamilton had done were subjected to noisy and uncompromising if not convincing censure. Such an assault might have been withstood, not only with equanimity but success. Unfortunately, however, a more formidable hostility was encountered from Madison, who, having the interests of Virginia in his mind, firmly refused to be reconciled to the measure unless it could be saddled with a preposterous rider, assuming the amount of all State debts discharged by any of the States since the peace. In the division the opposition prevailed.

On March 17, 1792, Hamilton sent in another report to the House concerning certain additional supplies required to meet the costs of St. Clair's disastrous and expensive Indian campaign. He suggested three schemes from which Congress might make their choice: first, the sale of the government's shares in the Bank of the United States; second, a new funded loan; third, taxation. He himself was decidedly in favor of the last of these expedients, and he sketched an amended tariff which would satisfy the purpose. Some items in this fortunately pleased the southern members. For example, a duty upon hemp and cordage, though objected to by the navigating interest, highly gratified Madison because it brought one branch even of agriculture within the fostering reach of protection. The retention of a duty of three cents per pound upon cotton also was agreeable to the planters ; and by such conciliation Hamilton secured the passage of his measure. Indeed, he was by no means inclined to be incredulous concerning the probable value of the cotton culture. Long ago he had maintained its value at a time when his fanciful rival, Jefferson, was devoting himself with much assiduity to building up a great silkworm industry in Virginia.

The manner in which in these two reports Hamilton had not only done his best to prevent the increase of the national debt, but had suggested and urged schemes for its prompt extinguishment, very clearly showed the groundlessness of certain virulent attacks which had been made upon him. He had been loudly and persistently accused of having constructed the whole funding scheme for the sake of perpetuating the debt, and keeping it in existence as a very powerful " hoop to the barrel." Under color of a mere financial arrangement he was said to have brought in a great measure of domestic statesmanship. Men said that he was resolved that the debt should for ever remain to secure the hearty support of the capitalists and to make large revenues necessary, which in turn would bring power and influence to the central government. If these accusations had been made in good faith, the recommendations contained in these two successive reports must have utterly dissipated the notion in the minds of all candid men.

Had Hamilton contented himself with vague generalizations he might have been suspected of disingenuousness, and of a design to hoodwink the people with fair pretences while he led them along the dangerous road towards his own ends. But here he appeared proposing definite and practicable schemes whereby the debt should not only be prevented from increasing, but should be steadily diminished.

Soon, too, he had a more conspicuous opportunity of vindicating himself from aspersions of this nature, and quite confounding all among his opponents who were capable of undergoing such a process. Congress directed him to report a plan for the redemption of so much of the public debt as the United States had reserved the right to redeem. Every effort was made by the opposition to prevent this call upon him, for they dreaded not without reason the loss of one of the most valuable weapons in their armory of offence. The contrivance by Hamilton of an effective plan for the redemption of the debt, so fast as the law of its creation would permit, would at once rob the Republicans of an admirable cry and add immensely to Hamilton's reputation both for ability and integrity. But it was to no purpose that Madison and his followers fought hard in this contest; they were well answered by Ames, Sedgwick, Gerry, Fitzsimmons, and many others. It could not be gainsaid that the reference fell within the direct language of the act establishing the treasury department. It was finally carried by a vote of thirty-two to twenty-five, furnishing not a bad test of the strength of the Republican party in the House.

On Dec. 3, 1792, in response to this call Hamilton

presented a scheme which was at once ingenious, simple, and practicable. Unwilling to rely upon any surplus of the current revenue above expenses, but preferring to leave this to meet unforeseen contingencies, he started afresh with entirely independent propositions. Payments upon the deferred debt could not be begun until 1801. In the interval the United States were entitled, if they saw ·fit, to redeem the six per cent debt in instalments of annually increasing magnitude. The secretary now proposed, so fast as these instalments should respectively become redeemable, to borrow such amounts as should be necessary to pay them. These new loans, which would thus supersede the old ones, could without doubt be contracted at a lower rate of interest, whereby a national saving would accrue. But the secretary also proposed to fund the new indebtedness in such a manner that the revenue appropriated to it would suffice not only to pay the interest, but also to discharge the principal within a short, definite term of time, say in periods ranging from one to five years. The date with reference to which these periods ought to be arranged was said to be the first day of January, 1802, being the earliest day at which payment on account of the principal of the deferred debt could be begun. Then by making the appropriations permanent the same funds could after that date be applied to the reduction and discharge of the deferred debt.

The secretary thought that the requisite sums could be raised by reasonable taxation. The same revenues already appropriated to pay the interest upon the six per cent loan would form the basis in the new arrangement. A great outcry had been raised in favor of a prompt discharge of the national obligation. Such authorities as Madison, and other leaders of the opposition in Congress, had alleged the readiness and even the desire of the people to be heavily taxed for the purpose of rescuing the country from debt with the utmost possible speed! It was by no means necessary to take these gentlemen at their word in order to carry out the secretary's present plan, which suggested only moderate and tolerable taxation. He indulged in no unpleasant reminiscences however, simply declaring his purpose to be " the final exoneration of the nation." If the business of redemption was to be undertaken in earnest, the establishment of additional revenues was unavoidable ; " and a full confidence," he thought, could be " reasonably entertained that the community would see with satisfaction the employment of those means which alone could be effectual for accomplishing an end in itself so important and so much an object of general desire."

The plan of this report was unexceptionable as a means to the end proposed. But the fate of the measure is indicative of the truth that the end had been proposed rather than desired. So it happened that a scheme, in many respects one of the most excellent in the records of national finance, was debated for a few hours in the House in committee of the whole, and was then relegated to entire neglect and forgetfulness. The anti-federalists who had clamored for it killed it, not by argument, but by the simple process of abandonment. Indeed some of the recommendations of the secretary were especially distasteful to them. Heretofore, when he had been dealing out taxes his hand had seemed to rest most heavily upon his own supporters, upon the mercantile communities. The excise alone had formed a material exception to this practice. Now for the first time he sought some slight revenue from the southern planters, men who abused him without cessation, but had hitherto escaped as if by especial grace from contributing a fair share to the public income. It was just that the more intelligent and rich class of the party which had cried out so vehemently for this reduction should bear a portion of its cost. So Hamilton recommended a tax on saddle-horses and on all horses used in vehicles for pleasure-driving. If objections should occur to the imposition of this horse tax, then, he said, a tax upon pleasure-carriages might be substituted for it. It was said that not a horse or vehicle of this description was to be found in New England, and not many even in the middle States. So the indignant southerners rallied against the measure.

It cannot be questioned that Hamilton and the Federalists had the redemption of the debt honestly at heart as a favorite object. It would have been a second achievement not less glorious than the great assumption and funding measures, to organize a machinery which should discharge the debt within a short period and without imposing upon the people any excessive burdens. Hamilton individually would have been highly gratified to have seen his plan put into effective operation. If he was patriotic he could accomplish no greater good for his country. If he was selfishly ambitious he could have done nothing which would have more exalted his reputation. But the anti-federalists, having refused to meddle with the project themselves, were resolved that their opponents should steal no glory from it, and by a not very creditable manœuvre, which will forthwith be explained, they managed to keep the secretary and his friends abundantly busy for the rest of the session, and so render them quite unable to revive this topic.

The remainder of this report had relation to the payment of the loan from the bank. The plan was to make this payment from a loan of two million dollars borrowed abroad at a rate one per cent lower than was being paid to the bank, and thereby to save in interest the sum of $35,000 per annum. The circumstances which made this transaction especially feasible at this moment were as follows: Certain loans had been negotiated in Holland — as doubtless more could be — at the rate of five per cent, while the rate payable to the bank was six per cent. Part of the moneys thus raised abroad had been designed for use in discharging certain overdue instalments of the French debt. But the deposition of Louis XVI., the dissolution of the Legislative Assembly, and the general political chaos which supervened in France, made it unsafe to undertake the payment. It was questionable whether any authority existed in the country, which could lawfully receive the money and acquit the debtor. Yet the funds had been provided and it was expensive to keep them idle. If used immediately in paying the bank, they could surely be replaced, when needed, by a loan on better terms than those of the present loan from the bank.

When the discussion came up in Congress the question of the financial wisdom of the scheme was soon lost sight of, and the debate taking a partisan aspect turned upon the questions whether Hamilton meant to aid the bank with ready money; to what extent the French government was legally established; and whether the government of the United States had not better sell its bank shares at a sacrifice, simply in vindication of its right to sell them. The result of the discussion of these important issues was another triumph for the opposition, which succeeded in reducing the amount named in the bill to $200,000, or precisely the sum actually due to the bank as the yearly instalment on account of the loan.

Such was the fate of these honorable and earnest efforts of Hamilton to relieve the country from its indebtedness. The least that could have been expected from them, even in their failure, was that they should for the future free him from the charge of seeking to perpetuate the debt for party purposes. But even this end was not accomplished; and long after the accusation had been actually proved to be shamefully false the enemies of the secretary would again and again renew it, to their own dishonor more than to his hurt. It is indeed somewhat strange to find the anti-federalists greatly jubilant over what they were pleased to call their triumph over the great secretary. They seemed to forget that in thus triumphing over him they had triumphed over their own principles. They had conquered him only when he undertook to do that which they had long asserted that he ought to do, and had maligned him for being as they said reluctant to undertake. It was a victory indeed, but bringing the most singular and illogical cause for rejoicing!

For a long time the assaults upon Hamilton's personal integrity were confined to vague and general allegations of corruption. Specifications were never furnished, and the language was of a kind so common in party warfare that no distinct vindication was necessary or possible. Such innuendoes were only useful to prepare men's minds, and unless followed by some definite accusations would amount to nothing. This the Republicans well knew, and eagerly did they watch for the needed opportunity. Meantime so sedulously did the leaders reiterate the broad allegations, that the subalterns began to believe them. It seemed impossible that there should be no truth in what so many persons said every day; the obstinate repetition seemed able to transmute falsehood itself into truth. Nor were the better informed Republicans who were, or ought to have been, well aware of the deficiency of any real foundation, altogether without hope that some weak point might be discovered by a severe and searching attack. Had not the whole complicated machinery of the treasury department been constructed and set in motion under circumstances of extreme difficulty and exceptional complication, amid a chaos of unliquidated arrears of debts, broken-down credit, assumption of new debts, schemes for new loans? Was it conceivable that, in bringing order into all this confusion, nothing had been done which was, or could by distortion be made to appear to be, unauthorized, irregular, illegal, even dishonest? It seemed not unduly sanguine to hope for some gratifying result from a minute investigation. At least, even if this should not be attained, the secretary and his friends could be kept so busy going over this extensive ground, that they could have no time left them in which to win fresh prestige by the consummation of their scheme for redeeming the debt. Altogether the chiefs of the Republican party thought that with little danger of loss there was a tolerable chance of gain.

It is significant that, though the plan was concocted by Jefferson and Madison, yet it was not deemed wise to risk the reputation of a first-rate leader in initiating the attack. Some of the principal resolutions offered in the course of the debates were preserved in the archives of the state department embodying alterations in the handwriting of Madison. But Parker, of Virginia, was thrown forward in the first skirmish. He offered a simple resolution calling upon the secretary of the treasury to lay before the House an account showing the application of the moneys borrowed in Antwerp and Amsterdam for the United States during the current year. He then retired, and the gentleman who had been selected to do the hard fighting stepped forward.

The champion chosen for this hazardous duty was another Virginian, the redoubtable Giles, a man quite invaluable to his party; who upon occasions like the present was found to be ever ready for any thing and competent for any thing in the way of dirty work, being loud of speech, voluble in abuse, careless of the limits of truth or decency, insensible of disgrace, and incapable of defeat. This personage was proud of the distinction, as he deemed it, of being selected to conduct the battle against the dread secretary. He began by submitting resolutions asking for information concerning the loans which had been effected, their terms, the application of the proceeds, the balance remaining unapplied, the dates at which interest began to run on the loans, and the times at which interest was stopped by payments.

Hamilton promptly furnished full replies to these interrogatories. At first he construed the resolutions to relate only to foreign loans ; but directly afterward conceiving a broader application to be possible he sent in a supplementary report, embracing all the loans negotiated at home. No sooner was this information furnished than Jefferson hastened to point the moral ; for if the devilry which lurked in the reports was not explained it might fail to attract notice. So the secretary of state wrote to the president concerning his comrade of the treasury in the following language : " The most prominent suspicion excited by the report of the secretary of the treasury of January 3, 1793, is that the funds raised in Europe, and which ought to have been applied to the payment of our debts there in order to stop interest, have been drawn over to this country and lodged in the bank, to extend the special items and increase the profits of that institution."

A few days after the date of this report certain resolutions of inquiry were passed by the Senate. The information which they called for was in a great measure furnished by sending to them the books of account of the department. But a letter which accompanied these showed that the two loans contracted in Holland under authority of the two Acts of August 4 and August 12, 1790, had been negotiated without discrimination between them, and the proceeds, though appropriated by the Acts to separate purposes, had apparently been commingled. A new scent was opened.

Giles forthwith introduced into the House still another series of resolutions. The first called for copies of the authorities under which the foreign loans had been negotiated. The second called for the names of the persons by whom and to whom the instalments on account of the French debt had been paid; also the dates of the drafts drawn against these foreign loans and of the payments of the proceeds of those drafts. The third called for the account of balances between the United States and the bank and branches. The fourth called for a particular account of all moneys which had come into the sinking-fund, whence they had been received, how invested, and where deposited. The fifth called for an account of the balance of unapplied revenue at the end of the preceding year, 1792, whether in money or bonds; also an account of all unapplied moneys obtained from the several loans, with designation of the places where they were deposited.

Taken in connection with the resolutions already offered, these were fitted to draw forth a full narrative of the doings of the treasury department in all matters save the detail of customs and excise. The minuteness of the inquiry thus instituted and persevered in, no less than the tenor of the resolutions themselves, sufficiently indicated their purpose. The information sought was useless for any other end than to impeach the secretary's honesty. Yet there was nothing in the language of the resolves which avowed or demonstrated this fact, and therefore if nothing should come of them it was at least open to the Republicans to express satisfaction at this result, and to deny that they had expected to detect corruption, malversation, or illegality. But Giles could not contain himself within such prudential bounds. As if assured of the gratifying disclosures which in his heart he both hoped and anticipated, he boldly and instantly showed his whole hand. In a very vehement speech he assailed the secretary for having held back in making his former reports the information now sought, which the orator had the audacity to assert had been called for in the resolutions to which those reports undertook to reply. Having thus charged wilful concealment, he proceeded to state part at least of that which he thought had been concealed, and in so doing for the first time gave public and definite shape to the innuendoes against the secretary. He stated that the second resolution had reference to the fact that money, borrowed to pay certain debts owing to France, had been allowed to lie long unused for this purpose, so that the United States had been paying double interest. The third resolution concerned a like condition of things in connection with the Bank of the United States, money having been needlessly borrowed from the bank when the abundant proceeds of foreign loans were lying idle in the bank, whereby the United States had been caused to pay a total interest of fifteen or seventeen per cent. The fourth resolution sought an explanation of a very singular circumstance; namely, the drawing large sums from Holland for the alleged purpose of making purchases of the public debt at home, when it was quite obvious that without the aid

of such drafts the sinking-fund was already overflowing from domestic sources, and when the probability of accomplishing such purchases was much
diminished by the rise in the market price of the
debt and the limitations set to the buying. The last
resolution touched upon an alarming matter, nothing
less indeed than the absolute disappearance of a sum
exceeding a million and a half of dollars, — betrayed
by a great discrepancy existing between the secretary's report of drafts against the foreign loans and
the bank account of the same.

Giles closed his fulminations by declaring that
" candor induced him to acknowledge " that he cherished impressions decidedly unfavorable to the gentleman at the head of the treasury department. Still
he generously held himself " open to conviction,"
and avowed that if he were mistaken " his acknowledgment of mistake should be at least commensurate
with any conviction produced." The reader who shall
have the patience to follow this subject to the close
will not see this noble pledge fulfilled. Nor when
Giles uttered the words did he expect to be called
upon to make them good. He was assured of success; his whole speech was but a sort of preëmption
of victory and triumph. That the battle could result
in the discomfiture of any person save Hamilton he
evidently did not seriously imagine to be possible.

The task imposed by these inquiries was enormous.
Hamilton and all his subordinates in the department,
whether guilty or innocent, were subjected to no
slight punishment in being obliged to prepare in a
short time such a *résumé* of elaborate accounts and
complicated narration. They made common cause

together, and by night as well as by day they all labored assiduously until the whole information required was laid before Congress in time for consideration before the close of the session. Had they chosen to reply, as they might have done with some reason, that the labor was too onerous, and that time was wanting to them in the short interval between the date of the introduction of the resolutions and March 3 which would close the term of Congress, it would have been no unfair response. They might well have displayed reasonable industry and yet have been behindhand. Had there been any thing to be concealed they would doubtless have pursued this course. On the contrary, however, their main purpose was to complete their exculpation in sufficient season to have it examined, tested, made public. So they all worked with desperate energy. Hamilton, especially, intended to suffer no derogatory inferences to be based upon any appearance of reluctance upon his part. While engaged in preparing his replies he shut himself up in his own house, attending only to such affairs as could not be postponed, and laboring incessantly until he became actually haggard with his unremitted exertion. Toiling in this manner he sent in his answers to the several interrogatories by instalments, as fast as he was able, furnishing a report concerning any topic so soon as he could complete it, and then entering upon the next in order. It was impossible to say that he did not do his best to confer upon Congress the freest scope for inspection and study. The celerity with which these reports were made was a remarkable feat.

Considering the provocation which he had received

he kept his temper remarkably well. Ordinary political hostility he had to expect and was bound to meet with dignity; but when it came to being called, upon specific charges, a law-breaker, a corruptionist, actually a vulgar money-thief, the defamation of his personal character had been carried to such an extreme point as might have excused a burst of indignation. "I trust," he wrote to Washington, "that I shall always be able to bear, as I ought, imputations of errors of judgment; but I acknowledge that I cannot be entirely patient under charges which impeach the integrity of my public motives or conduct."

It has since been admitted by all persons — even those most opposed to Hamilton the statesman, and most inimical to Hamilton the man — that in all matters of money and business he uniformly displayed an integrity altogether irreproachable, a sense of honor delicate to the last degree. Against all insinuations of wrong-doing in the conduct of the affairs of his department he has long since been acknowledged to be impregnable. To one whose sentiments were so rigidly upright the villanous accusations of Giles must have appeared especially odious. Hamilton was only thirty-six; his detractors love to dwell upon his inexperience, and when they can find no other fault it is with singular complacency that they charge him with the "atrocious crime of being a young man." Yet he was old enough and experienced enough to have achieved the difficult task of a perfect mastery over his own temper even upon an occasion so trying as the present, and to appreciate that an infusion of ill-blood into grave business is usually a blunder.

Naturally Hamilton first disposed of the most offensive charge, that of the disappearance of one and a half million dollars. It was an easy explanation. The whole amount of income, or more properly of receipts including proceeds of loans — except such as had been borrowed in Europe and left for use there, which were accounted for independently — was $17,879,825.33. The amount of disbursements to the end of the year 1792, that is up to a point only thirty-five days prior to the making of this report, was shown to be $12,765,128.83, leaving a balance of $5,114,696.50. The secretary then stated where this sum was. Part was in the treasury in cash; part on deposit in the Bank of the United States and elsewhere, not yet passed to the account of the treasurer; part was the proceeds of Amsterdam bills sold but not yet received; part, nearly $2,500,000, consisted of bonds not yet due given for duties; part was an uncollected residue of excise-duties. Such were the chief items in the schedule which not only accounted for the sum to be accounted for, but even for a slightly larger one; namely, $5,116,897. The suspicious circumstance thus made apparent of his having *too much* money was readily explained. "In a case where estimates must necessarily supply the deficiencies of ascertained results, differences of this nature are of course." Nor was it easy to contradict him when he expressed the opinion that it was just cause for satisfaction that "the estimates heretofore communicated are proved by the official documents already received to have been essentially correct."

This seemed a very gratifying excess to contemplate, — receipts amounting to upwards of five millions of dollars beyond outlay. What business had the secretary to be borrowing money and taxing the people in order to create such a surplus? But the secretary promptly responded to the query, and reminded the House that only a very small part of the sum was a real surplus of income. Appropriations had been made of which the full amounts had not yet been called for, and which would surely in good season reduce this fund to the neighborhood of $400,000. Then this real ultimate surplus would be embraced in the appropriations for the service of the next financial year.

How had it happened that Giles had ventured to assert that Hamilton's own reports betrayed so large a deficiency as $1,500,000? Partly it had happened, without doubt, because Giles had either in ignorance, haste, or malice taken reports and documents which together did not profess to contain full information, and had drawn inferences from them as if they had been exhaustive. It seemed also that he was not capable of comprehending a financial exhibit, did not understand accounts, and was grossly uninformed concerning the laws and regulations governing the treasury department. Hamilton laid bare his imbecilities, which, if otherwise uninteresting, at least show the manner in which the accusations had been prepared.

In a recent statement the secretary had mentioned that, on January 3, "there remained *to be received*" upwards of $600,000 as the proceeds of certain foreign bills. Hamilton explained to Giles that what was "to be received" "could not be considered as *in* the treasury." Again, reference had been made to an account rendered by the bank concerning the proceeds of the sales of certain Amsterdam bills. The document indicated that " this sum was in bank over and above the balance of the treasurer's cash account." But the skilled detecter of frauds included it in the cash account, and so made that account too small by precisely this large sum.

Among the items making up the surplus of $5,000,000 Hamilton had included certain bonds given for duties, which bonds had not yet matured. As assets of the government on deposit in the treasury he had thought it proper to mention them, though they were in no sense money. Among the misconceptions which had obtained, " not the least striking " had reference to this matter. " The *laws* inform," said the secretary, with ever so slight a touch of satire, " (and consequently no information on that point from this department could have been necessary) that credits are allowed on the duties on imports " for periods ranging from four months all the way to two years. The account of receipts and expenditures to the end of the year 1791, laid before Congress, showed that no less than $1,828,289.28 of the antecedent duties were outstanding in bonds. " How then could it have happened that the surplus of 1792 was sought for in the treasury *at the very instant of the expiration of the year?* I forbear to attempt to trace the source of a mistake so extraordinary." It was noted however that of this surplus $172,584.82 were actually not due and payable even until April and May, 1794. Certainly such exposures required no comments.

One other matter the secretary disposed of in this report. A discrepancy had been noted between a memorandum in the treasurer's bank book and the secretary's statement of the amount of bills drawn at the treasury upon the foreign fund, — a discrepancy to the alarming extent of more than five and three quarters millions of florins or guilders. " This disquieting appearance " was sufficiently explained in this wise. The Act incorporating the bank authorized a subscription to be made on behalf of the United States for shares to the par value of $2,000,000, and provided that the money should be taken from the proceeds of either of two loans to be raised in Europe for certain other specified purposes. The same sum was then to be borrowed by the government from the bank and sent abroad again for account of these same foreign loans in order to reimburse the deficiency. Such was the theory of the congressional scheme ; but obviously to have gone through all the details — the actual drawing of money from Europe, depositing it in the bank, drawing it at once from the bank again and retransmitting it to the starting point — would have been not only absurd but costly to the government, not alone in interest but in the probable loss arising from overstocking the market with foreign exchange. The youngest banker's clerk would not have concealed his ridicule at the transaction. It was mere matter of book-keeping, and the principle could be pursued and the end achieved at a great saving by entries in the accounts and the exchanging of vouchers. Thus the transaction was in fact arranged ; and thus it happened that a memorandum appeared on the treasurer's bank book when no corresponding statement occurred in the treasury schedule of bills drawn. For the treasurer had been credited, but the bills had never really gone abroad. Hamilton had been charged with corruptly favoring the bank at the expense of the country; but in this case, where he had slightly stretched the strict letter of the law to save money to the government at some loss of the bank, he had reaped his reward in being charged with downright dishonesty. It seemed a little hard. "Could no personal inquiry," he said, "of either of the officers concerned have superseded the necessity of publicly calling the attention of the House of Representatives to an appearance in truth so little significant? Was it seriously supposable that there could be any real difficulty in explaining that appearance, when the very disclosure of it proceeded from a voluntary act of the head of this department?"

On August 4 and 12, 1790, two Acts had been passed authorizing the contracting of two several loans abroad. The purpose of the one was to pay off arrears owing in France; that of the other was to facilitate certain purchases at home of the domestic debt. Immediately upon being invested with authority, Hamilton entered upon the requisite arrangements to place both these loans upon the markets in Holland. Indeed in anticipation of such action by Congress the negotiation had already been entered upon by the banking houses abroad. But instead of presenting to the money lenders these two distinct loans, it was simply announced that the United States wished to borrow the joint amount of the two, upon a pledge of funds.

Giles having charged this commingling to be unlawful, the secretary now explained that he had been induced to it by considerations of expediency. The offer of two different loans simultaneously was contrary to custom, and was likely to be in many respects (which were pointed out) prejudicial to the borrower. Hamilton had therefore written to the foreign bankers intimating his wish to place the loans distinctly if they thought that it could be well done, but permitting them in their discretion simply to call for the total amount of the two. The bankers were decidedly of opinion that the latter was the better and cheaper method, and accordingly pursued it. It was true that one loan might have been filled before the other was offered ; but if the proceeds were to be kept separate and applied thus individually to their respective appropriations a double loss would have ensued, in the want of money applicable to the one purpose at a time favorable to its use, and in an idle surplus of money applicable to the other purpose at times unfavorable to its instant employment. Especially was it necessary that the purchases of the domestic debt should be made at such various points of time as they could be made to advantage. It was farther explained not to be the custom of business in the department to keep a specific sum set apart by itself to meet its appropriation, but to draw all sums from whatever sources received and to whatever uses destined into the grand balance of the treasury, to make such drafts as were needed for any purpose from this general reservoir, and to charge the amount so drawn to its specific appropriation.

Hamilton did not deny that he had been aware that

this course of procedure might be open to criticism as not strictly regular. But, considering the matter carefully at the time, his action in view of the reasons prompting it had seemed to him to be right. Subsequent reflections had not led him to any change of opinion. He now believed, after having given the question very close attention, that his action was perfectly lawful. Others might differ from him. The case was undeniably one in which a difference of opinion was perfectly possible. But any such discrepancy, if it should exist, must be wholly confined to the technical propriety of the proceeding. The question was of the character to make it properly determinable by a court of law, wherein a decision upon either side would be capable of support by ample argument and abundant reason. In respect of the substantial merits there could be no doubt that the course adopted by Hamilton was very advantageous to the United States; that it was in the highest degree adapted to secure the ends proposed by the legislation of Congress; that it was in every practical point of view wise and excellent. Surely it was to be hoped that it was within the permission of the law, and every effort of construction might kindly be made to render it so.

One other consideration the secretary acknowledged to have weighed much with him in drawing the proceeds of these loans directly into the general balance in the treasury. The first instalment of interest on the reformed indebtedness fell due April 1, 1791, and the chief part of the revenue to meet this payment " was only to begin to accrue " on January 1 of the same year, and was liable in great part to credits of four, six, and twelve months. No experience enabled the secretary to judge how promptly these indispensable supplies would be forthcoming. One grand fact only stood forth predominant over all else, — that a failure to meet these first demands with perfect punctuality would be fatal to the dawning credit of the country; would probably return it to financial ruin and possibly to political chaos; against a national calamity so dire the manager of the national finances could not be excusable if he neglected to strengthen himself beforehand by every just means in his power. If there was a very nice and doubtful question of law in the way, surely he was entitled to demand, nay, it was his duty to take, the benefit of that doubt. Hamilton was not the man to be wanting in such an emergency.

"If," he said, "a doubt had occurred about the strict regularity of what was contemplated as a possible resort, a mind sufficiently alive to the public interest and sufficiently firm in the pursuit of it would have dismissed that doubt, as an obstacle, suggested by a pusillanimous caution, to the exercise of those higher motives which ought ever to govern a man invested with a great public trust. It would have occurred that there was reasonable ground to rely that the necessity of the case and the magnitude of the occasion would insure a justification; and that, if the contrary should happen, there remained still the consolation of having sacrificed personal interest and tranquillity, no matter to what extent, to an important public interest, and of having avoided the humiliation which would have been justly due to an opposite and to a feeble conduct."

The next accusation was, that the contracts for the foreign loans had been neither honorable nor advantageous for the United States. Whether these allegations had been made in ignorance of facts, or whether with a knowledge of the facts they had been thrown out simply in malice, is matter of speculation. But the choice lies between these two explanations, for the facts stated by Hamilton in reply were such as every man engaged in public affairs ought to have known. In the first place, the whole borrowing under both the Acts of August 4 and 12, 1790, had been effected upon conditions equally favorable with those attending the loans of contemporary borrowing powers of the most tried resources and the best established credit ; indeed, upon conditions more favorable than were obtained by some powers of great respectability. In the second place, the United States had taken the lead in the market in subsequently obtaining reductions of interest, and in this respect had gained either earlier or more complete success than any other power. In the third place, the rate of interest and charges had been so far reduced within the brief period of a single year, that, whereas the interest on the net sum received (including an indemnification for charges) had in the beginning slightly exceeded the rate of five and one-half per cent per annum, the negotiations at the close of the twelve months were effected at the rate of somewhat less than four and one-half per cent. " When this state of things," said the secretary, " is applied to a government only in the third year of its existence, and to a country which has so recently emerged from a total derangement of its finances, it would seem impossible to deny

that the issue is not only honorable but flattering, —
unless indeed it can be denied that a sound and vigorous state of credit is honorable to a nation." Hamilton
gave the honor and the glory to the country, though
for the condition of the country which rendered the
achievement possible the credit in no small measure
belonged to himself.

It is interesting to compare the borrowing power
of the United States at three different periods of its
existence. Under the Congress of the Confederation, after independence and peace had been conquered in 1784, a nominal four per cent loan was
negotiated. In fact it was a loan at the rate of
6.6468. In the contracts entered into in the latter
part of the year 1790, "the highest *real*, not *nominal*,
rate of interest" which was given by Hamilton did
not exceed 5.5012, while the lowest real rate which
was reached within twelve months later by the same
secretary was 4.4951. During the late rebellion,
what between the depressed value of government
securities and the high price of gold, the Germans
bought our bonds bearing six per cent interest at
forty dollars upon the hundred, in gold. The loan
recently accomplished is understood to be a net five
per cent loan. It is true that our present loan is
great, and the loan of 1790 was small; but the figures
cannot be set beside each other for comparison, simply as absolute sums. The facilities for governmental
borrowing have been immensely improved in the interval; the amount of capital seeking such investment
now is vastly greater than it was then ; and to both
these considerations is to be added the farther and
very weighty one, that in those days the domestic

resources available for such loans were, as will shortly be seen, very small, whereas the present domestic demand is very large and is almost wholly an addition. Such substantial facts constitute Hamilton's monument as well as his defence.

Some fault had been found with this negotiating of loans abroad, because it was said that the drain of specie to pay the interest, and especially the ultimate redemption of the principal, must prove too exhausting to the slender resources of the country. It was said to be better to pay seven and one-half per cent at home than five per cent abroad. Those who put forward these arguments seemed to forget that these new loans were in great part raised to pay off over-due foreign loans already contracted. To have obtained the money for this purpose at home, and remitted it, would have brought the evil day of excessive drainage of money into instant existence at a most inopportune moment. The very danger which was deprecated would have been precipitated. But the simple truth was that any such process of domestic borrowing was impossible. There was not accumulated capital enough in the country to furnish a considerable supply for investment in government securities. What funds there were found ample occupation in the much more attractive and remunerative channels of business, which were rapidly increasing in every direction. Moreover, even if the loans should be put upon the home markets at rates sufficiently high to attract purchasers, yet foreigners would be equally or even more attracted. They would send over their orders to purchase securities bearing so high a rate of interest at prices which would induce domestic owners to sell, and "our specie would be carried away so much the faster" as the instalments of interest would be greater at the advanced rate.

It was alleged against the secretary, that on divers occasions he had permitted the proceeds of the loans to lie idle so long as to cause a material loss in interest. The first instance, he now explained, arose from his unwillingness to draw upon the bankers of the United States abroad until he had received from them certain information that they had made sufficient collections to honor his drafts. He did not care to commit the public credit by a premature operation. The second instance arose at the breaking out of the Indian war, when for a short time he held in hand a little larger surplus than usual, to be prepared for the sudden extra drain to be anticipated for military outlay. The third delay had occurred in Europe, and was chargeable to the agents of the United States there, for whose appointment and proceedings the treasury department was not liable; and, moreover, for this it could be shown that those agents had ample justification.

It was further shown that the practical result of these delays had been a gain by exchange, which constituted a full offset against any loss in interest.

The opponents of the secretary, after having charged him with not having drawn the proceeds of the foreign loans into the United States with sufficient promptitude, immediately followed the accusation with another, to the effect that he had drawn such funds when there was no necessity for doing so. They said that he had brought over money from Europe to buy up the domestic debt when there was an ample supply, lawfully applicable to that purpose, in the control of the treasury at home; also that he had borrowed money from the bank when his abundant deposit account rendered the transaction wholly needless. The motive was found in his corrupt favoritism towards his darling institution, which of course benefited by such a large deposit of funds and such a liberal borrowing without withdrawal of the borrowed money. But the loss to the United States in double and treble interest running against her all the while was said to be obvious.

The most manifest blunder underlying these accusations lay in treating as part of the treasurer's cash resources the immature bonds given for duties, as has already been explained. The next error was in the supposition that the proceeds of the loans were kept as a separate item of account and specific accumulation of money, and so existed *in addition* to the treasurer's reported balance of cash; whereas in fact they constituted part of the aggregate balance in the treasury.

By references to the accounts of the department at frequent intervals during the period to which the charges related, the secretary showed that it was only by this borrowing from the bank and these drafts upon Europe that the treasury had been able to furnish the means for making the purchases of the domestic debt which had been made. Even in a time of complete peace he thought an average balance of about $500,000 not too much to keep on hand in the treasury. But during the period under consideration a war was pending; the revenues also were problematical; the exchange of the old indebtedness for the new was going forward with fitful rapidity, and rendered it impossible for him to know long beforehand what sums he must be ready to pay out in interest upon the regular pay-days ; and, moreover, there were thirteen different headquarters for making these payments, far removed from each other and with slow and laborious intercommunication. Then too there were sundry extra disbursements to be made : the foreign officers were to receive $200,000; the first repayment on account of the loan from the bank was about to fall due. Considerable arrears might be called for at any moment, and it concerned the credit no less than the honor of the country not to be unable to pay upon demand an over-due debt. Yet moderate as was the balance of $500,000 to be kept in view of all these regular and exceptional liabilities, and dubious as were the resources whence it must in part be obtained, it appeared that Hamilton had purchased the public debt so freely, as generally to have had on hand a less sum rather than a greater. He demonstrated that he had not drawn moneys from abroad to buy the domestic debt when he had resources at home practically available for the purpose, except upon one occasion to be explained forthwith ; and that he had never kept large collateral funds in existence, under pretence that one of them was needed for this purpose, when in fact the other would have sufficed. On the contrary he proved that he had figured so closely, had always used his funds so fast in the prevention of idle and costly accumulation, and had kept his balances so narrowly pared down, that few men would have been willing to have endured the constant watchfulness and anxiety of the situation.

The last of the series of vindicatory communications, bearing date February 19, 1793, dealt with the charge of undue favoritism towards the bank. A few dates are important in this connection. The receipts on account of the drafts upon the European bankers began in March, 1791, and concluded in March, 1792. The bank did not go into operation until December 12, 1791. Consequently, during about three quarters of the whole period pending which these moneys were coming in, it was altogether impossible for the bank to derive any manner of benefit from them. As matter of fact, the secretary stated that "the banks of North America and New York were the agents of the treasury for the sale of the bills in question. They sold them, collected, and, with the exception which will be presently stated, disbursed the proceeds." When the Bank of the United States began business, a concentration of the public deposits in it grew naturally out of the relationship established between it and the government. Yet instead of effecting this condition of things with any extreme haste, the change had been effected not by a direct transfer of funds, but by the natural and gradual drawing for the public disbursements upon the deposits in the other banks. So far indeed had the secretary carried his precautions against causing any annoyance to the older corporations, that he had subjected himself to the animadversion of the friends of the Bank of the United States.

A schedule of the sums on deposit with the several banks at various dates during the period in question fully confirmed these statements of the secretary. On December 13, 1791, the treasury balance was:

In the Bank of the United States $133,000.00
In other Banks 820,862.75

On February 1, 1792, —

In the Bank of the United States 456,278.90
In other Banks 408,992.94

During February a state of affairs took place between the Bank of the United States and the Bank of North America, which rendered a more expeditious transfer convenient to both. Consequently there was, on March 1, 1792, —

In the Bank of the United States $692,959.06
In other Banks 138,795.10

On April 1, 1792, —

In the Bank of the United States 359,643.64
In other Banks 391,733.70

Moreover there were at these periods considerable sums lying in the other banks not yet passed to the treasurer's credit, which would really have largely swelled these nominal balances; whereas there were for some time no such items in the account of the new bank. It was tolerably plain that the favorite institution had not been very well treated; and that it certainly had reaped no benefit from the foreign loans.

There was only one period at which a considerable sum appeared to have lain idle for a short time. This arose from the fact that the treasurer had drawn for a considerable amount, intending to use it for the purchase of the public debt, the price of certificates being at the time low. But it was a long process then to realize upon European drafts, and ere he was in a position to control and use the money the speculation had set in, and the debt certificates had risen to such an absurd height that he had to wait a short time for them to fall back again to a reasonable figure. This they did in good season, and the delay incurred was well compensated by the prices at which investments were soon afterward made. Thus was there presented an abundant excuse for permitting a considerable sum to lie idle for not more than four months at the longest.

But the secretary had not yet exhausted his vindication. When he found this large unemployed and unemployable balance in the national coffers, the surplus of which had been intended to be used in the reduction of the national debt, but was not immediately available for that purpose, he cast about for some means of making the accumulation useful. Its original destination constituted, according to his views, part of a general plan for the regular redemption of the public debt in pursuance of the right reserved to government. It now occurred to him that by using this sum to discharge at once the debt to the Bank of the United States, and replacing it, when the time should again become favorable for purchasing the public debt, by a loan contracted at a lower rate of interest than was payable to the bank, an annual saving of $20,000 at least could be achieved. This sum was not inconsiderable in those economical days, and it was obvious that the transaction was feasible and that the country could have two millions of dollars cheaper from other quarters than from the bank. It was therefore by no means an undue spirit of favoritism which led the secretary to urge this scheme upon the consideration of Congress. At the time of the rendition of this report Congress had come to no decision concerning the recommendation, but subsequently, as has been seen, rejected it.

It was a farther and important explanation, that the secretary did not really have an immediate control of such large sums as these deposit accounts would imply. This was chiefly due to a peculiar practice which had obtained for the purpose of simplifying the treasurer's bank account. The bills drawn by the treasurer upon distant places and deposited with the bank for sale were immediately passed to his credit as cash, though they were allowed to be sold on credits of from thirty to sixty days, and though it was therefore understood that the proceeds were not demandable from the bank until they had been collected. Hence the apparent sum in the bank was always in excess, often largely in excess, of the real sum.

It is significant of the knowledge which his opponents manifested concerning financial affairs, that in this connection Hamilton found it incumbent to make the elementary explanation, at considerable length, that the notes given for these bills and payable in thirty, forty-five, or sixty days were in no sense the "same thing to a bank as *cash*. 'Tis evident that it could not pay its own bills with these notes," &c. Is it surprising that men who needed such lessons and elucidations failed in an attempt to overthrow the first financier of the age?

Such were the main points of Hamilton's explanatory reports. All detail, even many arguments, have been necessarily omitted in order to avoid tediousness in a narrative which at best can hardly now be regarded as of a lively character, in spite of the eager concern and the deep feeling which invested the controversy and all that pertained to it in the days when the hot party warfare was actually waging. ·These elaborate financial exhibits, at the time of their publication, were fraught with an intensity of interest to the minds of our forefathers, which, unfortunately for the historian who has to deal with them, has by no means survived to the present generation.

By the Federalists the documents were received with extreme gratification, but with no surprise. Their great leader had done no more than they expected of him. He had inflicted a Waterloo upon the unfortunate Giles ; but then nothing else had ever been looked for. The work too had been done in a masterly manner, with perfect thoroughness and with perfect temper. The secretary had scarcely deigned to notice the mass of invective which had been accumulated by his adversaries, only occasionally mentioning a specific charge in order to show the direction and bearing of his defence. Had he been otherwise minded, the oratory which was indulged at the time of the moving of the resolutions in the House of Representatives, and which he was quite justified in regarding as a part of the *res gestæ*, would have furnished an excellent point of departure for a rejoinder in an indignant tone. But he had contented himself with preparing a plain, straightforward reply to the requests for information. He had dealt with the matter in a simple, business-like fashion. He had been drawn aside into no generalizations, no displays of eloquence, but had narrated facts and the course of affairs in his department in a shape as condensed as was compatible with sufficiency. The very completeness of his defence consisted in the perfect intelligibility of its every item. The more fully he could make himself understood, the more clearly he could make every transaction stand out for the comprehension of every one, the more lucidly he could display the working of his department, the more exhaustively he could show the results of his operations, the more obvious he could render his motives, — so much the more confidently could he anticipate acquittal, and, beyond acquittal, the universal approbation. Thus the very theory and principle upon which he conducted the contest furnished a strong presumption that he was in the right. He who was laboring with the extreme of assiduity to cast light upon every detail of a complicated subject could not reasonably be suspected of having much to conceal.

Throughout the country these reports had the inevitable effect of greatly enhancing the secretary's reputation. If any persons had seriously doubted his integrity, they now saw it mathematically demonstrated. If any had doubted his ability, they now saw how impossible it was to criticise his transactions. Even those who dreaded the general political bearing of his policy were obliged to admit that his management of affairs in subordination thereto could not have been improved, and that the business of the nation could not have been conducted with greater skill, economy, or integrity. Hamilton's statesmanship was not touched by these discussions, which referred only to matters of practical administration;

the former might be condemned, and yet the latter might consistently be admired: and so indeed it did extort admiration even from the most reluctant.

The effect of this series of reports upon Congress was striking. The extreme Federalists were jubilant. Their enemies had been beaten upon measures of importance many times, but never yet had been subjected to such personal humiliation as had now been inflicted upon them. The whole party watched with undisguised amusement the embarrassing situation of the accusing phalanx, waiting to see what movement they would undertake to make. The anti-federalists who had not become too deeply implicated in this sorry undertaking wisely held aloof from their more unfortunate comrades. But Giles and a few more discerned for themselves no honorable retreat. Grimly but slowly, and with obvious unwillingness, they came forward to close the battle; but they waited to do so until four days before the third day of March would put an end to the Congress. A subject of so great importance and complication could not of course be properly debated and disposed of in these closing days of the session, at least if there was any foundation for the sweeping charges of these gentlemen. But their delay had been based upon the double incentives, that the exiguity of time would prevent at once so ample a public examination and triumph of the secretary as his partisans would desire, and so complete an exposure and castigation as they themselves dreaded.

Hamilton had sent in his several reports with the utmost possible despatch and in the clearest shape, for the express purpose of furnishing every possible facility to Congress for studying them. The latest was dated on February 19. Familiar as he had professed to be with the subject, and readily comprehensible as the secretary's exhibits had been, Giles took nine days after this latest report was in his hands wherein to con and digest it and to prepare his action. When however the action which he wished to have taken was explained to Congress, there seemed nothing in it which should have required such delay in the conception.

On February 28 he presented nine resolutions of censure against the secretary. Out of the imposing array of original criminations it is somewhat ludicrous to see what a feeble remnant was preserved in this conclusion. The first two simply stated certain abstract rules concerning the inviolability of specific appropriations. The third charged the secretary with having misapplied a part of the proceeds of one of the foreign loans in using it to make payments of interest, and with having drawn part of the loan into the country without the president's order. The fourth found fault with him for commingling the loans contracted under the Acts of August 4 and 12. This was the only one of all the nine resolutions, which really amounted to any thing. The fifth censured the secretary for failing to give official information to Congress concerning the moneys drawn from Europe, and the progress of the drafts. The sixth accused him of improperly drawing from abroad, without the president's orders, more money than the Act authorized to be drawn; also, with not keeping the commissioners of the sinking-fund informed as to the progress of the foreign drafts. The seventh charged

him with having needlessly borrowed from the Bank
of the United States $400,000, when he had else-
where a larger sum on deposit. The eighth charged
him with indecorum towards the House in undertaking to judge of its motives in calling for information,
and in failing to give fully the information demanded.
The ninth declared that the resolutions should be
transmitted to the president.

Giles moved to refer the resolutions to a committee
of the whole. The motion was opposed by Van
Murray as involving a useless waste of time at the
end of the session, and not without strong expressions of reprobation of the whole transaction, and
contempt for the mover. If the secretary was to be
censured at all, it was said, he should at least be
allowed a hearing before a committee. A contrary
course of procedure was discourteous, unjust, and
contrary to established rules and precedents. But
Hamilton's supporters were on the whole inclined to
be amused at the ridiculous position into which his
assailants had fallen, and were willing to be entertained by seeing them flounder in the mire and wade
even deeper into it. Every thing about the matter
was eminently satisfactory to them, and was likely to
grow more so to the end. Their chief's prestige had
only been increased by the malicious attempt to destroy him. The spectacle of the shrivelled charges
against him was highly edifying, and might as well
be gazed at a little longer. Altogether, the Federalists were in such high good humor with the doings
of their adversaries that they would on no account
check the humor of those unfortunate gentlemen.
So the discussion in committee of the whole was

permitted to take place, and it continued for two days. The first two resolutions were, however, first thrown out entirely from consideration, as containing only abstract propositions; and the ninth was also refused commitment. The only noteworthy element in the debate was the fervor with which Madison entered into it. He had been a party to this attack upon the secretary in its earliest stages, and though his complicity was not generally known, yet the scheme had so heartily engaged his good wishes, and he was in honor so far bound to stand by Giles, that he was obliged to speak. But the task was so eminently disagreeable as to ruffle even his calm and equable disposition. When the fate of the resolutions was decided he fairly lost his temper, and for once in his life, forgetful of the respect due to the body of which he was a member, he declared that the opinion of the House was impotent to change the truth of the facts, and that the public would ultimately decide upon the criminality of the secretary's conduct.

The first vote was taken upon the third of the nine resolutions, being the earliest in order of the six which had been committed. The division showed thirty-eight nays against fourteen ayes. After such a trial of strength Giles was satisfied, and proposed to withdraw the remaining resolutions without more ado. But a vote being demanded, the chairman ruled that after reference to a committee it was too late to withdraw resolutions, and that it was necessary to proceed and obtain a report. The fourth resolution was lost without a division. The fifth was lost by thirty-five to sixteen. The seventh and eighth were lost without a division. This action in committee of the whole was conclusive of the fate of the grand movement from which many anti-federalists had been led to anticipate such happy results. On March 1 the report was considered in the House, and the demoralized assailants made even a much feebler showing than before. On the third resolution the division was forty to twelve; on the fourth, thirty-nine to twelve; on the fifth, thirty-three to fifteen; on the sixth, thirty-three to eight; on the seventh, the same; on the eighth, thirty-four to seven.

Great must have been the relief of Hamilton when the crisis had thus passed away. Undoubtedly he had quite confidently expected to accomplish the discomfiture of his detractors. He had the facts upon his side; he was familiar with them all, and could prove them all. The gravity of the occasion, however, lay in the doubt whether sufficient opportunity would be given to him to admit of proof and elucidation. That it would not be allowed if his assailants could prevent it was obvious from the tactics pursued by them from the outset. They had devised a clever plot for accomplishing by indirection the end which ought properly to have been accomplished by an impeachment. They sought to have Hamilton convicted of illegal doings, of corrupt practices, even of actual theft of money, through the medium of resolutions adopted by the House of Representatives after debates, and then to report this conviction formally to the president. The only possible consequence would have been the expulsion of Hamilton from the cabinet with a stain upon his name, not wholly removable by the most complete refutation which he could offer in unofficial and *ex parte* explanations. Such a blot is never wholly wiped away; to prove that it ought never to have existed is not quite equivalent to obliterating all trace of it.

Had Giles or his co-laborers in this disgraceful cause sincerely believed that they could prove what they ostensibly professed to expect to prove, it was their duty to have undertaken to accomplish an impeachment. If there were obstacles in the way of this course, at least they could have recurred to the usual and effectual instrumentality of a committee. An investigation of minute and searching thoroughness, which nothing could have escaped, would then have been unavoidable. Had it been intended to conduct the conflict upon the principles of fair fighting, Hamilton would have been allowed an opportunity of defence of a very different kind from that which was permitted to him. Nothing could have been more oppressive and unjust than to call upon him for a series of written replies to certain specific interrogatories however wide in their scope, and then upon such construction and misconstruction, apprehension and misapprehension as could be brought about in respect of these replies, to find him guilty of heinous offences not only against the laws and statutes, but against honor and morality. Very severely were the calumniators taken to task for this disingenuous behavior, and it is certain that among the people at large they lost by so ignoble and cowardly an assault much more than they could possibly gain, by the show of a few votes against Hamilton and the questionable technical lawfulness of one of his transactions. There is no pity for their humiliation, when they were obliged to witness the throngs flocking to the house of the secretary to congratulate him upon his happy issue out of unmerited afflictions.

CHAPTER III.

FOREIGN RELATIONS — GENET'S MISSION.

So soon as the United States had assumed the character of an independent nation, the manner in which she was to be received and treated by the old established powers of Europe became matter of deep concern. The subject touched nearly both the pride and the interests of the new people. With much care and anxiety did the government seek to select the first envoys to the foreign courts from among the very best men that the country could show. Nor was it without a lurking sentiment of grave misgiving that the gentlemen upon whom the choice fell departed upon their arduous mission to meet the trained and accomplished diplomatists of the trans-atlantic courts. The trial was severe, but it cannot be denied that our representatives acquitted themselves with an admirable skill and success. They had little occasion to ask indulgence to their inexperience. The only minister whose subtlety occasionally confounded their native shrewdness was the Count de Vergennes, and he was aided in the process of covering his purely selfish machinations by the unfair advantage which arose from the fact of his representing a nation to which we were under great obligations, and the kindly motives of whose rulers it seemed ungenerous to distrust.

Betwixt the United States and Spain specific causes of difficulty subsisted, which survived long after the adoption of the new Constitution to vex and embarrass the administration of Washington. The boundaries of Florida remained in dispute, and, far worse than this, the question of the right of citizens of this country to navigate the Mississippi to the Gulf of Mexico kept the United States for many years upon the brink of foreign hostilities and domestic disturbance. Spain, holding both sides of the lower portion of the river, claimed as appurtenant to that ownership the exclusive right to command the stream itself, and to prohibit the passage of vessels from the territory lying above. The residents west of the Alleghanies, regarding this river as the natural, necessary, and cheap outlet for their commerce, were greatly exasperated at the assertion of a right to close it against them. They soon reached a frame of mind in which they were ready at any moment to plunge the country into war in order to acquire the privilege which seemed essential to their prosperity. But if their less nearly interested fellow-citizens east of the mountain chain should prove unwilling to back them to this extent, and should refuse to bring the matter to the arbitrament of arms, then they were resolved to shift for themselves as best they could. At times they seriously talked of military expeditions to be set on foot by themselves without regard to the action of the rest of the country. For a brief period certain troubles and disagreements threatened to produce war between Great Britain and Spain, and at once the idea of marching to the mouth of the Mississippi in company with a British force gained favor among the inhabitants of the West. Thus the government was kept continually agitated with a variety of fears. Now it seemed that a portion of the citizens of the United States would take upon themselves to inaugurate with a foreign power an unauthorized and unlawful war; now a secession of the western country and the formation of an independent State appeared imminent; again an alliance of the inhabitants of these regions with the troops of an unfriendly and dreaded power was darkly threatened. And all the while at not unfrequent intervals desperate men were heard to mutter that the navigation was a necessity of life to them; that it must be had; and that, if it could not be otherwise obtained, then it would be well not only to sunder themselves from the United States, but to go to the length of attaching themselves to Spain as her voluntary colonists.

Menacing as was this condition of affairs the government, at least after it had acquired solidarity by the adoption of the Constitution, might have felt confidence in its power to cope with such difficulties had they stood by themselves and not been complicated by the unfortunate condition of our relations. with Great Britain. That power was certainly not friendly towards its quondam provinces. That it would not be backward to indulge even in hostile machinations in the advancement of its own interests and for the division of the Union could not but be suspected. In discussing the attitude assumed by the mother country toward the people so lately her colonists during the first quarter of a century after their independence, it is difficult to be sure of arriving at a perfect fairness. It was the era, as is well known, when the most rigid and narrow principles of protection were believed to constitute the sure means of promoting commercial and industrial prosperity. The theory not of Great Britain alone, but of all civilized nations, was in every respect selfish and illiberal to the extreme degree which ingenuity could devise. Colonies were to the mother country what the roots are to the tree; they were expected to feed the prosperity of the central empire, and in turn to draw from the same centre their sustenance, which they were to pay for by every means in their power. So long as the cis-atlantic settlements had continued dependants of Great Britain they had not been ill pleased with this condition of things. They fancied that they found substantial advantages in forming a part of the greatest national commercial system in the world, while the benefits which might be derived from a freer condition of trade were altogether matter of speculation and utter uncertainty. The removal of colonial restrictions might be dreamed of as a blessing fraught with vague and vast advantages; but it was dreamed of only, not hoped, expected, or demanded. The doctrines of the day in government and trade were acquiesced in as each generation of men acquiesces in the stage of knowledge then arrived at by the world at large. The American merchants took it quite as matter of course that Great Britain should monopolize their commerce. Indeed it seemed no great hardship. A large market was open in the mother country and her extensive dependencies; nor were some compensating advantages wanting to them. If they were commercially restricted they were in turn commercially protected, and by the most powerful and useful commercial protectress that the world afforded. A great and remunerative trade rapidly grew up between the two lands; and besides this a very lucrative resource was found in the privilege of intercourse with the British West Indies, a privilege enjoyed by the provinces solely by virtue of their own British character. A large and prosperous business was established in this direction, and important branches of home industry were cherished by it. The product of the eastern fisheries was taken to the islands, molasses was brought back, and the manufacture of rum from this furnished a comfortable livelihood to a great number of persons.

But the independence of the United States changed all this. The new country, no longer a part of the British nation, lost by this assumption of a new character the rights which it had long enjoyed. The United States now found themselves suddenly placed by their own action outside of the magic circle, and occupying the position of any other foreign nation. Indeed they occupied a worse position than most foreign nations, for no treaty stipulations secured to them any rights. They were at the mercy of all the arbitrary and illiberal orders in council which might be issued any day and on any day again revoked. Great Britain wished to keep the greatest possible amount of maritime carrying for her own marine. Great Britain wished to monopolize the markets of her West Indian dependencies. She jealously guarded herself from infringement in these respects on the part of Holland, of France, and of all other foreign powers, and only occasionally peddled out some special privilege in a bargain by which she expected to receive at least as much again. Was it reasonably to be expected that she should break through her established principles, operating towards all the friendly peoples in her neighborhood, in favor of distant persons whom she regarded as her own revolted subjects?

For a little time indeed some hopes of concessions were entertained. A course of business relationship so intricate and long established could not be severed at a blow without grave damage to both parties. But erelong the policy of the English cabinet was developed ; first by orders in council, and then by the more permanent acts of parliament. The American merchants saw themselves subjected to restrictions apparently almost ruinous. It was useless to say to them that no peculiar or exceptional policy was adopted towards them, that they fared like other nations, unless perhaps in one or another particular some nation might by a bargain have secured special advantages. Under the circumstances it was impossible for them to be logical or moderate. The treatment shown towards them might be the same in principle as that shown towards others, but it did not affect them as it affected others. The case of the United States was not like that of the old European nations. Our merchants in losing essential privileges which they had long been wont to enjoy could not but feel that they were being very unjustly used and were fully persuaded that they were being destroyed. American commerce had long been trained to run in certain channels, and the narrower these were the deeper they had been worn; when now they were to be suddenly dammed up, it was no easy matter to divert the streams or dispose of the water elsewhere. A large and important proportion of the population felt obliged to recognize the plain and unwelcome truth that irretrievable disaster was imminent.

Under such circumstances logic could not subdue ill temper. The omnipotent law of self-preservation asserted itself. The conduct of Great Britain was denounced upon all sides as oppressive, hostile, intolerable. The United States it was said could amply pay Great Britain for all that they asked from her, and it was conceived that this statement presented an argument which proved beyond an answer that it was the duty of Great Britain to comply with American requests. It was forgotten that Great Britain had a right to refuse the bargain, to decline the price proffered for that which she did not choose to sell. Without any *casus belli*, the people were yet almost ready to renew hostilities with their old enemy when she so coldly and firmly declined to abandon her right to do what she would with her own. If technically right, yet morally she was felt to be altogether in the wrong.

These commercial difficulties were by themselves a sufficient cause of alienation between the two countries, but others scarcely less effective were not wanting. Great Britain refused to make compensation for the many thousand negroes carried away in her ships at the close of the Revolution in direct contravention of the stipulations of the treaty; she still held the western posts years after the compact had been signed which required their surrender, long after Washington had been inaugurated as President of the United States. It was not alone because this last infringement was unjust and insulting that the people became bitterly indignant about it, but because also these military positions formed dangerous bases from which to stimulate forays on the part of the Indians, or expeditions of the western inhabitants down the Mississippi. Yet to all remonstrances and demands English ministers presented the ready reply, that the stipulations of the treaty on the part of the Americans had not been fulfilled, for that it was still impossible to collect in the courts the ante-Revolutionary debts, principal and interest, due from American to English merchants. But soon after the adoption of the new Constitution a suit was brought upon a claim of this nature in one of the courts of the United States, and judgment was recovered in due course. It was farther stated that no legal obstacle remained to prevent such collections. Creditors might for reasons of their own neglect to sue, debtors might be insolvent, but the judgments could be obtained in the courts if they were properly sought; and this was all that any person, foreigner or native, could expect or require. These facts, especially the actual result of the test case, were declared to prove conclusively that the United States no longer remained in default in this respect. Unfortunately, however, the practical obstacles which still remained were such that the British were not willing to accept this single judicial achievement as indicating with accuracy the true condition of things.

Not less important in its results was a very intangible yet a very powerful source of irritation. This lay in the treatment accorded by the British ministry and other persons of rank and influence to the United States and the envoys of that country. George III. indeed, making one great special effort of manliness and courtesy, gave to Mr. Adams a frank and sufficiently courteous reception. It was a trying occasion, and the monarch had the spirit and breeding to show himself equal to it. But this was an episode altogether exceptional. The character of his majesty did not suffer him to continue a course of conduct which would have done such constant and extreme violence to his most sincere convictions, his most intense feelings. Soon afterward he publicly and pointedly turned his back upon the American envoys. This settled the question of their treatment. Thenceforth superciliousness, coldness, and neglect were their lot, and the superciliousness of English aristocrats what pen shall venture to depict! There was that element in the temper of both peoples, that at the end of a long hard war they might have shaken hands and declared an honest and substantial friendship, with only slight and transient vestiges of ill-will rankling upon either side. Whether or not this should be done necessarily depended chiefly upon Great Britain. Certain it is that the United States were not unwilling to establish such a relationship. It is true that their interests prompted them to it, but their sincere feelings did not lag far behind their shrewder motives. Great Britain unfortunately was in a different frame of mind; the sentiment, not indeed universal but widely prevalent in that country,

was very sullen and even revengeful. So she turned
an insolent and frigid shoulder to American advances,
and appeared deliberately and decidedly to prefer to
establish hatred rather than good-will betwixt the two
peoples. Perhaps it was not a difficult task to accomplish, but she set about it in such grim earnest
and with such needless persistency, that the feeling
aroused by her in the breasts of Americans survived
to subsequent generations.

So long as the States were struggling in that
wretched chaos which intervened between the treaty
of peace and the adoption of the Constitution, Great
Britain stood aloof, careful however to lose no opportunity of expressing her great delight at the painful
spectacle before her eyes. She thought that she saw
the process of disintegration and the first stages of
decay, and she did not conceal her opinion or her satisfaction. The first Congress which met under Washington's presidency was accordingly in the humor to pass
any legislation which might promise to put a useful or
vindictive pressure upon England. It was with much
difficulty that the more cool and calculating members
prevented the passage of an act discriminating expressly and severely against the commerce of that
country. It was said that in this way and in no
other could we surely bring her to terms. We gave
her much that she wanted, and took from her a great
amount of what she had to sell.

The more moderate party, among whom Hamilton
was prominent, deprecated proceedings which would
open wider the existing breach. They had in view
rather by patient argument and pacific influences
to accomplish the end of a commercial treaty,

and to achieve a substantial and permanent benefit to the country, than to give vent to wrath or to effect retribution. Pressure and injury did not seem to them the wisest course to pursue in order to induce negotiations; such measures might be necessary in time, but for the present should be held in reserve. The United States could press hard, yet England might be able to press the harder and to resist the longer of the two. A declaration of a commercial war should be withheld as a last resort. Moreover, important results were hoped for from the aspect presented by the reorganized nation, and by the working of affairs under the new system. These expectations were far from being disappointed. England had never condescended to send a minister to the Congress of political entities heretofore calling themselves collectively the United States; but being sounded by Gouverneur Morris under instructions from Washington, she now readily expressed her willingness to enter upon the wonted diplomatic status. All approaches looking towards the establishment of altered commercial arrangements were however still kept at a distance. The new minister, Mr. Hammond, was empowered to inaugurate negotiations to this end; but he had no power to conclude them, or actually to do any thing practical or definitive. Patience and perseverance were necessary for this achievement.

But time, it was urged, could be safely trusted in this matter. England needed only a brief period to enable her to reflect, in order to appreciate fully the situation and opportunities of both parties. The Americans were quite right when they said that British and American commercial interests were not hostile but harmonious; that the two peoples working in accord could do each other infinite good, but that if they should work at cross-purposes the resultant injuries might well prove to be not unequally distributed. In the councils of trading nations business interests are omnipotent, and exert a steady pressure before which the most substantial legislative barriers inevitably go down. The native capacity for adjustment to circumstances, which the commerce of an energetic country possesses, also came to the rescue. Aided by these facts affairs were coming into better train, and would surely in good season have righted themselves. Under the influence of Hamilton's financial measures prosperity became general. The vision of ruin was removed from before the terrified eyes of the merchants. A cheerful spirit began everywhere to supersede melancholy forebodings. People were growing rich and good-humored. Great Britain was not starving American prosperity, nor were the orders in council and the parliamentary enactments causing our vessels to rot at their wharves, our products to accumulate in the warehouses, or the grass to grow upon our exchanges. Retaliatory legislation, indeed, still seemed to a large party to be wise and proper, and the course to be adopted was still in discussion and undetermined, when suddenly a new and powerful element was imported into the controversy by France.

With that country, as may be conceived, the relations of the United States were very friendly. A strong sense of gratitude to her for her valuable services in the Revolution was but slightly if at all diminished

by the reflection, that in aiding us she was consulting
and furthering her own interests. Neither was the
selfish policy pursued by the Count de Vergennes at
the time of the negotiations for peace known by the
people at large. France appeared as an ally who had
freely poured forth blood in our behalf, as a friend
who had generously lent us money in our need, and
afterward had refrained from dunning a debtor who
had fallen sadly into arrears. Yet it could not be
denied that the commercial liberty accorded by France
was no greater than that obtained from Great Britain.
In vain had Jefferson during his mission at the French
court sought to induce the statesmen with whom he
became familiar to enter into more liberal arrangements. In vain did he show to them with the clearness
of demonstration, that the changes which he asked
would benefit their countrymen no less than his own.
The monopoly on tobacco was regarded with that
jealousy which is wont to guard a sure and lucrative
source of revenue. To no purpose did Jefferson show
that an even larger sum would flow into the royal
coffers, if the monopoly should be abolished. Nor concerning fish-oils and other burdened articles could
the Virginian, for once quite right upon a question of
political economy, secure a favorable consideration
of his views. His failure disappointed him, but caused
him to bear no malice. For the errors and short-
comings of France he had an inexhaustible fund of
long-suffering. His last act as secretary of state,
the promulgation of his elaborate but incorrect report
upon the commerce of the United States, was a strong
effort to show that France treated the United States
better in matters of trade than did Great Britain.

This position, of which the falsehood was known to none better than to him who assumed it, was vigorously controverted by Hamilton. The comparison was difficult to make. But a not incorrect and a quite sufficient result of the investigation may be stated to have shown that both countries pursued the old-fashioned, protective, thoroughly illiberal system with much rigidity, and that in point of success in this pursuit there was so little to choose between them as to render the inquiry useless. It was however an important consideration that the strictures of French regulations did not bear nearly so hard as did the English, for they did not operate to break up the old-established course of trade. There were comparatively few producers, merchants, or ship-owners in the United States who cared what the French system of customs was. Consequently no such feeling of anger was aroused towards France as was so vehemently manifested towards England. France was not putting American merchants in a worse position than they had been wont previously to occupy. She was not ruining any one. She was only pursuing an economical theory which in the darkness of those days was generally accepted as sound.

The outbreak and early career of the French Revolution did not so much alter as simply exaggerate the condition of feeling in this country. For a time it seemed that a new and powerful bond of amity was to be established between two free nations, achieving emancipation so nearly simultaneously. For a time a warm sympathy was the universal sentiment cherished in the States towards the new *régime* in

France. It was entertained no less by Washington and Hamilton, who were afterwards so bitterly accused of extreme anti-Gallicism, than by Jefferson and Madison, who in time became what was called " Gallo-maniacs." So long as moderation ruled the counsels and advance of the French revolutionists all was kindly harmony in the United States. One of the earliest acts of Hamilton as secretary of the treasury was to expedite certain payments to France, on the expressed ground of friendship towards that country in her then interesting situation.

Erelong, however, as the more dispassionate and watchful observers saw the alarming acceleration of the revolutionary pace, many of them began to fear the result. They became more inclined to silent scrutiny than to loud admiration. On the other hand, the party of French sympathizers — by far the more numerous of the two among the people at large — became proportionately more vehement in their expressions of regard. Even the cool head of Madison became so heated by the wonderful fire of enthusiasm which that great event kindled in every quarter of the civilized globe, that he declared it to be his opinion that though the French Constitution might possibly be " not exactly conformable to perfect wisdom," yet he believed it to contain more wisdom than any instrument that had fallen under his eye. This statement, which might be criticised as extravagant if not as disloyal, was uttered before the famous tenth of August, 1792.

The dethronement of the king, his execution following hard thereon, the hideous massacres of September, all the events which attended the unhallowed ascendancy of Danton and his bloody *confrères*, changed the complexion of men's minds in the United States. The more thoughtful portion of the community, already rendered doubtful, now became altogether alienated from a cause which assumed so revolting an aspect. Nor was their alarm and distrust in any degree allayed when they saw the more excitable among their own fellow-countrymen not so much shocked, silent, or questioning, as fired, sympathetic, almost emulous. *Liberté, égalité, fraternité* were no more to be kept from crossing the Atlantic than any physical epidemic, and threatened to rage with a fury which would be feebly compared even to that of the cholera or the small-pox. It was a strange and unprecedented state of affairs when Gallicism seemed about to supersede patriotism, and love of France to stifle love of the United States. The more ardent American admirers of Robespierre altogether lost their heads, and bade as reckless a farewell to every sentiment, except the passion of revolution, as if they had been Frenchmen of the craziest quality. Even Jefferson — who showed afterward that he was by no means incapable of self-restraint and of the exercise of common sense — said that he deplored the slaughter indeed, but that he mourned for the victims as he would for men fallen in war. It had been necessary to use the arm of the people, — an agency less blind than shot and steel, but not much less blind. Those who had been sacrificed by that arm seemed to him to be not ill-likened to those who die upon a field of battle.

It may easily be conceived that Hamilton did not fall into a similar frame of mind. So long as the revolution paused at the stage of the national convention, it had his sincere approval and kindly goodwill. When, however, erelong "The Mountain" and the Jacobin club began to prevail, and a murderous frenzy ruled the hour, he became utterly opposed to the movement which no longer appeared in any other shape than as a bloody chaos. The cruelty shocked him; the absurd social and political theories disgusted him. He distrusted any happy exit out of such calamities voluntarily encountered, wherein no remnant of humanity or of reason could be discerned. Even should he refrain from speculating upon the possibilities or probabilities of the future, which in an entirely novel condition of things it was totally useless to seek to forecast with accuracy, he could not bring himself to regard the present spectacle otherwise than with the horror common to all who had escaped the French infection.

The two parties had already worked far asunder; feeling had already begun to run high; the friends of France had already begun to accuse the government of lukewarmness towards a dearly loved ally; and those of opposite sentiments were already accusing the French sympathizers of a willingness to reduce the United States to a mere appanage, if not even to an actual copy of revolutionary France, — when the news of the declaration of hostilities between France and Britain came to fire the excitement of the one faction, to strengthen the convictions of the other. For a long while afterward the passions which raged in this country were scarcely less violent than those which prevail during actual war. The French and the anti-French factions hated each other with much more animosity than had been cherished between Englishmen and Americans in the war of the Revolution, or than that which soon afterward marked the war of 1812. Very singular and wonderful was the capacity for maddening men all the world over which these events in France possessed!

A vessel arriving at Philadelphia from Lisbon, on April 5, 1793, brought the first rumors of the declaration of war uttered by France against Great Britain. Three days later newspapers coming to hand from England confirmed the news. Washington was at Mount Vernon, whither with all haste Hamilton despatched the important tidings. The president immediately wrote to his secretaries, requesting them to consider what measures it would be advisable to take in order to prevent citizens of the United States from "embroiling us with either of those powers," and to enable the government to perform its duty of "endeavoring to maintain a strict neutrality." Speedily following these letters Washington came to Philadelphia. By Jefferson he was met with advice to summon Congress; by Hamilton with a series of interrogatories for discussion and answer in a cabinet meeting.[1] The meeting was held April 19, but only

---

[1] Nearly all these interrogatories were furnished by Hamilton. The last was added by the president for the purpose of covering the only suggestion received by him in this emergency from the secretary of state. They were as follows: —

Question 1. Shall a proclamation issue for the purpose of preventing interferences of the citizens of the United States in the war between France and Great Britain, &c? Shall it contain a declaration of neutrality or not? What shall it contain?

Question 2. Shall a minister from the republic of France be received?

Question 3. If received, shall it be absolutely, or with qualifications; and if with qualifications, of what kind?

Question 4. Are the United States obliged, by good faith, to con-the briefest intimation of the doings thereat remains. It appears to have been unanimously agreed that a proclamation should be issued by the president forbidding our citizens to take part in any hostilities on the seas, on behalf of or against any of the belligerent powers; and warning them against carrying to the dominions of any such powers any of those articles deemed contraband according to the modern usage of nations; also generally enjoining them from

sider the treaties heretofore made with France, as applying to the present situation of the parties? May they either renounce them, or hold them suspended till the government of France shall be established?

Question 5.   If they have the right, is it expedient to do either, and which ?

Question 6.   If they have an option, would it be a breach of neutrality to consider the treaties still in operation ?

Question 7.   If the treaties are to be considered as now in operation, is the guarantee in the treaty of alliance applicable to a defensive war only, or to war either offensive or defensive ?

Question 8.   Does the war in which France is engaged appear to be offensive or defensive on her part, or of a mixed and equivocal character ?

Question 9.   If of a mixed and equivocal character, does the guarantee, in any event, apply to such a war?

Question 10.   What is the effect of a guarantee, such as that to be found in the treaty of alliance between the United States and France ?

Question 11.   Does any article in either of the treaties prevent ships of war, other than privateers, of the powers opposed to France from coming into the ports of the United States, to act as convoys to their own merchantmen ? Or does it lay other restraints upon them, more than would apply to the ships of war of France ?

Question 12.   Should the future regent of France send a minister to the United States, ought he to be received ?

Question 13.   Is it necessary or advisable to call together the two Houses of Congress, with a view to the present posture of European affairs ? If it is, what should be the particular objects of such a call?

all " acts and proceedings inconsistent with the duties of a friendly nation towards those at war."

Declarations of this character issued in similar emergencies have received the common name of declarations of neutrality, but Mr. Jefferson objected to the use of this precise phraseology upon the present occasion. We had a treaty with France, the obligations of which might, under certain circumstances, involve us in any war to which she should be a party. Therefore, since a " declaration of neutrality was a declaration that there should be no war," it could not properly be issued. Nor was the executive competent so to commit the people. Control over the questions of peace and war did not rest with the president, yet by declaring neutrality he must assume that power. These absurd suggestions were so far accepted as to prevent the actual use of the alarming word " neutrality " in the document, which nevertheless asserted in every substantial particular the condition of things signified by that word. The duty of the United States was said to require upon their part " a conduct friendly and impartial " toward the belligerent powers. Citizens were warned " carefully to avoid all acts and proceedings whatsoever which might in any manner tend to contravene " this principle. Notice was further given that punishment might be expected by all individuals who should commit, aid, or abet hostilities against any of the warring nations, and that prosecutions would be instituted against all persons who, being within the cognizance of our courts, should " violate the law of nations with respect to the powers at war or any of them." But even this language did not prove satisfactory to the French partisans. Madison wrote to Jefferson to say that he "should still doubt whether the term '*impartial*' in the proclamation is not stronger than was necessary, if not than was proper." Freneau's "Gazette," crediting the spirit if not the form of the document to the much-hated Hamilton, called him "the Legislative Dictator of the Union."

In course of time Jefferson forgot his nice verbal scruples, and in his diplomatic despatches and private correspondence was wont freely to use the word neutrality in connection with and as descriptive of this declaration. Under that name it was subsequently bitterly reviled by the Democratic party. By that title it has since been known to historians and publicists. But it will not seem surprising that Jefferson and Hamilton were not agreed upon this point when their respective opinions concerning the duty of the United States are known. Hamilton saw a war newly broken out between European nations, endangering no possessions or interests of the United States, and in which they had no cause or excuse for interference unless as voluntary participants. Neutrality therefore seemed to be our duty, and the issue of an official proclamation to that effect seemed a natural, proper, and customary act. Jefferson, on the other hand, thought that "it would be better to hold back the declaration . . . as a thing worth something to the powers at war"! He expected that "they would bid for it," and that the United States "might reasonably ask a price for it"! It will hardly be denied that his views seem somewhat peculiar ones to be entertained and frankly acknowledged by an experienced, diplomatic, and upright statesman; and that he would not have put the country in a very admirable attitude in causing her to haggle for a compensation in return for doing right.

It was further unanimously agreed at this same cabinet meeting that a minister from the republic of France should be received. Heretofore M. Ternant, a gentleman who belonged to the moderate party of the earlier stages of the revolution, had represented France in this country. But news had lately arrived that he was superseded by the citizen Genet, who came to us as the accredited envoy of the republic, the latest form of government evolved by the turnings of the political kaleidoscope. Indeed, M. Genet had already arrived at a southern port, and M. Ternant found himself so far out of sympathy with the now ruling powers at home that he was making preparations to remain in the United States, after the arrival of the minister of the republic should reduce him to the position of a private gentleman with the privilege of consulting his personal interests. The tenure by which people held their heads in France at this time was too precarious to render that country inviting to him. The second question in the list therefore was answered in the affirmative, vastly to the comfort of Jefferson, who designated it as " the boldest and greatest that ever was hazarded, and which would have called for extremities had it prevailed." This was as far as the president and his advisers succeeded at their first sitting in advancing in the disposition of the thirteen queries. The third question was a pendant to the second, and the warmth of the discussion called forth by it is foreshadowed by the foregoing remark of Jefferson.

Should the reception of the minister of the republic be absolute or qualified? That a reception should be accorded to him had been agreed apparently upon the principle that he represented the actual government of France for the time being; and whatever might be the origin, probable duration, form, or character of an established and existing government, there was believed to be a right upon the part of other governments to receive its envoys. Business must be transacted with it; peaceful relations should be maintained with it. Communications through a minister constituted the customary means for accomplishing these purposes. But there was ground for saying that the circumstances of the present case were exceptional and might demand a deviation from the usual forms. There might be danger that the reception of the minister absolutely, without a word of qualification, would be construed into such a recognition of the new government as to commit us tacitly to more than we might be either obliged or willing to be committed to. Hamilton was of opinion that it would be only fair and friendly to apprise M. Genet beforehand of the intention of the United States not to conclude itself by the act of receiving him, but to reserve for farther consideration certain important questions; more notably the question whether or not the treaties formerly entered into with the King of France should be considered as abrogated, or at least as temporarily and provisionally suspended by reason of the new condition of things.

Our treaty with France bound us to certain stipulations which could not be lightly regarded. For example it bound us to guarantee to her, in all wars defensive upon her part, the integrity of her dominions in America. We were also to admit her privateers with their prizes into our ports to remain so long as they should choose. The general rule must be acknowledged to be that " real " treaties, of which nature this one was, are not abrogated by changes in the form of government of a contracting party. Yet, argued Hamilton, the rule must be construed reasonably; and the right of a nation to manage its domestic politics in a manner to suit itself does not give it a right to involve other nations, with whom it has connections of earlier date, absolutely and unconditionally in the consequences of any and all changes which it may see fit to make, no matter how great and sweeping. Such an utter upheaval and destruction, such a political earthquake, as had taken place in France, followed by the erection of a government in every point of form and principle diametrically different from that with which the treaty had been made, might fairly, must reasonably, give to the other party the right to abrogate its undertakings of elder date. It might so happen that in spite of this complete change of circumstances, resulting wholly from the voluntary act of France, totally beyond the possibilities of contemplation when the compact was made, the United States would not after due consideration wish to renounce her agreements. But that France had given her the right to do so could not be questioned by any reasonable man.

The right ultimately to renounce must imply the preliminary right to suspend. It was Hamilton's opinion that it would be both frank and prudent to declare explicitly at the outset in establishing diplomatic relations with the new republic, that the United States would claim these rights. He feared that by a reception of M. Genet without a word of this import we might, should we subsequently see fit to exercise our rights, be accused of insincere and unfriendly concealment, perhaps even of an actual implied surrender of the privilege. He was therefore decidedly of opinion that we had better openly and honestly declare that we claimed this right, though possibly we might not finally conclude to avail ourselves of it, of renunciation of our preëxisting treaty obligations. For a brief immediate period we would refrain from renouncing, and would only hold back our decision until it should be demanded, or until a fuller knowledge of events should make us ready to announce it. Such startling occurrences could not yet be comprehended, their ultimate bearing and permanent consequences could not be forecast without careful deliberation; a foreigner must be permitted to consider even the stability of the present government as in some measure doubtful. "Every thing is *in transitu.* This state of suspense as to the object of option naturally suspends the option itself." Nor is it right that, "during a pending revolution," an ally in a "real treaty" should be held to "pronounce between the competitors."

Upon the basis that the United States was entitled to the option of eventual renunciation, and therefore of present suspension, Hamilton conceived it to be clearly the wise course not to jeopard so valuable a privilege. The king had been our friend and benefactor, and with him the treaty had been made. It was impossible to say that the present government had been set up " by such a free, regular, and deliberate act of the nation, and with such a spirit of justice and humanity, as ought to silence all scruples about the validity of what had been done and the morality of aiding it, if consistent with policy." The reputation of the United States was at stake in this matter. Surely she should pause long enough to see what was the true character of the new government in France before perpetuating with it those close and friendly relations which had bound the kingdom to our republic. Hamilton was not enough of a Gallicist to consider that the character of Robespierre's ascendancy, though wearing the honorable title of republic and invested for the moment with a more terrible and absolute power than that of an oriental despotism, was of such assured excellence as to demand the instant fastening of the bonds of an unusually close international amity.

Moreover, if sound principles of international law would confer upon the United States such an option as was claimed for her, was she not bound by her duties to other nations to use it? Using it, she would be a neutral; voluntarily declining to use it, she would pass into the condition of an ally. Needlessly to renew obligations would be equivalent to entering into them afresh. Yet it is now, and was then, a well-recognized rule, that it is a breach of neutrality, pending a war or in contemplation of war, to enter into treaties containing engagements for military aid and succor in circumstances likely to occur in that war. We might therefore retain the treaty only at the cost of becoming parties to hostilities. Yet it must be acknowledged that the treaty itself was far from being of such value to the United States as to make it worthy of preservation, even at a much less price. It was now keenly felt that the United States had pledged themselves to perform for France extreme and embarrassing acts of friendship. To be rid of their engagements by any just and honorable deliverance would bring a substantial advantage offset by no material loss. In this connection Hamilton already evolved and laid down that wise rule of American politics, since so famous under the name of the " Monroe doctrine." " The military stipulations," he said, " are contrary to that neutrality in the quarrels of Europe which it is our true policy to cultivate and maintain."

Simple as this truth may seem, there were many persons in those days who thought that in order to vindicate her position among the great civilized nations it was incumbent on the United States not to stand aloof from a general European war.

But if for these reasons the enemies of France might, if they were so minded, consider as an act of hostility our immediate and unhesitating observance of the old treaty as a subsisting compact still of binding force, it seemed clear upon the other hand that France could not look upon the suspension or even abrogation of it in the same light. Her own strictly analogous conduct would furnish our justification. For she herself had " formally declared null various stipulations of the ancient government with foreign powers," and this she had done upon the strength of precisely the same doctrine laid down by Hamilton ; namely, the principle of the inapplicability of those stipulations to the new order of things. If there was any reason left in France it would seem that these, her own modern precedents, must be allowed to rule in our case with the like force as in hers. Indeed, though the news had not yet reached the United States, it was soon afterwards learned that at this very time France herself was abrogating parts of this very treaty. It expressly provided that as between herself and the United States free ships should make free goods. Yet, almost simultaneously with the discussion in our cabinet, orders were issuing from her government for the capture and forfeiture of enemy's goods in neutral bottoms, without any exception in favor of the vessels of this country.

A supposed emergency suggested by Hamilton toward the close of his argument is too ingenious not to be mentioned. The treaty had been made with Louis XVI. Great Britain and Holland might not improbably capture some French island in the West Indies, and formally proclaim that they held it for the future king of France, the lawful successor of this same monarch, to be returned to him so soon as their arms should place him on his ancestral throne. "Can it be possible that a treaty made with Louis XVI. should oblige us to embark in the war to rescue a part of his dominions from his immediate successor?"

Such are in brief shape the main arguments in a very elaborate cabinet opinion prepared by Hamilton. The secretary at war was of the same mind. Jefferson was naturally of the contrary persuasion. He held to the rigid rule of international law, which lays it down that a change in the form of government of a nation does not affect the validity and binding force of its "real treaties;" he denied that any such exceptional condition of affairs existed as to stay the operation of this rule in the present juncture, or to confer upon the United States the power to renounce or suspend the French treaty. He did not apprehend serious danger from holding the treaty still in force, nor did he conceive that this could constitute a breach of neutrality; but he did think that to abrogate it, or even temporarily to suspend it, would give "just cause of war to France." These views finally prevailed, and it was determined that the reception of M. Genet should be absolute.

A few days later Hamilton sent to the president his opinion concerning the obligations imposed by the treaty with France in the present crisis and condition of affairs, upon the basis of considering it to be still in force. The treaty was entitled, "Traité d'Alliance éventuelle et défensive." The guarantee upon our part of the integrity of the dominions of France in America was therefore limited to wars which were defensive on the part of France. It is well known that France claimed that the present hostilities were in fact, though not in form, strictly defensive upon her part. Certainly they assumed that moral aspect and that practical character in much of their future progress; but their technical character, for the purposes of construing treaty stipulations, was to be derived from their inception. The strict adherence to the international code which had been fatal to his arguments on the preceding point was now favorable to Hamilton's views. He gave his opinion that the war was offensive upon the part of the republic. The arguments of France went only to show that the war was *just;* an offensive war, however, may be as *just* as a defensive war, and may be undertaken for as good and as lawful a cause. The declaration of war and the commencement of hostilities proceeded from France as toward every nation at war with her, with the sole exception of Portugal. The best authorities upon international law laid down the rule, obviously reasonable, that in determining the nature of the war it was not proper or possible to go behind the plain facts of declaring it or beginning it. To inquire into the matter of its prudence or its righteousness, to ask whether it had been forced upon the nation by pressure of threats, or of aggressions fairly provocative of war, but yet falling short of actual hostilities, was to judge concerning the right of the quarrel. This no neutral nation could be expected to do; or indeed would be entitled to do.

Moreover, Hamilton was far from accepting the doctrine asserted by the French republicans that they were fighting only in self-defence. If they had seen alarming symptoms of a willingness and preparation on the part of the European powers to combine for the use of force against them, had they not themselves openly, repeatedly, formally uttered no less violent and even more outrageous threats of interference in the domestic affairs of these very neighboring nations? On Nov. 19, 1792, the National Convention had passed and had caused to be printed in all languages a decree declaring in the name of the French nation that they would "grant fraternity and assistance to every people who wish to recover their liberty," and that they charged the " executive power to send the necessary orders to the generals to give assistance to such people, and to defend those citizens who may have been or who may be vexed for the cause of liberty." Hamilton asserted that it was " not justifiable in any government or nation to hold out to the world a general invitation and encouragement to revolution and insurrection, under a promise of fraternity and assistance."

But if it be thought that the language of this decree was too vague to found upon it serious objections, more direct and definite instigation to rebellion was not wanting. To a deputation of seditiously minded English and Irish citizens at Paris the French Convention said, that the moment was without doubt approaching "in which the French will bring congratulations to the National Convention of Great Britain. . . . Let the cries of friendship resound through the two republics! . . . Royalty in Europe is either destroyed or on the point of perishing on the ruins of feodalty; and the declaration of rights placed by the side of thrones is a devouring fire which will consume them." On December 15, last past, the French nation had farther declared, no longer to Great Britain alone, but to the world, that she would " treat as enemies the people who, refusing or renouncing liberty and equality, are desirous of preserving their prince and privileged caste, or of entering into an accommodation with them. The nation promises and engages not to lay down its arms until the sovereignty and liberty of the people, on whose territories the French armies shall have entered, shall be established, and not to consent to any arrangement or treaty with the prince and privileged persons so dispossessed, with whom the republic is at war."

It was impossible to disregard these incendiary proclamations as being hollow words and rhetorical outbursts which would not upon fair opportunity be followed by acts. The French were in wild and deadly earnest, and so far were they from talking emptily that they were inclined to let their reckless actions outrun even their extravagant language. The sparks from the great blaze had fallen among every people of the civilized world, and zealots abounded in every land who made it their task assiduously to blow these sparks into a consuming flame. Hamilton's friendly feeling towards the earlier struggles of revolutionary France had by this time given place to a feeling of strong disgust and reprobation. " Sullied by crimes and extravagances," said he, " it loses its respectability." The French was frequently compared to the American Revolution. Hamilton owned that he had no taste for the comparison when he gazed at the carnage, blasphemy, and fanaticism of the foreigners.

It would be a waste of time to discuss whether or not he was right or wrong in these sentiments. The French Revolution in all its stages is now matter of familiar history, concerning which every reader of this volume has doubtless long since formed his own opinion. But if any person is inclined, in view of the generations of despotism which preceded the uprising, to look upon all its stages with sympathy and condone even those hideous crimes which disfigured a part of it, let him recollect that he has seen also the subsidence of that brief madness

as well as its paroxysm, and that he knows it only by
report, and sees in it only an episode in a career
otherwise not especially blameworthy.   At the time
of which we are now treating the chaos of bloodshed,
brutality, unreason, and atheism was seething at its
greatest heat.   All the world was gazing at it, not with
that philosophical criticism which time and distance
lend to the worst possible spectacle, but with an intensity of immediate interest and even of personal
concern strongly working upon the feelings of all on-
lookers.   Its duration, influence, results, were all
unknown, and in every respect the worst might be
feared.   When one found his neighbor in an ecstasy
of admiration he could not but find his own sentiment of disapprobation strengthened into revulsion;
and as one citizen wished to fraternize, his order-
loving fellow became filled with alarm.   The times
were not favorable for neutrality.   The spirit of
proselytism, rapidly developed, furnished just and
lively cause for apprehension to all who were satisfied
with the condition of things existing around them.
France and her friends throughout the world openly
went upon the principle that all who were not with
her were against her, and certainly pursued a course
of conduct eminently adapted to bring about this
system of demarcation and to make all outside of
the sympathizing circle the active foes of those
within it.

It was an onerous duty that was imposed upon the
president and his cabinet by the outbreak of actual
war.   Hamilton was perhaps the most agreeably
situated.   His feelings and his sense of duty worked
in happy unison.   He did not wish to see the United

States in any manner entangled with France. Personally he disapproved of the conduct of France; as a cabinet minister he believed that the interests of his country would be best subserved by a strict neutrality. He saw and dreaded the strong leaning towards France on the part of a large, active, excited party throughout the States. He was well assured that to great numbers among the people any pretext or opportunity for becoming a party to the contest would hold out an irresistible temptation to reckless action. Worse than this was the too apparent willingness of many individuals to precipitate hostilities in spite of the government, by their own lawless proceedings. He was firmly resolved that his exertions should be put forth to the uttermost extent that they could go for the preservation of peace. Nor was the task thus put upon him by his sense of public policy otherwise than harmonious with his private sentiments.

Jefferson occupied a far less agreeable position. In order to do his duty as secretary of state he was often obliged to do violence to his own predilections. He strongly and closely sympathized with France; finding excuses for her worst acts; pardoning where excuse seemed not altogether satisfactory; regretting rather than reprehending the bloodiest deeds, and looking for an early and a happy issue out of the present afflictions. He appreciated no less clearly than Hamilton that as matter of policy the United States ought not to become a participant in hostilities. He was disappointed that such was the case, but the fact that it was the case he honestly recognized. He thought the policy was selfish, but acknowledged it to be wise. The danger was that in attempting always to guide the nation too near to the brink he would in some unfortunate moment cause it to topple over. For he was resolved in all cases to go to the extreme limit which international law and treaty obligations would permit in favor of France. He was ready to disoblige and offend her foes up to the very point of creating for them a *casus belli*. It was necessary to watch him closely lest he should at some time commit an indiscretion, and overstep the dubious boundary which in such matters separates the barely justifiable from the unjustifiable. A sentence in one of his letters to Madison indicates well his state of mind. " I fear," he says, " that a fair neutrality will prove a disagreeable pill to our friends, though necessary to keep us out of the calamities of war." Thus he confidentially expressed his feelings. Yet Jefferson's *public* course in this period does him honor. He consistently and clearly carried out the pacific policy of the government. He did his duty, sometimes reluctantly, but always well. One is occasionally provoked at the absence of any marks of temper in his replies to a French minister who was casting the grossest insults upon our president and country, and who surely deserved no courtesy of treatment. Yet so long as President Washington saw fit to permit the minister to remain, and refrained from requesting that a rebuke should be administered to him, it was proper for the secretary of state to preserve the forms of civility.

The other two cabinet ministers were of little use to the president in these days of trial. Knox — a frank, honest, military man, little at home in questions of law or policy, a stanch Federalist and great admirer of the secretary of the treasury — could generally be counted upon to give his vote upon the side of that gentleman at the close of a discussion without having taken much original part in the discussion itself. Randolph, who should have furnished great aid in settling such legal questions as continually arose, usually succeeded in evolving an opinion manifesting both knowledge and legal acumen ; but his vacillation and uncertainty, his tendency to decide every matter both ways, his inability to lay out or abide by any definite policy, his habit so indignantly described by Jefferson of " throwing his oysters to his foes and the shells to his friends," made him of much less assistance than he should have been. It is a little amusing to look back at the working of feelings and politics now that the publication of correspondence enables us to put private confidences side by side with public demeanor. Randolph was supposed to be politically opposed to Hamilton, but in these French matters we find Hamilton not unfrequently persuading and using his enemy, and when unable so to do remaining quite careless of his opposition. On the other hand Randolph was supposed to be the political ally of Jefferson, whereas in fact it is now well known that, so far from lending any efficient aid to that secretary, this unfortunate attorney-general was continually disappointing and exasperating his apparent friend. " I can by this confidential conveyance speak more freely of Randolph " — thus does Jefferson unbosom himself in a moment when the cup of his vexation had been made to overflow by his untrustworthy ally : — " He is the poorest creature I ever saw, having no color of his own and reflecting that nearest to him.   When he is with me he is a Whig. When with Hamilton, he is a Tory.   When he is with the president, he is what he thinks will please him."   If only Randolph were "in the woods where he could see nobody," Jefferson would have hoped to control him altogether; but unfortunately the national affairs were transacted not in the forest, but at Philadelphia.   In spite of the bad behavior of the attorney-general the secretary of state still made the effort necessary to refrain from breaking with him.   He ingenuously writes: "I have kept on terms of *strict friendship* with him hitherto that I might make some good out of him, and because he has really some good private qualities; but he is in a station infinitely too important for his understanding, his firmness, or his circumstances."

Presiding over this inharmonious quartette, Washington succeeded in preserving that coolness in judgment and equanimity in temper which mark him preëminently among all the illustrious men who live in history.   His predilections and sympathies were with Hamilton rather than with Jefferson.   But they did not lead him into partisanship.   He was now no more than ever before that character in which he so dreaded to appear, a party man.   He seems to have regarded these two gentlemen as the advocates pleading upon opposite sides of a cause; he kept to himself any private opinion he might entertain as to where the better merits lay; and in the many interlocutory judgments which he was called upon to give, he decided sometimes in favor of the one, sometimes of the other.   The general bent of his policy was towards strict neutrality and the careful preservation of peace. In this he was able nominally at least to combine all his secretaries, — Hamilton and Knox heartily, Jefferson less willingly, Randolph with such fluctuating measure of consistency as his wavering temper would permit. The disagreements which arose concerned matters of detail and the methods of carrying into practice upon each specific occasion this acknowledged general theory of action.

In the councils of this imperfectly accordant administration Hamilton enjoyed a sense of conscious strength and influence. His logic and his energy could be brought directly and strongly to bear in shaping results. Jefferson on the other hand felt in need of external support. It was this desire which had led him in the first instance to suggest and afterward to reiterate the advice that Congress should be convened in extra session. The excited temper of the people would probably find expression in that body; and in the House of Representatives he well knew that he should have an ardent and uncompromising ally. But this true cause of his urgency was not of course proclaimed by him, and the reasons put forward were simply that such an extraordinary emergency existed, involving such novel and important questions, that the advice of Congress might well be expected to be of service to the executive.

The anticipation which was present in Jefferson's mind as an incentive was also present in Hamilton's; but naturally it there exerted precisely the opposite influence. To preserve a neutral course was likely at the best to require all the resistent power of the government. If to the pressure of popular opinion should be added the pressure of a Gallicized House of Representatives, the labor might prove beyond the measure of the executive strength.   Hamilton accordingly asserted that no sufficient cause existed for summoning Congress to meet in an extra session.   No questions had yet arisen with which the president and his cabinet had not found themselves perfectly able to cope both in respect of deliberation, decision, and action.   Nothing required to be done which the executive was not empowered by the Constitution to do. There was no action which Congress would be asked to take if it should assemble ; therefore why oblige it to assemble?   This indeed was so far true that no specific purpose to be achieved by the aid of Congress had been suggested.   Jefferson's recommendation was therefore left to rest upon the assertion of the desirability upon general grounds of having the legislative body in session in troublous times.   The language of the Constitution, however, seemed hardly to leave it open to the president to convene Congress for no more definite purpose than that of enabling it to express its sentiments concerning matters appurtenant to his own separate function.   So whenever this proposition was renewed it failed for want of a proper necessity, and the legislators were not called from their homes until the regularly appointed day.

If the cabinet discussions following the news of war were not harmonious, the events which this body was immediately afterward called upon to consider did not serve to allay the differences of sentiment. Genet, the new minister, arrived at Charleston on the eighth day of April, 1793 ; and no sooner was his foot upon American soil than he entered upon a

series of unjustifiable, unlawful, and insulting transactions, which appear unequalled in the diplomatic
history of the United States. If ever envoy came
charged to send not peace but the sword among the
people it was this young Frenchman. It was from
no want of experience or knowledge that his conduct
was so reprehensible. On the contrary, he was a man
of excellent natural ability, and of an exceptionally
thorough training in diplomatic affairs and international obligations. For seven years he had been exercised at home under the astute Count de Vergennes,
and afterward had filled positions in London, Vienna,
Berlin, and St. Petersburg. More recently he had
been revolutionizing Geneva, and affiliating it with
France. He could not plead ignorance in excuse for
any portion of his behavior; on the contrary, his
skill and zeal made him more than ordinarily dangerous. The simple difficulty was that the intoxica-
tion of the Revolution had thoroughly possessed him,
and ruined the usefulness of a man who under other
circumstances might have accomplished a brilliant
success. But unhappily the world seemed to him
only a field for French exploits, and its nations to have
no other destiny in the present age than to be either
allies or foes in French hostilities. That a country
should seek to pursue its own interests in a peaceful
career in this era of universal warfare seemed to him
monstrous and unnatural. That the free and friendly
republic of the United States should be satisfied with
any other part than that of warm coöperation with
republican France was odious and incredible. If the
government was not prepared to go to any necessary
lengths in behalf of its great benefactor, then was

this government no less false to its duties, no less at variance with the will of the governed masses, than were the effete and wicked tyrannies of Europe. Never doubting the temper of the people, never questioning their readiness and their power to support him in all which he should undertake, Genet at once began to make use of the United States more as if they constituted a province or appanage of France than an independent empire.

It was in pursuance of this design that he had landed at Charleston, far from the seat of government, where he could get his schemes fairly under way before interference could be possible. He had brought out with him to this country three hundred blank commissions, to be distributed to such persons as would fit out cruisers in our ports to prey upon British commerce, especially in the neighboring West Indies. Within two days after landing he had commissioned and sent forth two privateers, manned chiefly by Americans. He opened a headquarters for the enlistment of American sailors into the French service. By virtue of a decree of the French Convention, he actually had the audacity to constitute the French consuls' resident in the ports of the United States courts of admiralty for the trial and condemnation of prizes brought in by the French privateers. By our treaty of commerce with France the privateers of that nation with their prizes were entitled to shelter in ports of the United States, and the prizes might also be sold in this country. But these were the extreme privileges thus specially allowed to them ; and no one was better aware than the well-trained Genet of the utter illegality of endowing a consul of a foreign country with the functions of a court of admiralty in the place of his residence. Yet within five days the privateers, sailing into the neighboring waters which were covered with the British mercantile marine, had captured merchantmen both of that country and of Holland, had brought them into the port of Charleston, and had procured their condemnation by their prompt and private tribunal.

Having paused in Charleston long enough to set matters in good train there, the minister prepared to advance upon the national capital. The vessel which had brought him from France was commissioned as a privateer, and then ordered to sail around to Philadelphia. But he himself preferred to proceed by land, not without good and sufficient motives. In April Jefferson had written to Madison that Genet's arrival would "furnish occasion for the people to testify their affections without regard to the cold caution of their government." This dangerous hint thus early given of the possibility of the people separating from the government, and refusing to give it their countenance and the moral support of their approbation, was only too thoroughly followed out. The reception accorded to the Frenchman at Charleston, both by the populace and by the members of the State government, was pointedly cordial. Similar manifestations marked his journey northward. The Democratic newspapers sedulously stimulated the popular sentiment. The news of his approach to Philadelphia brought out a great crowd to escort him into the city. It seemed to be resolved by the French sympathizers that the warmth of the citizens should more than atone for any calmness in the tone of the government officers. Deputations hastened to wait upon the minister, and to present to him fervent addresses. A great feast was given in the evening, at which the Marseillaise was sung, the red cap of Liberty was sent round from head to head, the sailors from the frigate which had brought Genet to this country were introduced to the revellers and received the fraternal embrace, and were presented with the intertwined flags of France and the United States. Altogether the festivity appears to have been very wild, very ardent, and in very bad taste. Such displays deceived while they gratified Genet, and unquestionably urged him to proceed to extremities which in the absence of such ill-judged encouragement might have been avoided, to the advantage of all the countries concerned. He could hardly be blamed for taking an erroneous view of things when he found respectable merchants upon all sides zealously adopting and glorying in the name of Jacobins; when he saw the staid men of Anglo-Saxon blood about him aping the excitability of the Latin races, throwing their arms around each other in the public streets, and ostentatiously exchanging the typical " kiss of fraternity." In our own generation we have seen stirring times, moving the deepest feelings of our human nature ; but the manifestations of sentiment in the civil war hardly enable us to believe the truth of the sketches which have come down to us from credible sources concerning the behavior of people in 1793.

Thus did those who felt themselves agreeably untrammelled by responsibility conduct themselves. But not so could the rulers of the people act; even

Jefferson, with all his longing for French affiliations, felt his private aspirations checked by the gravity of the occasion. At the present rate of progress, a few short weeks would see the country involved in a war of a peculiarly relentless character, having demented France as her only ally and all the rest of Europe banded against her. Jefferson had an instinctive and civilized shrinking from the destructiveness and brutality of warfare; it was one of the best traits in his character, and it now made him reluctant to join in hostilities, even to aid beloved France. Washington was resolved to keep the country moving along the path of prosperity by every honorable means in his power so long as he was in control of affairs. Hamilton would have seen almost any catastrophe with more tranquillity than the spectacle of the United States taking active part with the unhallowed government of Robespierre.

So when this French zealot, Genet, newly heated by the fumes of popular incense and civic orgies, came in contact with the national officials he seemed to experience a sudden chill, which was any thing but agreeable to his overwrought senses. How painfully vapid appeared the words of the president when the presentation of the new envoy took place! It was only a few days since the Marquis de Noailles and other illustrious *émigrés*, with whose blood the constituents of Genet would gladly have reddened their hands, had been admitted to the like honor by this impartial chief magistrate. Nay, the very room in which the reception took place had among its decorations some " medallions of Capet and his family." All this was painful to the sensitive envoy; but much more painful were the results of the cabinet conferences, which were held in these same busy and anxious days, concerning his privateers and his prize courts.

News of the doings at Charleston was no sooner received than the government felt itself obliged to take with promptness a decided position. The English minister immediately sent in his protests and demands for restitution. Among a number of wrongs the case of the " Grange " appeared especially unjustifiable. This vessel — a British merchantman — had been captured in American waters, actually within the Capes of Delaware, by the " Ambuscade," the same frigate which had already done its share of mischief by bringing M. Genet in safety across the ocean.

A cabinet opinion, given in writing by Hamilton on May 15, 1793, treating of these matters, can hardly fail to be of interest, in view of the operation of its doctrines as applied to the recent cases of Confederate cruisers fitted out in British ports during the late civil war. The transactions of Genet were indeed barefaced and outrageous to a degree far in advance of any thing which could be proved to have occurred in the more modern instances. But the principles of international law, invoked in 1793 by Great Britain and in 1861–65 by the United States, were so far similar as to render the older cases still very interesting. Little difficulty was found in coming to an unanimous conclusion that the " Grange " ought to be restored, and that to that end a demand should be made upon the French minister for her delivery to our national authorities. The requisition was subsequently urged and somewhat reluctantly complied with. It was also unanimously agreed that the erection of the French consuls into courts of admiralty, for the purposes of jurisdiction in questions of prize, was altogether illegal and not to be permitted. Against this rule Genet loudly protested, supporting his position by the most flimsy and preposterous semblance of argument. But the administration, conscious of being in the right, refused to withdraw or modify its declaration. The commissioning, equipping, and sending forth of armed privateers, and the enlistment of American sailors and marines to serve on board the same, were also declared without dissent to be contrary to the law of nations. In accordance with the opinion of Hamilton, and against that of Jefferson, it was also asserted to be unlawful for a foreign armed vessel to increase her complement of men while in a port of the United States, even by enlisting citizens of her own country commorant at that port.

These decisions were reached without serious difficulty. But much discrepancy of opinion was elicited by the demand of Mr. Hammond for restitution of the British vessels captured by the illegally despatched privateers and brought into our ports. Hamilton was of opinion that the restitution should be made. His reasoning in some parts expresses, as well as it has ever been put, the theory upon which the United States based her claims against Great Britain for reparation for the ravages of the Confederate cruisers. The liability of a nation for the acts done within its territory wherein it alone is sovereign, and the impossibility of justification upon the ground of the insufficiency of its internal arrangements of police or law to meet the emergency, are very clearly laid down.

"The jurisdiction of every *independent* nation within its own territories naturally excludes all exercise of authority by any other government within those territories, unless by its own consent, or in consequence of stipulations in treaties.

"The equipping, manning, and commissioning of vessels of war; the enlisting, levying, or raising of men for military service, whether by land or sea, all which are essentially of the same nature, are among the highest and most important exercises of sovereignty.

"It is, therefore, an injury and an affront of a very serious kind, for one nation to do acts of the above description within the territories of another, without its consent or permission.

.   .   .   .

"The obligation to prevent an injury usually, if not universally, includes that of repairing or redressing it when it has happened.

"If it be contrary to the duty of the United States as a neutral nation to suffer cruisers to be fitted out of their ports to annoy the British trade, it comports with their duty to remedy the injury which may have been sustained, when it is in their power to do so.

"If it be said that what was done took place before the government could be prepared to prescribe a preventive, and that this creates a dispensation from the obligation to redress, the answer is, —

"That a government is responsible for the conduct of all parts of a community over which it presides; that it is to be supposed to have at all times a competent police everywhere to prevent infractions of its duty towards foreign nations; that in the case in question the magistracy of the place ought not to have permitted what was done, and that the government is answerable for the consequences of its omissions.

"It is true that in a number of cases a government may excuse itself for the non-performance of its duty, on account of the want of time to take due precautions, from the consideration of the thing having been unexpected and unforeseen,

&c.; and justice often requires that excuses of this kind, *bonâ fide* offered, should be admitted as satisfactory.

"But such things are only *excuses*, not *justifications;* and they are only then to be received when a remedy is not within the reach of the party.

"If the privateers expedited from Charleston had been sent to the French dominions, there to operate out of our reach, the excuse of want of time to take due precautions ought to have been satisfactory to Great Britain. But now that they have sent their prizes into our ports, that excuse cannot avail us. We have it in our power to administer a specific remedy, by causing restitution of the property taken; and it is conceived to be our duty to do so. It is objected to this, that the commissions which were issued are valid between the parties at war, though irregular in respect to us; that the captures made under them are therefore valid captures, vesting the property in the captors, of which they cannot be deprived without a violation of their rights, and an aggression on our part."

Jefferson fully agreed with Hamilton as to the illegality of the fitting out and sailing of the capturing vessels, but he could not bring himself to the point of agreeing with him also concerning the propriety of restitution. To take a vessel from a French captor and give it back to an English owner taxed Jefferson's official impartiality too severely. It was, he said, an act of *reprisal;* it could only be done by force, and being substantially an act of war it must be expected to result in war. He thought that an apology for the past, a promise to prevent repetition of such transactions in the future, ought to be satisfactory to Great Britain. He would have been satisfied to excuse the United States on the ground of want of time to take sufficient precautions to prevent the escape of these vessels, and he did not subscribe to the doctrine of the liability of the government for all acts which took place upon its territory and arose from the insufficiency of its domestic arrangements of police and law. Jefferson's argument was rather an appeal to the magnanimity of Great Britain not to exact a penalty which, under the circumstances, too much resembled a hardship than a logical demonstration of her lack of lawful right to do so. Yet it was certain that France would consider the effort to make specific restitution as unfriendly, needless, even wrongful upon our part.

The question was of novel as well as of grave import; its decision either way might involve very disagreeable consequences. The dilemma in which Washington found himself placed was difficult. He was anxious to do right, but was not perfectly sure what was right; he was desirous to avoid giving offence, yet he felt assured that he could not well avoid it. Finally he adopted a middle course, not so easily defensible upon purely logical grounds as might have been desired, yet which practically relieved the country from the immediate embarrassment.

Mr. Jefferson sent to Mr. Hammond a letter in which he said that, if the commission of the capturing privateer was valid, then "the property, according to the laws of war, was by the capture transferred" to the captors, and "it would be an aggression on their nation for the United States to rescue it from them." If the commission was not valid, then the property was not transferred, and a suit for its recovery would be cognizable in our courts. But in any event the transaction could not be imputed to the United States. "It was the first moment of the war, in one of their most distant ports, before measures could be provided by the government to meet all the cases which such a state of things was to produce; impossible to have been known, and therefore impossible to have been prevented by that government. The moment it was known the most energetic orders were sent to every State and port of the Union to prevent a repetition of the accident."

It is impossible to view, without some amusement, the position which Jefferson assumed in regard to these matters in his communications with the British minister. Reciting the information given to him by that gentleman concerning the condemnation of an English prize in Charleston by the French consul, "you justly add," he says, "that this judicial act is not warranted by the usage of nations, nor by the stipulations existing between the United States and France. I observe further, that it is not warranted by any law of the land." Comforting words these; and as Mr. Hammond read them he must have anticipated that they were the preamble of a promise to make restitution, or at least reparation. Such was Hamilton's doctrine, who had no desire to see a government shirking its responsibility, a nation refusing to make good unlawful acts wrongfully committed within its own domain. "A government," said he, "is responsible for the conduct of all parts of the community over which it presides. It is supposed to have at all times a competent police everywhere to prevent infractions of its duty towards foreign nations. The magistracy of South Carolina ought not to have permitted what was done, and the government is answerable for the consequences of its omissions."

Not so, however, Jefferson. The transaction, he continued kindly to explain, "is consequently a mere nullity; as such it can be respected in no court, can make no part in the title to the vessel, nor give to the purchaser any other security than what he would have had without it. In short it is so absolutely nothing as to give no foundation of just concern to any person interested in the fate of the vessel; and in this point of view, sir, I hope you will see it." Here was consolation! A French official had invaded the jurisdiction and insulted the nationality of the United States; had undertaken to set up a judicial tribunal in a principal seaport of the country; had gone through the forms of judicial process, condemned and sold the vessel of the subject of a friendly kingdom. To a request that the United States would vindicate her sovereignty and repair the wrong done upon her territory, the reply is that the whole proceeding is "nothing." So the British owner can rest happy in the reflection, that if he has lost his vessel through the inability of the United States to prevent France from setting up courts in American cities, yet the whole matter is a "mere nullity," and not fit to give him any "foundation of just concern." What a chapter for Martin Chuzzlewit! The English government was far from resting satisfied with Mr. Jefferson's logic and with his advice, that recourse should be had to the local courts of the country. A breach of international obligation had occurred in the United States, and to the government of that country the government of the injured country looked for reparation. In good time these views prevailed. A few months later, Washington's increased familiarity with questions of international law made clear to him the soundness of Hamilton's views. He then caused the British minister to be assured that restitution, or at least reparation, should be made; and the French minister was notified that either the captured property or its value must be returned by France to the United States. Settlement was finally made upon this basis with Great Britain in Jay's treaty.

But the truth was that a serious difficulty did exist in the way both of curing and of preventing these wrongs and injuries. The idea was vaguely wandering in Jefferson's mind when he wrote the foregoing sentences, and erelong circumstances brought it forward and gave it shape. He was quite right in thinking that the instrumentality should exist in the courts; his error lay in refusing to acknowledge the liability of the government and nation for the non-existence of that instrumentality. The lesson was but imperfectly taught by the prize cases, but soon afterward was more distinctly shown by the trials of Henfield and Singletary. These persons were prosecuted upon a charge of having unlawfully enlisted in the United States in the service of France. They were defended by counsel, whose fees were paid by Genet. The case was supposed to be a test case; and when the defendants were acquitted great was the rejoicing of the French faction.

At last these frequent experiences showed where the difficulty lay. Hamilton had well said that he believed the courts were incompetent to deal with these matters.[1] There was no law in the

[1] "The effects of captures under the commissions are in a legal sense valid as between the parties at war, but have no validity

land under sanction of which the judicial tribunals could interfere to prevent or punish, or make reparation in cases of breach of international obligations. Therefore it was that Hamilton thought that the executive should intervene and do that which plainly ought to be done. The nation of the United States owed certain duties to Great Britain; the government of the United States must see to it that those duties were performed, or must face the consequences of a breach of them even if those consequences should be the outbreak of war. It was no excuse for us to say to Great Britain that we had not the proper domestic legal machinery to enable us by due form in our courts to satisfy our obligations to her. Humiliating and unworthy of a powerful nation as such an excuse might be, it would also be totally unavailing. The duty must be fulfilled, and the United States must provide the necessary instrumentalities or make amends for their non-existence, whether that non-existence arose from inexperience, neglect, oversight, or a false estimation of the efficiency of the means provided. Precisely this ground did our country take in the " Alabama " controversy. Whether the internal legislation and police arrangements of England were or

against us. Originating in a violation of our rights, we are nowise bound to respect them.

" Why then (it may be asked) not send them to the animadversion and decision of the courts of justice ? Because, it is believed, they are not competent to the decision; the whole is an affair between the governments of the parties concerned, to be settled by reasons of State, not rules of law.

" 'Tis the case of an infringement of our sovereignty to the prejudice of a third party ; in which the government is to demand a reparation, with the double view of vindicating its own rights, and doing justice to the suffering party."

were not such as to enable her to discharge her duties was matter of indifference to us. We simply held her to those duties, and she must fulfil them or make compensation. Hamilton quickly comprehended this principle, and therefore advised that the executive should make due reparation by an imperial act, a necessity by reason of the fact that the courts were " not competent." Very soon Jefferson's eyes were opened to the same light. Then the knowledge spread ; and, after the lapse of a year crowded with examples, it came to be understood by everybody that a statute was desirable to form a basis upon which the judiciary could work. Accordingly the celebrated Act of June 5, 1794, was at last passed. It was .called at the time the Neutrality Act, but the term Foreign-Enlistment Act has since become more common. It was the first statute of this kind which had ever been known, and has formed the model of all subsequent legislation upon the subject both in Great Britain and in this country.

Genet was an obstinate man, and the first rebukes which he received in this privateering business were far from sufficient to reduce him to a due subordination to the lawful requirements of the government. He entered into a correspondence, and in his vehement epistles he mingled argument and rhetoric with all the fervor of his race. He questioned the soundness of the doctrines of international law asserted by the cabinet; he declared that apart from and superior to such doctrines were the special stipulations embodied in the treaty between France and the United States. Embarrassing as those stipulations were, however, and too probable as it seemed that if they should be observed they would involve us in war with Great Britain and the other allied powers, or if they should not be observed that the infraction would precipitate hostilities with France, yet they did not go the length to which M. Genet sought to stretch them. Nor was General Washington the man to be intimidated by the bombast of the overwrought envoy. On June 5, 1793, Mr. Jefferson wrote to Genet and informed him that, after due deliberation upon his suggestions, the opinions previously entertained by the cabinet had undergone no change. Privateers must not be commissioned and armed in, or despatched from, our ports. More than this, by way of " reparation to the sovereignty of the country " for previous breaches of duty in this respect, it was now required that " the armed vessels of this description should depart from the ports of the United States."

Boundless was the indignation of Genet at this condition of things. When Henfield and Singletary, subjects of the United States, were indicted for enlisting at Charleston on board a French privateer, he wrote to the secretary of state one of his most feeling and eloquent despatches : " The crime laid to their charge," said he, " the crime which my mind cannot conceive and which my pen almost refuses to state, is the serving of France and defending with her children the glorious cause of liberty." Declaring himself ignorant of any law or treaty depriving Americans " of this privilege," and authorizing " officers of police arbitrarily to take marines in the service of France from on board their vessels," he called for the intervention of Jefferson and of the President of the United States, " in order to obtain the immediate releasement of the above-mentioned officers, who have acquired by the sentiments animating them and by the act of their engagement, anterior to every act to the contrary, the right of French citizens if they have lost that of American citizens." Genet obviously came from a people neither addicted to the study of logic nor penetrated by the doctrines of Blackstone. The cabinet were unable to see that a change of citizenship could be lawfully effected by cherishing a sentiment even if that sentiment should develop into an unlawful act. Jefferson tranquilly replied that the offenders were in the hands of the judicial authorities for trial, and that the executive could not interfere, — a principle so plainly appurtenant to a free government as to be quite unintelligible to the representative of the despotic republic of France. Jefferson concluded his letter with the expression of a hope that the trials would terminate favorably to the defendants. Hamilton criticised the propriety of language too easily capable of being "construed into a wish that there may be found no law to punish a conduct in our citizens, which is of a tendency dangerous to the peace of the nation and injurious to powers with whom we are on terms of peace and neutrality." In accordance with this suggestion the questionable phraseology was stricken out, and without any mollifying clause the missive was despatched to add to the rage of the thwarted envoy, and to inspire him with a distrust of Jefferson as a friend in profession rather than in fact.

Some objection had been taken by the British minister to the freedom accorded to the French to purchase arms in this country. But the cabinet were well agreed upon this question. Arms might be contraband of war, but that was the most that could be said. The manufacture and sale of them was a branch of industry not to be interfered with by reason of the outbreak of war between foreign friendly nations. Either belligerent might lawfully purchase, of course taking its chance of safe delivery.

Another difficulty was involved in the question, whether or not an armed vessel arriving here should be prohibited from enlisting into her employment as seamen or marines natives of the country to which she belonged. Jefferson was opposed to such prohibition; Hamilton and Knox were in favor of it. The president adopted the latter view, and directed the secretary of state to give notice to that effect to M. Genet. For a time, however, it was judged best not to institute prosecutions against foreign subjects acting in contravention of this rule, and orders were given to the government counsel to confine their legal proceedings to the cases of American citizens. After a little while, however, persistent infractions of these regulations on the part of Frenchmen, and the obvious resolution of the minister to disregard the rules established by the government, induced the president to withdraw this too liberal immunity, and to order the prosecution of foreigners as well as of our own citizens.

Thereupon Genet fell into a wild fury. He had brought two cases before the attention of the cabinet, demanding reparation, instead of which he had encountered a rebuff, the justice of which he could hardly be expected fully to appreciate in his present mood.   He sat down and wrote a singularly insolent letter, pardonable only on the ground of his partially demented condition.   He had presented demands, he said, and in return had received " the private or public opinions of the president.   This ægis not appearing to you sufficient, you bring forth aphorisms of Vattel to justify or excuse infractions of positive treaties.   It is not thus the *American people* wish we should be treated."   Had Hamilton had the answering of this tirade, and this unseemly setting of the opinion of the people against the action of the government, Genet would certainly not have been pacified by the reply he would have received.   For Hamilton was deeply incensed.   But Jefferson was not easily provoked to anger against the French envoy, and prudently kept the indefensible letter to himself, answering it in a manner fitted to turn away wrath.

The troublesome frigate " Ambuscade," carrier of Genet and capturer of the " Grange," was about this time lying in New York harbor watching a British packet-ship with the purpose of pursuing her so soon as she should set sail.   The governor notified the French consul that the armed vessel must not depart until twenty-four hours should have elapsed next after the British ship should get under way.   The rule is tolerably well established as a principle of international law.   Genet however sent instructions to the consul, denying the lawfulness of the order, and bidding him " oppose it with energy."   This was bad, but worse was to come.

The case of the " Little Sarah," *alias* " Le petit Démocrat," tried the temper of the administration beyond any which had gone before. She was one of the prizes of this same ill-omened breeder of contention, the mischievous "Ambuscade," brought into Philadelphia and there increased in her armament and equipped to depart as a privateer. News of this coming to Governor Mifflin he sought, through Mr. Secretary Dallas, to persuade Genet to detain her. The minister refused in language of extraordinary import, declaring significantly that he should soon have three French war ships at his control in our waters, and deprecating an attempt to stay the vessel, since it would inevitably be resisted by force. Mifflin — after consultation with the members of the administration then present in Philadelphia — ordered out the militia to take possession of the vessel. Jefferson, much exercised at this threatening condition of things, called on Genet upon Sunday, in hopes by his influence to bring that gentleman at least temporarily to his senses. The Frenchman however was equally deaf to argument and to entreaty. He had begun to suspect half-heartedness on the part of Jefferson,—who had told him all sorts of political secrets and all the private partisan slanders of the cabinet; who was enduring daily anguish for his sake in the discussions of the secretaries! But Genet did not appreciate this condition of things, and now by his gross ingratitude placed his friend in a very awkward position. To the persuasions of Jefferson he replied by a series of insulting remarks; and finally, refusing to give any pledge in the matter, simply expressed his opinion that the obnoxious craft probably would not be ready to depart before the following Wednesday. Washington, now absent from the city, was expected to return in this interval. He would then assume the responsibility, and give such orders as he should see fit under the circumstances. Jefferson, relying on the slender assurance to be elicited from the minister's declaration of probability, caused the interference of the militia to be dispensed with. The consequence was, that the privateer quickly dropped down the stream and put herself beyond all danger of farther interference. Washington, returning to find affairs in this very unsatisfactory condition, fell naturally into extreme dudgeon, and at once sent for Jefferson; but the secretary had "retired indisposed to his seat in the country." The president, not much appeased at this intelligence, wrote to the fugitive with some sharpness of expression. But the mischief was done beyond the power of president or secretary to cure.

These events had not been allowed to succeed each other without exciting warm discussion and much difference of opinion in the cabinet. In the absence of the president the secretaries had been obliged to define the course to be pursued in the immediate emergency. Hamilton, seeing the vessel drop down stream and having little faith in the ostensible reasons given for her doing so, had proposed to bring some guns at once into position on Mud Island and thus, if need be, to prevent her actually getting off to sea. This he urged as a "provisional measure, only to take effect if the vessel attempts to depart, in which case France would justly have nothing to complain of." Jefferson had strongly opposed any such scheme, alleging that, since the application of force was sure to meet with resistance on the part of the privateer, the result would prove to be the inception of a war with France. He refused to believe that the United States was ready to go to war with France simply because, as he saw fit to put it, a French vessel had bought and was carrying away two guns. Such "little subjects of displeasure," being merely "the acts of an individual," seemed to him by no means intolerable. He could not bring himself to "gratify the combination of kings with the spectacle of the two only republics on earth destroying each other for two cannon," nor would he by adding the United States to that royal combination "let it be from our hands that the hopes of man receive the last stab." To this sentimentality Hamilton replied that he also deprecated war, nor did he expect it. To show a firm front in this matter, to do our duty courageously, to cause our laws and ourselves to be respected, might be expected to avert rather than to precipitate war. For the case was a clear one ; and if we should tamely suffer this gross indignity and infraction of law to pass unchecked worse would quickly be attempted, till, if we had a tittle of independence left, we should be fairly driven to resentment, resistance, and war. It is hardly necessary to discuss the merits of this controversy for the instruction of a generation which has seen Great Britain make restitution for the ravages of the confederate cruisers. Not one of those vessels was released from actual seizure in order to enable her to sail from beneath the very eyes of the government. Further, the supposition may be fairly ventured that, if the escape of any one of those craft had been accompanied with such circumstances of outrage and official insult as distinguished the departure of "Le petit Démocrat," the chances of a patient delay by the United States and a final peaceful settlement would have been seriously reduced.

But if this event was eminently disgraceful to the United States, it was at least open to them to point to one matter in which they had not been remiss in the performance of their duties. Another vessel was at this same time increasing her armament in this same port of Philadelphia. Orders were peremptory not to let her pass the fort. There was no question made about firing upon her; by any necessary means she was to be stopped. Fortunately she did not seek to evade the detaining mandate. The characteristic distinguishing her case from that of "Le petit Démocrat" lay in her nationality; for she was an English vessel. This fact was enough to render the secretary of state fully alive to the obligations of international law, and the propriety of using batteries.

The irrepressible Genet, much encouraged by his success in despatching "Le petit Démocrat" and in escaping the censure which he so richly merited for his behavior in that matter, now proceeded to another flagrant and insolent violation of law. He posted hand-bills throughout the city of Philadelphia, which the president and his secretaries could not stir abroad in the streets without seeing upon every side of them, urging people " to enlist in the service of the republic and engage in the cause of liberty." Nay, he actually took steps to organize in the western country a military expedition to invade the Spanish-American possessions. He also sent a letter to Jefferson containing a demand which he well knew ought not to be complied with. It was then the acknowledged principle of international law that enemy's goods in a neutral bottom were lawful prize. Between the United States and France a special treaty-stipulation had established the doctrine that free ships should make free goods. Genet now demanded that the United States should arbitrarily assert this rule as against all other countries. To do so would have been equivalent to a general declaration of war; and the cause of such a war would have been nothing else save that the maritime nations of Europe would not permit the United States at their own sole option to alter established principles of international obligation in the very day of their important operation. The epistle embodying this extraordinary demand was couched in language appropriately unbecoming. A long tirade was closed by the assertion that the French "are punished for having believed that the American nation had a flag, that they had some respect for their laws, some conviction of their strength, and entertained some sentiment of dignity. If our fellow citizens have been deceived, if you are not in a condition to maintain the sovereignty of your people, speak! We have guaranteed it when slaves. We shall be able to render it formidable, having become freemen." These words the long-suffering administration read and still controlled their temper, refrained from rebuke, and answered in the ordinary course of business and in the tone of diplomacy.

But with all their wonderful self-restraint and persevering courtesy they abated nothing in the substance of their proceedings, as will appear by the following code of rules which was adopted unanimously in a cabinet meeting early in August, and forthwith made public. Of these rules the second and sixth were suggested by Randolph, the others were drawn by Hamilton.

1. The original arming and equipping of vessels in the ports of the United States by any of the belligerent powers for military service, offensive or defensive, is deemed unlawful.

2. Equipments of merchant vessels by either of the belligerent parties in the ports of the United States, purely for the accommodation of them as such, is deemed lawful.

3. Equipments in the ports of the United States of vessels of war in the immediate service of the government of any of the belligerent parties, which, if done to other vessels, would be of a doubtful nature, as being applicable either to commerce or war, are deemed lawful; except those which shall have made prize of the subjects, people, or property of France, coming with their prizes into the ports of the United States, pursuant to the seventeenth article of our treaty of amity and commerce with France.

4. Equipments in the ports of the United States by any of the parties at war with France, of vessels fitted for merchandise and war, whether with or without commissions, which are doubtful in their nature, as being applicable either to commerce or war, are deemed lawful, except those which shall have made prize of the subjects, people, or property of France, coming with their prizes into the ports of the United States, pursuant to the seventeenth article of our treaty of amity and commerce with France.

5. Equipments of any of the vessels of France in the ports of the United States, which are doubtful in their nature, as being applicable to commerce or war, are deemed lawful.

6. Equipments of every kind in the ports of the United States of privateers of the powers at war with France are deemed unlawful.

7. Equipments of vessels in the ports of the United States which are of a nature solely adapted to war are deemed unlawful; except those stranded or wrecked, as mentioned in the eighteenth article of our treaty with France, the

sixteenth of our treaty with the United Netherlands, the ninth of our treaty with Prussia; and except those mentioned in the nineteenth article of our treaty with France, the seventeenth of our treaty with the United Netherlands, the eighteenth of our treaty with Prussia.

8. Vessels of either of the parties not armed, or armed previous to their coming into the ports of the United States, which shall not have infringed any of the foregoing rules, may lawfully engage or enlist therein their own subjects, or aliens not being inhabitants of the United States; except privateers of the powers at war with France, and except those vessels which shall have made prize, &c.

A marine league from the shores of the United States was established as the extent of their jurisdiction over the sea, within which limits they acknowledged their duty and asserted their right and intention to enforce observance of the rules of neutrality.

The course pursued by the administration of Washington during the first trying months of the European war has ever since called forth the eulogiums of students of international law. A series of questions had been presented in rapid succession before our government, involving nice and dubious questions of obligation; and the men who were called upon to decide them had had but slender occasion or opportunity at any previous times in their busy lives to render themselves familiar with the doctrines and principles applicable to such emergencies. Indeed the theory of the rights and duties of neutrals was itself in a formative stage rather than already a definite and complete code. Upwards of three quarters of a century which have since elapsed have only advanced it towards certainty without yet fully bringing it to that desirable and difficult consummation. But the action taken and the principles and rules enunciated by President Washington and his cabinet in the spring and summer of 1793 have borne examination and criticism so well, have been found so reasonable, just, and impartial, that no better precedents can be cited in argument.

Yet, though such is the opinion which dispassionate after-generations have been able to adopt, it was very far from being the contemporaneous sentiment of the day. For a time no one was pleased. Great Britain complained bitterly and justly of the manner in which France continually repeated her attempts, attended too often with at least the temporary appearance of success, to wrest from the United States important and unlawful privileges. France, utterly deaf to the sound dictates of that reason to which she was erecting altars and performing a ridiculous and disgusting worship, was incensed at the interposition of any obstacles to her free over-riding of all manner of laws. At home an excited faction, which for some little time undoubtedly included far the larger part of the people, was scarcely less indignant than were the Frenchmen themselves at the policy of neutrality so resolutely adhered to by the president and cabinet. An extreme unpopularity for a time beset the persons to whose influence this policy was quite justly attributed. The wrath so deeply felt was violently expressed ; yet the strongest phraseology of vituperation failed to bring relief to those who used it, so inadequate did it seem for the expression of their sensations. Hamilton was overwhelmed with the grossest abuse that tongues and pens well skilled in the art could cast upon him. Nor as time went on was Washington himself any longer held sacrosanct.

He at last found himself placed by the French sympathizers in that position which of all others he had
so keenly abhorred, so often deprecated, — the chief
of a party instead of the head of the nation.

The language of the Democratic press, more notably of the newspapers of Freneau and Bache, had
respected nothing. They had welcomed Genet with
the triumphant prognostication that by his aid and
influence it would be brought to pass that "the
gorgeous trappings of monarchy would be no longer
substituted for republican simplicity." Even Jefferson
allowed himself to descend to the same kind of language. "The satellites and sycophants" surrounding
the president had, he said, "wound up the cere-
monials of government to a pitch of stateliness"
which nothing but Washington's personal character
could have supported, and which even that might soon
fail to support "in the appeal of the times to common
sense as the arbiter of every thing." He somewhat
ungrammatically declared of Washington that "naked
he would have been sanctimoniously reverenced, but
enveloped in the rags of royalty, they can hardly be
torn off without laceration." The only fault which
these enthusiastic scribblers of welcomes to Genet
afterward found with him, when he was advancing in
mid career of lawlessness and insolence, was to charge
him with comporting himself "too tamely" and of
being "too accommodating, for the sake of the peace
of the United States."

A rumor arriving that the ambassador of the United
States had been murdered in Paris, the newspapers
commented upon it by expressing their astonishment
that he had been suffered to live so long, under the

protection of an American diploma, "to triumph in unexampled folly and impertinence." The proclamation of neutrality was branded as an act "disgraceful to the American character." The arrest of Henfield and Singletary and their commitment for trial was denounced as a proceeding of despotism. The judges who presided at the trial were accused of having been guided by political motives, and of having taken "the most alarming measures to stifle the calls of justice and to intimidate an American jury into a verdict consonant with the wishes of the court party or British faction." American citizens were said, "like some European subjects," to be "*slaves* attached to the soil," unable "without leave from their *masters*" to enter into foreign service. All the offensive slang of the day in France was ferried across the Atlantic. Actions were commended or denounced according as they were or were not "fraternal," and persons were approved or condemned by granting or withholding the sobriquet "citizen" in connection with their names. As a sample of the rodomontade which pleased the readers of the public prints of the day, the following address to Hamilton may not be uninstructive: "O votary of despotism! — O abetter of Carthaginian faith! — Blush! Can you for a moment suppose that the hearts of the yeomanry of America are become chilled and insensible to the feelings of insulted humanity, like your own? Can you think that gratitude, the most endearing disposition of the human heart, is to be argued away by your dry sophistry? Do you suppose the people of the United States will (instigated thereto by duty and interest) prudently thumb over Vattel and Puffendorf to ascertain the sum and substance of their obligations to their generous brethren — the French? No! no! Each individual will lay his hand upon his heart and find the amount there! He will there find that manly glow, both of gratitude and love, which animated his breast when assisted by this generous people in establishing his own liberty and shaking off the yoke of British despotism!"

The frame of mind indicated by these extracts from the opposition press of that year was unquestionably that of a large proportion of the people throughout the States. It may be conceived in what an anxious and embarrassing position the government was thereby placed. Established only a few brief years since, founded upon the grand principle of the right of the people to govern themselves, yet apparently in a serious crisis already deprived of the sympathy of a majority of the people ; obnoxious therefore to the charge of governing in their despite, ignorant of the measure of its own untested power to stand upright against the tempest of popular passion, — the government of the United States has never but upon a single other occasion found itself in equally trying jeopardy. Nothing but the confidence reposed in Washington carried it through without shipwreck. Even towards him many became inimical in their secret feelings ; and in time, as has been said, a few ventured by innuendo, occasionally by open assault, to express this sentiment. But for the most part the semblance of respect was retained towards the chief magistrate.

This painful reticence was however made up for by proportionately fierce onslaughts against that unfortunate gentleman who was popularly supposed to be the most influential adviser and the closest friend of Washington. Bitter was the hatred and unmeasured the distrust manifested by the Democrats towards Hamilton. He was stigmatized as the foe of France, the friend of her foes. Nor could a weightier or more conclusive condemnation be uttered than was contained in this description. From this fact of chief importance followed as matter of inevitable implication the secondary facts, that he was therefore the apostle of tyranny, the determined enemy of the Gallic trinity, " Liberté, Égalité, Fraternité." His strong and masterly purpose to establish the line of our neutral obligations distinctly and rigidly, to force compliance with it in every instance without fear or favor, was a policy the most offensive to the popular wishes that could well have been devised. The people were not prepared for a full, candid, and upright performance of their duties. They were better pleased to define their obligations with the utmost possible degree of laxity, and then to break even those acknowledged obligations on every occasion when it could be done without precipitating immediate war. Not a few would have been well enough pleased to have shared side by side with their adored France in the conflict itself. The more general feeling however did not reach quite to this point, but was content to come close to this utter extremity. It hardly admits of a doubt, that had Hamilton's line of conduct been in all cases strictly pursued, and had the people believed that his counsels were altogether supreme in the cabinet, the government would have been set at defiance, with what results it is impossible to prognosticate. To this criticism he must be acknowledged to be open, that his policy would have imperilled the domestic tranquillity, possibly even the stability of the government.   Yet in no instance can it be said that he wished any thing to be done by the United States, which it was not the strict duty of the United States to do, save perhaps the suspension of the treaty; and that was a privilege fairly to be demanded.   But he was uncompromising, and nothing but compromise would avail in such an emergency. The administration lost something of its dignity by temporizing more than he approved of; but by not temporizing it might have lost its existence.

The people somewhat exaggerated the measure of Hamilton's influence with Washington.   It was greater than that of any other individual, but it was not paramount.   No external influence ever subjugated the independent common sense of the president.   Nor did he now fail to listen with respect to the antagonistic arguments of Jefferson, or the suggestions of Randolph, the trimmer.   The consequence of this mingling of counsels was obvious in the manner in which he often softened the too sharply edged outlines of Hamilton's logical and stern uprightness.   The student of the history of those times will not deny that Washington deserved the title of savior of his country by his conduct in this year at least as fully as by any of his military exploits.   A notable instance of this working of things is furnished by the matter of restitution to Great Britain for vessels captured by the Charleston privateers.

There can be no doubt that the presence of Jefferson in the cabinet during this perilous summer was a very fortunate circumstance.   It is true that he sometimes failed to reach sound conclusions by reason of his French proclivities; it is true that his presence caused serious divisions in a cabinet which without him would not have proved very inharmonious. But the mischief arising from these circumstances was more than outweighed by the fact that his presence and arguments undoubtedly preserved an equilibrium in the mind of Washington and in the decisions of the conclave, which otherwise could hardly have been hoped for; and also by certain external and incidental advantages. France and all the great body of French sympathizers throughout the United States felt that the interests of that country were at least powerfully represented at every cabinet meeting. They had the privilege of a hearing, and an eloquent and trustworthy advocate to urge their cause. The leader of the opposition party, beyond a doubt the shrewdest politician in their ranks, was ever present to argue, to persuade, to protest in their behalf. More than this, he did not scruple to undertake the singular task of supplying them freely with all manner of private information. He was spy as well as friend. If they seemed to see him too little successful, too much over-ridden, yet he still retained the chief secretaryship, he still signed his name to the despatches. It was impossible to effect a complete severance from an administration in which he was content to remain, and in which he was known to play an important and influential though so often an imperfectly satisfactory part. If Jefferson had resigned before the arrival of Genet — as he had threatened to do — Washington's task would have been infinitely more difficult; his success would have been grievously imperilled.

All admirers of Jefferson, and many of those who do not admire him, unite in praising much of his conduct in this portion of his career. He has been assailed for forming part of an administration, notwithstanding that he could not shape and too often could not agree with its policy. But such criticism is hardly fair. He stayed in a crisis of grave importance to do all that he was able by his most strenuous endeavors aimed toward the promotion of what seemed to him sound measures. If he was not in sympathy with his fellows, yet his views occasionally prevailed, and still more often tempered the result. Publicists have generally praised his letters to Genet very highly; the principles enunciated in them have been respected; their language is often quoted. Yet it is somewhat strange to see to how great an extent this praise and distinction have been thrust upon him. The doctrines which he so ably elucidated were by no means always the doctrines in which he believed. Often they were distasteful to him; often they had been determined upon by the cabinet against his contrary arguments; often they were but imperfect expressions of his belief. It is probable that nearly every one of these famous despatches to the French minister was penned by him with half-hearted reluctance. He may be said to have had distinction as a diplomatist in some measure made for him and actually forced upon him. So unwelcome was his task to him that erelong he tired and utterly sickened of it. In the midst of the vexatious difficulty caused by the departure of the " Little Sarah " or " Le petit Démocrat," he sent to Washington a letter stating his intention to resign at the close of the quarter, that is to say at the end of the month of September. It was like resigning a command in the midst of battle. But he could endure the tax upon his feelings no longer; he had been tried too severely, and no consideration, he said, could induce him to retain a post, the irritations of which conquered his philosophy. Washington begged and insisted upon his staying at least a short time longer; and at last he yielded so far as to extend his term for one more quarter and to postpone his retirement to the close of December. Afterward he bitterly regretted his concession. He wrote to Washington that he wished to withdraw from scenes for which, said he, " I am every day more and more convinced that neither my talents, tone of mind, nor time of life fit me." But it was well understood at the time, and subsequently confessed by himself, that his real incentive to retirement lay in his unwillingness any longer to put his name to documents, of the purport and contents of which he disapproved.

But the pendulum which had swung so far over upon the French side began at last to fall back. The sanguine and reckless minister in time overstrained a sentiment which he had thought capable of limitless stretching. Repeatedly he had found fault with the government upon the alleged ground that it was persistently disregarding the will of the people, which should be the supreme law. He had reiterated against Washington the charge of obstinately refusing his reasonable request to summon an extraordinary session of Congress, in order to obtain an expression of its sense concerning the foreign policy of the country. Insolent and indefensible as this conduct was, it had been long endured; and this very endurance perhaps helped to deceive the mistaken zealot. He was tempted at last, in the discussions concerning " Le petit Démocrat," to threaten that he himself would appeal from the president to the people ! This crowning instance of his mad insolence sealed his fate. His vexed and troubled friends sought to suppress the unfortunate tale. But it gradually found its way to the knowledge of the public. The pride of the people was at last touched, and on every side arose the outcry of their indignation. Startling indeed was the wrath which was aroused. The astonished minister found himself all at once not less generally assailed than a short time before he had been commended. The Democratic press, fairly driven from its first ill-advised efforts to defend him, at last had desperate recourse to disowning the truth. The controversy became very bitter, and distinct denials of veracity were freely interchanged. At last Chief Justice Jay and Senator Rufus King, who formed an early link in the chain of evidence against Genet, and whose truthfulness had been directly denied, published a letter over their own signature relating their knowledge concerning the matter. Genet, greatly excited, wrote to the secretary of state demanding the prosecution of these officers for libel. Jefferson had previously written to Madison, saying, " You will see much said and gainsaid about Genet's threat to appeal to the people. I can assure you it is a fact." Now, however, he carried Genet's request for a prosecution before the president and persuaded him to request the attorney-general to comply with it. Fortunately when the matter came before Randolph his French prejudices did not deprive him of his legal

acumen.   His clearer insight into the law, as well as
the proprieties of the case, led him to decline to proceed; and the result was that Genet was relegated to
the right of action which pertained to him, as to any
other individual, in the courts of the country.

Already, without waiting for the change in public
sentiment which this indiscretion and gross insult on
the part of the French minister produced, the cabinet
had resolved to request his recall.   Twice did Washington suggest this step before it was adopted.   Hamilton, indeed, would have been not loath to see a
direct dismissal; but the constitutional power of the
executive to dismiss was regarded as doubtful, and the
measure was thought imprudent.   Jefferson had stood
by his friend so long as he could.   He had received
the envoy with open arms upon his first arrival, and
wrote enthusiastically to Madison that it was "impossible for any thing to be more affectionate, more mag-
nanimous than the purport of his mission."   Slowly
and reluctantly had these feelings given place to distrust and indignation.   But Genet had loaded Jefferson too heavily.   It had been impossible for the shrewd
secretary not to see that his "incorrigible" friend was
rapidly bringing not only himself, but the French cause
in the United States, to the brink of destruction.
Complaint succeeded to praise, and grew very hearty
and sincere as events moved quickly on in mischievous
career.   At last Jefferson frankly acknowledged that
the true "purport of the mission" was to involve this
country in the war as an ally of France; that Genet's
"object was evidently, contrary to his professions, to
force us into the war."   He declared that it was
"true wisdom" for the party "to abandon Genet

entirely." So when, early in August, the propriety of requesting a recall was again mooted in the cabinet, Jefferson was found more malleable. The step was resolved upon, and the secretary of state himself signed the letter. The elaborate explanation of the condition of things which had led to this request, sent to our minister, Gouverneur Morris, at Paris, was the joint labor of Hamilton and Jefferson. Therein it was stated that Genet had undertaken to " use our force, whether we will or not, in a military line against nations with whom we are at peace ; . . . to direct the civil government, and especially the executive and legislative bodies; to pronounce what powers may or may not be exercised by the one or the other ; " . . . to charge the president with having " been too hasty in deciding certain questions," for which Congress should have been convened. Thus had Genet made " himself and not the president the judge of the powers assigned by the Constitution to the executive," and had " dictated " to the president " the occasion when he should exercise the power of convening Congress at an earlier day than their own act had prescribed." " If our citizens," it was said, " have not already been shedding each other's blood, it is not owing to the moderation of M. Genet, but to the forbearance of the government."

This application to his government was very reluctantly, and only in pursuance of a direct order of the cabinet, communicated by Jefferson to the minister. Genet, instead of being thereby brought to his senses, was only fired to wilder demonstrations. He was highly incensed against Jefferson, accusing him of double-dealing, of holding " a language official and a language confidential." He quite alarmed that functionary, who by no means relished the prospect that his "language confidential" might be published by his quondam friend, whom he had initiated with imprudent kindness into the "mysteries" of the government. The infatuated minister afterward undertook to make that very appeal to the people which he had denied that he had threatened to make. He demanded the publication of what had passed between himself and the government, in order that the nation might judge for itself with which party lay the right, with which the wrong.

In other respects he abated and caused his subalterns to abate nothing of their previous arrogance. A prize, taken by a French privateer within a mile of our shore, was brought into the harbor of New York. The marshal was ordered to serve process upon her. Genet ordered the French squadron to protect her by force. Another prize, in the port of Boston, was held by the marshal of that district by virtue of a writ of replevin. She was rescued by a body of marines under the command of the lieutenant of the French war-ship "Concorde." This war-ship had lately arrived in the harbor, and had been welcomed by salutes and a military parade, under orders of Governor Samuel Adams. She had returned the civility by hanging from her mainmast a conspicuous list of merchants in the town who supported the government, and were therefore in this fashion denounced as aristocrats. In such insults and lawless violence did Genet persist to the very last moment of his career, ruining his cause in the United States, sowing with thorns the path of his unfortunate patron, the secretary of state, placing his enemies undeniably in the right, and shifting to their side the advantages to be expected from popular favor. " Was there ever an instance before," quoth the irritated Jefferson, " of a diplomatic man overawing and obstructing the course of the law in the country by armed force ? " The very last day that Jefferson remained in office he was compelled by a peremptory command from Washington to undertake an unwelcome task, which he had intended by wily procrastination to devolve upon his successor. He was obliged to administer a rebuke to Genet for endeavoring to publish, and actually to use the secretary himself as a medium for distributing, copies of his instructions. It was the minister's purpose to put them forth as a political document, and to follow them with others which he hoped to disseminate by the same means.

The government had not resolved to ask the recall of Genet without grave misgivings as to the manner in which this action would be received in France. But no difficulty was encountered. The shifting character of affairs in that country left no man long either popular or powerful there, and fortunately averted all evil consequences to the United States. A successor to M. Genet was sent over in the person of M. Fauchet, a gentleman of more moderation, who pushed the advantages of France with not less zeal but with more discretion and consequently more success. Genet sank beneath the surface, but he left behind him a vicious reminiscence of his presence in the shape of the democratic clubs and societies. These bodies had been formed throughout the United States, in affectionate imitation of the political clubs of France. One of them had, upon motion of the infamous Collot d'Herbois, been formally adopted by the Jacobin club at Paris. These institutions had been nourished by the especial attention of Genet. They needed no fostering care to assist their evil growth, but in the fulness of his zeal he had bestowed upon them all the patronage and encouragement in his power. They had been the ardent supporters of his career, the ready instruments of his schemes. From no other source did such manifestations of insubordination appear as from these noisy and active bodies. In many of them, if not in all, the spirit of insurrection was scarcely smothered. They were as dangerous elements as the body politic could well contain within itself. Well-affected citizens regarded them with alarm, and even the soberer persons of French proclivities looked upon this irregular enginery with disfavor. Yet organizations of this kind were in accordance with the spirit of the times, and in spite of frowns and discountenance they continued to thrive after Genet had disappeared from the scene. When the whiskey disturbances in western Pennsylvania gradually grew into insurrection, it was well known that the disorderly spirit was sedulously fomented by these societies.

At last an official rebuke was administered to them. In his message to Congress, in November, 1794, the president referred to the existence of " self-created societies " which had made it their business to criticise and condemn the government and to stimulate resistance to law. The Senate, in its reply, assailed these societies with much warmth, declaring them calculated " to disorganize our government." In the House a long and eager debate ensued as to the mention which their address should contain concerning this clause of the message. The democratic societies found no friends who dared to come forward and openly name and defend them. The opposition leaders could not make up their minds to this. Yet the vague and general language which had been used made a covert defence possible. The Federalists sought to make it a battle for and against the democratic clubs ; the opposition-strove to make it a contest concerning the general right of the people to form voluntary associations, and to discuss the measures of an administration. It may be fairly considered that the result was a drawn battle. But one important fact at least was made clear, and that was that the democratic societies could find no one among their supposed political friends who was willing to advocate them without disguise. The discredit which was thus brought upon them was happily aided by the overthrow of the Jacobin club itself, at Paris, which opportunely occurred about this time. Thus, after having been the cause of much trouble and yet having actually accomplished nothing, this longest-lived fruit of the labors of Genet in the United States withered away and fell out of sight, within about eighteen months after the close of his mission.

CHAPTER IV.

THE WHISKEY INSURRECTION.

IN that first and famous report upon the public credit which Hamilton made to Congress in January, 1790, he recommended the laying of duties upon spirits of domestic manufacture, and upon stills. So many other and more immediately interesting topics were discussed in this report, that the proposition for the establishment of an excise tax attracted comparatively small attention. When, however, it was touched upon in the debates in Congress it met with warm opposition and was finally defeated. If the State indebtedness should not be assumed, it was said, the United States would not need this resource, while the States would find it indispensable.

But assumption was destined to success, and with that success the necessity for an increased taxation in some shape became inevitable. Commerce could not bear the whole burden. Accordingly in December, 1790, Hamilton again reiterated his previous advice. The schedule which he proposed established rates which varied according to the class of proof of the liquor, ranging from nine cents per gallon as a minimum to thirty cents per gallon as a maximum. Each still, employed in distilling spirits, was to be taxed annually sixty cents per gallon of its capacity.

The secretary stated that he was encouraged to renew the suggestion because he believed that the objections which had been previously made to it had originated in collateral considerations, subsequently obviated, rather than in objections to the measure itself. But it must be confessed that the course of the debates in Congress manifested the existence of a wide-spread and bitter antipathy to the principle of such a tax. It was denounced as among the worst of all possible forms of raising money; as oppressive, inquisitorial, demoralizing. A large proportion of the opponents of the measure were obviously stimulated neither by abstract opinions concerning the propriety of such legislation, nor by distrust of the financial merits of the scheme, but by considerations of a wholly local bearing and by the special interests of their constituents. As is always the case, these motives led to a great amount of vehement and earnest oratory and to the display of a degree of insubordinate animosity which augured ill for the smooth working of the law. Findley, who came from western Pennsylvania where distilling was the chief occupation of the people, distinguished himself by a singular exhibition of dangerous temper, declaring that he would have such a law met by complete social ostracism of all concerned in its enforcement. He would have their neighbors hold these unfortunates in contempt, refuse to associate with them, speak with them, buy, sell, deal, or have any kind of communication with them. He pronounced against them a ban in temporal effect not unlike a papal bull of excommunication. But a tax upon ardent spirits is defensible upon so many just grounds, that oratory like this was unavailing and the bill became law, taking effect in the following spring.

The first year of the operation of the law showed receipts much below what they should have been, due in part to its unpopularity, in part to some few defects in its provisions. A reference to Hamilton for suggestions to cure these defects was opposed by the anti-federalists who wished to keep the law as hateful as possible, and so to lay the greater odium upon the secretary who was responsible for it. But the reference was carried and the amendments were made, leaving the act open to no objection in matters of detail. In truth, if an excise were justifiable at all it could not have been put into more liberal shape. Yet the result was only a partial restoration of goodwill. In certain regions the people were simply and plainly resolved to submit to no excise tax whatsoever, however moderate the tariff or generous the regulations.

The most determined spirit of opposition was manifested in the western portion of Pennsylvania, beyond the Alleghanies. From this central hot-bed the insubordinate temper began in time to radiate in all directions, crossing the Virginia line and even finding its way over the mountain-chain to other counties of Pennsylvania. But nowhere else did matters come to the extremity to which they were carried in the four transmontane counties. This neighborhood had been settled originally by Scotch-Irish Presbyterians, men with a native aptitude for the consumption of whiskey, stubborn of temper, prone to violence in their moments of excitement, and by no means easily amenable to the control of government. Disputes as to the jurisdiction over this territory, long waged between Virginia and Pennsylvania, had not led to a reverence for law and order. Indian conflicts had been conducted upon singularly vindictive and bloody principles, and not many years had elapsed since a massacre had occurred in which the whites had slaughtered Indian men, women, and children, to the number of nearly one hundred, with circumstances of shocking barbarity.

Beneath the leadership of Gallatin, Findley, and Smilie, it was hardly to be wondered at that these people turned out apt and zealous soldiers; and soldiers in no figurative sense they showed a strong disposition to become. On July 27, 1791, a meeting was held at Red Stone Old Fort, at which it was agreed that county committees should be convened in the four malcontent counties. About a month later one of these committees passed denunciatory resolutions, declaring among other things that all officials under the excise law were "inimical to the interests of the country," and advising their outlawry by unanimous combination of their neighbors according to the threat of Findley. A meeting of delegates from the four counties was held in September following, which passed further inflammatory resolutions. Intemperate words could not long be reiterated among a population so reckless without leading to more substantial forms of disapproval. Accordingly it happened that in this same month of September the collector of revenues for the counties of Alleghany and Washington was waylaid in the latter county by a body of armed and disguised men, who cut off his hair, tarred and feathered him, took away his horse, and left him in this plight to make the best of his way for a long distance on foot. This first case of violent outrage was brought before the district court, and processes were issued against three persons charged with implication in the crime. But to issue process was easier than to serve it, and the deputy who undertook this duty, making up his mind that he would never return alive from its performance, sent a messenger in his own stead. This poor fellow could make no legal service, but he was seized, whipped, tarred and feathered, robbed of his horse and money, blindfolded and left tied in the woods for several hours.

Many other persons suffered in a similar manner. Not alone those engaged in aiding the execution of the law, but in some instances even distillers who submitted to it became the victims of the popular vengeance. A tarring and feathering was inflicted as punishment for the imprudent remark that the people of the county could hardly expect protection to be afforded them by a government whose laws they so strenuously opposed. There was freedom neither of speech nor of action. Two persons who had had the misfortune to be witnesses of one of these scenes of violence were seized and secreted, to make sure that they should not give testimony against the rioters. A wretched maniac, who wandered through the country proclaiming himself to be employed by the government to make certain inquiries concerning the distilleries, was pursued by some persons in disguise, dragged from his bed, stripped naked, branded in several places with a hot iron, then tarred and feathered, and in this horrible condition was at last turned away at daybreak to shift for himself. Though his insanity was perfectly apparent, yet the abuses to which he was subjected were said to have "exceeded description," and to be "sufficient to make human nature shudder."

Amid these outrages the position of the government was embarrassing in the extreme. Prejudices and misrepresentations against the law had been industriously disseminated throughout the whole country. The processes of the courts were proved to be inefficient, while Congress had not yet organized the means by which the executive could come to the aid of the judiciary when the latter arm was found incompetent to the execution of the laws. Further, the government dreaded for obvious reasons to resort to force until it should become absolutely necessary, and the uselessness of all milder means should be indisputably demonstrated. Accordingly some delay was submitted to, and for a brief interval a more submissive spirit seemed to be returning. But the appearance was delusive, and matters soon fell back into the old train.

The threats of destruction to property made it almost impossible for the government to hire offices. An unfortunate man who ventured to let his premises in Washington county for such a purpose was directly compelled, by threats of scalping, tarring and feathering, and the burning of his house, to expel his unpopular tenant, and to give public notice of his action in the Pittsburg Gazette.

On Aug. 21. 1792, a meeting of "sundry inhabitants of the western counties of Pennsylvania" was held. Gallatin acted as clerk. A series of resolutions were passed condemning internal taxes in general and the excise tax in particular, and declaring it to be a duty to oppose every legal obstruction to the operation of the law ; phraseology which afterward called forth much severe ridicule from critics of these proceedings. A committee was appointed to present an address to Congress, and another committee was charged to correspond with such other similar committees as might be created elsewhere concerning this same subject, and also empowered to summon general meetings of the people or conferences of the various committees. It was again urged upon the people at large to follow the example, which those present at this meeting agreed to set, in completely isolating the excise officials and cutting them off from all communion with their kind. This organization of corresponding committees reminded men of the times immediately preceding the Revolution, when a similar machinery had been organized and set in very effective motion against Great Britain. A course which so recently had led to such serious results could not be renewed without arousing alarm. Nor was the clause of excommunication to be made light of ; for it was truly said that an outlawry pronounced in such bitter terms of invective could not fail to operate as a " signal to all those who were bold enough to encounter the guilt and the danger to violate both the lives and the properties " of the designated victims.

At the time when news of this meeting and its doings reached Philadelphia, following hard upon the reports of acts of violence, Washington and Jefferson were both absent. Hamilton, however, being upon the ground set zealously to work to meet the requirements of the occasion. The excise had been his child, and now that it had fallen into trouble no other member of the cabinet seemed inclined to deprive him of his parental privilege or duty of extricating it. Neither upon his part did he betray any inclination to shirk or divide responsibility. Accordingly with the progress of events he is to be found writing proclamations to be issued by the president; preparing letters to be signed by the attorney-general; and later, when military movements began, in the absence of the secretary of war, exercising the functions of that official, and accompanying the army on the march. In the present exigency, Hamilton urged Attorney-General Randolph to institute prosecutions against some of the more conspicuously guilty parties. That gentleman, however, was not in sympathy with the secretary, and the victims were so erroneously selected that the legal proceedings came to nought.

Hamilton was inclined to enter upon vigorous practical measures at once, but Washington preferred to issue a proclamation. Hamilton accordingly drafted one, accepted some few amendments suggested by Randolph, and then forwarded it to Washington, with an intimation that by a slight change in the formal clause at the end he could avoid the necessity of sending it to Monticello to obtain Jefferson's countersignature. But Washington wrote to Hamilton that preferring to follow the previous practice, " and for another reason which had some weight in his mind," he had sent the document to the secretary of state. Jefferson was hardly grateful for this deferential regard for his dignity. He countersigned the paper, indeed, but in a letter to Madison declared this to be another instance of his being forced to appear to approve what he had uniformly condemned from its first conception. What was this "other reason" which Washington refrained from explaining can only be conjectured, and the sole facts which suggest any ground of conjecture are to be found in the dates, which show that this step was taken only about ten days after the famous letters of Sept. 9, 1792, written to the president by Jefferson and Hamilton respectively in reply to his effort to conciliate them.[1]

Civil means of coercion being the policy determined upon, Hamilton concocted a scheme for bringing a pressure to bear upon the non-compliant distillers. He proposed to proceed vigorously with prosecutions, but only in clear cases of non-compliance; to seize the produce of the distilleries of non-complying counties wherever it could be done peaceably upon the way to the markets; to purchase for the army, not through contractors as formerly, but directly from law-abiding manufacturers, and by cash payments, to help to do away with the argument that want of ready money rendered payment of the taxes impossible. But, unfortunately, many difficulties in the way of the thorough execution of this plan prevented it from having the measure of success which was hoped for it. The lawlessness and violence continued. A collector's house was broken into by a party of disguised rioters, and the sheriff refused to execute the warrants for their apprehension. This indeed was nothing to be surprised at, for the pre-

1 *Vide ante*, vol. ii., page 7.

vailing spirit of the officers, whose duty it was to aid in the enforcement of the laws, had been either lukewarm or actually hostile ; and " the weight of an unfriendly official influence had been one of the most serious obstacles " with which government had been obliged to struggle. In June, 1793, an inspector was burned in effigy. In November a collector was compelled, by threats of his life, backed by presented pistols, to surrender his books and resign his office. In January following, a barn, with its stores of hay and grain, belonging to a person who had given information against a rioter, was burned by incendiaries. The same fate befell the property of a complying distiller, who had always spoken favorably of the law. It was openly menaced, that in Alleghany county not a house should be left standing belonging to any person who had obeyed the law. To show that the threat was no empty one the work of destruction was vigorously entered upon. A series of night attacks upon the government offices was inaugurated by armed men, who fired volleys at them, broke into them, and in one instance seized the owner of the house, tarred and feathered him, and left him bound naked to a tree in the forest.

At last, in this same month of June, a law was passed establishing such provisions for the practical enforcement of the law, that the executive felt able to proceed with good hopes of success. The experiment of forbearance and delay had been tried with ample thoroughness and wholly unsatisfactory results. It was accordingly determined now to conquer the disaffection at any cost. As the first step, a batch of thirty legal processes were issued, both

against non-complying distillers and against rioters.
But the malcontents seemed resolved to meet this
crisis and final struggle with no less spirit than the
government. This time the marshal set forth to serve
the warrants in person. He had unusual success, and
served twenty-nine of his papers without serious interruption, but as he was proceeding to serve the
thirtieth he was fired upon by a body of armed men.
On the following morning another armed body, about
one hundred strong, attacked the house of the inspector, Colonel Neville, near Pittsburg. But the
place was barricaded and defended by armed servants
and negroes, so that the assailants were beaten off.
A renewal of the attack being quite surely anticipated, application was made to the local authorities
— the judges, generals of militia, and sheriff of the
county — for protection. Their reply was not reas-
suring. They said that the combination of the people
against the revenue law was so powerful that it was
impossible to furnish the required assistance; and
that if the *posse comitatus* should be ordered out, the
great majority of the force would be found to side
with the rioters. The day following five hundred
men returned to storm the obnoxious building, led
on by a notorious rioter, who had assumed the nick-
name of " Tom the Tinker." The dwelling was now
garrisoned by a major, with eleven men, from Fort
Pitt; but the odds were so great that it was deemed
best for the inspector to escape secretly. This he
succeeded in doing, and the major then began a par-
ley with his foes. They insisted, unconditionally,
that the defenders should march out and ground their
arms, a humiliation to which the military man would

by no means submit. So the attack began with vehemence. In spite of the odds the soldiers were making good their defence, and had killed the leader and wounded several others, when the agreeable scheme of burning them out was suggested. The extensive out-houses were straightway fired, and the flames rapidly approaching the main house at last compelled the garrison to come to terms.

Upon this same raid the marshal and a son of Colonel Neville were captured. Both of them were men of courage and spirit. But the violence and menaces to which they were subjected induced the marshal to promise, and the young man to guarantee his promise, that he would undertake to serve no more processes west of the Alleghany mountains. This compliance procured their release, but demands were the next day made upon them requiring the inspector to resign his office, and the marshal to surrender his warrants. This they refused to do, and finding themselves in a condition of imminent and increasing peril, with no prospect of protection from the lawful authorities, they finally felt obliged to escape by flight down the Ohio river, and by this circuitous route and ignominious means to make their way through the wilderness to the safer regions of Philadelphia.

The malcontents meantime called a meeting at Mingo Creek Meeting-house, at which however they transacted little business, except to arrange for a monster assemblage of the four western counties, the counties next east of the mountains, and the adjoining counties of Virginia, to be held on August 14, 1794, at Parkinson's Ferry, in Washington County. Prompted partly by an anxious curiosity, partly by a desire to have some material for inflaming those who should gather in response to this summons, the United States mail was stopped, some three days later, on the road from Pittsburgh to Philadelphia, the bags were cut open and the letters were taken out and examined. The contents of some of them were said to be, and doubtless were, eminently unsatisfactory to the agitators.

Upon the strength of alleged discoveries in these stolen epistles it was resolved to forestall the meeting proposed to be held on August 14. A summons was issued calling the people together upon August 1 at Braddock's Field on the Monongahela. They were requested to come armed, accoutred, and bringing provisions for four days. The call was addressed to the officers of militia, who were urged to bring with them as many recruits as they could. In every respect a military and even belligerent aspect was studiously assumed, and a demonstration of an unprecedented character was generally understood to be in preparation by the leaders.

Meantime the government was upon its part far from idle. Chiefly through the instrumentality of Hamilton the plan was maturing whereby this prolonged defiance of the law and the constituted authorities was to be finally and completely crushed. The law recently passed provided that if an associate justice after receiving evidence should notify the president that the execution of the law was obstructed by combinations too powerful to be suppressed by the ordinary course of judicial proceedings and the means at the disposal of the regular officers of the law, then the militia might be called forth; and if the militia of the State where the disturbance prevailed should be incompetent to quell it, then the forces of the neighboring States might be summoned. In accordance with the advice of Hamilton the facts were now laid before Justice Wilson, who readily made the necessary certificate. Hamilton computed that the four insurgent counties contained upwards of sixteen thousand males above the age of sixteen years, of whom about seven thousand might be expected to be armed. This force might receive some accession of strength by detachments from Virginia, and from disaffected counties in Pennsylvania east of the mountains. To make success a certainty twelve thousand militia should march. The governor of Pennsylvania, in an official conference on August 2, explicitly stated to the president that the militia of Pennsylvania alone would be found incompetent to the suppression of the insurrection. This Hamilton deemed a sufficient foundation for summoning at once the militia of the neighboring States.

Requisitions were made upon Pennsylvania, Virginia, Maryland, and New Jersey. Thirteen thousand troops were called for, and this number was afterward increased to fifteen thousand. Dubious confidence could at first be placed in the efforts of the Pennsylvanians. Governor Mifflin, by reason of political affiliations, was very far from being in sympathy with the government. It required a series of conferences and letters, expostulations and arguments on the part of the president and Hamilton, to bring him to a willingness to perform his duty. At last, however, when the crisis came and he was called upon to act, he threw off all farther hesitation and displayed an ample zeal and energy. It was found to be feasible to permit the quotas to be filled by volunteers, and Washington afterward wrote with no small satisfaction of the alacrity and good feeling which were displayed. There were even seen " instances of general officers going at the head of a single troop and of light companies ; of field officers, when they came to the place of rendezvous and found no command for them in that grade, turning into the ranks and proceeding as private soldiers under their own captains ; and of numbers possessing the first fortunes in the country standing in the ranks as private men, and marching day by day with their knapsacks and haversacks, sleeping on straw with a single blanket in a soldier's tent during the frosty nights." Many of the Quakers even conceived that the occasion was one upon which they might properly sacrifice their peculiar tenets to the common welfare, and appeared in the ranks under arms. The government were much gratified to see that so soon as the real feeling of the community could be tested, the loyalty and content were proved to be all that could be desired.

The law required as preliminary to the actual employment of force, that a proclamation should be issued by the president. The secretary of state having but little stomach for this task, it was undertaken by Hamilton. He drafted the proclamation of August 7 ; Washington signed it, and Randolph, with what unwillingness may easily be conceived, countersigned it.

Governor Lee of Virginia was requested to accept the command-in-chief. Hamilton at one time contemplated acting with the army in a subordinate capacity. This however seemed hardly practicable, and he was finally content to ask leave from the president to attend the troops on their march. He based this request upon the ground of public advantage, in consideration of the "connection between the immediate ostensible cause of the insurrection" and his own department. "In a government like ours," he said, "it cannot but have a good effect for the person who is understood to be the adviser or proposer of a measure which involves danger to his fellow-citizens, to partake in that danger; while not to do it might have a bad effect." Permission was readily granted, and towards the end of September the president and secretary left Philadelphia together for Carlisle, where the troops had rendezvoused and were ready to start.

The insurrection had meanwhile been rapidly expanding. At Braddock's Field there had assembled on August 1 no less than seven thousand armed and excited "citizens of the western country," which designation was studiously assumed by them to distinguish them from citizens of the United States. In political matters words are often things. The intention of the leaders of this body, as it was rapidly developed and subsequently freely acknowledged, was to attack the national forces posted at Pittsburgh, and in the anticipated event of success to unite with certain of the neighboring counties of Virginia and Pennsylvania, secede from the Union and establish an independent State! "The first step," wrote Brackenridge, a prominent and influential man among the rioters, "will be the reorganization of a new government. . . . Should an attempt be made to suppress these people, I am afraid the question will not be whether you will march to Pittsburgh, but whether they will march to Philadelphia, accumulating in their course and swelling over the banks of the Susquehanna like a torrent — irresistible and devouring in its progress.   There can be no equality of contest between the rage of a forest and the abundance, indolence, and opulence of a city. . . . An application to the British is spoken of, which may God avert! But what will not despair produce !"   Such were the purposes admitted in writing early in August.   Such was the oratory which inflamed the subalterns.

The numbers gathered at the trysting-place passed a sleepless night around their camp-fires, inciting each other to deeds of violence.   In the morning, after a short time consumed in the reading of the intercepted letters and in debate, they organized as a military force by the choice of officers.   Then without more ado they at once attacked the fort, and threatened Pittsburgh.   But Colonel Butler in command of the garrison offered stout resistance, and the less courageous among the insurgents retreated, leaving their more desperate comrades to hover around, after the Indian fashion, and to fire the dwellings of the officials and law-abiding persons in the neighborhood.

Soon afterward was held the meeting which had been regularly summoned for August 14, at Parkinson's Ferry.   A liberty pole was set up and flags were hoisted, bearing a red stripe for each insurgent county and sundry inflammatory and seditious inscriptions.   It was proposed to appoint a "Committee of Public Safety."   But just at this stage of proceed-

ings news came of the approach of five commissioners, three of whom had been deputed by the national
and two by the State authorities, to undertake to
bring the insurgents to their senses. It was the last
step to be expected as preliminary to the application of force. The more cautious among the rebels,
notably the cool-headed and probably indifferent
Gallatin, saw that the fatal extremity was at hand;
for no reasonable man could question what would be
the result of a military encounter in the field. It
was possible to avoid the consequences of a destructive overthrow and severe castigation afterward only
by a real or a fictitious submission.

The former was as yet impossible; nor could even
the latter be easily effected. The mass of the people were quite earnest and honest in their convictions
of the rectitude and probable success of their demonstrations. They had placed implicit confidence in
the orators who had assured them of the unconstitu-
tionality and wickedness of the excise laws. They
had fully believed all that had been so often told to
them, and which they had been so long repeating to
each other, of their own power to oppose the militia,
and to meet any force which the government could
bring to bear. Firm in these convictions, and wrought
up to a pitch of violent excitement, the populace
was not easily to be brought to a just appreciation
of the real condition of things. The meeting could
barely be prevailed upon to appoint a sub-committee
of fifteen to confer with the commissioners. All
Gallatin's art and influence were required to moderate
the tone of the resolutions so far as to obtain the
striking out of a direct refusal to obey the excise

laws, and the insertion of a promise to submit to the State laws.

When the meeting of the fifteen delegates with the commissioners took place, the requisitions on the part of the government were presented and were certainly beyond criticism in point of mildness. Submission to the law, continued long enough to prove its substantial sincerity, was to issue in a general amnesty. The members of the committee were to declare their own personal submission to the law, and to recommend the like conduct to the people in general, also the abstention from any direct or indirect opposition by actual violence, or by threats against excise officers and complying distillers; meetings of the citizens were to be held for obtaining signatures to declarations of this tenor. Upon receipt of these terms, which the committee of conference had thought to be reasonable, the committee of public safety was undecided. Some counselled acceptance; but others said that with a sufficient supply of fire-arms the insurgents were quite capable of holding their own against the United States. An armed body of the people, incensed by rumors of an intended yielding on the part of some of their leaders, and suspicious that bribery had been practised, broke into Red Stone Old Fort, and undertook to overawe the meeting. They were persuaded to retire and leave the deliberations ostensibly free; but under such untoward auspices it was not possible to accomplish much. A vote by secret ballot showed a small majority in favor of acceding to the demands of the commissioners. But the members present neither made for themselves, nor recommended to the people, the stipulated pledges. Another and smaller committee was nominated to hold another interview with the commissioners. These new representatives demanded delay until October 10, which all concerned well knew would be so late in the season that it would be difficult or impossible for the militia to cross the mountains. Of course such a demand was refused, but the proposition to take the sense of the people in primary meetings was renewed.

The folly of undertaking to treat soon however became thoroughly manifest. After this last conference, by the advice of the committee, meetings of the people were summoned about the middle of September to express their sentiments on the question of submission; and, in order to guide them so far as might be, the opinion of the members of the committee was declared in favor of that step. In Gallatin's township the assemblage over which he presided wisely voted to accept the proffered amnesty, and very generally signed the required papers. But this action was exceptional. Everywhere else the gathered bodies gave expression to resolutions of unmitigated hostility. Even freedom of discussion was forbidden under pain of vengeance. In Findley's township the declarations of submission were torn to pieces without having a signature attached to them. The frenzy of the irresponsible multitude had escaped from the control of those leaders whom either fear or wisdom would have inspired to moderate courses. Another proclamation was wasted by the government. An effort to deceive the administration into a belief that quiet was returning was made by the crafty ones among the insurgents. Both efforts were alike futile. Findley and another were sent on a mission to the president, to explain to him the state of the country, and offer a qualified and deceptive submission. They approached Carlisle, where lately the malcontents had been in the riotous ascendant, burning a magistrate in effigy, setting up a liberty pole, and offering to the peacefully inclined citizens the option between liberty and death. Now, however, the place was alive with soldiery. The two delegates, fearing for their lives, preserved a careful incognito till they came beneath formal military order and protection. The frigid reception which Washington accorded to them increased their fright. They returned well convinced of the inevitable conclusion, and in terror and humiliation did their best to undo the mischief they had so long and sedulously concocted.

Washington stayed to see the expedition fairly launched at the close of the month of September, and then, being much needed at Philadelphia, returned thither, leaving Hamilton in general superintendence, — a charge not so distasteful as it was responsible. From this moment he was ever among the troops, encouraging them, watching every thing, untiringly alert and vigilant. The march was a hard one. The Alleghanies were crossed in the middle of October, amid continued stormy weather, causing much hardship and ultimate mortality. But as the army advanced the spirit of resistance died away. On November 9 the famous rendezvous at Parkinson's Ferry was reached. But there was no one there to oppose the troops. The armed men had thought better of the situation, and had sought safer retreats in which to utter their sedition. General Lee issued a proclamation, renewing the promise of amnesty, and calling on the people to take the oath of allegiance. These offers were not readily accepted. The spirit was still bad, violent, and menacing, and continued to be manifested until the troops were actually at hand, and then just in time to escape a real collision the malcontents would reluctantly become tranquil and submissive. Prominent men came in with deprecatory and repentant assurances. Brackenridge, who had lingered even till after the eleventh hour, finally signed the submission the day after the last appointed day. But upon the strength of this tardy yielding he came to cast himself upon the mercy of the government. "I was received," he wrote, "by Hamilton with that countenance which a man will have when he sees a person with regard to whom his humanity and sense of justice struggle. He would have him saved, but was afraid he must have him hanged." Hamilton himself often said, both publicly and privately, that he had saved Gallatin's neck. Yet he received but slender gratitude from that gentleman, who accused the secretary of forming a part of a "Star Chamber" court at Pittsburgh. That Hamilton should be inclined to show leniency towards Brackenridge or Gallatin, or any other intelligent person among the insurgents, was indeed an extremity of forbearance and forgiveness hardly to have been expected. For not only was it his measure that they were assailing, so that their success must involve his political destruction, but he personally had been to a peculiar degree singled out as a mark for every sort of abuse and malignity. The insurrection had been carefully instigated and guided by his personal foes as a useful weapon against him, in the hope that if it failed of all else it might at least achieve his overthrow and irremediable disgrace. But his moderation in this temptation is not the first instance of Hamilton's power of preserving the coolness of his temper as well as of his head amid political embroilments.

There were no military exploits for the troops to perform. Nowhere did any body of men present itself within their reach. Individuals were arrested and handed over to the civil authorities for trial. An overawing show of force was made; and the army spread itself as widely as possible throughout the disaffected region. It was made so manifest that not the most stupid or bigoted man in that neighborhood could fail to see that the entire insurrection was a contemptible fiasco. The leaders, thoroughly frightened, were begging for mercy. The armed men were only too careful to keep out of the way of those national forces which they had so lately proposed to annihilate. The whole affair was at once humiliating, ridiculous, and disagreeably dashed with substantial peril. Hamilton remained with the army long enough to become assured that the work was thoroughly and effectually done. He made himself useful by acting as counsel for the United States in the conduct of some few examinations of prisoners in the United States Court before Judge Peters. Then finding no farther necessity for his presence he returned to Philadelphia about the middle of November. The main body of the army followed not much later, but a detachment about twenty-five hundred strong went into winter quarters in the transmontane region to make sure that the old spirit should not again blaze forth, or gain headway in any spot.

Such was the ignominious end of a rebellion among the most absurd that history records, and yet by reason of the time and circumstances of its occurrence fraught with a really grave danger to the integrity of the government. It had originated and advanced in the idea that the new government was not established with sufficient firmness to dare to act with resolution against an audacious and extensive combination. Feebly as the insurgents behaved when actually brought to the test, they yet created a crisis which was potentially very perilous. It was a question what the government would venture to do, and what it could safely do, in the face of threats appearing to be so earnest, violence apparently so determined. Had feeble counsels, which were not wanting, prevailed, not western Pennsylvania alone, but the whole country would have regarded the imbecility of the government as a demonstrated fact; nor could the unity of the nation have long survived such a reputation. Fortunately neither Washington nor Hamilton could be terrified or deceived into allowing the processes of demoralization and disintegration to proceed without interruption. They brought it about that the government emerged from this jeopardy with a great and valuable accession of strength.

CHAPTER V.

FOREIGN RELATIONS—JAY'S TREATY.

FROM this episode of domestic insurrection we must return to the consideration of the complications of the United States in European politics. The hatred felt towards England at this period may be not inaccurately measured by the affection shown towards France. Every one who loved the latter felt in duty bound to detest the former with corresponding intensity. The converse of this proposition however did not hold true. The opponents of the French faction were far from feeling towards Great Britain an enthusiastic or subservient attachment. They were indeed accused of entertaining such sentiments to a degree far beyond the truth, partly because such exaggeration was the natural result of the bitterness of the controversy, partly because the charge of predilections for that unpopular country constituted an excellent political weapon. But in fact her ungracious demeanor, her commercial restrictions, and her persistent non-compliance with the treaty of peace had left England few warm adherents in the United States.

Hamilton and Adams were especially singled out as obnoxious to this offensive accusation of Anglicism.

Yet familiarity with the lives and writings of both these distinguished men makes it abundantly clear that neither of them gave more than a fair appreciation to the excellence of the social and political system of England. "I must confess to your majesty," said Adams to George III., "that I have no affection save for my own country." The blunt remark continued to tell the truth to the latest moment of the speaker's long life. Not less perfectly did it express the sentiments of Hamilton, though he never had occasion to put his feelings into an aphorism rendered so famous by the circumstances attending its utterance.

Great Britain did not for several months after the outbreak of the European war furnish much pretext for fault-finding. She for the most part observed with tolerable fairness the obligations under which she was placed by our neutrality. She protested, as indeed she was in duty bound to do, against the constant breaches of international law committed by France within the jurisdiction of the United States, but she did not attempt to retaliate or imitate the outrages of her enemy. Yet she still held the western posts; she still granted no relaxations in favor of American commerce; she exercised the vexatious right of taking French merchandise out of American vessels; above all she insolently persisted in boarding our vessels for the sake of impressing those whom she might see fit to call her own subjects. These ample causes of complaint were kept by the Democratic press constantly before the eyes of the public, though in good truth there was little disposition in any quarter to forget or condone such flagrant injuries.

One would think that English statesmen would have seen the obvious policy of doing at least all that they conveniently could, occasionally even of stretching a point, to aid the sorely pressed party in the States, which was doing its best in great stress to prevent the country from engaging in actual hostilities on the side of France. But stubborn, proud, and dull-witted counsels prevailed. England could not be civil to the successful rebels, no matter what price she might have to pay for the privilege of insulting them.

On June 8 instructions were issued to the commanders in the British navy to " stop all vessels loaded wholly or in part with corn, flour, or meal, bound to any port in France, or any port occupied by the armies of France." The cargo was to be sold in the nearest British port for the benefit of the owners, and the vessels were to receive a fair freight ; or the master might release his cargo by giving bonds to sell it at the port of some " country in amity with his majesty." English statesmen undertook at the time to defend the lawfulness of this measure, by which a paper blockade of an entire country was declared to extend over all the waters of the world. They claimed to have a fair prospect of reducing their enemies by famine, and under such circumstances they insisted that food on the way to those enemies might properly be treated as contraband of war. Some English publicists still feebly sustain the order as justified by the extraordinary character of the war, the scale on which it was conducted, and the purpose and supposed possibility which prompted it. It cannot be denied however by an unbiassed judge, that the measure was high-handed in the extreme, and really founded upon no better basis than the arbitrary doctrine of might making right. The United States, whose merchants suffered much by the operation of the instructions, officially protested against them with much warmth, but little effect.

If this feather was not altogether light, one of much more considerable weight was soon after cast upon the already sorely burdened backs of the party of peace and neutrality. On the sixth day of November, 1793, an order in council bade the British cruisers to seize and bring into the ports of that country all vessels which they should find laden with the produce of any French colony, or carrying provisions or any supplies for the use of such colony. The order was kept back for a time, but was promulgated about the end of the year. It was designed to stop all neutral trade with the French West Indies; nor was it likely to fall much short of effectually accomplishing this purpose. For it was part of a grand scheme for the conquest of all the West Indian possessions of France, to which end a powerful squadron was at the same time despatched to those seas. News of the order reached the United States on March 7, 1794. It had unfortunately been preceded by intelligence of a great number of captures of American vessels made by the British cruisers in the neighboring seas.

Fierce was the outburst of wrath with which the news of this unjustifiable proceeding was received in the United States. It was asserted and believed that the commerce of the country had been deliberately doomed to extirpation by the greatest maritime power in the world. There were no friends of England who dared or even wished to excuse, to palliate, to deprecate in her behalf. It was great good fortune that in such a paroxysm of rage war did not at once ensue ; for the disagreements between Federalists and anti-federalists now resolved themselves into the question, which party should originate and carry through the most effectual measures of resistance.

In this spirited emulation the Federalists outstripped their competitors, much to the chagrin of the leaders of the Democratic party. Within twenty-four hours next after the arrival of the news Hamilton had defined his position. He had stigmatized the order as " atrocious," and had written to the president advising the fortification of the principal seaports in the several States, so far as should be necessary to enable them to resist a maritime attack ; the raising of ten thousand auxiliary troops ; and the investiture of the president by Congress with power to lay a partial or a general embargo, and to stay, partially or generally, the exportation of commodities. Two days after the date of this letter Sedgwick — one of the most prominent Federalists in the House, and having intimate political connection with Hamilton — introduced a series of resolutions of the same purport. But these schemes, in spite of their very hostile aspect towards Great Britain, were highly distasteful to the opposition ; partly because the popularity attendant upon originating them seemed to have been shrewdly secured by the Federalist party, partly because any steps toward the raising of a military force was objectionable to politicians who wished the minimum of vigor and power to pertain to the national government. The favorite object of the Republicans seemed in danger of being achieved both by persons the most odious and by means the most objectionable to them.

The followers of Jefferson had recently been putting forth vigorous exertions to defeat the initial efforts toward the formation of a navy. They had done this without hesitation at the very moment when they were doing their utmost to promote war with the greatest maritime power in the world. Most of them did not change their course in this juncture, when a few weeks or days even might see the navy of Great Britain actively engaged against the United States. But the present crisis had come in good season to rob them of any faint anticipations of success which they might previously have cherished in this ill-advised undertaking; and on the same day upon which Sedgwick brought forward his resolutions the bill for the frigates was passed by a majority of eleven. Not many days before the majority in its favor had been only two, and the influence of the British policy was seen in this increase.

Such was the singular policy of the Republicans; to preach war, but to prepare for peace. The avowed policy of the Federalist party, dictated by Hamilton, was to get ready with all speed for war, but not by threats or offensive language to render it inevitable. They acknowledged that it was imminent, and if it was indeed to come about there was no time to be lost in putting the country in a condition to meet it. Certainly there was enough to be done. England was in complete fighting order; while the United States could not be more completely unprepared for actual hostilities than they were at this juncture. At the same time the Federalists deprecated war ; they did not believe it to be absolutely unavoidable, nor cease to hope that it might be averted. The best basis upon which to found efforts to avert it seemed to them to consist in a resolute demeanor; a manifestation of vigor ; a state of readiness. To show firmness without bluster, power without violence, was the policy which Hamilton assiduously urged upon persons of whom many were in too much need of the lesson. The principles of the opposition were less simple. Not more resolved to fight, if need should be, they were yet less unwilling to see that need brought about. At the same time, however, that they contemplated the chance of war not wholly without favor, they could not well take part in preparations for it. Two obstacles to this course were conclusive with them : in the first place, their opponents had originated the measures ; in the second place, the result of the measures might not improbably prevent the outbreak of hostilities.

The policy of the Republican leaders was at once more mild in aspect, more dangerous in fact, than that of the Federalists. They had before the House a proposition for legislation looking to establishing severe retaliatory restrictions upon British commerce. This had been originally based upon Mr. Jefferson's famous report concerning the commerce of the United States. Soon after that document had been submitted to Congress, Mr. Madison had brought in a series of resolutions founded upon it, whereby duties upon various articles had been raised with the ingenious purpose of changing the principal channel of our commerce from a British to a French direction. In vain had it been urged that a severe system of protection not for the benefit of our own people but of foreigners would be thereby established, and Americans would be heavily taxed to encourage French industry. The opposition pressed the measure warmly, and long and interesting debates ensued. An amendment was adopted by which the increase of duties was confined to British merchandise only, and in this shape the bill seemed too likely to pass. Yet it could not be denied that its passage would almost inevitably have led to such a degree of irritation and complication that war could hardly fail to result under all the circumstances. It was abundantly proved that pressure of this kind, however it might provoke, was totally incompetent to bend the British cabinet.

The contest in the House was warm and of doubtful result. First the Federalist proposition for an embargo was defeated by a hostile majority of two. Then the Democratic commercial project was negatived. Then the Federalist resolution for raising an auxiliary corps of troops was voted down. But it was at once followed by another of like tenor, which Sedgwick offered for the declared purpose of ascertaining the sense of the House as to " whether any extra provision for the protection of the country was deemed necessary." The opposition did not dare to appear upon the negative side of such a question, and this time the result was that the House resolved that "measures ought to be taken to render the force of the United States more efficient." A committee of nine, upon which Sedgwick was chairman, was directed to arrange the details. Encouraged by this success the embargo resolution was renewed, and at last was carried. It was concurred in by the Senate, approved by the president, and forthwith put into operation. Thus by virtue of these two hardly won victories the Federalist policy became substantially triumphant.

In the midst of this excitement came another exasperating piece of intelligence. On February 10, 1794, Lord Dorchester, governor-general of Canada, held a council with the Miami Indians. He told them that he found the boundaries obliterated, and that he should not be surprised if the conduct of the people of the States should bring on war in the course of the present year, in which event the lines must be drawn by the warriors. The people, long since suspicious of the manner in which the British influence over the savages was supposed to be exerted, were greatly incensed at this language. Especially it was believed that the obstinacy with which the north-western tribes had lately refused to make peace, and had insisted upon the Ohio as a boundary, had been attributable to the arts and· intrigues of the English.

The Democratic party, not intending a second time to appear behindhand in zeal, took advantage of this new provocation to cause one of their more violent members to propose in the House the sequestration of all debts owing in the United States to British subjects. These sums were to be paid into the national treasury, and the amount thus secured was to be appropriated as a fund to indemnify the owners of vessels and merchandise unlawfully seized by the British. The proposition was monstrous. Even when war is declared it has been the rule, rarely infringed since the middle ages by any civilized nation, that debts owing to individuals of the hostile nation shall not be interfered with. But here was no war to excuse what even war could not reasonably be said to justify. The scheme was little if at all raised in its moral character above the level of theft. Yet it was with extreme difficulty that the United States was rescued from the dishonor which this measure must have induced. The people were excessively enraged. Many even among the Federalist representatives were inclined to give their votes to this nefarious resolution. With them Hamilton anxiously exerted himself to assuage their vindictiveness and to bring them to a just sense of the nature of such legislation. He spared no pains to obtain interviews and to present arguments for this purpose. The notorious Giles distinguished himself by his vehement exertions upon the other side. It was nothing save reprisal, he said; and " reprisal is a right, reprisal is a duty." Happily sufficient sense remained in the House to prevent the success of such rhetoric. The resolution did not indeed meet the summary condemnation it deserved, and was defeated only through the indirect means of a postponement. But even thus the stigma was fortunately escaped.

Another scheme, a favorite with the late secretary of state, was soon broached. If less objectionable than the foregoing on the score of morality, it was certainly not wiser as a stroke of policy. On April 2 it was moved, that until restitution should be made to all American citizens who had suffered loss or injury by reason of any acts done or countenanced by Great Britain in violation of our neutral rights, and until the surrender of the western posts, no farther commercial intercourse should be had with that country in any articles of her growth or manufacture. This suggestion was exceedingly distasteful to the more temperate members of the Federal party, because it appeared to them fit only to widen the chasm which they were not altogether without hopes of bridging over if not actually of closing. In time it might become wise, but at present it must be regarded as hasty, premature, injurious.

To justify this opinion there came in good season welcome intelligence from Europe, which materially aided the Federalists and justified the moderate element in their policy. Two days after the last resolution had been offered in the House, the president communicated the important news that a new order of Jan. 8, 1794, had rescinded that of Nov. 6, and that instructions had been issued which would leave unmolested all such trade with the West Indies as citizens of the United States could lawfully have conducted prior to the war. Pending hostilities, France had opened to American vessels the right, never before accorded to them, of carrying the produce of her islands to Europe. But Great Britain denied the lawfulness of such extension of extraordinary privileges in time of war, and vessels engaged in such transportation were still held to be subject to seizure. For this however there was some fair ground in reason. The satisfactory arrangement as to the future was supplemented by the declaration that no condemnations would take place in cases of previous seizure except where it would be justified under the new order. The British ministry, it was farther explained, had never intended that the instructions should be construed so sweepingly as had been supposed. Nor was it long before the good faith of this last action of the British government was put beyond a question, by information of the actual release of several vessels which had been taken under the earlier order. At the same time it was announced that Lord Grenville had indignantly disavowed the sentiments of Lord Dorchester's speech to the Indians, and had declared in parliament his hope by a course of friendly action to restore harmony between Great Britain and the United States.

All this was very gratifying to the Federalists, and helped them materially when indeed they stood in great need of help. Nothing more was heard about sequestration of debts. But the non-intercourse resolutions were still urged with much persistence. They were finally carried in committee of the whole by a handsome majority, were then put into the shape of a bill, and in that shape also had equal success in the House. In the Senate, however, the casting vote of the vice-president fortunately prevented the bill from becoming a law. This pressure on the part of the opposition was especially exasperating to the Federalists, because before the conclusion of the debate was reached the nomination of Chief Justice Jay, as envoy extraordinary to Great Britain, had actually been sent in to the Senate by the president. The establishment of a system of non-intercourse simultaneously with the despatch of the minister would have reduced almost to nothing the prospects, already sufficiently small, of any successful issue of his mis-

sion.   No more irritating mode of opposition could
have been resorted to.   The purpose seemed to be to
win by indirection ; and the whole course of the Republicans in this matter was considered unmistak-
able proof of their unchangeable purpose to bring
about war.

When the Federalists had said that they believed a
pacific solution to be still a possibility, and that preparations for war might well prove chiefly serviceable
in promoting peace, they were quite in earnest in
their intention to save the country, if it could be
saved with honor, from the threatening evil.   They
did not expect to do this simply by showing a readiness to fight, any more than they would have hoped,
like the Republicans, to achieve it by domestic legislation.   The warlike measures formed a background
against which the movements to secure peace could
stand out more effectively.   Their plan was to
send an extraordinary embassy to the Court of St.
James', of such a nature as should show, both in
respect of the person selected, his instructions, and
all attendant circumstances, that one great and last
effort was to be made in this grave crisis to preserve
tranquillity.   They hoped that such a demonstration
might lead the English ministry to a more thoughtful
consideration of the condition of affairs between the
two peoples, to a wiser appreciation of British interests.   It seemed incredible that the common sense of
the cabinet should be buried so deep that it could
not be reached by such a proceeding.

This project of a special mission having been conceived by Hamilton was communicated by him to
George Cabot, then a prominent Federalist senator

from Massachusetts. On March 10 this gentleman had a confidential interview upon the subject with other members of the party. The result was that Hamilton's suggestion met with their warm approval, and that they were farther unanimously agreed that Hamilton himself should be the envoy. Of the same mind was Washington when the project was broached to him. But, upon receiving a report of this state of feeling among his friends, Hamilton urgently deprecated the portion of the scheme which related to himself. He wished to be able to use all his influence, especially with the president, to insure the adoption of the plan ; and he could not with propriety do so if he was practically insisting upon his own mission.

There were also other objections in the way of this selection to which others certainly were not blind, and which Hamilton may have equally appreciated. It could not be doubted that the strong hatred of the opposition towards him personally would induce them to put forth extraordinary efforts to defeat the entire plan, if he were to be nominated. The chances of success were sufficiently dubious at best, to make it grossly impolitic to bring forward the name of any man who would be opposed on grounds of personal enmity. It could not be denied that such would be the case with Hamilton. Various communications received by the president manifested very clearly the spirit of hostility which the appointment would arouse. Randolph and James Monroe especially signalized themselves in this opposition, and Jefferson covertly aided the cause of his party and his friends. It was with much reluctance that the friends of the secretary at last yielded to considerations of this nature, backed by his own entreaties, and the supposed importance of retaining him in the cabinet.

It was the earnest desire of Hamilton that the chief justice, John Jay, should be selected. He was a man in every way fit for the position, while the fact of sending a person occupying so eminent a station might be expected to lend dignity to the mission and confer upon it that impressive character which was very important to its success. On April 14 Hamilton sent to the president a very long and elaborate review of the whole situation, concluding with a strong recommendation of the appointment of Jay. This settled the matter. Immediately after the receipt of this letter the president sent for Jay and offered the appointment to him. Jay expressed himself fully in sympathy with the scheme, but asked for time to consider the part proposed for him. In some anxiety as to his decision, Hamilton accompanied by several leading Federalists called upon the chief justice and strongly urged his acceptance. Under such pressure he consented, and on April 16 the nomination was sent in to the Senate. A discussion upon it was maintained during three days following, and a violent opposition was developed. It was declared that Jay held very erroneous views concerning the foreign policy of the country; that as secretary of state he had acknowledged that the United States had committed infractions of the treaty; that the mission was incompatible with the office of chief justice, and tended to undermine the independence of the judiciary. Monroe and Aaron Burr led the attack; but their tactics were unsuccessful, and the confirmation was made by the satisfactory vote of eighteen to eight. These numbers must be regarded as surprising as well as agreeable personally to the gentleman chiefly concerned, for almost immediately afterward the non-intercourse bill produced an even division. The course, therefore, pursued by several senators of the Republican persuasion must have been somewhat eccentric. While willing to send the envoy, they were yet ready to promote measures of a character gravely to embarrass him, if not to insure the uselessness of his mission.

Hamilton was much troubled at this spirit. The very fear, he said, which the war party entertained of the success of the mission proved the fair chance of that success; wherefore they were to be seen endeavoring to prevent its proceeding under right auspices, or to clog it with impediments which would frustrate its effect. So much did he dread the tendency to measures of an irritating nature, or fitted to bring the sincerity of our neutrality in question, that he suggested to Jay that it might be advisable to make an acceptance of the proffered embassy conditional upon the nominating message containing a request that Congress would " abstain for the present from measures which may be contrary to the spirit of an attempt to adjust existing differences by negotiation." It required the utmost skill, perseverance, and vigilance on the part of the Federalists to prevent the indirect defeat of the mission by legislation of a character to incense or humiliate Great Britain beyond the possibility of concession.

An example of the temper of the opposition in this respect is shown by the action of the House concerning the extension of the embargo for a second period of thirty days. The measure had been aimed at England, but it had inevitably injured other nations also, and among the rest France. This painful consequence the Democratic majority in the House sought to avert by amending the proposition so as to exclude from the operation of the embargo all peoples having treaties with the United States. By this means England was singled out and made the peculiar victim, as had been at first intended. Monroe further asked leave to bring in a bill providing for the suspension of the fourth article of the treaty of peace with Great Britain, until such time as that country should comply with all her stipulations therein written. But his own party deserted him on this occasion, and only one vote besides his own was cast in favor of the permission he requested.

This opportune moment was likewise seized upon by the Democratic party to try to send the congratulations of Congress to the Directory for the successes of France over Great Britain. It seemed to be forgotten that contemporaneously with the English orders, which were deemed a good cause for war, almost identical orders had been issued by the French, had been renewed after a brief revocation, and were still in force. With such ominous elements was the political atmosphere charged when an extraordinary mission of peace was in the very process of inauguration. The prospect was but too great that Mr. Jay's own countrymen would find means to defeat the purposes for which he had consented to cross the ocean. But the Federalists stood manfully by him and fought for the cause with untiring pertinacity and astonishing success.   One of the keenest among their opponents said to Senator King: "You are strange fellows! Formerly you did what you chose with a small majority; now, we have a great majority and can do nothing.   You have baffled every one of our plans." In truth the individuals composing the Federal party in Congress and in office were very able, had thus far continued to act together in perfect harmony, and had been admirably led.   The last two advantages they were soon to lose.

The appointment of the envoy having been duly consummated, Hamilton forthwith entered upon the task of preparing his instructions.   The labor did not fall within his department, but reasons enough existed for devolving at least a portion of it upon him.   The idea of the mission had originated with him; more than any other man he had secured the advancement of the scheme to the present stage; he had urged the selection of Mr. Jay; he was in full sympathy with the purposes in view.   The same could not be predicated concerning the secretary of state.   Mr. Randolph's views, subject of course to chameleon-like changes of hue, were for the present of a different complexion from those of his colleague. Hamilton submitted his "points" to the president, who handed them over to Randolph.   The final draft was decided upon in cabinet meeting of May 6.

It must have called for no small measure of moral courage in the more prominent promoters of this mission — in Jay, Washington, and Hamilton — to press it to this actual conclusion.   Vehement and frequent were the displays of popular indignation. It was difficult to compare the number of those in favor of the undertaking with the number of those opposed to it. Hamilton was of opinion that a handsome majority in New York and the Eastern States were well pleased with steps which tended to avert war. But it must be confessed that these moderate and sensible persons, as is very apt to be the case, were also silent and retiring. They did not come forward by a course of vigorous manifestations to sustain the public men who represented their views. On the other hand the opposition party contained a body of fiery and energetic zealots who pushed noisily to the front, and made a very gallant display, probably quite out of proportion to their real numbers or influence. Ten factious men in a community will make more show than an hundred orderly citizens, and so it was at this juncture in the United States. The friends of the mission held their peace and went quietly about their daily affairs. The enemies of the mission gathered in public conventions, made speeches, issued addresses, joined in parades, instigated mass-meetings to behave not unlike mobs. In Philadelphia an altar was set up and dedicated to liberty ; before it the people danced, sang hymns, vowed fealty, and went through other singular mummeries after the wonderful fashion of the French people. At Lexington an effigy of Mr. Jay was placed upon the platform of a pillory, and after having been sufficiently mocked at by the populace was guillotined, and the body, filled with gunpowder, was blown up. Everywhere the Democratic clubs were galvanized into vigorous life. The original organization in Philadelphia published an address, sounding the alarm against " domestic domination," and from all sides echoed the responses of the affiliated societies.   In Kentucky a great gathering, professing to represent " Western America," assailed the foreign policy of the government, accusing it of " tame submission," and of selecting as an envoy to Great Britain the man who was " the enemy of the western country."

With such mingled auspices, the virulent abuse of his opponents almost drowning the hearty godspeed of his friends, was it the fortune of the chief justice to set forth upon his voyage.   Almost simultaneously with his departure, Randolph gave a permit to a French vessel to pass through the embargo, the pretext being that she was to sail in ballast.   The British cruisers captured her and found her laden with a cargo of gunpowder.   A packet, speedily following that which had carried Jay, also took to England copies of some very irritating correspondence which had just passed between Randolph and the English minister at Philadelphia.

It could not be concealed from the reflections of the most sanguine, that the variety and importance of the matters in dispute between the two countries rendered the prospects of a successful negotiation very dubious.   The United States presented a large claim for damages for the deportation of negroes by the British vessels at the close of the war, contrary to the stipulations of the treaty of peace.   In times past the validity of this demand had been all but fully admitted by Great Britain.   But with lapse of years it had grown stale, and as if a statute of limitations could run against it England now appeared loath to recognize it.   The detention of the western posts was regarded in the States as an outrage altogether unjustifiable.   In England it was regarded as a fair offset against American defaults.   A great many seizures, condemnations, confiscations, detentions of American vessels and cargoes, had of late been committed by British vessels in contravention, as was alleged, of the rights conferred by international law upon a neutral nation.   For these infringements English orders in council, and decrees of English courts of admiralty, were held responsible.   The English claimed the right to take native-born subjects of the king from any vessel in any place except only in the ports of the country to which the vessel belonged. The United States not altogether denying the abstract right, yet complained bitterly and with ample reason of the unprincipled manner of its exercise; for the press-gangs would frequently seize not only naturalized but native-born citizens of the States, and even did not scruple to leave vessels to the mercy of the elements in mid-ocean or at a distant port almost wholly stripped of sailors.   American merchants were resolutely bent upon trading to the West Indies.   The British government could see no justice in the requisition made upon them to abandon their long-established commercial system.   Great Britain insisted upon compensation for debts owing to her citizens by citizens of the United States prior to the treaty of peace, and to the recovery of which legal impediments were declared to have been imposed in the States in contravention of the stipulations of the treaty.   The United States insisted that the recovery had long since become possible, if the creditors would but come into the courts and pursue their remedies with due diligence.   There should be added to all these subjects of quarrel a dispute as to the boundary line between the United States and the British territories upon this continent in one part of its course and uncertainty concerning it in another part.

The points which Hamilton made in considering the instructions proper to be given to Mr. Jay were substantially as follows: Indemnification should be made by Great Britain for losses caused by her unlawful depredations on our commerce. In determining what should be considered unlawful depredations, as near an approach as possible should be made to the fair rule of international law, which declares that only such articles are confiscable as are by general usage deemed contraband of war, and that carrying these shall not infect either the rest of the cargo or the vessel, unless there be an attempt at concealment. But provisions were certainly not "by general usage" contraband, and England having undertaken to make them so in this special war would doubtless demand a modification of the rule. Some concession might be made to meet the exigency, but as slight as possible. That the United States should stipulate not to allow sale to be made in her ports of British vessels brought in as prize would probably be insisted upon, and might properly be conceded.

It should be agreed that no armed force should be kept upon the great lakes by either party; and no garrisons, save small guards to protect trading houses, should be maintained within a certain distance of the boundary line. Citizens of each country should enjoy the right of free-trade with the Indians residing within the territorial possessions of the other. In case of war between the Indians and either of the contracting nations, the savages should receive from the other nation no greater supplies than were customary in times of peace.

Great Britain must be required to surrender the posts and make pecuniary reparation for the negroes carried away. The United States upon their part should grant indemnity for all losses arising from legal obstructions interposed to the recovery of the ante-revolutionary debts, not exceeding in the whole a certain sum to be named.

In the matter of commerce the existing condition of things should be subjected to a few innovations. Merchants of the United States should be permitted to carry to the West India Islands in American vessels of certain burden — say not less than sixty tons nor more than eighty tons — all such articles as could then be carried thither from the United States in British bottoms; also to bring thence directly to the United States all such articles as could then be brought thence to the States in British bottoms. Each nation should be permitted to carry in its own bottoms to the ports of the other articles of its own manufacture on terms of the most favored nation.

The instructions finally agreed upon differed much from the outline sketched by Hamilton. The tendency of the alterations was in favor of Great Britain and against the United States. In due time, when the treaty made in conformity with this final draft of the instructions was received and subjected to severe criticism and loud execration, the soundness of Hamilton's views was vindicated. Being then consulted concerning the propriety of publishing the instructions, he stated that in his opinion the publication would be hurtful to the executive and to the character and interest of the government. "The truth," he said, "unfortunately is that it is in general a crude mass which will do no credit to the administration. This was my impression of it at the time; but the delicacy of attempting too much reformation in the work of another head of department, the hurry of the moment, and a great confidence in the person to be sent, prevented my attempting that reformation." He then proceeded to point out a number of matters in which concessions to British prejudices and interests had been made, and sacrifices of fair American demands had been submitted to, far in excess of his opinion of what was right.

Upon his arrival in London Chief Justice Jay was received by the secretary for foreign affairs, Lord Grenville, with much courtesy and a profusion of amicable protestations. But when they came to actual business the British minister did not permit civility to interfere with the driving of a hard bargain. He now appeared as rigid as he had before been polite, and quite disappointed any pleasing anticipations which his conduct might at first have aroused in the anxious mind of the American envoy. That gentleman found that his task was to be not one whit less difficult and painful than he had originally had reason to expect. Mr. Jay arrived on June 15; within less than two weeks afterward negotiations were fairly initiated, and proceeded laboriously during the summer months. The result sufficiently shows the unaccommodating spirit in which the British ministry prosecuted their dealings. Between their unyielding temper and the impending danger of war, Mr. Jay was indeed between the upper and the nether mill-stone.

Not a word did the treaty say about impressment, not a word about indemnity for the deportation of the negroes. The western posts were to be surrendered, but not until June 1, 1796, since the British insisted that they needed this amount of time for preparation. The disputed and uncertain boundaries were to be determined by commissions; a fair enough arrangement, yet so ineffectual that the discussion was kept alive for half a century, brought the nations to the verge of war, and was at last and with extreme difficulty settled by the famous treaty agreed upon by Mr. Webster and Lord Ashburton. The United States were to make full compensation to British creditors for all losses fairly chargeable to legal obstructions which had prevented them from collecting their ante-revolutionary debts. Great Britain was to make compensation for all loss and damage incurred by American citizens, by reason of irregular or illegal captures or condemnations of their vessels or other property under color of authority or commissions from his majesty. The United States in turn were to make compensation to British subjects for all loss or damage sustained by them, by reason of the " capture of their vessels or merchandise taken within the limits and jurisdiction of the States and brought into the ports of the same, or taken by vessels originally armed in ports of the said States." Thus was made good the promise which Washington had caused to be made to Mr. Hammond. The advice originally given by Hamilton when the question was first raised in the cabinet constituted the basis upon which this settlement was finally made.

The recent disgraceful effort of the opposition in Congress to confiscate the debts owing in the United States to British subjects doubtless it was which gave rise to the insertion of an excellent article stipulating that in future no such action should be taken by either government. It was simply a promise not to act very dishonorably, but it was well to have the matter set down in plain words.

The British West Indian ports were opened to vessels of the United States of not more than seventy tons burden, bringing " any goods or merchandises, being of the growth, manufacture, or produce of the said States " upon the like terms and subject to like duties as if the cargo had been brought in a British bottom. The same description of vessels were permitted to carry from the same ports the growth, manufacture, or produce of the islands in like manner as British vessels might do, but to no other place save some port of the United States. It was also " expressly agreed and declared that during the continuance of this article the United States will prohibit and restrain the carrying any molasses, sugar, coffee, cocoa, or *cotton* in American vessels, either from his majesty's islands, or from the United States to any part of the world except the United States, reasonable sea stores excepted." This was the clause in the famous twelfth article of the treaty which afterward raised such a storm of indignation in this country, which even the warmest friends of the administration did not venture to defend, and which caused the Senate to make their ratification conditional upon its suspension.   The truth seems to be that at the time when it was made its full effect was not comprehended either by Mr. Jay or Lord Grenville. Neither of those gentlemen, it is said, was aware that the exportation of cotton from the southern States had already been undertaken, and gave every promise of becoming an important branch of American commerce.

Commerce between the European dominions of England and the United States was placed, for each country in the ports of the other, upon the footing of the most favored nation; and each was permitted to transport in its own bottoms articles of its own growth, produce, or manufacture to the ports of the other.

A clause established a list of articles which should be deemed contraband of war under all circumstances. But it was recited that whereas it was difficult always to agree upon the special cases in which alone provisions and other articles not generally contraband may be regarded as such, therefore such articles, though liable to seizure, should not be absolutely confiscated, but that indemnity should be made to their owners. Very fair stipulations were entered into concerning blockades, captures, privateering, foreign enlistment, and sundry other matters which it is needless here to rehearse at length. The chief topics in dispute, so far as they were disposed of by the treaty, were covered by the articles which have been referred to.

The signatures of Mr. Jay and Lord Grenville were set to the treaty in London, Nov. 19, 1794. It shows how slow was communication across the Atlantic in those days, that the instrument was not received at

Philadelphia until March 7, 1795. Ere that time Hamilton had ceased to be a member of the cabinet, and had returned to the city of New York, which through all the mutations of his public career he had ever regarded as his permanent home. He had long had this step in contemplation, but had postponed it until he could feel well assured of the success of the English mission. Had that miscarried he might have felt it his duty to remain at his post through the crisis in that case to be anticipated; but when he was advised that an agreement had been substantially reached by the diplomatists, he felt free to consult his personal inclinations. His official functions came to an end on the last day of January, 1795. Had he anticipated the storm which was soon to break, his resignation might have been deferred for a twelve-month. The clearing horizon in which he found comfort and release was delusive.

The Senate was summoned to meet in extra session on June 8, to consider and act upon the treaty. Their deliberations were secret; but they were known to be bestowing upon the important matter before them the careful consideration which it deserved. Upon the twenty-fourth of the month a conditional ratification was advised and consented to by a vote of twenty to ten, showing precisely the majority required by the Constitution. The president had already made up his mind in favor of ratification, for though he thought some of the stipulations open to objection, yet these seemed to him to be outweighed by the substantial advantage of the establishment of a peaceful understanding between the two powers. But the peculiar action of the Senate brought affairs into an exceedingly embarrassing condition. What had been done with the treaty? It had not been rejected. It had not been ratified. What was its legal status? What also were the president's power and duties? Should he notify to the British court a ratification subject to a condition? Such a nondescript transaction was unknown to international proceedings, and might be said to be meaningless and absurd. Should he renew negotiations upon the point covered by the condition? There were great objections to taking any step which Great Britain might construe into a general reopening of the discussion. Should he nevertheless take this course, what consequences would ensue thereupon? If the conditional requirement should be refused, was the treaty to be therefore regarded as definitively rejected? If the requirement should be acquiesced in, was the treaty then binding without farther action on the part of the Senate? Beneath the eye of a keen and bitterly hostile opposition, which had often shown a rare capacity for magnifying wonderfully the most minute constitutional doubts,[1] these questions gave more serious cause of anxiety than perhaps their intrinsic importance would have altogether justified.

The way was by no means smoothed by the receipt of certain news from England, which reached the president while he was engaged in anxious cogitations concerning the situation in which the Senate had left him. English newspapers came to hand containing

---

[1] Shortly before this time Fisher Ames had said that the Republicans questioned the constitutionality even of the daily motion to adjourn!

the intelligence, not official in form but doubtless trustworthy, that the "provision order" of June 8, 1793, had been renewed. In fact, this order was privately communicated to the commanders of the war ships, and was not known in London until vessels captured by virtue of it were brought in. This of itself would have been sufficiently annoying, but it became especially so from the fact that the article of the treaty concerning contraband was capable of being so construed as to recognize the lawfulness of such instructions, whereas the president was resolved that it should not receive such a construction. A ratification, made while the order was freshly issued and in force, would too strongly cast the evidence upon the question of construction against the United States. The president took time to consider his course.

It was suggested that the ratification should be made conditional upon the withdrawal of the order. But it was said that to proffer a ratification clogged with one condition by the Senate, and another by the president, was a clumsy and unbusiness-like proceeding. Hamilton advised that the treaty be sent to the agent of the United States in England, ratified as advised by the Senate, and with the instruction, "That, if the order for seizing provisions is in force when he receives it, he is to inform the British ministry that he has the treaty ratified, but that he is instructed not to exchange the ratification till that order is rescinded, since the United States cannot ever give an implied sanction to the principle." At the same time a carefully considered remonstrance against the principle of the order should be despatched. One of the reasons upon which Hamilton based his opinion was, that to exchange ratifications pending such an order would give real cause of umbrage to France, because it would be more than merely to refrain from resisting by force an innovation injurious to her; it would be to give to that innovation a sanction in the midst of a war.

Meantime the curiosity and excitement of the people had grown to an extreme pitch. Upwards of fourteen months had elapsed since the much maligned mission had been inaugurated; the final consummation was upon the verge of taking place, and yet what were the main features of the contract only a few favored individuals knew. Federalists and Democrats were alike eager to pierce the mystery, and the latter added to their eagerness the darkest suspicions. They reviled the privacy of the transaction with great wrath, and declared that it marked the monarchical tendencies of the administration. On the last day of the session of the Senate permission was given to the senators to show their copies of the treaty to any persons for perusal, but not to permit any copy of the whole or any part to be taken. It was hardly to be expected that such liberty as this could be allowed without full information to the public speedily following. Accordingly, within three days after the adjournment of the Senate, an imperfect abstract of the document appeared in the " Aurora," a Democratic sheet. The impropriety of sending an inaccurate version abroad was immediately made the pretext by Mason, a Democratic senator from Virginia, for furnishing the full and correct text to Editor Bache. At once a vast batch of copies were stricken off at the office of the " Aurora" and circulated with exceeding despatch, especially toward the North and East, the mercantile sections,

The conduct of Mason has been criticised as a breach of confidence. He subjected himself to the reproach needlessly, for upon the very day that the copy of the treaty was printed in the newspaper, over Mason's signature, Washington directed the instrument to be published. But if the good name of a Republican suffered, at least the opposition had not miscalculated the effect of the publication. Everywhere that the treaty went it was accompanied or speedily followed by comments, which Washington soon afterward quite justly described as " arrant misrepresentation." The seed thus widely sown and sedulously watered fell upon no unkindly soil; and the abundant crop of discontent was not long in maturing. Boston led the way with a public and formal announcement of her disapproval. A town-meeting was called; a vote of censure against the treaty was passed without dissent; an address to the president, setting forth twenty objections, was adopted without opposition, and received an official complexion by being forwarded by the magistrates of the town.

In New York better things might have been hoped for, Jay having at the recent election been chosen governor of the State. In the city a meeting was convened with the purpose of following the example set by Boston, but was found to contain a large proportion if not a majority of persons of a contrary way of thinking. Discord prevented any thing being accomplished. But the enemies of the treaty, resolved not thus to be defeated, gathered afterward and passed resolutions enumerating no less than twenty-eight causes of dissatisfaction with the treaty. It was full of concessions to Great Britain; it secured nothing of equal value for the United States ; it was "hostile and ungrateful to France." Philadelphia and Charleston followed with similar action. Everywhere the cry was, " the violation of our engagements with France." Unfortunately men of excellent standing had taken the lead at these several gatherings, and had given to them a somewhat higher character than they deserved. For it was noticed that few of the more intelligent merchants had connected themselves with the movement. Beneath the leaders, who were engaged from political motives, the assemblages were for the most part made up of the lower orders of the people. This characteristic of the opposition was farther evinced by the tendency to displays of foolish violence. On sundry occasions the treaty was burned, the British flag was trailed through the streets, effigies were carried in procession, and tumultuous gatherings were with difficulty prevented from becoming mobs. The example set by the leading places was rapidly followed by the smaller towns and villages, and from every neighborhood the tokens of indignation found their way before the president.

The purpose of all this elaborate display and extreme pressure was to deter the president from ratifying the treaty. There have been few statesmen in countries having a popular system of government, who would have had the nerve demanded by such an occasion. But Washington in his thorough, deliberate way had pondered upon the subject until he had reached a clear and firm conclusion. From such a conclusion he was never once driven in the course of his long public life.   In the present crisis some persons feared that the stability of the government might be shaken by a ratification; even anarchy might be a not distant though an indirect result.   Yet the president did not waver.   During his administration of the government, he said, he had seen no crisis from which in his judgment so much was to be apprehended. If no counter manifestations in favor of the treaty should appear, he feared that the opposition to it must be considered " in a manner universal," which would " make the ratification a very serious business indeed." Men who were of " no party, but well disposed to the present administration," led him to believe that the prejudices against the treaty were more extensive than had been generally supposed.   Yet, said he, with that simple and gallant honesty of his, " it is not to be inferred from hence that I am disposed to quit the ground I have taken, unless circumstances more imperious than have yet come to my knowledge should compel it; for there is but one straight course, and that is to seek truth and pursue it steadily."

Washington was not without support in his position, in spite of the aspect presented by the country at large.   The cabinet with the exception of Randolph was with him.   With Hamilton he was in constant communication, and had that gentleman still been the secretary of the treasury he could have exerted no greater influence nor been more frequently consulted. Repeatedly in all the varying phases of the business did the president lay before his old assistant and trustworthy friend the doubts and questions which occurred to him, and with quick despatch and ample fulness were all such letters replied to. At one time, in the moment most nearly approaching to doubt which he seems to have experienced, Washington appealed to Hamilton, as the man most competent from knowledge, experience, and opinion, to give to him a sketch of all the important arguments upon both sides of the discussion. He wished once more to see them clearly arrayed against each other.

Hamilton's sentiments made him in an unusual degree an impartial adviser. He occupied concerning this treaty somewhat the same position which he had occupied concerning the Constitution. His views had been given in consultation and had but imperfectly prevailed ; the result was by no means wholly to his satisfaction ; yet he regarded it as the best which could be obtained, and very much better than the only other alternative which could be considered as presenting itself. The Constitution with all the short-comings which he conceived to exist in it he had vastly preferred to anarchy, and had accordingly supported it with warmth. The ratification of the treaty with all its inequalities and deficiencies was greatly better than war, and therefore this measure also he aided with his best exertions. Yet abundant evidence remains to show how far it fell short of what he deemed a satisfactory contract.

Washington was strengthened in his intention to ratify, by the fact that certain language at the close of the document seemed to show very plainly that both negotiators contemplated a subsequent contract for the purpose of disposing of some points left open by the present arrangement. He was disposed to enter at once upon this supplementary negotiation, and asked

Hamilton's advice as to the points which it should cover. Hamilton replied that the tonnage of the vessels permitted to trade to the British West Indies should be increased ; that the right should be given to American vessels to trade from the British territories in India to other parts of Asia, since " it is a usual and beneficial course of trade to go from the United States to Bombay, and take in there a freight for Canton, purchase at the last place a cargo of teas," and thence return home. A great effort should be made to secure the rule of free ships making free goods. At any rate naval stores and provisions ought, if possible, to be expressly excluded from the list of contraband, unless going to a place under siege or blockade, or to a fleet or army engaged in military operations. The least that could be submitted to in the matter of impressment would be the establishment of the principle " that no seaman shall be impressed out of any of our vessels at sea, and that none shall be taken out of any such vessel in any of her colonies, which were in the vessel at the time of her arrival at such colony." The affair of the negroes should " be retouched, but with caution and delicacy."

In the city of New York Hamilton's influence was marked and effective. When the meeting, already mentioned, was summoned for the sake of discussing the treaty, certain leading merchants published an address, stating that if such a meeting was to be held it should be as fully attended as possible, in order that the true opinion of the people might be obtained. The purpose of this movement was of course to outnumber and counteract the malcontents who had concocted the scheme, and it was so far successful that in spite of the vigorous exertions of the Livingston family, who had expected to control and direct the assemblage, the chairman was chosen by the friends of the treaty. Hamilton rose to move an adjournment, and was yet speaking when a riotous throng, fresh from burning the treaty on the Battery, came marching up Broadway with French and American flags flying side by side. The mingling of this new element in the crowd at once produced a tumultuous condition of affairs. Missiles began to fly, and a stone struck Hamilton on the head. " If you use such striking arguments," said he, " I must desist; " and the meeting broke up in confusion. Afterward the chamber of commerce of the city passed resolutions expressing a favorable opinion of the treaty, and a desire to see it ratified. But at the same time, by way of rebuke to the manner in which all sorts of gatherings throughout the country were assuming the constitutional functions of the Senate, these merchants expressed themselves quite content to leave the decision with those to whom the Constitution had confided it.

By way of farther effort to moderate the public excitement and enlighten the general intelligence concerning the treaty, Hamilton went busily to work with his pen and contributed to the newspapers the essays of " Camillus." The first of these papers was published July 22, 1795, four days after the public meeting at which Hamilton had endeavored to speak. Apparently they were not without their due influence upon the public sentiment, which soon appeared to be so far changing for the better that the supporters of the government thought it advisable to call another meeting. The people now came together in a very different mood from that which had caused the breaking-up of the previous gathering. Hamilton, no longer a mark for the peculiar arguments of a mob, delivered a long and elaborate defence of the treaty, and was listened to, not only with courtesy, but with approbation. Indeed public opinion had begun to turn also outside the city of New York; or perhaps it would more correctly describe the condition of things to say that the large number of sensible and thinking people, of that class who are always averse to demonstrative interference in public affairs, began to appreciate the necessity imposed upon them by the present crisis of taking some more active part. They accordingly began to assemble in meetings not less numerously attended and much more respectably conducted than those of their opponents, at which they made their speeches and passed their resolutions in favor of the treaty. This portion of the community, being at last thoroughly aroused, very soon made it evident that the opposition was not so universal as had been for a time supposed.

Some answers to "Camillus" of course appeared, and called forth the farther letters of "Philo-Camillus." But these replies were far from satisfactory, and the Republican leader contemplated the unequal strife with much disgust. He had no desire to come down into the arena himself: it was not his way; he was wont to express much contempt for the newspaper press. It was especially disagreeable to engage in a contest with Hamilton, concerning controversies with whom Aaron Burr once remarked: "If you put yourself upon paper with him, you are gone." Jefferson was doubtless of the same mind, for under the greatest temptation he always succeeded in restraining himself from breaking a lance in such a fray. But he was exceedingly desirous of seeing the task of refutation undertaken by some hand more nearly equal to the occasion than any which had yet essayed. As was his wont, when pressed by a need of this kind, he had recourse to Madison. "Hamilton," he wrote feelingly, "is really a Colossus to the anti-republican party. Without numbers, he is an host in himself. They have got themselves into a defile where they might be finished; but too much security on the Republican part will give time to his talents and indefatigableness to extricate them. We have had only middling performances to oppose him. In truth, when he comes forward there is nobody but yourself can meet him. . . . For God's sake take up your pen and give a fundamental reply to 'Curtius' and 'Camillus.'" But Madison had little stomach for the enterprise which . his chieftain urged upon him, and the "fundamental reply" so sorely needed was not forthcoming.

On August 12 a cabinet meeting was held, and the treaty was discussed; and on August 14 Washington ratified it, resolving however to accompany the exchange of ratifications with a vigorous memorial protesting against the "provision order." Probably one of the warmest enemies of the treaty indirectly hastened this final action of the president. Randolph alone of all the members of the cabinet had obstinately cast every obstacle which he could devise in the way of this consummation. It was on August 11 that the famous private despatch of the French minister, Fauchet, was put into Washington's hands. Lord Grenville wisely conceived that he could make no better use of the startling disclosures contained in this document than to divulge them to the government of the United States. The unfortunate epistle showed Randolph to be guilty at once of corruption and of treachery. The discovery of such motives influencing the mind of the chief opponent of the treaty naturally had the effect of destroying the force of his arguments, and the ratification instantly ensued. Randolph retired in disgrace ; and in private life set about the compilation of that " Vindication " which has not succeeded in rescuing his name from infamy.

Randolph was not the only victim who could connect his fall from an illustrious eminence with this bitter controversy. John Rutledge, of South Carolina, had been nominated by the president to the chief justiceship left vacant by Jay's resignation. Almost simultaneously with the act of nomination, and before news of it could reach him and possibly warn him to check or conceal his sentiments, he assumed a very conspicuous part in the public meeting which was held at Charleston to condemn the treaty. This unfortunate conjunction of circumstances was very embarrassing to the Federalists. They were loath to reject the president's nomination ; they were not less loath to confer so high a dignity upon one who had made himself so prominent an opponent of their politics. Hamilton was consulted. He gave it as his opinion that the president would not under the circumstances be annoyed should he be overruled by the Senate. Upon principle the rejection seemed right, and therefore it ought to take place. Objections of a personal nature, on the score of bad habits, had been also suggested, and these if well founded were entitled to conclusive weight. This view prevailed. The Senate refused to confirm Mr. Rutledge in the office, and after having held a single term of the court he was obliged to retire from the brief and imperfect possession of that high honor.

Congress came together in the following autumn, with a Republican majority in the House of Representatives. No disguise was attempted of the purpose of the party to stir up trouble concerning the treaty so soon as opportunity should offer. The instrument came back from Great Britain early in March, with the amendment required by the conditional ratification duly appended, and was forthwith published as law by proclamation from the president. Debate was at once opened in the House upon a motion introduced by Livingston, requesting the president to send in to the House a full transcript of the instructions to Jay, the correspondence, and all other papers relating to the treaty. A nice constitutional question had been raised as to the powers of the House. The treaty had been made by the president and Senate, and it now stood the perfected and supreme law of the land. Yet it dealt with and undertook to contract concerning many topics which the Constitution placed in whole or in part within the control of Congress and of the House of Representatives as a part of Congress. Especially it required an appropriation of money. The House, it was now said, was not deprived by the treaty of its constitutional powers, and might legislate as it should please, in contravention or neglect of any treaty stipulations. The president and Senate could not, it was argued, by ratifying a treaty, indirectly compel the House of Representatives to make an appropriation. This position the Federalists denied. The treaty-making power was supreme, as they thought, and, for any purpose of discussing the merits or constitutionality of the treaty, a call for papers was improper. For three weeks an eager discussion ensued. Then the resolution asking for the papers was carried by a vote of sixty-two to thirty-seven.

The president at once requested Wolcott to obtain an interview with Hamilton, and request his advice and assistance concerning the action proper to be taken. But Hamilton had left Philadelphia, and the president therefore sent to him a letter at New York. Hamilton's reply was prompt, and was followed a few days later by a full argument upon the constitutional question involved. Washington would not have been disinclined to comply with the request, could he do so without compromising his lawful right of refusal. He had no objection to the papers being seen. He did not consider that they contained any thing which it was desirable to conceal, and he was not without hopes that the submission of them to the House might soothe the temper of the majority and facilitate the needful legislation. Hamilton was of the contrary opinion concerning the question of expediency. The promulgation of portions of the instructions, to be subjected to the unfriendly distortions of the opposition, seemed to him unwise, and of the document as a whole he had no very high opinion.

He had said so before, and he repeated the criticism again. It had not been well digested, and in parts it was neither very definite nor very strong.

Upon the question of the right of the House to demand the papers, except as a basis for impeachment, he was of the same mind with the president and cabinet. The resolutions did not suggest an intent to impeach any one as a cause for the request; and Gallatin himself had admitted that, if the requisition was founded upon that ground, the fact should be openly set forth. The call, being " altogether indefinite and without any declared purpose," furnished to the executive " no basis on which to judge of the propriety of a compliance with it." Yet such a basis should properly have been furnished, for the matter was proper for the exercise of discretion on the part of the executive. It could not be that, after the treaty had been fully completed in the manner provided by the Constitution, it could be subjected to the House of Representatives and placed in jeopardy of being practically annulled by their disapproval of its provisions.[1]

[1] The following letter, though hastily written, yet contains so clear an exposition of the merits of this constitutional argument, · that it deserves to be carefully read : —

" I observe Madison brings the power of the House of Representatives in the case of the treaty to this question : Is the agency of the House of Representatives on the subject *deliberative* or *executive ?* On the sophism that the legislature, and each branch of it, is *essentially deliberative*, and consequently must have discretion, will he, I presume, maintain the freedom of the House to concur or not.

" But the sophism is easily refuted. The legislature, and each branch of it, is *deliberative*, but with *various* restrictions, not with *unlimited discretion*. All the injunctions and restrictions of the Constitution, for instance, abridge its *deliberative* faculty and leave it,

As matter of common sense, it is impossible to question the justness of the reasoning which leads to this conclusion, or to deny the absolute necessity

quoad hoc, merely executive. Thus the Constitution enjoins that there shall be a fixed allowance for the judges, which shall not be diminished. The legislature cannot, therefore, deliberate whether they will make a permanent provision, and when the allowance is fixed they cannot deliberate whether they will appropriate and pay the money. So far their deliberative faculty is abridged. The *mode* of raising and appropriating the money only remains matter of deliberation.

"So likewise the Constitution says that the president and Senate shall make treaties, and that these treaties shall be supreme laws. It is a contradiction to call a thing a law which is not binding. It follows that by constitutional injunction the House of Representatives *quoad* the stipulations of treaties, as in the case cited respecting the judges, are not deliberative, but merely executive, *except as to the means of executing.*

"Any other doctrine would vest the legislature, and each House, with unlimited discretion, and destroy the very idea of a Constitution limiting its discretion. The Constitution would at once vanish.

"Besides, the *legal* power to refuse the execution of a law is a *power to repeal it.* Thus the House of Representatives must, as to treaties, concentre in itself the whole legislative power, and undertake without the Senate to repeal a law. For the law is complete by the action of the president and Senate.

"Again : A treaty, which is a contract between nation and nation, abridges even the legislative discretion of the whole legislature by the moral obligation of keeping its faith ; *a fortiori*, that of one branch. In theory, there is no method by which the obligations of a treaty can be annulled but by mutual consent of the contracting parties, by ill-faith in one of them, or by a revolution of government, which is of a nature so to change the condition of parties as to render the treaty inapplicable."—*Hamilton's Works*, vi. 92.

The following points also were suggested by Hamilton as memoranda from which to elaborate an opinion :—

I. The Constitution empowers the president with the Senate to make treaties.

II. A treaty is a perfected compact between two nations, obligatory on both.

III. That cannot be a perfected contract or treaty to the validity of

of the conclusion itself, if the United States are
to expect foreign nations to enter into treaties
with them at all. The form of ratification required by the Constitution has been found to the
full as complex and cumbrous as is consistent with
the practical transaction of such business. If at any
time after the contract has passed successfully the
double ordeal of the presidential and senatorial judgment, the United States can still relieve themselves
with color of lawfulness from some essential por-

which the concurrence of any other power in the State is constitu-
tionally necessary. Again,

IV. The Constitution says a treaty is a *law*.

V. A law is an obligatory rule of action, prescribed by the competent authority. But,

VI. That cannot be such a rule of action or *law* to the validity of
which the assent of any other person is requisite. Again,

VII. The object of the *legislative* power is to prescribe a rule of
action for our own nation, which includes foreigners coming
among us.

VIII. The object of the treaty power is by agreement to settle a
rule of action between two nations, binding on both.

IX. These objects are essentially different, and in a constitutional
sense cannot interfere.

X. The treaty power binding the *will* of the nation must, within
its constitutional limits, be paramount to the legislative power, which
is that will, or at least the last *law* being a treaty must repeal an
antecedent contrary law. And,

XI. If the legislative power is competent to repeal this law by a
subsequent law, this must be the whole legislative power by a solemn
act in the forms of the Constitution, not one branch of the legislative power by disobeying the law.

XII. The foregoing Constitution reconciles the two powers, and
assigns them distinguishable spheres of action ; while

XIII. The other construction, that claiming that a right of assent
is a sanction for the House of Representatives, destroys the treaty,
making powerless and negative two propositions in the Constitution,
to wit: 1. That the president with the Senate are competent to make
treaties. 2. That a treaty is a law.—*Hamilton's Works*, vi. 94.

tion of their obligations, through a refusal of the House of Representatives to concur in certain necessary legislation, it would be the extreme of folly upon the part of any power to exchange any thing of value against so dubious a return. The difficulty, however, still survives. Washington and Hamilton established an admirable precedent founded upon sound reasoning ; but they could not remove the defect in clearness existing in the Constitution. It is still possible for an ill-advised or excited majority in the House of Representatives to encroach upon a function from which it was intended wholly to exclude that body.

The opposition party in the House, in 1796, did all that they could, without coming to really dangerous extremities, to keep this embarrassing question open for the vexation of posterity. It is impossible to defend their course in this respect. For had they considered the subsequent bearing of their action they could hardly have failed to perceive that even if the treaty was as bad as they declared it to be, yet it could not do the country such permanent and extensive mischief as the triumph of the constitutional principle for which they contended. How could some imperfectly favorable stipulations, most of them of brief continuance, an omission of some matters of right not thereby altogether lost but only remitted to farther negotiation, — how could such objections as these be set against the substantial destruction of the power of the United States to bind itself in treaty with any other people? The Republican doctrine indeed was lost in the folly of a *reductio ad absurdum*. For if the House of Representatives was entitled to freedom of legislation in the first instance, surely there was nothing to deprive it of that freedom afterward. If it could pass a law to further or to contravene the treaty in one year, it could repeal either or both of these laws at any subsequent session. Thus a contract between the United States and another nation would practically signify an obligation binding upon the one, but at any moment lawfully revocable by the other. But the Republicans, regardless of consequences, made the most of the possibility which the Constitution left open to them.

When the president declined to furnish the papers a resolution was brought forward wherein the right to any agency in making treaties was disclaimed; but it was asserted that if a treaty "stipulated regulations upon any subject submitted by the Constitution to the power of Congress," it must depend for its execution in this respect upon legislative action, as to the expediency of which the House might deliberate and adopt or reject the measures as it should see fit. A second resolution declared that when the House had a right to information upon any ground, it was not obliged in its application to the executive to state that specific ground as constituting the purpose for which the information was sought. The request might be made generally and should be complied with, for whatever other improper end the papers might really be wanted! The resolutions were supported by Madison, and passed by a vote of fifty-seven to thirty-five.

It became at once a serious question whether the House would exercise the right of interference which it so resolutely asserted. The doubt was put to the test by the introduction of a resolution to the purport that such laws as should be necessary to carry the treaty into effect ought to be passed. An acrimonious debate ensued, which was protracted during some weeks. Gallatin made a very able speech against the treaty, but was answered by Ames with one yet abler. The external pressure in favor of the treaty was strong and increasing. While this doubt hung over the action of the House, the merchants could no longer insure their vessels. Addresses began to pour in beseeching the requisite legislation. One came even from Gallatin's district, the disaffected region of the whiskey insurrection. The opposition became discouraged, demoralized, and also not a little sobered at the vision of the evils which they would surely precipitate upon the country should they venture to act upon their avowed principles. Some of them manifested an inclination to change sides, and when at last the vote was reached in committee of the whole it showed a tie, — forty-nine to forty-nine. Muhlenberg, the speaker, was a Republican. He quailed beneath the gravity of the crisis; reminded his party that the vote was not conclusive, since action was still to be taken by the House; deserted them and voted for the resolution. When the matter came before the House the resolution was saved by a majority of three; the numbers standing fifty-one to forty-eight. The split was sectional. From the commercial States of New England only four votes were given against the resolution. New Jersey went solidly in favor of it; the Maryland delegation threw only one vote against it. Two-thirds of the New York and Pennsylvania members were in favor of it. But from all the States south of the Potomac it obtained only four votes.

CHAPTER VI.

ADMINISTRATION OF ADAMS.

When all doubt was removed as to Washington's willingness to accept the presidency for a third term, much perturbation and excitement prevailed concerning the election of his successor. It was by no means certain which party would prevail in the contest. The Federalists hoped not without anxiety; the Republicans were anxious not without hope. The prospects of the opposition had been steadily improving for a long time past; and the House of Representatives, which seemed the most accurate test of the popular sentiment, had long shown a large Republican majority. If a majority of the people approved of the ratification of Jay's treaty, it was not so much because they thought well of it as because they considered war likely to be a worse evil than the sum of the defects of that instrument. Certainly the negotiation had not for the time being brought any accession of glory or popularity to the administration.

Thomas Jefferson was the candidate of the Republicans, and a man more sure to win if victory was a possibility could not have been selected. Years had certainly not diminished upon his head since he had given as a reason for retiring from the cabinet of Washington that his age unfitted him for the toils of office. In the interval he had reiterated his fixed resolve and unvarying desire to pass the remainder of his days amid the famous clover of Monticello. Yet all the while this untrustworthy moralist had been gathering and playing with consummate skill every card which chance or design had placed within his reach. If now it were written in the book of destiny that he should be president or even vice-president, he was meekly prepared to suffer the immolation, to forget the date of his natal year, and leave his fields of lucerne to his overseer.

The Federalists did not find their selection of a candidate so easy as did their opponents. In their ranks no man appeared preëminently satisfactory. Adams, Jay, and Hamilton were the three from whom they would naturally incline to choose. Each of the three had his just claims, and each his undeniable points of objection. Adams was vice-president; and the idea of a succession, since become altogether obsolete, was for a long time in the earlier age of the republic not without much force. Adams had deserved well of the party. Many and many a time had the equal division of the Senate left matters of the first importance to be decided by his casting vote, and on such occasions he had never quailed or wavered before the responsibility. Firmly and manfully, yet not in a manner to give needless offence, he had conferred success upon bill after bill, each one of which involved some cardinal principle of Federalism. His courage, his ability, his patriotism were beyond question; so in the main was his devotion to the party. Yet he was not thoroughly a party man; there was an element of independence in his character which his friends admired, but which induced those less friendly to call him headstrong. It was conceived not impossible that in some important conjuncture he might take the bit in his teeth and sheer quite off the party track. For this reason not a few of the Federalists, Hamilton among the number, were far from feeling altogether satisfied with the prospect of seeing John Adams exalted to the presidency by the votes of their party. That their sentiments were not without foundation was proved by his presidential career no less than by the open expressions of opinion on the part of the opposition. If the Republicans were to be beaten they were not ill-pleased to be beaten by Mr. Adams; for they plainly intimated their expectation that they might often be able to exert substantial influence over him.

John Jay — late chief justice of the United States, envoy extraordinary to Great Britain, and now governor of New York — certainly had a record, a personal character, and a measure of ability which would have amply justified an attempt to make him the successor of Washington. But the extent of the hostility to the treaty could not be accurately measured; it might detract from his chances of success, and in a close contest not a point could be lost.

Hamilton does not appear to have been seriously thought of. He was the leader of the party; he would unquestionably have been the first choice of the thorough-going Federalists of the eastern States, and would have been agreeable to those of the middle

States. But his financial measures had brought upon him the wrath of the planting and slave-holding interest in the South, and his success could not be anticipated. It has been well said, that the most illustrious among American statesmen have been great and admirable until they have reached that stage of success and distinction at which they begin to aspire to the presidency. That ambition becoming their predominant wish inevitably accomplishes their ruin. Hamilton escaped this mischief. No other statesman in this country, of equal prominence, has failed at some period to be named as a probable candidate, or to anticipate with more or less longing such a consummation of a public career. But Hamilton appears never to have aspired to this office, never to have been brought by his friends into this arena. This fact must be regarded as singularly fortunate. What might have been the influence upon his character or the effect upon his reputation of a contrary accident can only be conjectured. If it had not been deleterious, at least it probably would not have been advantageous. There was no opportunity for him to have succeeded in the rivalry, and defeat is a distinction which no friend could covet for another.

So the Federalists generally, with rather imperfect satisfaction, were settling down to the resolution to support John Adams as their candidate for the presidency, and Thomas Pinckney of South Carolina as their candidate for the vice-presidency. But the very crude system which the Constitution then prescribed for the election to these high offices rendered an accurate calculation of the chances of the several candidates impossible. Unexpected and unintended results were not improbable. The foreknowledge which the present simple plan furnishes was altogether impossible in those days. The electors cast their votes for two persons, not designating which was to fill the one position, and which the other. The person having the highest number of votes was president; the person having the next highest was vice-president. There was room for infinite ingenious manœuvring, and a single elector might determine whether a candidate should obtain the first or the second place.

Hamilton, feeling that he was justly entitled to exercise an extensive influence with his party, scanned the field with no small anxiety. His first object was to bring about a Federal victory, be the successful candidate who he might. If Adams could secure a greater number of suffrages than any other member of the party, then by all means let Adams win. Yet it cannot be denied that the success of Pinckney would have better accorded with Hamilton's personal inclinations. Mr. Adams was firmly convinced that Hamilton conducted secret machinations for the purpose of bringing him in second to Pinckney; and he regarded this as unfair dealing on the part of Hamilton, partly because he had been wont to consider and speak of himself as "heir-apparent," partly because he felt firmly assured that he was the first choice of the majority of the party. It can hardly be denied that if Hamilton was of opinion that Pinckney would make the better president of the two he was perfectly justified in stating this opinion to the correspondents who sought his advice, perfectly justified in casting such influence as he had into the Pinckney scale. More than this he certainly did not do; to say that he did even so much would be almost an exaggeration. Yet Mr. Adams always persisted in believing that Hamilton, by some occult and disreputable necromancy, had deprived him of votes to which he was fairly entitled.

Hamilton's real position was perfectly simple and fair. His cardinal motive was to secure success for the Federalist candidate. Every member of the party knew that this success would be very narrowly achieved; that the intervention of a little personal jealousy, a little clever intriguing to aid one or another individual, might turn possible victory into certain defeat. There was too much reason to fear that some of the New England electors, resolved that the triumph of the party should be the triumph of Adams, secretly intended to cast their second votes for some other person than Pinckney. Hamilton could not but see that this was a very dangerous game to play in the face of their powerful and skilful enemy. Ever so little retaliation on the part of the southerners might lead to the consequence of Jefferson securing the largest vote.

In view of this condition of things Hamilton urged a very plain and straightforward course. Every elector of Federalist persuasions should make it his first object to bring out the full strength of his party; to this end he should vote for Adams and Pinckney. Could such a programme have been perfectly carried out it would have resulted in a tie between these two gentlemen; an accident sufficiently provided for by the Constitution, and which would doubtless, as Hamilton well knew, have ultimately given the presidency to Adams. But it was not probable that this programme could be thus perfectly carried out. A vote here and there would be influenced by personal prejudice or other consideration, and one or other of the two candidates would have more than his rival. The reason why this course was distasteful to the Adams faction was because they anticipated defections from their candidate at the South, which they thought it necessary to meet and counteract by defections from Mr. Pinckney in the East. The fault which they found with Hamilton's recommendations was that they would not be followed by some of the southern electors; and because they did not expect his advice to be fairly taken they said that it was not fair advice.

Yet the accuracy of his opinion was quite vindicated by the result. It cannot be shown that he detracted a single vote from Mr. Adams which would otherwise have been cast for that gentleman. Mr. Adams levied all his forces. He won by three votes over Mr. Jefferson, by only one vote over the number required for a choice. Victory could not have been more narrowly saved. Surely Hamilton was justified in saying that the duty of every Federalist was, not to throw away a vote in the effort to draw distinctions between candidates from his own party, but to vote for both those candidates in order to increase the chance that one or other should come in over the Republican competitors. It is said that if the advice of Hamilton had prevailed Pinckney would have been elected, and the will of the Federalists would have been thwarted. The supreme will of the Federalists was doubtless to elect a president from their own party, and the Adams party imperilled this achievement to the very uttermost degree of hazard. Had two votes less fallen for Adams, what obloquy would have covered the men who did not follow the advice of Hamilton, who threw away their second votes and gave the game to their adversaries, or threw the choice into Congress !

Whether or not the breach which this affair opened between Mr. Adams and Hamilton could ever have been closed may be doubted. The new president was of an irascible turn, and not devoid of a certain egotism which led him not easily to brook any action which stood in the way of his preferment in the honors of public life. But as ill-fortune would have it, so far from any opportunity offering to mend the broken amity, the course of affairs throughout the presidential term steadily increased the mutual distrust. Hamilton and Adams held very different opinions concerning the policy of the party and the measures proper to be pursued in order to sustain the honor and the welfare of the country. The result was that the Federalists were divided between them, and the ruin of the party ensued as the natural and inevitable consequence of this dismemberment.

For this course of affairs it has been the custom of the friends of Adams to lay all the blame at the door of Hamilton, and for the friends of Hamilton to lay all the blame at the door of Adams. I confess that it seems to me that the fault was rather that of untoward circumstances than of either of these gentlemen. Washington had been twice made president by the will of the people. Adams had been made president by the will of the Federalist party. He naturally considered that this selection and preference implied something substantial in his behalf; it seemed to him that he was invested with the leadership of the party by virtue of having been chosen to fill the most prominent and dignified position in its gift. He thought that if Hamilton could not agree with him, then it was Hamilton's duty to preserve a discreet silence and keep his views carefully to himself. For all that Mr. Adams was so stanch a republican he was of an autocratic temper; and the combined force of his opinions and his impulses led him to act with no small degree of arbitrariness.

But a large proportion of the party were by no means content to accept the domination of Mr. Adams. They acknowledged him to be one of the most distinguished members of their party, and the most available candidate which it contained for the presidency; but they did not acknowledge him to be the leader of the party. It was one thing to occupy that situation which would attract votes, but quite another thing to be entitled to dictate a policy. Mr. Adams never yet had exercised this function; he had never at any moment or in any transaction *led* the Federalists. On the other hand Hamilton had led them from the very outset. He had been marked out as their leader not only by the manner in which they themselves followed his advice, but equally so by the manner in which the opposition had singled him out as the one preëminently dangerous opponent to be destroyed at all hazard. He it was who had in a measure created the party. His financial measures had first established distinctly the line of demarcation

in Congress and in the country. His schemes had
constituted the Federalist policy. His broad and
liberal construction of the Constitution had been
adopted by the Federalists as the theory upon which
the country was to be governed and all public affairs
to be administered. Anti-federalism — or, as it was
afterward called, Republicanism or Democracy — signified only contradiction of the doctrines and opposition to the measures of which Hamilton was either
the originator or the chief expositor. In earlier days
the very tactics of the party had been shaped by him
in all the more grave and dubious crises. The Federal leaders in Congress had been the lieutenants of
this distinguished captain. Able as they were, they
acknowledged his superior capacity to conduct a political campaign, and without a particle of reluctance or
jealousy they heartily took and obeyed his directions.
Later, when financial disputes had been superseded
by foreign complications, the influence of Hamilton
was but slightly less conspicuous, and his leadership
none the less unquestionable. What indeed can
constitute the leadership of a political party, if the
origination of its policy and an almost supreme influence, voluntarily submitted to by and exercised over
its chief workers in the active labor of the cabinet and
Congress, does not constitute it? Tried by this test,
Hamilton had been the leader of the Federalists from
the beginning of Federalism, and his reign continued
unbroken by his retirement into private life.

His withdrawal from the cabinet of Washington
might unquestionably have operated as an abdication
of his more vague but not less undeniable position of
chieftainship; it might have so operated had the

party been so inclined, or had he insisted upon it. But in fact his opinion in public affairs was not less sedulously sought, not more respectfully received, before than after this event. Continually did Washington consult him, and cause the secretaries to consult him in all matters of difficulty. It has already been seen how constantly his advice was sought concerning the treaty, its ratification, the submission of the papers to the House of Representatives, the proper subjects to be disposed of in a subsequent negotiation. This advice was not intrusively thrust upon persons indifferent to it, but was sent in reply to frequently reiterated requests for it. And this is but an example of what was continually going forward. At one time Washington begs him to assist with suggestions as to the formation of a new cabinet. "What am I to do for a secretary of state? I ask frankly and with solicitude; and shall receive kindly any sentiments you may express on the occasion." Then follows a long sketch of the disagreeable situation and of the difficulties environing the president. Again the president refers to him for an outline of his message to Congress. "Although," he says, "you are not in the administration,—a thing I sincerely regret,—I must nevertheless (knowing how intimately acquainted you are with all the concerns of this country) request the favor of you to note down such occurrences as in your opinion are proper subjects for communication to Congress at their next session"

So it went on from week to week during the remainder of Washington's presidential term. Whenever he was hard pushed for advice or assistance, he turned to Hamilton as to a friend in whose ability

and kindliness he could fully trust; and never did
Hamilton hesitate to put aside his own private affairs
and devote his time to the service of Washington.
At last, when the retiring president was considering
the subject of a farewell address, — a matter which
came very closely home to his heart, and which he
wished to make as nearly beyond criticism as a mortal
work could be, — he again had recourse to Hamilton;
and though that famous document cannot be said to
be wholly the product of any one brain, or the work
of any single hand, yet by far the greater part both
of its form and of its substance was contributed by
Hamilton.

What was done by the chief was done also by the
subordinates. Wolcott the new secretary of the
treasury was continually writing to Hamilton, not
alone about financial matters, but concerning politics
and party-affairs generally. Pickering frequently
corresponded with him. King, Cabot, and others of
the more prominent members of the party constantly
imparted to him their knowledge of what was passing
and requested in return his opinion and advice. So
long as Washington was at the head of affairs this
was a wholly unobjectionable proceeding, not in the
least imperilling the good-will, sympathy, and harmony existing between all concerned. But the
succession of Mr. Adams gave at once a different
complexion to the political relationship. The new
president would much more readily have taken counsel with those who dwelt in the tents of the opposition than with that evil disposed lawyer of New York,
who would not have been altogether unhappy had
Pinckney been in the first office. But Wolcott and

Pickering could not put off their habits, sentiments, convictions, in subservience to the will of a new master. Wolcott indeed offered to resign, but Mr. Adams declined to accept the offer, and continued all the members of the prior administration in possession of their offices. It was a mistake upon his part which he discovered and repented afterward; not because he could have filled their places with better men or sounder Federalists, but because with new officers of his own appointment he might have had a cabinet altogether sympathetic with and loyal to himself.

These gentlemen had fallen into certain established ways in the conduct of their official duties. They had been wont to turn to Hamilton for consultation, advice, and to a certain extent even for guidance. Not that they were not men of abundant ability and independence; but they had been wont to regard Hamilton as the man best fitted to lead their party, and they had deferred to him accordingly. They were not now ready to transfer this allegiance to Mr. Adams; they were not pliant to his arguments and were by no means ready to submit to his dictation. They still wrote, as before, to Hamilton; they still sought his advice; they still respected it beyond the opinion of any other person. When, as often happened, it militated against the doctrine of the president, it weighed much the more heavily in the scales.

For a long time Mr. Adams appears to have been unconscious that his secretaries were subject to any other influence than his own. When at last he made the discovery he was extremely enraged, and never could be persuaded that they had not acted in bad faith. It was a grave charge to bring against these men. It fell with heaviest gravamen upon Wolcott and Pickering, but with no light weight also upon Hamilton. Three men more upright in every particular of public life it would be hard to name in the history of any country. It was singular indeed if they engaged in a dishonorable course of behavior and long persevered therein. The charge against them is that they secretly united to thwart the policy of Mr. Adams; that to this end the discussions of the cabinet were reported to Mr. Hamilton, and his advice was given to the secretaries and was allowed by them to have a paramount influence over their action. But were not these secretaries not only entitled, but in duty bound, to advise according to their conviction and belief? And for the purpose of intelligently forming these convictions and beliefs were they not justified in discussing questions of policy with any member of the party with whom they wished? Probably no secretary since the government first went into operation has considered himself under any obligation to refrain from the political topics of the day either in conversation or correspondence. Only the correspondence of Wolcott and Pickering with Hamilton has been singled out for censure, though marked by no exceptional characteristic.

So far as Hamilton was concerned, the real claim of the advocates of Mr. Adams practically amounted to nothing else than this: That on all occasions when Hamilton did not agree with the president, Hamilton must preserve a strictly guarded silence, allowing no one to discover his opinions or to know his reasons for them. It was the old grievance of the

Republicans, that Hamilton's influence was so irresistible as to preclude intelligent action. Had he been a man of no more than ordinary intelligence, he might have sent letters by every mail to as many members of the administration as he saw fit, and no one would have imagined it to be improper. It was simply because the recipients of his letters read them attentively and pondered their contents deferentially, that his Federalist opponents thought he should be relegated to a political Coventry, and that he alone of all men in the free country should not be permitted to say what he believed, or why he did so believe. It was a strange and unprecedented interdict to publish against an able and upright gentleman and retired statesman!

If indeed the secretaries betrayed cabinet secrets and so committed a breach of honorable confidence, therein they did wrong. But that was an act altogether independent and distinguishable from the interchange of opinion. Nor does any evidence of such conduct upon their part exist. The general charge has never been substantiated by specific items. Yet even to such allegations the lax custom of the day might be pleaded in extenuation if not in full excuse. Mr. Jefferson had sent to Mr. Madison transcripts of the private doings of the cabinet, and in a small circle of intimate political friends and allies a strictly confidential intercommunication of state and party secrets was no more uncommon and probably no more common in those days than in previous and in subsequent times.

The real point of offence — the only point upon which a strong stand can be made by the critics of

Wolcott and Pickering — was, that they should not have remained in the cabinet when they had ceased to be in sympathy with Mr. Adams, when they were opposed to his measures and hoped to see his policy fail rather than succeed. This accusation would leave Hamilton altogether outside of the offence, except for such slight measure of wrong-doing as might consist in abetting the conduct of his friends. This charge involves rather a breach of good taste than of honor, and lies against the customs rather than the ethics of politics. Hamilton could scarcely be blamed for using such opportunities as were offered to him for honestly impressing upon the action of the party such characteristics as he deemed essential at once to its success and to the national welfare.

Neither is it by any means clear that the secretaries should have insisted upon retiring from office. Mr. Adams was well aware of their opinions. If the views which they urged, and arguments which they advanced, were offensive to him, he could at any moment have freed himself from their advice and replaced them with more congenial assistants in the administration. These views and arguments were neither more nor less in contravention of his own because they not unfrequently were the views and arguments of Hamilton. His hostility to the individual caused Mr. Adams to be highly incensed when he learned the measure of influence which had been exerted by the man whom he was pleased to hate as a bitter enemy. But this, however it might appeal to Mr. Adams' irascibility, had not altered the real character of the opinions and logic of the secretaries. It would be difficult even now to say that a member of a cabinet is bound to resign because he is not in full accord with the president.   It is not many years since the conduct of a cabinet officer who obstinately adhered to his post in direct despite of the president was not only defended but applauded.   In the earlier days of the country the composite cabinet was a favorite experiment.   Had not Washington's cabinet held Jefferson and Hamilton as coadjutors?   Had not the Republican Randolph long continued a member of a Federalist administration?   Surely it was not a point of honor or of obvious etiquette, in that age, for Wolcott and Pickering to resign because they belonged to a different wing of the party from that to which the president belonged.   Indeed the separation was rather in process than completed so long as they remained in office, and when the time had come for them to go Mr. Adams was not slow to open the door for them.   The whole connection was very unfortunate, especially for Mr. Adams; it could not fail to rouse a strong sense of indignation in him as he contemplated the unfavorable effect it had upon his administration.   But the indignation should rather have been entertained against that untoward fate which will sometimes make ripples in the stream of life, than against the other individuals who were found floating beside him in those ripples.

The embarrassments of Adams' administration grew out of the relations subsisting between France and the United States.   Simultaneously with the recall of Genet the French government had requested the recall of Gouverneur Morris.   This cool-headed man of the world had remained at much too low a temperature to be agrecable to the superheated republicans of France. Washington thought the opportunity a favorable one to show that the administration was not justly amenable to the charge of hostility to the " sister republic." He recalled Morris — though in a private letter expressing his entire satisfaction with the course of that gentleman — and sent out in his place James Monroe, a Gaul of the Gauls. This new envoy more than counterbalanced the unfavorable impressions left by his predecessor. He absolutely ran riot in enthusiasm. A grand pageant was gotten up to celebrate his reception by the Convention, and he seized the occasion to present a panegyric upon France, which was fittingly replied to by a rhapsody ; at the close of which Monroe and Merlin exchanged a typical embrace, to the gratification of the spectators. A rebuke from the government for this dramatic display did not check the propensity of the minister, whose next step was to send to the Convention an American flag to be intertwined with the French colors and suspended in their hall.

Monroe's instructions directed him to demand redress for the injuries inflicted by France upon American commerce in breach of the treaty stipulations for free ships making free goods. He applied for indemnity, and at the same time made his application ridiculous by stating that he did not found it upon the obligations of the treaty ; and that if the French order should be deemed productive of substantial advantage to that country, the inconvenience would be submitted to by the United States " not only with patience but with pleasure." For this officious blunder and wholly unpardonable misconstruction of his instructions he was soundly berated by Randolph. He next got himself into trouble in connection with the negotiation then pending in England. He sought to soothe the suspicious alarm of the French government by stating that Jay was only empowered to " demand reparation for injuries." Afterward when the much wider scope of that instrument, especially the important fact that it embodied a treaty of commerce, became known, the French were much exasperated. The unfortunate Monroe then did his best to obtain for them a copy of the treaty while it was still a confidential paper, even before it had been submitted confidentially to the Senate of the United States. Jay's firmness alone prevented the consummation of this astonishing attempt. The treaty indeed placed Monroe in a very disagreeable position, for in his reckless friendliness he had been assuring the French Convention that they should forthwith have a loan of five millions of dollars from the United States. The assurance had been equally unauthorized and absurd ; but it would now by the ratification of the British treaty lose so much as the possibility of fulfilment. So long, however, as that ratification seemed doubtful Monroe still clung to the hope of accomplishing the subsidy, and was even sufficiently infatuated to suggest an alliance with France, the seizure of the western posts by force, and an invasion of Canada. By such wild projects he acknowledged that he hoped to effect " a diversion in favor of France."

The singular course of Monroe, of which a few chief points only have been mentioned, was doubly unfortunate for him. The French government, finding that he could only hold out hollow representations, became vexed with him and regarded him as a rather useless humbug. The government of the United States, more seriously angry, recalled him. On his return he employed his leisure in writing a defence of himself, in which he bitterly assailed the administration for not standing by him in his unauthorized undertakings.

Monroe was succeeded by Charles C. Pinckney, a gentleman who was expected to prove not distasteful to the Directory, though certainly he was not such a Gallican as the enthusiast whom he superseded. But the French were much irritated at the behavior of the president, who had in their opinion withdrawn a minister for no cause except friendliness to the people to whom he was accredited, and who now sent in his place an individual who could not be so agreeably described. The result was that they refused to receive Mr. Pinckney, and the unwelcome news of this insulting measure came among the earliest tidings to vex the new president. This repulse, which Mr. Adams in his first message to Congress described as the " denial of a right," was accompanied with circumstances of singular insolence. The climax was finally reached by a notification to Mr. Pinckney that if he should remain in Paris he might expect to be the subject of the disagreeable attentions of the police. He accordingly retired to Holland.

News of the election of a Federalist president was no sooner received in France than a fresh decree was issued against American commerce. The treaty between France and the United States was declared to be so far modified as to subject the vessels and cargoes of the latter country to capture for any cause which was recognized in Jay's treaty with Great Britain as ground for capture. It was farther ordered that citizens of the United States found serving on board the armed vessels of any power at war with France should be treated as pirates, even though such service was compulsory. An American sailor was therefore liable first to be seized by a British press-gang, and then to be swung off at the yard-arm by a French captor. The decree was made to bear upon our commerce even more severely than its language would seem to authorize, by the construction put upon it; for it was held to direct the seizure of all vessels not having certain peculiar shipping-papers, called the *rôle d'équipage*, required under certain old French ordinances but rarely carried by American vessels, indeed almost unknown on this side the water. The French cruisers had shown little mercy toward American shipping, and little respect for laws of any kind prior to the issue of these instructions; but they now redoubled their former hostile vigilance, while indemnity from the French courts of law was never known to be obtained. In the midst of this state of things Jefferson's famous letter to Mazzei found its untimely way before the public, creating much consternation among the partisans of that gentleman.

The course which the government would pursue under these circumstances was the topic of anxious speculation. The French faction appeared grave and silent. Few men had the servility to defend the behavior of the Directory. The more respectable members of the party, deprecating war and yet acknowledging its imminence, were anxious to send an extraordinary mission to that government. Unfortunately it was well known that both Wolcott and Pickering were averse to this step. Monroe at the time of his departure from Paris had been informed that no successor would be received until the grievances which France professed to have against America should be redressed. These two secretaries, therefore, and with them no small fraction of the Federalist party, were of opinion that the United States could do no more than she already had done for the preservation of amicable relations, and that another mission would only furnish the gratuitous opportunity for renewed insults.

In this juncture Hamilton exerted himself vigorously to insure the success of moderate counsels. He was fully persuaded of the propriety of making the experiment of the extraordinary mission. He thought that the envoys might be received in spite of the declaration made by the Directory, which might properly be construed to signify only a resolution not to receive a minister resident, and not therefore to preclude a special embassy. At least even if the worst should happen, and the ambassadors should be treated as Pinckney had been, the clamors of the French party at home would be stilled, and a united sentiment might be expected to pervade and strengthen the community in the troubles which would too probably ensue. " As in the case of England," he said, "so now, my opinion is to exhaust the expedient of negotiation, and at the same time to prepare vigorously for the worst. This is sound policy. Any omission or deficiency either way will be a great error."

The difficulty of the occasion was much aggravated by the condition of affairs in Europe. The state of things which increased the insolence of France introduced the unpleasant element of alarm into the United States. Bonaparte's brilliant successes may have been in a measure the cause which had induced the Directory to manifest such intolerable insolence to our minister and hostility towards our commerce. While Adams and his cabinet were deliberating upon the course which they should pursue, each vessel which arrived from Europe brought fresh news concerning the rapid advance of the terrible ascendancy of France. Her arms seemed irresistible. Holland, Spain, and the northern states of Italy were practically only her frightened appanages; Austria was defeated and received at Vienna such terms of peace as the conqueror condescended to give. England herself was intimidated and seeking to open negotiations. She seemed none too soon to be paving the way for an extrication from hostilities, when intelligence was received of the mutiny in her fleet at the Nore and then of the suspension of specie payments by the Bank of England. With no small anxiety did the statesmen of the United States contemplate the possibility that within a brief period France might have beaten all Europe into timid peace, while the questions between that now invincible power and the United States should remain still unsettled. "Who indeed," wrote Hamilton, "can be certain that a general pacification of Europe may not leave us alone to receive the law from France?" Talleyrand had lately returned from his exile in this country, and as the result of the observations made while he was our guest had reported that the United States were of no more account than that little speck upon the map of Europe called Genoa, which Napoleon had, as it were merely in passing, recently terrified into obedience.

Hamilton used all his influence with McHenry, Smith, and other prominent Federalists, but above all with Wolcott and Pickering, to bring them to his way of thinking. He wrote urgent and elaborate letters; he depicted the dangers threatening from abroad, the necessity of promoting union at home. "If I were certain that they would not hear the commission," he said, "it would not prevent my having recourse to it. It would be my policy, if such a temper exists in them, to accumulate the proofs of it with a view to union at home. This union . . . appears to me a predominant consideration, and with regard to France more than ordinary pains are necessary to attain it." If the expedient of the embassy "be not adopted, it seems to me rupture will inevitably follow. . . . I cannot but add that I have not only a strong wish but an *extreme anxiety* that the measure in question may be adopted." Again he wrote: "I would try hard to avoid rupture, and, if that cannot be, to unite the opinion of all good citizens of whatever political denomination. This is with me a mighty object." These appeals were not without great effect. They did not convert the two gentlemen to whom they were more especially directed, and who were quite capable of adhering inflexibly to a conviction in spite even of the much talked of authority of Hamilton. But the force of the opposition to the mission was much blunted. Wolcott wrote: "You know that I am accustomed to respect your opinion, and I am not so ignorant of the extent of your influence as not to be sensible that, if you are known to favor the sending of a commission, so the thing must and will be." Thus, by the aid of Hamilton in overcoming the contrary sentiment in the cabinet, Adams, who had all along desired the mission, was enabled to bring it about. He was not angry at the action of Hamilton on this occasion, when the meddling furthered his own views, though the interference was really just as improper as if it had been for different purposes.

Of whom the embassy should consist was a matter of scarcely less importance than that of its despatch. Hamilton said decidedly: " To fulfil the ends proposed, it is certain that it ought to embrace a character in whom France and the opposition have full reliance." Of course therefore it must be composite, since after the experience had with Monroe it would hardly be safe to send a French sympathizer single and alone. Hamilton was for appointing Jefferson or Madison, with Pinckney and Cabot as coadjutors; and then for giving them " certain leading instructions from which they may not deviate." The proposition was so obviously wise that it could be gainsaid by no one. But unfortunately the canny Madison would not go upon an errand of such dubious auspices, and it was doubtful whether it would be constitutional for the vice-president to act. The president then wished to nominate Pinckney and John Marshall from the Federalist party, and Elbridge Gerry from the Republican ranks.

Gerry had endeared himself to Adams in the late presidential election, by declining to cast either of his two votes for Jefferson in order not to imperil the choice of his fellow-citizen from Massachusetts.   But he had long been an object of extreme dislike and distrust among the Federalists, by reason of having been a persistent opponent of the adoption of the Constitution.   Every argument was therefore resorted to with the purpose of inducing the president to forego his personal prejudice, and with such success that at last he consented to name Francis Dana, Chief Justice of Massachusetts.   But Dana declining, the president would make no second effort to find a substitute for Gerry and nominated that gentleman, very much to the disgust of Hamilton and his friends, but equally to the joy of Jefferson and his followers.

What leading instructions should be given constituted a farther point of discussion.   Hamilton at one time stated that he was " disposed to make no sacrifices to France.   I had rather perish, myself and family, than see the country disgraced."   Yet there was no use in sending a mission in such a juncture unless some concession from the strict rigidity even of justice was to be permitted.   Accordingly Hamilton expressed himself content " that indemnification for spoliation should not be a *sine qua non* of accommodation."   He could not however quite reach the length to which Jefferson went, who set forth his sentiments in a letter to Gerry in the following extraordinary language : " Peace is undoubtedly the first object of our nation.   Interest and honor are also national considerations ; but interest, duly weighed, is in favor of peace, even at the expense of spoliations past *and future (!) ; and honor cannot now be an object* " *! !*

The oft-repeated tale of this embassy need not be repeated here at any length. On the arrival of the envoys Talleyrand refused them an audience, refused to present their letters to the Directory, refused to tell them whether they would be formally received or not. At length, having long left them in this unworthy and embarrassing position, he sent to them certain private gentlemen devoid of any diplomatic character, acting as a sort of back-stairs emissaries from the insolent great man. These persons, first exacting promises that their names should not be revealed, made advances, of which some were preposterous, and others ignoble. The first step to be taken, as a basis to the opening of negotiations, they declared to be the distribution of a large sum — no less indeed than twelve hundred thousand livres — between Talleyrand and certain of the more prominent members of the Directory. After compliance with this pecuniary requirement, which was asserted to be equally customary and essential, it was intimated that the public business of the embassy might be approached. The chief feature, however, in this public business of the embassy, according to the opinion of the French minister, was a large advance of money to be made by the United States to France, with a promise of more so soon as more should be needed. As for any indemnity for the illegal seizures and condemnations of American vessels and cargoes, it would be made only on condition that the United States would lend the necessary amount to France; and then it was only to be paid over to the individual claimants upon their coming under obligations to use it in purchasing supplies to be sent to the French colonies. Nay, the ministerial rapacity extended even beyond this point. Holland had been obliged by the Directory to issue a great number of " inscriptions " for the benefit of France. Many of these were still on hand, and the market price had depreciated till they were worth only half their face value, with the moral certainty that erelong they would be worth nothing. The United States was now called upon to relieve France of a great quantity of this valueless paper at its full nominal value !

The envoys were aghast at such propositions, no less than indignant at the manner in which they were presented. Insolence and indignity could not, as it seemed, be pushed to a greater extremity. In vain did they repeatedly declare that a loan was an impossibility. The same ignoble go-betweens continued alternately to dun and to insult, to beg for money and to threaten as the alternative of compliance the subjugation of the United States, and their reduction to servitude. For many months this condition of things continued, the American ambassadors bearing much and persisting long, being inspired by the firm resolution that through no fault of theirs should this last grave effort to prevent a disastrous war result in miscarriage. But the limit of their patience was at last reached.

At this ultimate stage however Talleyrand, who had objects to gain by the negotiation, intimated that he could perhaps treat with Gerry, a gentleman amenable to French reason, though it was useless longer to traffic with such contumacious Anglicans as Pinckney and Marshall. This attempt to divide the embassy which the United States had

sent jointly was unfortunately in a measure successful. Gerry, whether through timidity, weakness,
or vanity, or yielding to the combined force of all
these influences, consented to remain behind. Marshall returned home, having obtained his passports
not without difficulty. Pinckney succeeded in obtaining a reluctant permission to remain a few months
in the south of France for the benefit of his daughter's
health.

While these vexatious and humiliating dealings
had been going on in France, a profound ignorance
concerning them had prevailed in the United States.
Vice-President Jefferson had indeed been conducting
a confidential and friendly correspondence with M.
Talleyrand, but that shrewd diplomatist had probably
not seen fit to explain to his American friend all
which was doing under his auspices in France. For
when the despatches came to hand from the envoys
containing intelligence of the overtures made to them,
and the manner of the making, the opposition clamored
loudly to have the papers laid before Congress. The
president, nothing loath, complied with the mistaken
request. The opposition triumphed and repented;
they were thunderstruck at the contents of the letters
which they had asked for. These epistles have since
become famous in history as the " X Y Z Correspondence," which initials were used to designate the persons who had been sent by Talleyrand to the envoys, in
compliance with the promise of secrecy given to them.
At the same time the president notified to Congress
intelligence of a new decree of the French government, more outrageous than any which had preceded
it. It declared that all neutral vessels carrying mer-

chandise and commodities, being the production of England or any of her colonies, were lawful prize. To add to the piquancy of this news the country soon heard of the burning of an American vessel by a French privateer in the harbor of Charleston, and of captures made at the very mouth of the port of New York.

News of the publication of these despatches created a great stir abroad. The English cabinet caused them to be printed in all civilized languages, and widely distributed through Europe. Talleyrand for a moment was taken aback. Then he burst into a violent rage. He denied all complicity with X, Y, and Z. He asserted that the whole story was a plot gotten up by the two Federalist envoys, who were well known to be inimical to France. He appealed to Gerry to corroborate what he said; and denying all knowledge of the persons signified by X, Y, and Z, he insisted that their names should be given up to him by that gentleman. Alas, poor Gerry! How bitterly did he repent that he had not had a little more moral courage! How gladly would he now have found himself on the stormiest seas that ever rolled, could they but be bearing him on his way home with Marshall! He was in a dilemma whence escape with honor seemed impossible; even escape in personal safety seemed by no means comfortably probable. He contemplated not without chagrin the unpleasant chance that he might soon see the inside of a French prison.

But if there was excitement in Europe over this astounding development, how much more was there in the United States! The nation burst into a great rage. Was it for this that they had been so long-suffering, so obstinately well-disposed toward France? Had they so long endured from her a series of wanton injuries, had they come to the very verge of war in her behalf, only to be plundered and insulted before the eyes of the whole civilized world?

There was no difficulty about taking vigorous measures. Hamilton and his party had been for some time past urging military and naval preparations, but they had been thwarted in nearly every measure of the kind. The obstacles in their way were now in a moment removed. Several of the Virginian anti-federalists retired temporarily from Congress; even Giles withdrew his brazen front, and Jefferson himself was abashed and discouraged. He wrote to Madison in a tone at once angry and desponding. The "first impressions" to be derived from the despatches he acknowledged to be very "disagreeable and confused." The dealings with the envoys "were very unworthy of a great nation (could they be imputed to it) and calculated to excite disgust and indignation in Americans generally." The Frenchmen, he complained, seemed to have so far mistaken the tenets of the Republicans of the United States as "to suppose their first passion to be attachment to France and hatred of the Federal party, and not love of their country." The Frenchmen certainly had not been thus deluded altogether without cause!

A bill for a provisional army was now passed without difficulty, obtaining in the House a majority of eleven votes. The regular forces also were enlarged; the navy was increased, and a department of the navy was established. Much auxiliary legislation

was passed. Liberal appropriations were made for
the purchase of arms, the equipping of ships, the
fortifying of harbors; and additional taxes were
imposed without demur to meet these extraordinary
expenses. Some persons were for contracting at once
an alliance with Great Britain. But this Hamilton
decidedly opposed. The interest of that country
assured the possibility of making such an arrangement at any time. The necessity for it was not yet
imperative, and it might well prove an entanglement.
Indeed, Anglican as he was said to be, he was by no
means kindly disposed towards England at this moment; that country, with a singular, dull-witted in-
fatuation, having seized this juncture to renew and
increase her depredations upon our commerce. Hamilton spoke with much asperity of this conduct,
whereof the stupidity was almost as exasperating
as were the actual injuries.

Talleyrand in dismissing Marshall and Pinckney
had appealed directly to the people of the United
States, assuming that they would not tolerate the
action of their constituted authorities. His blunder
was equal to his insolence. The people enthusiastically supported the government. From every quarter
came pouring in to the president addresses of the
most patriotic tone. Every city, town, and village,
every association of men in the country, seemed desirous of indicating their readiness to stand by the
administration heartily in this crisis. The president
replied in language of not less fervor; his impetuous
nature was thoroughly excited, and he spoke with
much fire and spirit. Yet though fully chiming with
the popular sentiments, his notes of encouragement fell

displeasingly upon some ears. In a letter to Madison Jefferson described his language as " the most abominable and degrading that could fall from the lips of the first magistrate of an independent people." All hopes of coalescing with the Federal president were for the time quite dashed.

It was this temper of the nation which inspired Hopkinson, who, beneath the stimulating influence, produced the lyric of " Hail Columbia." Though, says Mr. Hildreth, the song was " totally destitute of poetical merit," yet it expressed the sentiment of the people so well that it at once became exceedingly popular, and rang from one end of the land to the other. The patriotic tune quite drowned the feeble tones in which some of the Democratic newspaper writers ventured to advocate the payment of the gratuities to the French statesmen and the loans to France, for which course they found a noble precedent in the subsidies given to the Algerine corsairs. Other proofs of devotion more substantial than the chanting of ditties consisted in gifts of armed vessels, purchased and equipped by subscriptions raised among individuals, and then freely presented to the government.

In the midst of all this warlike preparation and spirited show Marshall arrived. He could corroborate and elaborate the tales told in the despatches. He was everywhere fêted, while letters of recall were at once despatched to bring Gerry back from his unjustifiable stay. The president, sending in the latest intelligence to Congress, used these famous and unfortunate words : " I will never send another minister to France without assurances that he will be received, respected, and honored as the representative of a great, free, powerful, and independent nation."

In these exciting times there were few men who succeeded in preserving their wonted coolness in thought or action; and the consequence was that some things were done which had better have been left undone. Of this description were the famous alien and sedition laws. Much alarm was inspired by the presence of a great number of malcontent foreigners in the States. Each succeeding change which had taken place in the government of France for several years past had rolled upon our shores a fresh wave of political refugees. A few of them doubtless were quiet citizens, seeking a tranquil home; but far the greater portion were turbulent, proselyting zealots, utterly incapable of any other occupation than that of political agitation. England had been prudently purging herself of the worst of her native Jacobinical fanatics: and large numbers of these exiles had flocked to the United States, more dangerous than the Frenchmen by reason of the similarity of language and more congenial habits of thought. The Irish also constituted a discomforting element, inasmuch as their intense hatred to England made them partisans of the French faction. If there was to be trouble with France, there unquestionably was a source of serious peril in the presence of these active, intriguing, foreign masses, with no steady occupation, no stake in the country, no affection for the land, no sympathy with the government. Not a little fear was felt that opportunity might produce an "internal invasion," as it was called. To meet and obviate this peril Congress passed an act giving the president authority to order out of the country all such aliens as should be "judged dangerous to the peace and safety of the United States, or concerned in treasonable or secret machinations against the government."

Soon afterward was passed the statute known as the sedition law. Purporting to define more precisely the crime of treason, and to define and punish the crime of sedition, it undertook to establish some very extreme regulations. Its first section embodied the singular declaration that the people of France were the enemies of the United States, wherefore adherence to them and giving them aid and comfort was declared to be treason and punishable with death. Fortunately this very reprehensible style of legislation was substantially corrected, and before the bill had passed the House and Senate it had been materially curtailed and altered. In its final shape this first section declared to be a high misdemeanor all combinations to oppose the measures of government, to impede the operation of the law, to intimidate persons in office, or to bring about any riotous or unlawful assemblage. This was not very bad; but the next section was aimed at the press, and punished with fine and imprisonment the printing or publishing "any false, scandalous, and malicious writings against the government of the United States, or either house of the Congress, or the president, with intent to defame them, or to bring them into contempt or disrepute, or to excite against them the hatred of the good people of the United States, or to stir up sedition, or with intent to excite any unlawful combination for opposing or resisting any law of the United States or any lawful act of the president, or to excite generally to oppose or resist any such law or act, or to aid, abet, or encourage any hostile designs of any foreign nation against the United States."

Unquestionably the passage of these laws was an error. They excited vehement opposition; they drew down much censure upon the government, and so soon as the immediate excitement which gave rise to them had passed away the reminiscence was very hurtful to the Federal party. They were not needed for any practical use; a crisis might have arrived in which they would have been necessary or at least not useless; but that crisis was not at hand and did not afterward arise; nor is there any good reason to suppose that it was in any substantial measure warded off by this legislation. The statutes did nothing except show how thoroughly in earnest the administration and Congress were, and to what lengths they stood ready to go. It was hardly worth while to pass a sweeping edict of banishment and a statute for muzzling the press, — two measures so totally at variance with the whole spirit and theory of American polity, — simply to prove that government would be equal to a grave emergency.

The policy which found expression in this legislation has been laid at the door of Hamilton. Admirers of the gentlemen who defended the laws on the floor of Congress, of the president who signed instead of vetoing them, have spoken of them with condemnation as the offspring of Hamilton's brain. For the purpose of foisting the responsibility for such obvious blunders upon his devoted shoulders it is found convenient to assume, not only that he occasionally advised leading Federalists, but that he dictated the

Federal movements upon all occasions; and solely upon this vague and incorrect general assumption the blame pertaining to the conception and passage of these statutes has been most unjustly fathered upon him. In truth he was not consulted in either case until after the measure had been initiated. He had less to do with either law than with almost any legislation which took place at this period. The alien act is only mentioned in his correspondence with Pickering, in order to be criticised as too wholesale and severe; and it was probably in consequence of this stricture that the rigor of the bill was much softened, until even Gallatin himself expressed contentment with its provisions. Concerning the sedition bill, so soon as he heard of it, he hastened to write to Wolcott in the following terms : —

"I have this moment seen a bill brought into the Senate, entitled 'A bill to define more particularly the crime of treason,' etc. There are provisions in this bill, which, according to a cursory view, appear to me highly exceptionable, and such as, more than any thing else, may endanger civil war. I have not time to point out my objections by this post, but I will do it to-morrow. I hope, sincerely, the thing may not be hurried through. Let us not establish a tyranny. Energy is a very different thing from violence. If we make no false step we shall be essentially united; but if we push things to an extreme, we shall then give to faction body and solidity."

It is with no small satisfaction that admirers of the statesmanship of Hamilton are entitled to note his position in these matters. It shows what a clear and cool brain he had, how little liable to be led into error by the anxiety or the excitement of stirring and perilous times. The same sensible and moderate habit of thought appeared in his opinion concerning another proposition advanced at this time by some members of his party. It was thought that foreigners had found naturalization too easy, and it was now proposed that notification of intention to become a citizen must be made five years, and residence in the country must continue fourteen years, before citizenship could be granted. In debate it was actually suggested to forbid naturalization altogether; and even John Jay was inclined to think that no person of foreign birth, not having already acquired the rights of citizenship, should be allowed to hold any civil office of honor or profit. Hamilton was by no means in accord with these extreme sentiments. He did not approve the long residence required by the statute, "which of itself," he said, "went far to a denial of the privilege." Five years he considered a proper minimum of residence, but only political privileges should be postponed to the end of this term; rights peculiar to the conducting of business and acquisition of property should be at once conferred upon proof of the intention to become a citizen.

Before the passage of the bill for raising a provisional army, to which the Republicans were driven to accede, Hamilton had written to Washington, predicting that once more the veteran commander would be called into active life, and insisting that the sacrifice of his personal comfort would be imperative. Washington replied deprecating the necessity, but saying that if the contingency should indeed be imminent he should wish, before determining upon his own course, to know who would be his coadjutors, and whether Hamilton would be disposed to take an active part. Hamilton answered that he should be content to serve in any station in which the service he should render would be proportional to the sacrifice he would be obliged to make. "If you command," he said, "the place in which I should hope to be most useful is that of inspector-general, with a command in the line. This I would accept. The public must judge for itself as to whom it will employ; but every individual must judge for himself as to the terms on which he will serve, and consequently must estimate, himself, his own pretensions."

After the passage of the Act the president and the secretary of war both wrote to Washington, sounding him as to his willingness to accept the highest post created by the law, that of commander of the army, with the rank of lieutenant-general. In the Revolution he had been general and commander-in-chief, so that strictly speaking he was now invited to fill a position of less dignity than that which he had already held. Considerations of this kind, however, had little weight in Washington's mind. His reply stipulated only that he should not be called upon to take an active part until it should be absolutely necessary, and that his wishes should be allowed to control in the appointment of the general staff. Before the letter to the secretary containing these statements had come to hand, Adams somewhat precipitately sent to the Senate his nomination of Washington. Of course it was confirmed. McHenry, the secretary of war, was then at once despatched by Mr. Adams to Mount Vernon to confer with Washington. The result of the interview was that McHenry advised the president that Washington consented to serve upon the stipulation that "the general officers and general staff should not be appointed without his concurrence." McHenry declaring that there could be no difficulty about this matter Washington gave him the list, first upon which stood the name of Alexander Hamilton as inspector-general, with the rank of major-general; second and third were C. C. Pinckney and Knox, as major-generals. It was with a knowledge of these facts that Mr. Adams informed the Senate that Washington had accepted the position.

It was inevitable that the order of this selection should create some comment. Knox who stood last should have been first, and Hamilton who stood first should have been last, if the relative rank in the Revolutionary army was to be regarded as determining seniority. This shifting of the positions was making a completely new departure. There was some excuse for it to be sure, by reason of the fact that Hamilton had been out of the line of promotion during nearly all his service in the last war; but even had this been otherwise there was little chance that Knox would not have been his superior in rank. The truth however was, that in the many years which had passed since the treaty of peace the relative ability and reputation of these three gentlemen had been greatly changing. Hamilton's powers had developed and become known to a striking degree. Had there been little to choose between the three, the reference to their relative rank in times gone by might have been permitted very properly to adjust their present positions. But in the interval Hamilton's intellect had grown apace, till it could not be denied that he was now a far abler and greater man than either of his coadjutors. Upon a return to an old calling, after the lapse of so long a period, a new distribution based upon present actual merit seemed not unjust. In any such comparison the surpassing fitness of Hamilton could not be questioned.

Another consideration, always of much weight in this country, lay in the popular wish. It was beyond a doubt that the country expected and desired Hamilton to stand second in the organization of the forces. From Jay, Wolcott, Pickering, McHenry, indeed from all quarters, the evidence of this sentiment accumulated before the president. Mr. Pickering doubtless spoke the truth when he wrote: "Even Colonel Hamilton's political enemies, I believe, would repose more confidence in him than in any military character that can be placed in competition with him." Indeed, it could not be denied that if every officer who outranked Hamilton in the Revolutionary army were to be therefore permitted to outrank him in the new army, he would have been put in a position altogether absurd.

Mr. Adams by no means shared this general sentiment concerning Mr. Hamilton. He frequently expressed his opinion that Knox and Pinckney were entitled to precedence, and he secretly resolved to arrange the matter in his own way if he possibly could. Yet he sent in the three nominations to the Senate in the order named by Washington; and in that order they were confirmed, with the express understanding that custom, based upon a resolve of the old Congress and ever since followed, would determine the order of seniority by the order of confirmation. But no sooner had this stage been reached than the president threw off the mask and asserted that in his opinion the order now " legally " was, Knox, Pinckney, and Hamilton. He therefore ordered the commissions to be made out and to be so dated as to give this relative precedence.

When this resolution of Mr. Adams became known a great outcry and indignation arose. From every quarter evidence rapidly accumulated that Hamilton was marked by an almost universal wish as the incumbent of the next position to that of Washington. Secretaries Wolcott, Pickering, McHenry, and Stoddert were all in his favor. So was Jay. Ames, Cabot, and Higginson joined in a formal representation to the president. " Every public man," wrote Pickering to Washington, " except the president, feels that no officer ought to intervene between you and Colonel Hamilton. Of all the senators and representatives from New England whose opinions I have heard, not one ever entertained the idea that Hamilton should be second to any but you." Those who had doubted whether Washington would consent to act at all, had expected Hamiliton to be commander-in-chief.

The gentlemen most nearly concerned behaved with much good feeling and propriety. When the question was first, mooted Hamilton repeatedly assured Washington that he was not inclined to be contumacious in the matter ; that he would be governed wholly by the wishes of his old friend and commander ; that it should never be said that his ambition or interest had stood in the way of the public welfare. " I shall cheerfully place myself at your disposal," he wrote, " and facilitate any arrangement you may think for the public good." He even directly intimated his willingness to serve under General Knox, and did not refuse to serve also under General Pinckney. Thus he felt and expressed himself in the earlier stage of the controversy, in spite of the fact that he knew that both Washington's wish and the widespread opinion would give him the next rank to that of the commander. Later the complexion which Mr. Adams gave to the difficulty, and the manner in which Hamilton's friends were obliged to maintain his cause, put him in a situation in which he felt in honor bound not to forego his just claim.

Knox was placed in an awkward quandary by the ill-advised partisanship of the president, and was in a manner forced to stand upon his dignity and insist upon his supposed rights. But General Pinckney very magnanimously and patriotically recognized the propriety of Washington's arrangement. I declare, he wrote, that " it was with the greatest pleasure I saw his name at the head of the list of major-generals, and I applauded the discernment that had placed him there. I knew that his talents in war were great, that he had a genius capable of forming an extensive military plan, and a spirit courageous and enterprising equal to the execution of it." Hamilton could not fail to be touched even more than flattered by such conduct and sentiments. But the less fortunate relationship into which he was thrust with General Knox was very distressing to him. " There is no man," he regretfully wrote, " in the United States with whom I have been in habits of greater intimacy, no one whom I have loved more sincerely, nor any for whom I have had a greater friendship."

Surely it was a blunder to promote instead of seeking to heal discordance and jealousy among prominent military men upon the apparent verge of a great
and perilous war. But Mr. Adams was warmly interested in this matter. In spite of every adviser he
was stubbornly bent upon subordinating Hamilton.
Previously inimical to that gentleman, he grew actually to hate him as this quarrel advanced.[1] He
refused to refer the question to General Washington,
or to take any steps for an amicable accommodation.
He said that to do so would only produce exaspera-
tion and bring the matter back again to himself, and
that his mind was unalterably made up. He lost his
temper in writing about the vexatious controversy,
and said, " There has been too much intrigue in this
business both with General Washington and with me.
If I shall ultimately be the dupe of it I am much
mistaken in myself." For these words and innuendoes he was severely taken to task.

General Washington was not of opinion that Mr.
Adams was entitled to complain of intrigues in this
matter. For his part he was, upon the contrary,
quite convinced that Mr. Adams had acted very un-
fairly by him in receiving his acceptance of the com-
mandership strictly conditioned as it was, and then
seeking practically to annul the condition. He justly
considered that his terms after having been ratified
by the president were now being wholly ignored. To
such treatment Washington was not prone to sub-

---

[1] Pickering wrote : " The fact is that the president has an extreme aversion to Colonel Hamilton ; a personal resentment; and
if he followed his own wishes and feelings alone would scarcely
have given him the rank of a brigadier."

mit placidly. He wrote a long letter to Mr. Adams, rehearsing what had passed between them, and requesting to be informed whether Adams' "determination to reverse the order of the three major-generals" was final. It was sufficiently clear that an answer in the affirmative would be instantly followed by Washington's resignation.

Up to this extreme point Mr. Adams had been firm in his resolution; but the limit of safety had been reached. He did not dare to draw down upon himself the open wrath of Washington, and to be held responsible by the country for the resignation of its hero. Pride, anger, and hatred could not supply him with courage to face such direful consequences of persistence in his course. He yielded. He replied that the three commissions had been dated on the same day, and that he hoped for an amicable adjustment or acquiescence among the gentlemen themselves. He added, not very ingenuously nor indeed very consistently, the following awkward sentence: "But if these hopes shall be disappointed and controversies should arise, they will of course be submitted to you as commander-in-chief. I was determined to confirm that judgment."

Knox declined his appointment. Pinckney accepted frankly and with good feeling. Thus was this sorry business brought to a close, though it could hardly be expected not to leave some animosities rankling long afterward. Mr. Adams, having been beaten in a dispute to which he himself had succeeded in giving a personal tone, not only experienced the sense of public humiliation, but could not feel much gratification in contemplating the manner in which

he had conducted the contest. He did not profess
to be a good intriguer, yet could hardly feel otherwise than mortified at being foiled where he had
hoped by a little shrewd management to secure his
end. Naturally his antipathy to Hamilton was increased ten-fold; and henceforth he was quite rancorous against his victor. Naturally also Hamilton
could not be conciliated towards Mr. Adams by the
display of such a strong prejudice against himself.
The hostility between two such men could not but
be hurtful not only to each of them but to the country, and the traces thereof have long survived.

The dispute settled, Hamilton was at once called
into service. The labor before him was enormous,
for whatever may be thought of the possible capaci-
ties of the nation for military achievement, it must
be acknowledged that at that period it was at the
farthest possible point from a state of readiness. Not
only were there no troops but there was no organization; there was no skeleton army which might be
filled out to imposing proportions by recruiting. The
few veterans of the Revolutionary campaigns, who
were still fit for service, monopolized all the knowledge which the country had in the art of war. Hamilton, therefore, found himself obliged to create a
system, not from component parts which fell readily
into familiar places, but from material utterly devoid
of shape or arrangement. What he had done for the
treasury he had now to do for the military department. Fortunately the task was altogether congenial
to his taste, and without forcing his native inclinations he was able to set about it with all his wonted
ardor and thoroughness.

A minute sketch of the duties which occupied him during several months would be tedious. He had to plan and superintend fortifications ; to arrange all the details for the organization, discipline, and command of an army of fifty thousand men, in a country which had seldom had so many hundred in service. He had to organize the commissariat department ; to provide arsenals, magazines, arms, and camp equipage. Often he had to draft bills to be passed by Congress, in order to secure the necessary legislation. More interesting occupation he found in scrutinizing the general military situation and the probabilities in case of the outbreak of war. A scheme for conducting it was devised by him with much thought, and bore the impress of his energetic and enterprising temper. If the people must fight, he resolved that they should at least fight for something worth having. A mere war of defence was unsatisfactory. The expenditure of money and of blood, the check to the national growth, the injury to the general welfare, should obtain some better compensation than the mere successful resistance to unjust oppression or the securing unquestionable rights. If aggressive enemies put the United States to such outlay, loss, and vexation, Hamilton was inclined to recover something substantial in the way of recoupment.

A brilliant campaign opened before his vision. The war, if it came, should settle for ever the question of the navigation of the Mississippi, and should leave Louisiana and the Floridas in the hands of the United States. His provisions looked "to offensive operations." He wrote to the chairman of the Senate committee on military affairs : "If we are to engage in war, our game will be to attack where we can. France is not to be considered as separated from her ally. Tempting objects will be within our grasp." Spain indeed was rather the valet than the ally of France, and in every matter followed the bidding of the Directory, as afterward of Bonaparte, with perfect servility. War with the master was war with the servant. Indeed, Spain had herself already given direct and sufficient cause for war. The commanders of her harbor-fortresses allowed American vessels, departing from the ports, to be captured by French privateers under their very guns. Craft thus taken were condemned in the Spanish towns as prizes. American captives were marched in chains through the Spanish dominions to French prisons. Nay, even Spanish privateers had captured American vessels carrying government property, and had consigned their officers to jail. The treaty of alliance between France and Spain would have dragged the latter country into a war begun against the former, even had Spain been reluctant. But she was not reluctant; she was forward. For this bearing part in a quarrel not her own why should she not pay a heavy price? Hamilton was well resolved that she should, and after hostilities should have been once commenced he would not advise to cry quits till she should have made over to the United States all her American possessions coveted by that country. "I have been long," he said, "in the habit of considering the acquisition of those countries as essential to the permanency of the Union;" and indeed the subject was one upon which he had already not unfrequently and very decidedly expressed sentiments akin to his present purpose.

An unprovoked war of conquest could never commend itself to him ; but an opportunity furnished by the wanton folly of the foreign owner of these regions should not be thrown away.

Beyond this, he even entertained vast though somewhat shadowy purposes for organizing a revolt of the dependencies beyond the Isthmus of Panama, which should be encouraged to achieve their freedom and establish a great sister republic in the southern hemisphere. It was a grand dream, and appeared to the thoughts of others beside Hamilton in those days. For a short time General Miranda seemed likely to find efficient coadjutors in his bold projects of South American liberation.

Immensely absorbing and exciting were all these fine aspirations for the brief period during which the course of events suffered them to endure. But they all came to nothing. The stage of preparation was not succeeded by so much as that of attempt. As every one knows we had no war with France, no war with Spain ; we did not conquer Louisiana nor the Floridas. Hamilton had been quite right when he said that to show a determined front and a readiness for war was the best way to preserve peace. Whether France had ever seriously intended or even been willing to come to an open rupture with the United States may be doubted. But if she had, that mood had been of short duration, and ere this had quite passed over. No sooner did she see that she was actually overstepping the limit of endurance than she drew back from her advanced position, and again took her place just within the line of safety.

When at last Gerry was compelled to leave Paris,

and in spite of his Gallic prejudices was leaving in no very good temper, he was at the moment of departure requested to become the bearer of some *quasi*-formal relenting messages, to the vague purport that France wished negotiation and deprecated hostilities. She no longer insisted upon a loan, and she modified some of the more outrageous of the regulations heretofore governing her privateers. No sooner did the wrathful spirit of the people of the United States become known in France than Talleyrand enveloped himself in an impenetrable fog of falsehood, whence he caused to emanate a series of the most audacious and bewildering of those peculiar weapons of diplomacy which in private life are described by a brief and uncourteous word. It speedily became evident that he did not mean to fight, preferring to resort to other processes of which he was a better master. But the question was whether or not he should be allowed to escape and to rest with impunity behind this shameful protection which he had sought. What alternative had the United States, if any, besides that of war?

It was all very well for the Directory to issue decrees slightly alleviating the gross oppression of our commerce; and very well also for M. Talleyrand to write to Van Murray at the Hague, laying all the blame for the failure of the last embassy at the door of the unfortunate Gerry, and suggesting still another mission from this country. "I think," he wrote with an admirable assumption of the character of the offended party, "if the American government has the intentions that it ostensibly professes, it ought to abstain from any new provocation and send a plenipotentiary favorably known in France." The last words were not the least significant in the epistle of the wily diplomatist. Van Murray, transmitting the letter, expressed his opinion that it was a snare which had been arranged under the influence of the alarm generated by the display of resolution in the United States. Surely there was nothing in this dishonest trifling to remove the *casus belli*.

The message of the president, sent in to Congress at the opening of the session, Dec. 8, 1798, well expressed the sentiment of the people. Something less than two months before he had been gravely pondering whether in this communication it would be expedient for him " to recommend to the consideration of Congress a declaration of war against France." This he had finally and wisely enough determined not to do. Yet his language was spirited and resolute. " Nothing as yet," he said, " had been discoverable in the conduct of France which ought to change or relax our measures of defence. On the contrary, to extend and invigorate them is our true policy." The United States still, as in the past, desired peace ; and even now harmony could be restored at the option of France. " But to send another minister, without more determinate assurances that he would be received, would be an act of humiliation to which the United States ought not to submit. It must, therefore, be left to France to take the requisite steps." A more just exposition of the situation could not have been given.

The answers of the Senate and of the House echoed the sentiments of the message. But some great men were ill-pleased both with the address and the reply.

" The Senate," Madison sneeringly wrote, "as usual perform their part with alacrity in counteracting peace by dexterous propositions to the pride and irritability of the French government. It is pretty clear that their answer was cooked up in the same shop with the speech." To whom Jefferson replied: " The president's speech, so unlike himself in point of moderation, is supposed to have been written by the military conclave, and particularly by Hamilton." The distinguished leader of the opposition was not gratified at beholding the progress of a policy which was giving to France the dangerous opportunity of putting herself quite irreparably in the wrong. Nor were the suspicions of these two gentlemen as to the paternity of the utterances of Mr. Adams altogether without foundation. Precisely these views had been recently expressed by Hamilton in a letter to the secretary at war, and singular coincidences existing between the language of the letter and that of the message have given rise to the supposition that the secretary had dexterously transferred to the mouth of the president the ideas and even words of that man whom beyond all others the president hated with an extravagant animosity.

So the preparations for war went actively forward, and the United States maintained a dignified attitude awaiting a proper advance on the part of France if peace was to be preserved, and showing very plainly that they would fight if farther wrongs should be done to them. Such was the policy which Hamilton approved, and which he urged with much warmth upon certain members of the party high in place and power, and so exasperated as hardly to rest content with any measure short of a positive declaration of war. Though a rupture might seem inevitable, yet he was loath to precipitate it, and his influence was used for the purpose of restraining his too eager friends. Had he been in truth, as he has been charged with being, anxiously concerned to promote an irrevocable breach of the peace there is little doubt that he could have succeeded. The Federal party was making great and rapid gains throughout the country, and a large proportion of its most able leaders were openly committed to measures of hostility. Hamilton's weight cast into the same scale would have determined the matter. But he would not thus cast it. With his wonted coolness of judgment he counselled yet a little longer pause upon the brink. Visions of personal aggrandizement, which a war could hardly fail to realize, neither bewildered nor betrayed him. He persisted in his old theory, — the same which he had advocated prior to Jay's mission, — to present a firm front, to make every preparation for extremities, and to allow to the foreign ministry the uttermost moment for the recovery of their senses.

The people at large were well pleased with this course of procedure, and the opposition, identified with the French faction and losing great numbers of adherents, was soon fairly outnumbered in both houses of Congress. But in truth it must be acknowledged to have been one of the most irrepressible parties that the political history of any country can show. It seemed to gain audacity by defeat, and its struggles now were marked with grim desperation. Jefferson, Madison, and many others seemed more ready to see the government annihilated and the country dissevered, than to see the United States at open war with France. It had been necessary to solicit a new loan to meet the expenditures caused by the military preparations. Jefferson at once expressed a wish that the Constitution should be amended by " an additional article taking from the federal government the power of borrowing "! It was in very mild language that he rebuked the aspirations of certain of his enthusiastic followers for secession. All he had to say was that he thought it was not yet quite time for this step. He gave also a somewhat amusing reason for wishing to keep New England as a part of the Union, even though it was the stronghold of Federalism and full to overflowing with the admirers of Hamilton and the supporters of Adams. " We must have somebody to quarrel with," he said, and " I would rather keep our New England associates for this purpose." In his opinion they were peculiarly well fitted for this sphere of usefulness, being a full population circumscribed within narrow limits; " their numbers will ever be the minority, and they are marked, like the Jews, with such a perversity of character as to constitute, from that circumstance, the natural division of our parties." From such utilitarian rather than sentimental motives was Jefferson willing to endure the unwelcome companionship, although he could not but assert that the southern States were " completely under the saddle of Massachusetts and Connecticut, and that they ride us very hard, cruelly insulting our feelings, as well as exhausting our strength and subsistence."

He soothed his lacerated spirit however by writing at this time the first draft of the famous Kentucky resolutions.   These embodied that doctrine of nulli-fication afterward so eloquently elaborated by Mr. Calhoun, and in a more developed stage defended in arms by Mr. Jefferson Davis.   The Constitution was declared to be a compact to which the States, as such, were integral parties.   Each party, that is to say each State, therefore had " an equal right to judge for itself as well of infractions as of the mode and meas-ure of redress."   Whenever in the judgment of any State such an infraction should take place, " nullifi-cation of the act is the right remedy."

Some portions of this instrument outran even the zeal and courage of the legislators for whose benefit it had been prepared.   The clauses whereby this asserted right of nullification was intended to be exercised in respect of the alien and sedition laws were stricken out before the passage of the resolves. But Jefferson could afford to be a little reckless, for with his usual cowardice he had taken good care to guard himself against any bolts of vengeance which might follow this objectionable procedure.   He had extracted from the gentlemen to whom he transmitted his draft of resolutions a " solemn assurance " that it " should not be known from what quarter they came." The secret was long honorably kept.

The example thus set by Kentucky was soon fol-lowed, though in more cautious form, by Virginia. But fortunately the contagion spread no farther. On the contrary the legislatures of nearly all the other States pointedly condemned these destructive doctrines, and gave the author of them good reason to rejoice that his pusillanimity had led him in good time to protect his reputation with the veil of secrecy.

Little as he approved of the two statutes which constituted the immediate provocation for these measures, Hamilton was deeply moved at the formal and public annunciation of such doctrines. The State legislatures had voted that their proceedings should be laid before Congress. Hamilton wrote to Sedgwick then in Congress, urging that if this step should be taken the matter should be sent to a committee. He advised that a report should then be made showing " the tendency of these doctrines . . . to destroy the Constitution of the United States; and with calm dignity united with pathos, the full evidence which they afford of a regular conspiracy to overturn the government;" also their effect and probable intention "to encourage hostile foreign powers to decline accommodation and proceed in hostility." To Speaker Dayton he wrote that this attempt to bring about "a direct resistance to certain laws of the Union can be considered in no other light than as an attempt to change the government." He had even received information that the faction which had carried the resolutions had entered upon an " actual preparation of the means of supporting them by force."

Thus matters stood for a brief period. Federalism appeared triumphant and in the right; Republicanism was waning and in the wrong. For a few weeks, or more properly perhaps it should be said for a few days, the members of the former party looked forth upon a brighter prospect than had gladdened their eyes for a long time; unfortunately it was but a passing glimpse, and the sunshine was as evanescent as it was grateful. The channel of communication which had been opened through Van Murray speedily brought a second letter to the president. M. Talleyrand wrote to M. Pichon, French agent at the Hague, who handed over the letter to Van Murray, who transmitted it to Mr. Adams. By this circuity did the French diplomatist undertake at once to accomplish his purpose and to avoid a formal act of humiliation. He made no promises to any American, but intimated in a sort of stage whisper to his friend Pichon what were his feelings, and what under certain circumstances would be his actions. Recurring to the noted words of the president, and even repeating them, he told his correspondent that a new envoy, should one come from the United States, would be received as the " representative of a great, free, powerful, and independent nation." This promise, for which M. Pichon himself could have no possible use, that gentleman assigned over, as it were, by the agency of Van Murray to Mr. Adams.

But since using the language thus cleverly quoted by the French diplomatist, farther information and developments had induced the president to use other language not quite so striking in form, yet not less distinct and positive. He had declared that the next ambassador must come from France, and the declaration had, as he knew, given very general satisfaction and expressed the sense of the people. Upon this ground he had nearly all the nation united at his back, and he could well afford to stand firm.

Yet he did not stand firm, and the manner of his change of position was even more astonishing than the fact. He took counsel of no one ; and indeed it must be admitted that, with the purpose which he had in his mind, it would have been folly to have taken any member of his own party into his confidence. Without the slightest premonition, then, upon Feb. 18 he sent in to the Senate the nomination of Van Murray as minister to France. He accompanied it with the assertion that Van Murray should not be actually ordered to Paris until unequivocal assurances of his honorable reception should be given. But what value was to be placed upon this assertion? Was not the president, in and by the very act of making it, breaking other recent and equally public and solemn assertions? He did not see fit even to give such reasonable color to his action as it might have received from Van Murray's despatches, but preferred to withhold those documents, showing them only to a few persons quite privately.

To nothing else can this nomination be likened than to the falling of a thunderbolt from a clear sky. Utter confusion was produced by it. The Federalists were in a terrible rage. Some said the president was mad; others that he had fairly gone over to the opposition; others that he was throwing out a lure for Republican suffrages at the next election. But in truth the Republicans were not less astounded, though more pleased, than were their adversaries. They had not been prepared for such a defection, and had not agreed to pay any price for it; but if it had indeed been undertaken then should their tents be open to receive the unexpected comer. Whatever might be the motive, the step at least was welcome. Nor could it well be regarded by the most suspicious Democrat as a snare, as was shown by the extreme and perfectly honest wrath of the Federalists. In vain was information sought from the members of the cabinet. They could not tell what they did not know. They could only say that their advice had not been asked, and no information had been imparted to them.

After two days of excited querying and interchange of suspicions the Senate rallied from its surprise sufficiently to refer the nomination to a committee of five, — all Federalists. These gentlemen, somewhat at a loss as to the report which it behooved them to make, at last determined to take a course, unusual doubtless, but certainly quite justifiable under such exceptional circumstances. They waited upon the president for the purpose of talking the matter over with him and obtaining some knowledge of the motives of his action. The president insisted that he could neither withdraw nor modify the nomination. A direct decision upon it he considered indispensable in order "to defend the executive against oligarchic influence." This language was significant of what had been perhaps his chief inducement to the action he had taken. He was beginning to suspect that the influence of Hamilton was superior to his own, that it had even been exerted over him without his own knowledge. His haughty and irascible nature chafed at the thought, and he resolved to vindicate his independence and his power at the same moment. "The British faction," he said, "was determined to have a war with France; and Alexander Hamilton at the head of the army, and then president of the United States." Such a vision destroyed his equanimity. He forgot that he had lately said that, "if France should send a minister to-morrow, he would order him back the day after."

The result of the interview was that the rejection of Van Murray became a certainty. Apart from the question of the propriety of the mission, it was beyond a doubt that this gentleman alone was not of sufficient calibre or reputation to undertake the whole burden of so weighty an embassage. Again acting hastily and without advising with any of his constitutional counsellors, the president anticipated adverse action upon his previous message by sending in a second one nominating Chief Justice Oliver Ellsworth and Patrick Henry as colleagues with Van Murray. This made such improvement in the scheme as it was capable of receiving, and freed it from all exception arising from the character or ability of the gentlemen named. Mr. Henry declined to serve, but his place was well filled by the nomination of Governor Davie of North Carolina.

There can be no doubt that the first instinctive impulse of the leading Federalists at the capital would have led them to reject the nominations, even though such a course would have been the repudiation of the president of their own party. Certainly they were angry enough to take the step if it could be done without appearing too great a blunder. In their quandary they turned as usual to Hamilton for advice. He was not better pleased than they were with what had been done. The day, the hour, before the president sent in Van Murray's nomination the prospect had been that long forbearance, a wise policy, much loss and expenditure of money were about to bring to the country a good return. The course of the

United States during the last few months had brought France to her senses. Reverses in Europe, too, had clouded her horizon. She had shown very plainly that she was bent upon negotiation, and the instant that the United States had shown a determined front she had manifested a tendency towards concession. "When from considerations of policy France could brook the ignominy which the publication of the despatches of the commissioners was calculated to bring on her, and stifling her resentment could invite the renewal of negotiation, what room can there be to doubt that the same calculations would have induced her to send a minister to this country?" Such were Hamilton's sentiments. The policy which led up to this honorable conclusion had been sedulously advocated by him, and was now to be abandoned when the conclusion seemed the next and certain stage. It was trying indeed to see the country "waive the point of honor," and obtain by humility what might have been not less surely won with dignity.

Thus did Hamilton feel as a statesman. As a politician his sensations were not more agreeable. It was not to be concealed from observers less shrewd and experienced than he was that a dangerous chasm had been opened in the Federal party. Adams would not stand quite alone upon his side of it. Men who loved peace and economy at any price, and who might doubt whether these main objects would have been secured by any other course, would probably adhere to him. His influence and position would attract others. The bulk of the party would not go with him; but even a limited secession would be perilous in the not very unequal division of parties. The only chance of a contrary result lay in the possibility of an ignominious failure of the mission. This would leave Mr. Adams naked to his enemies, but it would also fill the cup of national degradation to an intolerable fulness. The consequence which in fact ensued was that which at this time was generally anticipated as probable, — the breaking up of the Federal party.

Naturally enough, both as a patriot and as the champion of Federalism, Hamilton was incensed to a high degree. What had been done offended his judgment no less than his temper. Yet his coolness of head did not forsake him. He saw that too obstinate an opposition to measures looking towards the preservation of peace would be injurious, and would go far to fasten upon those who should be concerned therein the reproach of constituting a British faction. He replied to Sedgwick's request for his advice, that, much as he was astonished at the step, yet "as it has happened, my present impression is that the measure must go into effect, with the additional idea of a commission of three. The mode must be accommodated with the president. Van Murray is certainly not strong enough for so immensely important a mission." Thus, as has been seen, it was finally arranged. The three commissioners were approved by the Senate, with the express understanding that they should not present themselves in Paris until a direct and official promise to receive them as ministers should have been made by the French government.

The official assurance of a becoming reception was forthcoming in good season; and the commissioners negotiated a treaty, defective in some respects, yet much better than a war. But Mr. Adams had committed political suicide. Had he indeed fallen a noble sacrifice to his sense of patriotism and to the welfare of the country? The question is a difficult one to answer. His admirers will have it that he did ; that he fully appreciated the situation, foresaw the probable consequences of his action, and by an admirable effort of moral courage saved his country from all the manifold evils of war at the cost of his own farther political success. They paint him like an American Curtius, in the full career of power and ambition, plunging into the obscure gulf of private life in order that the United States might have peace.

It is as impossible for those of a contrary mind to prove that this picture is false as it is for those who paint it to prove that it is truthful. Too many incognizable elements are involved. It is impossible to know Mr. Adams' true motives. Perhaps unalloyed patriotism did not constitute the entire incentive. That dread nightmare of Hamilton " at the head of the army, and then president of the United States," may have not a little contributed to form the president's resolve. He was an honest man, and would not with a full comprehension of the character of his motives have yielded to such an influence. But he was egotistical and impetuous, and may not improbably have been unwittingly affected by sentiments of a personal nature. Certainly it is difficult to explain why the pendulum of his mind should have swung with such exceeding rapidity from the extreme upon one side to the extreme upon the other, if its movements were governed wholly by a statesman-like judgment. Of the fact of the swinging there is no doubt; and in seeking an explanation where shall we find one more probable than the rapid growth of his enmity towards Hamilton, caused by the triumph of the latter in the question of military precedency, and also by the first vehement suspicion, which seems just at this time to have been finding its way into his mind, of the superiority of Hamilton's influence over his own in the counsels of the leaders of the party? It is uncharitable to seek for an ill motive when a good one is at hand. Nor is it probable that the personal prejudice was more than a portion, perhaps an unrecognized portion, of the amalgamation of causes which led to the nomination of Van Murray. That it was present in that amalgamation it is hardly possible to doubt; and to the extent of its effect it must derogate from the president's right to claim commendation.

Then, again, it is a question whether Mr. Adams really did save the country from war. That calamity certainly did not occur; but in order to say that he saved the United States from it there must be proved, in addition to the fact of non-occurrence, the farther fact that it would have occurred had not the president's action been what it was. Of course this can be only matter of speculation. It is altogether impossible to *know* whether France would have sent a minister before the United States felt compelled to declare war, or whether she would not. It may be acknowledged that Hamilton's policy was less conciliatory and more apt to promote war than was that of Mr. Adams. It required a certain appearance, though by no means an improper appearance, of humiliation on the part of France; and at this brilliant and high-wrought period France was not in a humor to humiliate herself before a young, distant, long-suffering people. Hamilton himself had not very long before feared that war was inevitable. Yet the prospect had rapidly changed for the better within a short time past, and his unfavorable prognostications were giving way to cheerful hopes. France had endured quite tamely the first invasions upon her pride, and there was every reason to think that she would in time come to the required point. Hamilton, who was a good judge in such matters, was beginning to look for such a consummation.

A third question to be solved, before it is possible to come to a determination concerning the merits of Mr. Adams' action, relates to the measure of concession which a nation should make, beyond the line of strict justice, in order to avoid war. Supposing that he did save the United States from war, did he pay too high a price for their salvation? The country was young, and for its firm establishment in a course of prosperity it needed peace; it would enter upon a war with France, having a strong and enthusiastic French faction and also many foreign elements of danger among its own population; it was not a military power, and France was the conqueror of Europe. Add to this, that every civilized man must utterly hate and abhor warfare, and must feel that it is difficult to say what is not better than that brutal ill. Mr. Adams undoubtedly "waived the point of honor;" he took a step which the country, in her present day of arrogance and conceit, would not for an instant so much as contemplate. Yet upon this portion of the question civilized men may be content to praise him. And could the two former points only be established in his favor; could it be shown that his action was prompted by no other incentive than an unmixed and perfect patriotism, and that he actually prevented the happening of a war inevitable by any other course of procedure,— then we might be content to cry well done, even though the country did spare a little of its dignity, and though the Federal party was broken into discordant fragments. But turning from all these contingencies and suppositions upon which the defence of Mr. Adams is based, how vexatious is it to reflect that the rejected Hamiltonian policy bid fair to achieve for the country all which the commissioners' treaty achieved for it, without raising any delicate and dubious questions concerning the national honor!

CHAPTER VII.

ELECTION OF JEFFERSON.

Now might the Federalists cry, "*Actum est!*" for indeed it was all over with them. Whether justifiably or unjustifiably, Mr. Adams had succeeded in dividing the Federal house against itself, and it was about to meet the fate which awaits all edifices in that precarious condition. What had been a great party, singularly united and well-disciplined to have appeared at so early a period in the career of the country, was now split into two factions, which hated each other almost more warmly than they hated their common Republican foe. It was very vexatious to encounter such a disaster just at this moment, for apart from these dissensions the prospects of Federalism had never before been brighter. Ever since the birth of the party, almost coeval as it had been with the birth of the nation, it had been maintaining a desperate and doubtful ascendancy. Many and many a time had it been saved from a demoralizing defeat by a single suffrage. How often had Mr. Adams, now its destroyer, preserved its prestige by his casting vote when he presided over an evenly divided Senate!

A large part of the time the Republican or Democratic party had had a majority in the House; it has often been asserted and is not improbably true, that if the mass of the people could have been polled the result would have shown a decided minority of Federalists. Yet with such odds against them the party had succeeded in shaping the policy of the State in every important respect for a period of nearly twelve years. This wonderful success could be attributed only to the ability of the leaders and the character of the rank and file. Washington's influence was generally with them, though he had carefully abstained from assuming the *rôle* of a partisan. Yet in nine cases out of ten he had been known to approve their measures, and this was a great advantage to them. Hamilton was their acknowledged leader, and under so many disadvantages had won battle after battle, and proved himself a Napoleon in politics. He worsted Jefferson so often as to drive that discouraged Democrat into private life, and he might have continued in the same course had it not been for the fatal division in his own camp. Only when a third at least of his forces had marched off under another banner did he encounter defeat. No leader, it must be said, was ever better supported. For many years Mr. Adams was a stanch and useful Federalist; and there were also John Jay, Gouverneur Morris, Timothy Pickering, Oliver Wolcott, McHenry, Ames, George Cabot, Sedgwick, and many another entitled to take place beside him in point of ability and zeal. The voters of the party among the people were never denied to comprise far the greater portion of the intelligence and wealth of the land. In those days these qualities were still weighty and influential, and secured a success which has not ever since attended them. So by dint of untiring energy this brilliant band of statesmen had held their own, though with inferior numbers at their back, and had thrust off defeat in one desperate struggle after another equally to the surprise of themselves and their foemen. Only within a few months past had they really seemed to be gaining substantial ground in the country; they had been attracting new recruits by their spirited policy towards France: they actually counted a comfortable majority upon their side in the House of Representatives. There seemed reason to hope that the favorable change might be permanent. It was cruel that this very time should be marked by their destruction.

But the truth was that Federalism had accomplished its peculiar labor. Its function had been in the first instance to protect the new Constitution and the infant country. It had stood *in loco parentis* to them, and had to train them up in the way they should go. This task was accomplished by giving to the Constitution that liberal construction which has ever since prevailed, and preserving to the central government that degree of power which was necessary to its stability and independence in respect of the individual States. This was the true *raison d'être* of Federalism; and this duty had been thoroughly completed, so thoroughly that the result could never afterward be undone or seriously impaired. Then afterward ensued the secondary labor of saving the country from sinking, under color of being an ally, into a mere servile appanage of revolutionized France. This duty fell upon the Federals simply because they happened to have cooler heads than the French faction, and sounder ideas of government; so that they were naturally led to view *sans-culottism* with other sentiments than that of emulous admiration. This task also they had performed; and as a sort of supplement thereto they had even succeeded in inducing the United States to preserve so firm and resolute an aspect towards France as to wring a tardy and reluctant justice from that insolent and treacherous friend. But the purpose for which Federalism had been first created had been fully achieved before it fell in a ruin which was never retrieved. Its ascendancy had at first been essential to the very existence of the united nation, but before Mr. Adams ceased to be president this was no longer the case. That peculiar necessity, that exceptional period had passed, and the Federalists were now like any other political party. They could defeat or be defeated without seriously imperilling the life or even the prosperity of the country. Their fall was followed by no other results than such as are wont to follow any similar changes in the United States or in Great Britain. There was no convulsion, no indirect but serious danger of national dissolution,—which there surely would have been ten years earlier.

During the remainder of Mr. Adams' presidency, after the appointment of the ambassadors to France, the two factions then created advanced rapidly along the diverging lines upon which they had been respectively launched with such an unfortunate impetus by this imbroglio. The instructions to the envoys were considered and substantially agreed upon in cabinet meetings, but the question of their actual departure remained in abeyance. News came of a change in the French Directory, materially altering its political complexion. It seemed not improbable that the commissioners might find that the old policy toward the United States had again become prevalent, in which case they would too surely be repulsed with contumely. The cautiously minded members of the party were inclined to defer the day of sailing until some intelligence could be received of the sentiments of the new rulers in the councils of France. But Mr. Adams willed otherwise; and again suddenly, without a word spoken to his ministers, of his own sole motion, though within a few hours only after the close of a cabinet meeting, he issued orders that the gentlemen should set sail at a near day.

A fresh burst of indignation ensued. "The United States," wrote Wolcott, "are governed as Jupiter is represented to have governed Olympus." Again also Mr. Adams did not escape the charge of interested motives. The order for departure was sent out on Oct. 16, 1798. Just a month before, upon receipt of news of the revolution in the Directory, he had said that this fact, together with the general aspect of France, seemed "to justify a relaxation of our zeal for the sudden and hasty departure of our envoys." The significant event which had occurred in this intervening month was the election in Pennsylvania. On the twelfth of October it appeared that the Federals had been beaten in that State. Was the president indeed cannily casting another lure to the opposition? So his enemies said, and doubtless fully believed.

The end of this matter, though not reached for

upwards of a year, may as well be told at once. The commissioners arrived, to find that still another change had taken place in the shifting government of France, and that Bonaparte, with the title of first consul, was substantially dictator. But by good luck he was not at the moment in a bellicose humor, and condescended to nominate three commissioners to treat with the Americans. The game, however, was really played on the part of France by M. Talleyrand with all his wonted adroitness. After much discussion, it appeared that the ultimate instructions given to Van Murray, Ellsworth, and Davie involved some points to which France would not consent. She was in no condition to make compensation for past injuries to the commerce of the United States, nor did she wish to abrogate all prior treaties and conventions between the two countries for the sake of making an arrangement *de novo* by a fresh treaty. It being impossible therefore for the negotiators to conclude a binding and permanent contract, they were content to enter into a convention of unlimited duration, by the second article of which these two topics of dispute were set aside for future determination at a convenient time.

The point of indemnity was one upon which the people of this country had been very resolutely bent. Their interest and their honor were equally involved. Consequently, when it was found that no satisfactory stipulation in this matter could be elicited from France, a great sentiment of anger was aroused. No small proportion of the senators were inclined to reject the instrument, which altogether omitted the disposition of this point of difference. The Federalists, as usual, had recourse to the counsel of Hamilton, and by so doing placed him in a position which, to any other than an upright and evenly minded man, would have been pregnant with great temptation. What an opportunity for punishing Mr. Adams! The nomination and despatch of the envoys was precisely one of those measures which would finally be thought praiseworthy only if it should be successful. Its favorable result would insure from many persons all that laudation which has since been showered upon it in such abundance from some quarters; but its failure would overwhelm its projector beneath a burst of popular indignation at what would then surely be deemed the gratuitous humiliation of the country. By this appeal of the Federalists Mr. Adams' reputation was substantially placed in Hamilton's hands, to make or mar as he should see fit. To his honor it may be recorded that he appears not even to have been tempted by so rare an opportunity for revenge, not to have regarded for an instant the probable effect which the action of the Senate, for or against the treaty, would have upon Mr. Adams. His thought was solely for the country. He was of opinion that the interests of the people required that the convention, though imperfect, should be ratified. " Reason should govern," said he, very coolly; forgetting such military aspirations as he had doubtless cherished, condoning the wrongs which Mr. Adams was even then inflicting upon him personally. For the president was in the habit of talking about the existence of a British faction scarcely less extravagantly than Jefferson had been wont to do, and never hesitated to intimate that Hamilton was the inspirer and the leader of this unpatriotic band. Hamilton wrote to him once and again upon the subject perfectly courteous and very earnest letters, seeking to set him right; but Mr. Adams would deign no reply to these communications. He showed the same temper of personal acrimony which soon afterward led him to ride away from the capital in the night-time, in order to show a direct incivility to his successful competitor for the presidency.

Hamilton was a man of a widely different spirit. Personal feeling he kept sedulously removed from affairs of state; and though now under no burden of official responsibility, but acting as an individual, he declined to throw his powerful influence into the scale, which by prevailing would, in his opinion, injure the country in the process of ruining his own enemy. He wrote to Sedgwick urging that the convention should be ratified. He wrote to the secretary of state a letter to the same purport. He wrote to Gouverneur Morris, and, when his first letter failed to persuade that gentleman, he wrote another and elaborate one. He took very great pains in the business, and put himself in the uncomfortable position of disagreeing with some of his most powerful friends, whom he sought to convert to his way of thinking. The result was that the convention passed the Senate, with the erasure of the second article, and a limitation of its validity to the term of eight years. Bonaparte submitted to the modifications; and the reputation of Mr. Adams, by the essential aid of Hamilton, was delivered from a severe and imminent blow.

With the disappearance of any strong likelihood of a campaign the zest departed from the military occupation in which Hamilton had been engaged. This had been so rapacious of his time as to leave him but little opportunity to pursue his professional career, which the condition of his finances rendered really necessary to him. Yet for a long time it was obviously necessary to keep up the appearance of vigor as an invaluable *point d'appui* for the negotiations, which could hardly be expected to advance favorably under any substantial symptoms of relaxation in the national spirit. Hamilton was accordingly obliged to continue at his post and to work as hard and sedulously for the mere purpose of ostentation as if there were a prospect of serious work ahead. The task was irksome enough to him, but he recognized the duty and fulfilled it with perseverance and thoroughness. Nor was it until July 2, 1800, that he was at last permitted to resign, and again to retire from the public service to private life.

Meantime the question of who should be the next president was agitating the people and especially the more prominent men of both parties in public life, who, as was the custom in those days, expected to discuss and settle the matter for their respective followers. Allegiance was not then due to the popular caucus, but the chief men of the party in conclave agreed upon whom they would support as their candidate, and it was generally understood that he would be voted for by all electors of that political persuasion ; though no small measure of individual freedom was still, in accordance with the true intent of the Constitution, both claimed, allowed, and exercised in the electoral college.

That party to which the titles of Republican and Democratic were applied without discrimination, lately discouraged, now gathered renewed and lively hopes from the dissensions of their opponents. They prepared for a hard fight, and it could not be concealed that they stood a very good and a daily improving chance of winning it. A careful study of the field led most observers to the conclusion that the division of strength was singularly even ; it was asserted that the vote of New York would turn the scale, and that here the vote of the city would determine that of the State. For the presidential electors were chosen in New York by the joint vote of the two houses of the legislature, and the delegation from the city would determine upon which side the majority should be.

The State election took place in the spring of 1800, and with what spirit the canvassing was conducted under the circumstances may be well imagined. Hamilton exerted himself untiringly, and occasionally even at personal risk, for the prevalent temper was such that violence often obtained partial sway. But his labors were vain. The predilections of the city were originally rather with the opposition than with the government; and with so favorable a basis for his operations the industry and intrigues of Aaron Burr were invincible. The manner in which he manipulated the city was unquestionably the most thorough, most painstaking, and most successful that has ever been seen in this country. How far it was honorable or creditable to him is a question less easily settled, and for its determination must depend upon the very uncertain and varying notions which different persons entertain as to what is fair in politics. Having succeeded by his own efforts rather than by any previous reputation as a statesman in making himself the most prominent candidate of his party for the vice-presidency, Burr now arranged to be himself returned to the Assembly by a country constituency.

But however the means might be criticised the result could not be denied. New York was lost to the Federalists, and their cause was tottering. Mr. Adams saw that the event very greatly diminished Hamilton's influence in the coming struggle; for a Federal delegation from New York would have been almost or quite subject to Hamilton's advice. It was therefore less necessary now to continue to stand well with the Hamilton wing of the Federalist party. The freedom of action thus acquired was speedily and summarily exercised. Three members of the cabinet had long been obnoxious to the president as being more amenable to alien influence than to his own. They were now ejected in rapid succession. McHenry, secretary at war, was taken first; a courteous and amiable gentleman, with whom it was difficult to quarrel, but who was unlikely to make a disagreeable scene. The president requested an interview with him, grew angry with him, charged him with many offences whereof the most heinous would appear to be that he " had eulogized General Washington in his report to Congress, and had attempted in the same report to praise Hamilton." It is not surprising that this colloquy closed with a request from the president that the secretary would resign, which was promptly complied with on the following morning.

Mr. Pickering's turn came next. He was charged with being " so devoted an idolater of Hamilton that he could not judge impartially of the sentiments and opinions of the president of the United States." The secretary of state was a man of firm and independent temper, a little opinionated and very resolute. He failed to see that it was his duty to resign, believing that he had in every respect properly discharged his functions. Without due cause, the existence of which he denied, he would not voluntarily quit his post in troublous times. Let the president, if he should see fit, take the responsibility of dismissing him, and let the matter appear before the world what in plain truth it was, — the action of the president, not that of the secretary. So Mr. Pickering declined to resign, and Mr. Adams, seldom alarmed at the spectre of responsibility, dismissed him. Wolcott was probably a more stanch admirer of Hamilton than either of his fellows. But he had made an admirable secretary of the treasury, nor would it be easy to fill his place. He was therefore retained a little longer until the matter could be arranged without prejudice to the public affairs, when he also was compelled to retire.

In spite of this misfortune in New York the Federalists were by no means prepared to give up the game as altogether lost. An expedient was suggested at a meeting of the Federal members of the legislature whereby even this disaster might be retrieved. It was calculated, with great accuracy as the event proved, that the votes for Jefferson, including the twelve cast by New York, would not exceed seventy-three. Seventy were necessary for a choice. Could four be subtracted he would be defeated. The next legislature, which had just been chosen and of which the term would begin in time to give to it the choice of electors, would send twelve Republicans. But if the governor of New York could only be persuaded to convene an extra session of the present legislature in which there was a Federal majority, it might be possible to change the law concerning the choice of presidential electors, to take that function from the legislature and give it to the people by districts. From many districts, probably more than four, it would then be possible to send Federal delegates.

The promoters of this scheme — distinguished Federalists in the State — met in caucus and sought to enlist Hamilton's aid in urging it upon Governor Jay. They found it the more easy to prevail with him, because the proposed system was that which he had always approved. In the old days when the Constitution was under discussion, he had strongly favored a clause directing the choice of presidential electors to be made in every instance directly by the people. He now wrote to the governor advocating the summoning of the legislature to meet for this purpose. He met the issue fairly, grounding his appeal upon a great political necessity. The measure was to be "justified by unequivocal reasons of public safety." Nor should any colorable incentives be assigned. The truth should be told; "the motive ought to be frankly avowed." He urged the plan as the only remaining means of saving the nation, and was doubtless sincere even in this strong expression. But Mr. Jay, less deeply moved by the vehement partisanship of the moment, was not able to view the proposed act in the same light as his friend. A grave official responsibility rested upon him, from which Hamilton was free. He would not comply with the request, — very properly as it must be acknowledged, — and this last hope was taken from the Federalists.

Yet apart from its immediate political bearing the principle involved in this proposition to the governor was so far sound, that Hamilton was not content to drop it simply because it could not serve his purpose upon this especial occasion. It would have the effect of drawing closer the connection between the president and the people, by doing away with the possibility of the intervention of the State governments. It was a step toward a single nationality, and away from the dangerous composite system. It would leave the choice of members of the State legislature to be made without that mischievous complication which must inevitably be introduced if, in addition to their proper and natural functions, they were to be burdened with the responsibility of sharing in presidential politics. A resolution originating with Hamilton was shortly afterward introduced into the legislature of New York by De Witt Clinton, wherein this reform was declared to be proper to be embodied in an amendment to the Constitution. Another lesson also had been learned by the time that Jefferson had been elected, and an accompanying resolution suggested a second amendment requiring the electoral college thereafter to designate which of the two persons voted for was named for the presidency and which for the vice-presidency. Both resolutions passed in the State legislature very easily, and being thence introduced into Congress were passed also by the House of Representatives by a handsome majority. But when they reached the Senate they failed by a single vote. In less than two years afterward the latter of the two proposed amendments was adopted, and has ever since been the law of the land. The former has never been made a part of the Constitution, though its propriety has been tacitly acknowledged by the conduct of the people of the several States.

As the outlook grew steadily more unpromising for the Federalists Hamilton became very urgent to pursue again the course which he had marked out for the previous election, and the deviation from which had brought Jefferson so prominently forward in the place of succession. It was now more than ever necessary for the party to determine to support Adams and Pinckney equally. That policy alone could save them from defeat, and Hamilton entreated the prominent men to come to a "distinct and solemn concert to pursue this course *bonâ fide*." His preferences were strongly for Mr. Pinckney, yet he would gladly have seen this plan carried out with entire honesty, though such ideal good faith must have resulted in a tie vote, and might in that case have made Mr. Adams, by a sort of right of preëmption, a second time president. Yet he mistrusted some of Mr. Adams' followers, and feared that their defection from Pinckney might imperil the whole result.

Matters standing thus in the party, Hamilton was induced to take what must be acknowledged to have been an unfortunate step. He composed a letter for the purpose of showing the unfitness of Mr. Adams for the presidential office. To this end he freely and severely criticised both the political character and the official career of that gentleman. His conduct as president was not incorrectly said to have been "an heterogeneous mass of right and wrong," and the wrong was very mercilessly exposed. Many of Hamilton's friends were far from satisfied that he was not falling into an error in this transaction, and rather deferentially deprecated the project. Had they ventured to speak more boldly and undertaken to dissuade him, it would have been better for all concerned; but they were so wont to yield to his judgment that they only intimated a mild distrust instead of a strong disapprobation. Hamilton would not desist from the project; but he promised that the epistle should be kept very carefully private, should be sent only to trustworthy friends and members of the party, and should be guarded in its distribution so as not to take away a vote from Mr. Adams. The purpose was to persuade friends of that gentleman not to withdraw their votes from Mr. Pinckney; and it was only in order to influence persons inclined to take this course that the scheme was devised. Toward the close of the letter the writer distinctly stated that he did "not advise the withholding from Mr. Adams a single vote;" but that he claimed "an *equal* support of Mr. Pinckney with Mr. Adams."

It was chimerical to expect to preserve the secrecy or to limit the effect of such a document emanating from such a source, and Hamilton would doubtless have been disappointed in the attempt. Yet even the attempt was rendered impossible. Burr, who always found out every thing which was especially intended to be concealed from him, became aware of the existence of this paper. It was an act quite to his taste to purloin it and turn it to his own uses. He did so. To the infinite chagrin and embarrassment of Hamilton and many more this confidential letter was suddenly and to their utter surprise made public, with much flourish and malicious merriment, by the Republican prints. The effect was very bad. Not a few even of those who subscribed to its sentiments were vexed and annoyed at this expression of them. A project which at its best was questionable, at its worst became extremely mischievous. The Adams faction was very naturally enraged. The Pinckney cohorts, if a little chapfallen, were certainly not improved in temper.

Under the circumstances it cannot but be matter of surprise that the Federal electors behaved so well as they did when it came to the actual casting of their votes. Then it appeared that in spite of that unfortunate letter Hamilton's activity and influence had produced an effect hardly to have been expected. The compact was sacredly respected by every delegate save one. He, a member from Rhode Island, cast his vote for Adams and Jay. Otherwise the Federalists voted solidly for Adams and Pinckney, giving to the former sixty-five and to the latter sixty-four votes. But Jefferson and Burr were quite safely in advance with seventy-three votes apiece.

This tie left the result to be determined by the House of Representatives, voting by States, and at once there began a most eager and exciting canvass. There could be no question that Jefferson was fairly entitled to receive the presidency at the hands of his party at the first moment when it should be in their power to dispose of that coveted reward. It was equally beyond a doubt that the great mass of the party throughout the country was inclined to deal fairly by him, and yield him his just due. But it was no less clear that Burr would not be restrained by any consideration from using every means in his power to secure the prize to himself. Such political and personal influence had he succeeded in obtaining, so consummately successful was he in intrigue, that it was by no means improbable that he might gain his object. His great opportunity lay in compassing a bargain with the Federalists; and it is the least honorable thing that can be said of that party in the whole narrative of its existence, that too many of its prominent men now showed a tendency to listen to such overtures.

Burr's not very enviable reputation seemed likely in this juncture to do him more useful service than he could have gained from a better name. Whatever else might be said for or against Jefferson, at least it could not be denied that he was a Republican to the very core. In this political creed he had been stanch and true alike in adversity and in prosperity. He had manifested that he had firm convictions concerning the policy of the country, and that he would not materially depart from them. Burr on the other hand was already so well understood, that few men gave him credit for having any convictions whatsoever in affairs of State, or for believing in any other policy save that of pure selfishness. He was thought to espouse such principles—if the word may be applied to any expression of political belief on his part—as were likely to further his own ends. He was therefore quite open to propositions of barter. He could doubtless be persuaded to exchange some important Republican measures against Federal support. His election would triply please the Federalists. First, because it would involve the defeat and the bitter disappointment of Jefferson; and there were men in the party who would have been content to raise any human creature to power, provided he could be established upon the attractive basis of the total ruin of Jefferson's aspirations. Second, because the triumph of Burr would be much more like the triumph of an independent candidate than like the establishment of a pure and unalloyed Republican ascendancy. Third, because it was supposed that terms could be extracted from Burr much better than from Jefferson, who indeed might not improbably altogether refuse to trade.

Hamilton was shocked and alarmed at the prevalence of these feelings among the influential members of his party. He had a thorough distrust of Burr. It was an old and apparently an instinctive sentiment with him. Washington had shared it. It is traceable as far back as to the earlier days of the Revolution; and during the interval it had rather gained strength than been surmounted. It was not by any means a peculiar notion. Nor is it possible to observe without surprise the behavior of the Republicans in this regard. The closeness of the vote between Jefferson and Burr had been anticipated so soon as the composition of the electoral college was known. , At once, every one of whatever political complexion surmised that Burr would resort to every measure of art to secure his ascendancy. There was a suspicion that he had tampered with one of the New York electors, and how to circumvent him was the problem which vexed the minds of the well-disposed Republicans. The object was achieved by a vote that the secret ballot should be dispensed with, and that each elector should deposit his vote openly on the table. If the suspected individual had been corrupted he had not the hardihood to carry out the plot when his agency would be thus exhibited, and the project, if it ever really existed, failed. But whether the scheme had been in fact concocted or not is matter of little consequence; the moral lies in the fact that these very Republicans who dreaded such treacherous dealing deliberately voted for the very man whom they at the same time insulted by the manifestation of this opinion concerning his honor. In such estimation was Burr held even by persons who were yet willing from motives of political expediency to become his supporters for the vice-presidency, and possibly even for the presidency.

The contest in the House of Representatives could not fail to be close and dubious. The Federalists, though vanquished, suddenly found themselves masters of the new situation which their opponents had blunderingly created. They had no chance of bringing in their own candidate, but they might bring in whichever of the Republican candidates they should see fit. Jefferson was sure of eight States, but there were eight others upon no one of which he could count, and without some one of which he could not secure a majority. Bayard, sole representative from Delaware, and a Federalist, had more power in his hands than any one man. He singly cast the vote of a State. He could give the presidency to Jefferson by making Delaware the ninth State. Vermont, with two representatives, was divided. Morris, the Federalist, might join with his colleague, who was a Jeffersonian, and give the election to Jefferson. Maryland had more representatives, but was so divided that any one of the Federalists could give the choice to Jefferson. On the other hand there were certain of the eight States counted for Jefferson that were but slenderly saved by him. A very slight change — the votes of two or three individuals — might give them to Burr; and the persons were named who were but lukewarm in Jefferson's favor, and might at any moment accomplish this diversion. Altogether it was an uncertain and anxious period for all concerned.

The Federalist predilection for Burr steadily waxed stronger. At a private meeting a majority of the representatives belonging to that party expressed their intention of voting for him. Never, probably, was Hamilton more thoroughly aroused, more indignant, more energetic. Had he indulged in any feeling of personal vindictiveness, he could in no way have gratified it better than by defeating Jefferson. Some persons thought that the vehemence of his opposition to Burr must be stimulated by personal hostility growing out of political and professional rivalry in New York. But it was not so. Hamilton had not a tithe of the personal motives for enmity toward Burr that he had for enmity towards Jefferson, and so he himself felt and said at the time. From private malevolence it must be believed that he was altogether free. The only feeling which he is known to have expressed in all the eagerness of the hour, in confidential letters or unguarded conversation, points wholly toward the political aspect of the question. "If there be a man in the world I ought to hate," he wrote, "it is Jefferson. With Burr I have always been personally well. But the public good must be paramount to every private consideration." Again he said: "To contribute to the disappointment and mortification of Mr. Jefferson would be on my part only to retaliate for unequivocal proofs of enmity. But in a case like this it would be base to listen to personal considerations." It seemed to him an odious and a wicked act on the part of the Federalists to promote to the presidency a bad and dangerous man from any of the interested motives which alone could induce them to that measure. He wished to found their action, not upon partisan grounds, but upon a broad and honorable basis of patriotism and statesmanship. No portion of his career more fully proves him an honest man, or entitles him to higher respect, than does this.

He wrote very urgently to every one whom he could hope to influence for good in this matter: to Wolcott, to Otis, to Sedgwick, to Gouverneur Morris, to John Marshall, to Bayard of Delaware, to John Rutledge, to Senator Ross. The mails daily carried his repeated adjurations to the members of his party to play the honorable part in this momentous game; not to sacrifice their country in order to divide their opponents; not to imperil the republic in order to get terms from a rascal; not to give the presidency to an unprincipled and dangerous man simply to spite an able foe. With Bayard, whose singular position made his views of peculiar interest, Hamilton's efforts were exceedingly strenuous.

As a party measure he insisted that adherence to Burr would be a blunder. Failure would only leave Jefferson both triumphant and needlessly incensed, and would expose the party to the "disgrace of a defeat in an attempt to elevate to the first place in the

government one of the worst men in the community."
Success would never win Burr to Federalism. He
was too ambitious and too bad a man for that. "Every
step in his career proves that he has formed himself
upon the model of Catiline, and he is too cold-blooded
and too determined a conspirator ever to change his
plan." Moreover should the Federalists make Burr
president, the whole responsibility for every bad
measure of his administration would be shifted upon
them by a party which would say with truth that it
had intended him only for the insignificant place of
vice-president. Beneath such an incubus the party
could never again arise.

To Wolcott he wrote: "There is no doubt but
that upon every virtuous and prudent calculation
Jefferson is to be preferred. He is by far not so
dangerous a man; and he has pretensions to character. As to Burr, there is nothing in his favor. His
private character is not defended by his most partial
friends. He is bankrupt beyond redemption, except
by the plunder of his country. His public principles
have no other spring or aim than his own aggrandizement, *per fas aut nefas.* If he can, he will certainly
disturb our institutions to secure himself *permanent
power*, and with it *wealth*. He is truly the Catiline
of America."

To Morris he said that Burr was "sanguine enough
to hope every thing, daring enough to attempt every
thing, wicked enough to scruple nothing." He
warned Sedgwick of the folly of seeking to make
terms with Burr. "No agreement with him could
be relied on. His private circumstances render dis-
order a necessary resource. His public principles

offer no obstacle. His ambition aims at nothing short of permanent power and wealth in his own person. For Heaven's sake let not the Federal party be responsible for the elevation of such a man!" Hamilton owned himself both proud and fond of the Federal party. Its past career had been noble; he had trust and faith in it for the future. The danger of its humiliation in this grave crisis affected him deeply, and more than once he spoke of this dreaded consummation with deep and touching sadness.

History has shown how accurate was his estimate of Burr's moral character, nor has it disproved his opinion of the capacity of the man. "As to his talents, great management and cunning are the predominant features; he is yet to give proofs of those solid abilities which characterize the statesman." Those proofs Burr never did give, though he was long in politics and died an old man. "Daring and energy" Hamilton allowed to him; "but these qualities under the direction of the worst passions are certainly strong objections, not recommendations. He is of a temper to undertake the most hazardous enterprises, because he is sanguine enough to think nothing impracticable." The words were actually prophetic. Indeed, in reading the many letters written by Hamilton at this period one is struck with the fact that he gave at that time, with perfect accuracy and aptitude of language, the very description of Burr which history in possession of his whole career would now give. Scarcely a word would be altered, except perhaps occasionally for the purpose of adding even greater strength to the expression.

Intense excitement prevailed when the business of

a choice was actually entered upon by the House of Representatives.   It was voted that the session should continue without adjournment until the election should be accomplished.   The president and senators had seats given them upon the floor of the chamber, but the public was excluded.   Certain sick members were brought in upon their beds.   The balloting began, and the result of the first vote showed eight States for Jefferson, six for Burr, Vermont and Maryland divided.   The members gallantly sat out the first night according to the spirit of the resolution against an adjournment, but afterward they contented themselves with respecting the letter only of this resolve, and took recesses of abundant length.   Day after day the voting continued, without any nearer approach to a result.   People began to grow anxious, and rumors were rife of a determination on the part of the Federalists to prevent any choice.   No doubt some persons seriously contemplated such a scheme.   President Adams wrote to Gerry: " I know no more danger of a political convulsion if a president, *pro tempore*, of the Senate, or a secretary of state, or speaker of the House, should be made president by Congress, than if. Mr. Jefferson or Mr. Burr is declared such.   The president would be as legal in one case as in either of the others in my opinion, and the people as well satisfied."   So felt the present incumbent of the presidency, but not so felt most other persons.   The general opinion was that if the dead-lock could not be brought to an end by some means, and a choice made by the House, then the Constitution and government would be subjected to a very perilous strain.

At last on the sixth day of the balloting a general meeting of the Federalists was held. In an informal sort of way terms were demanded and obtained from Jefferson. A friend of that gentleman assured them that Jefferson, in the event of his election, would make no serious innovations in the Federal policy already established concerning the important topics of the public debt, commerce, and the navy; also that he would make no removals of worthy subordinate officials on the ground of their political views. Many of the Federalists were by no means well pleased to see their comrades come to the support of Jefferson. But fortunately there were a sufficient number of gentlemen who had the wisdom to approve this course, and the courage to pursue it. Hamilton's tonic medicines were having their effect. At the second ballot, taken on the seventh day, — being the thirty-sixth ballot since the beginning, — Morris, the Federalist, who divided the Vermont delegation, absented himself. Two members of the party from Maryland gave blank ballots. The divided States were thus brought in upon Jefferson's side; and by a vote of ten States he was made president, and Burr was obliged to content himself with the inferior place. To what extent this result was attributable to Hamilton's influence can only be surmised. Certain it is that to the majority of the members of his party in the House his advice had been distasteful. But on the other hand it can hardly be doubted that if instead of opposing the general sentiment of this body he had fallen in with their predilections, and had been as energetic in rallying them in favor of Burr as he was in stimulating them against him, that candidate would probably have won the success which he so coveted. Burr at any rate furnished a bloody and memorable proof of his own opinion concerning the effectiveness of the part played by Hamilton in this exciting contest; and Burr was as competent to judge correctly as any person could be.

With the inauguration of Jefferson Hamilton's prominence in public affairs in a great measure ceases. During the brief remainder of his life he continued to feel much interested in the many political questions which arose, and his opinion was sought and respected by a large circle of followers. But he ceased to exercise any power in the administration. He occasionally took up his pen, and thus made himself felt. He severely criticised the principles laid down in Mr. Jefferson's first message. He strongly advocated the acquisition of Louisiana, long a favorite project with him, and defended the constitutionality of the measure. But as he now ceased all efforts to mould in any respect the policy of the country, we may properly here take farewell of him as a public man.

CHAPTER VIII.

PROFESSIONAL AND PRIVATE LIFE.

No reputation is more notoriously ephemeral than that of a distinguished lawyer. In his own generation he fills a large space in the public eye; in the next a few reminiscences handed down in the profession alone rescue his memory from oblivion; the third generation scarcely preserves the hollow sound of the once famous name. Hamilton's distinction as a lawyer has of course been completely overshadowed by his distinction as a statesman; yet he enjoyed the no small glory of being the leader of the New York bar. So says that excellent authority, Chancellor Kent, who farther adds that, being "a very great favorite with the merchants of New York," Hamilton "was employed in every important and every commercial case." The industry and thoroughness of research which he displayed in preparing his causes seems to have made a great impression upon the chancellor, who speaks with admiration of his habit of always "ransacking cases and precedents to their very foundations," refusing to use the customary abridgments or translations, but going to the original works of Grotius, Emerigon, Valin, and the rest of the older and foreign writers, and carrying his " inquiries into the commercial codes of the nations of the European continent."

Such methods of labor were the more praiseworthy in Hamilton because he might naturally have fallen into the way of making his native talent and peculiar legal aptitude supplement the deficiencies of painful investigation. His mind fell easily into the course of professional argument, and his ability was thoroughly congenial to the pursuit of the law. No small proportion of his labors in the cabinet were of a legal nature, dealing with questions of constitutionality, many of which afterward came in one shape or another before the Supreme Court. Nor could that tribunal even with Marshall at its head often add much to a topic which Hamilton had discussed. When Jay retired from the position of Chief Justice of the United States the post was offered to Hamilton, but was declined by him. The greatness and usefulness of the office had then been but imperfectly developed, nor did the magnitude of its functions fully appear until the series of grave constitutional questions called forth during several consecutive years the luminous opinions of Marshall. Had Hamilton been at the head of the bench in those days it is certain that he would have left a reputation as a jurist which would have rivalled his reputation as a statesman, and would not have been equally subject to the cavillings of party. For though Marshall was a stanch Federalist and wrote thoroughly Federalist opinions, yet his greatness as a judge is not now questioned by writers of Republican proclivities.

Hamilton seems soon to have obtained the very

dangerous and perplexing reputation of being able to win any case, however desperate. A conscientious lawyer who knowingly holds this position must often be embarrassed as to the line of conduct which it is proper for him to pursue. The more unrighteous the cause, the greater the criminal, the more eager will be the effort to engage such counsel to triumph over the right. The rule of professional ethics which justifies the lawyer in accepting cases without regard to his opinion of their merits in a moral point of view is well known, nor does it demand discussion in this place. It does not appear to have satisfied Hamilton, who laid down for himself the strict principle that he would never undertake to defend before a jury an accused person of whose guilt, after a full and fair disclosure of the facts, he was in his own mind well assured. The members of the profession have a familiar line of argument which proves such a doctrine to be not only over-nice but even to be actually wrong ; yet a certain unconquerable human instinct, quite as satisfactory as the logic of the lawyers, supports Hamilton's determination.

Most advocates who have any criminal practice occasionally become concerned in melodramatic scenes. Mr. John C. Hamilton has preserved the following anecdote of such an occurrence in which his father was engaged. The body of a young woman was found in a public well in the city of New York, and a young mechanic of good character, who had been paying his addresses to her, was suspected of having murdered her. Hamilton was retained for the accused, and investigated the case with minute care. In so doing he became convinced not only of the innocence of his own client but of the guilt of a principal witness for the prosecution. But he was somewhat singular in this sentiment, and the community having prejudged the case and found decidedly against the prisoner were by no means well pleased to witness Hamilton's efforts to secure an acquittal. Hamilton, however, was thoroughly resolved not only to save the life but to restore the reputation of an upright man so unjustly defamed. As the evidence went in he strove hard and not unsuccessfully to show that the deed must have been done by some other hand than that of the supposed offender. At last the witness whom he himself profoundly suspected, bearing the unpleasant name of Croucher, was called to the stand. The night was far advanced, and the insufficient illumination of candles had been resorted to in the court room. When Hamilton's turn for cross-examination came, he took two candles, placed one on each side of the witness' face, and then confronted him with a fixed and keen gaze. It was not an agreeable process for Croucher, and he appealed to the court to forbid it; but Hamilton said impressively that he had " special reasons, deep reasons, which he dared not express — reasons that when the real culprit is detected and placed before the court will then be understood." The judge permitted the proceeding in consideration of the extraordinary circumstances of the case. Hamilton turned to the panel: " The jury," said he, " will mark every muscle of his face, every motion of his eye. I conjure you to look through that man's countenance to his conscience." Amid the breathless and awe-inspiring silence of the spectators Croucher was obliged to answer the interrogatories put to him; and in so doing he "plunged on from one admission to another, from contradiction to contradiction." When he was dismissed from the stand, the "spectators turned away from him with horror." The jury acquitted the defendant without leaving their box.

It may be thought that the position in which Hamilton placed Croucher was hardly justifiable. Had he sought to throw suspicion upon him as a merely strategical move, simply in order to shift the burden from his own client, the criticism would be fair. But if, as was the fact, a thorough knowledge of all the circumstances had fully convinced the counsel that the defendant was altogether innocent, and that another man was guilty, he was surely bound in strict duty to use such means as the cause afforded him and the court should declare proper to save his client upon this theory. As for the arrangement of the candles and his own impressive manner, these were only such accessories as were probably necessary if he was right, and if applied to a man of average intelligence and character would have proved altogether harmless if his belief was erroneous. The chance of his being quite right, and having saved an innocent life at the cost of a suspicion cast upon a guilty man, is largely increased by the story of Croucher's subsequent career. He was afterwards convicted of rape upon a young child, obtained a pardon, went to Virginia, there committed a fraud, fled to England, and there finally is supposed to have been executed "for a heinous offence."

Never exorbitant in his fees for professional services Hamilton was on many occasions romantically generous.   At a time when partisan feelings were much excited a deserving young man, the son of an aged farmer belonging to the Democratic party, by a combination of unfortunate circumstances and malicious tale-bearing was brought into serious difficulty. The matter taking the shape of a case in court the father came in great distress to Hamilton, anxious to retain him, but doubtful whether he could pay the fee. Hamilton evaded the old man's inquiries as to the probable cost, and becoming thoroughly convinced of the righteousness of the defendant's cause threw himself into it with much ardor.   He exerted all his powers of oratory, deprecating the introduction of politics into a question of justice, and speaking with alternate vehemence and deep feeling.   His words were the more effective because his client belonged to the party to which he himself had been all his life opposed.   Apparently both the speaker and his hearers were wrought to a high pitch of sentiment in the course of the address; the acquittal followed readily, and Hamilton immediately left the court room.   The venerable father with tears streaming down his cheeks pursued the deliverer, but could persuade him to accept no fee whatsoever.   " I would not," said Hamilton, " in such a cause tarnish my hands with gold!" The cool and business-like lawyer may smile at this; but the tale well illustrates the honest and generous sentiment which Hamilton carried into public affairs, and the exalted view which he took of the obligations and duties imposed upon those who occupy prominent and responsible positions in the framework of society. There was a grand principle not of law but of public morals at stake in this cause, and the result might exert a far-reaching influence; he preferred to undertake such tasks without financial reward.

On another occasion, being asked what would probably be the fee for conducting a cause in which a large property was involved and a protracted litigation was apprehended, he named one thousand dollars. He was employed and brought the case to a successful termination, though only after much greater labor than either he or his clients had anticipated. They offered him two thousand dollars. He wrote in reply: "I must decline it. When I undertook this cause I mentioned a thousand dollars. It has given me more trouble than I expected. It might have given me less. I cannot think of accepting this additional sum under the flush of grateful feeling on gaining a doubtful cause."

Hamilton's principles in practice at the bar were described by a member of the brotherhood as being "candid and liberal towards his brethren, utterly abhorring trick and chicanery." Another eminent professional writer said of him: "His manners were gentle, affable, and kind; and he appeared to be frank, liberal, and courteous in all his professional intercourse." In this respect he differed widely from Aaron Burr. The two were in a certain sense rivals, not because they had clashing interests, — for, as Hamilton said, each had his peculiar clientage, and few of those who employed the one would even in his absence have naturally sought the other, — but as to their relative success in winning causes there was some division in the popular opinion. Burr was a consummate master of all the artifice of the profession, nor did it concern him by what means he achieved victory ; a shrewd device, a sharp manœuvre, served his turn even better than a forensic encounter. Hamilton on the other hand was no strategist, but won his causes by honest weight of legal argument, by thorough preparation, and by his admirable eloquence. He always preferred a broad legal principle as the basis of his exposition. Chancellor Kent says: " He never made any argument in court in any case without displaying his habits of thinking, and resorting at once to some well-founded principle of law, and drawing his deductions logically from his premises. Law was always treated by him as a science founded on established principles."

 In spite of his small stature he was a very effective speaker.   Many proofs of this fact have occurred incidentally in the narrative of his life, but the direct evidence of his contemporaries remains in very forcible shape.   Indeed I am afraid to reproduce the language used by Chancellor Kent, Colonel Troup, and others in describing his oratory, lest it should seem like such extravagant panegyric as not to command belief. His air was open and animated, gaining the confidence of his hearers in his fairness and honesty in conducting the cause, nor was this confidence ever shown to be misplaced by the discovery of any approach towards deception. His bearing was dignified and imposing ; but his manner was warm, animated, and enthusiastic, and in the play of his features " the very workings of his soul " were visible. His eye was a very striking feature often spoken of by those who had known its influence ; it was very large, dark, and full of brilliant light. His voice too was powerful and melodious, having a great compass, so that he

spoke by turns in strong deep tones or in low and
soft utterances. He could overawe at one moment
and persuade in the next with surprising flexibility
of power. Many a tale is told of his control over his
auditors, holding them at one time in solemn silence,
again moving them to copious tears, and then trans-
porting them with lofty enthusiasm. He has failed to
retain that widely known distinction as an orator to
which he was amply entitled, only because he never
had the fortune to speak upon the floor of either
chamber of Congress, — the only forum in the country
which is sufficiently public, and where topics of sufficient general interest are discussed to insure to the
speakers in debate a permanent fame. Men who
speak well to a jury do not always show equal power
in legislative assemblies; but Hamilton's peculiar line
of argument and form of oratory was far better suited
to a Senate chamber than to a court room. In this
respect he resembled Daniel Webster. He descended
upon the jury-box and the throng of listeners, and
took complete and masterful possession of them by
force of his commanding greatness. He did not simply fill this lesser space with familiar ease, and then
when removed to a larger field find himself unequal
to the demands of more critical hearers and grander
subjects of discussion. On the contrary, the greater
province was that for which by nature he was the
better adapted.

It was not easy to stand against him when he was
once thoroughly aroused. Upon one occasion a farmer
came to him from the country with a tale of having
been induced by a rich speculator in the city to part

with his farm in exchange for a deed of land in Virginia. The transaction had obviously been a gross fraud upon the aged rustic, and Hamilton sent for the other party. The citizen appeared, and upon hearing what was the demand made upon him demurred, saying that it must first be shown that the title to the Virginia land was defective. "Sir," cried Hamilton, "you must give me back that deed! I do not say that you know that the title to these lands is bad, but it is bad. You are rich: he is a poor man. How can you sleep on your pillow? Would you break up the only support of an aged man and seven children?" Walking up and down the room for a moment in much excitement, he again burst forth: "I will add to my professional services all the weight of my character and powers of my nature; and you ought to know, when I espouse the cause of innocence and of the oppressed, that character and those powers will have their weight." The man requested time for consideration. Hamilton bade him take an hour. He took it, and at its expiration returned and executed the reconveyance. Hamilton declined to take any fee from his client.

In another instance Hamilton declined to take a fee from a political opponent who had written sundry severe invectives against him, but who nevertheless ventured to employ him. The client was acquitted, and as may be supposed was quite overcome by Hamilton's magnanimity, not only in consenting to undertake the case, but in conducting it to a successful termination gratuitously.

The family of Mr. Cruger, the friend and patron of his boyhood, having fallen into a quarrel and lawsuit in which a large property was in dispute, Hamilton undertook to act as mediator. It was a delicate matter to arrange family differences, but he had the good fortune to be successful. A fee was offered to him, but he refused to accept it, saying, " When I was young your father was kind to me. I have never had an opportunity before of showing that I remembered it; I beg you will not now withhold it from me."

One of the chief triumphs recorded of Hamilton in his legal career was that which he won in the case of Le Guen v. Gouverneur and Kemble, a suit which had been litigated in many courts, and had at last become famous. Gouverneur Morris was on the other side, and he delivered a long, brilliant, and telling speech, toward the close of which he made some rather personal points against Hamilton. On the next day Hamilton rose to reply, and in an exceedingly clever and brilliant harangue returned to his opponent somewhat more than a Roland for the other's Oliver. No small measure of interest had attached to this professional duello, and a throng of auditors, among whom were many quite competent to judge, decisively awarded the superiority to Hamilton. He gathered also the substantial fruits of it in winning the cause. The grateful client, whose whole fortune had been at stake, and who had recovered one hundred and twenty-five thousand dollars, tendered to Hamilton a fee of eight thousand dollars. Hamilton declared that one thousand was sufficient, and would receive no more. Le Guen next went to Burr, — for it was one of the rare occasions when Hamilton and Burr were together in a cause, — and offered to him the like sum, eight thousand dollars. Burr accepted the amount without reluctance.

The case of Croswell *v.* The People was one of those political causes which are apt to excite much feeling, and to involve no small danger of the prostitution of justice to partisan feeling.

In the little village of Hudson there were published two newspapers of opposite political creeds, the Federal sheet bearing the menacing name of the " Wasp ; " the Democratic rival more mildly styling itself the " Bee."   One day the " Wasp " remarked that its contemporary had declared the " burden of the Federal song " to be that " Jefferson paid Callender for writing against the late administration. This," said the spicy little insect, " is wholly false ! The charge is explicitly this : Jefferson paid Callender for calling Washington a traitor, a robber and a perjurer ; for calling Adams a hoary-headed incendiary ; and for most grossly slandering the character of men who he well knew were virtuous. These charges not a Democratic editor has yet dared, or will dare, to meet in open and manly discussion."

The substance of this venomous outburst was said to have recently appeared in the " New York Evening Post," a paper inaugurated and conducted under the auspices of Hamilton, Gouverneur Morris, and other distinguished Federalists of the city and neighborhood.   But there was a design on foot among the Democrats to repress the abuse of the Federalist press through the instrumentality of the courts, and upon the wise principle of making the experiment upon a weak defendant they preferred to bring the first case — a precedent for others which might follow —

against the country editor rather than against the powerful city journal. The attorney-general drew up an indictment and gave it into the hands of a Democratic sheriff; a grand jury consisting wholly of Democrats instantly found a true bill. The trial was to be had forthwith before the justices of the county court of sessions in Columbia county, gentlemen who held their appointments from the Democratic party, and whose term of office about to expire would leave them to expect reinstatement from the same political organization.

Many circumstances of oppression towards the defendant — especially in refusing him a sufficient opportunity to read the indictment before compelling him to plead, also the denial of a slight delay requested in order to enable him to procure the attendance of Callender — excited much popular indignation. Endeavors were made to secure Hamilton's services; but imperative engagements prevented his attendance. The cause went to trial in his absence, and the judge instructed the jury that their only function was to find whether or not the defendant was the publisher of the libel, and whether the innuendoes laid in the indictment were true; that whether the publication was true or false, libellous or innocent, and whether the intent was innocent or malicious, were questions with which they had nothing to do; for that after they should have found the publication the court would determine the matter of malice, and the truth could not be given in evidence by the defendant. The verdict of guilty was brought in after a night spent by the jurors in deliberation. At once a motion for a new trial was made on the ground that the foregoing rulings of the judge were wrong, and that the truth of the libel was admissible. There was no question that there was good authority to be found in the English reports for the law as laid down by the bench, but there was a strong feeling that the principle should not be adopted in New York.

The case had now assumed such an aspect of public importance that Hamilton resolved at any cost of inconvenience to enter into it, and at the argument upon the motion he appeared on behalf of Editor Croswell. Ambrose Spencer was attorney-general, but had just received his appointment as judge of the Supreme Court. The extraordinary spectacle was therefore beheld of a gentleman first arguing a cause as counsel, and then at once upon the close of his argument taking the qualifying oath of office and assuming his seat upon the bench as a judge. He had administered a somewhat severe castigation to Hamilton in the course of his argument, having re-marked, in speaking of Lord Mansfield's opinion concerning the law of libel, that the fame of that nobleman would live when the name of every person engaged in this suit would be lost in oblivion. As he uttered these words he pointed significantly toward Hamilton. People said that his motive in so promptly donning the judicial ermine was to place himself in a position where etiquette would protect him from retaliation. But his adversary was not thus to be balked of his repartee. "The attorney-gen-eral," said he, "is far too modest; whatever may become of the fame of other men engaged in this suit, the attorney-general has secured a *notoriety* that *will never die.*" In spite of this passage-at-arms, we are told that Spencer and Hamilton were personally on friendly terms, and few higher tributes were paid to Hamilton's ability and achievements than fell from the lips of his "notorious" antagonist in this cause. Hamilton spoke for six hours, ranging over a wide field of law, politics, and morals, and achieving, as Chancellor Kent said, "the greatest forensic effort he ever made." The regular reporter of the court set about his task of taking notes of the speech, but became so excited by it that he threw down his pen in despair. The only report which remains consists of certain memoranda made by Chancellor Kent, and intended "merely to present to the profession the general course of argument and the legal authorities adduced on a very important and much litigated subject of jurisprudence."

Hamilton succeeded only imperfectly in convincing the court, which was equally divided in opinion, and therefore determined nothing. But he did succeed in convincing the public and the legislature, so that after some little discussion and delay a statute was passed embodying the doctrines laid down by him concerning the law of libel.

Many agreeable pages ought to be written concerning the private life, the habits, character, tastes, and pursuits of Alexander Hamilton; and it is with extreme regret that the biographer has to say that almost no materials exist for the task. Tradition preserves vague memories, which tantalize without in any degree satisfying the desire for an accurate and graphic sketch of him as he appeared in domestic and social relations. The foregoing pages have been but poorly written if they leave necessary any criticism or analysis of his principal moral and mental traits. The numerous circle of his devoted friends sufficiently attests the warmth and kindliness of his own nature, by which he could attract and retain such sentiments on the part of others.

Lively in his manners, brilliant in his conversation, there were few who could equal him in power of fascination. The sense of personal loyalty to him individually, which was cherished without break by men whose own abilities were of an order not deserving to be called second rate, was very singular and striking. Such tales of trusting and devoted following are told sometimes of military heroes, the greatest of whom seem able to inspire the like kind of feelings; so were kings sometimes in the days of the Stuarts. But not often does a statesman find a band of supporters combining with so much independence and ability on their own part such a deep affection and unvarying faith as were manifested toward Hamilton by the leading Federalists of his day. Without a shadow of envy or jealousy they always frankly acknowledged his supremacy. They took his commands, whether welcome or unwelcome, without reluctance. They loved him even when they could not fully concur with him. Not a vestige of secret or rankling enmity subsisted towards him. An open, generous, and straightforward spirit upon his part naturally called forth the sympathy of men of similar temper; and even persons of anti-federal proclivities must admit that the Federal chiefs were men of noble and upright spirit. Whatever faults were laid to their charge were not of the mean or ignoble type. Aristocratical, monarchical, domineering they were often said to be; but as demagogues, time-servers, and backbiters no one ever sought to describe them. The Republican newspaper, the "Aurora," did indeed once say that Washington was neither a soldier nor a statesman, and that he was a peculator; but the respectable men of the party would not have indorsed such language. Timothy Pickering and Oliver Wolcott were inferior in intellectual capacity to Jefferson and Madison, but they were an hundred-fold more independent and outspoken; and it was the like element of bold sincerity in· Hamilton, which made them repose in him such implicit confidence and perfect regard. Seldom has a party, so comparatively weak in numbers as were the Federalists, been managed with such an absence of chicanery and questionable manœuvres.

The personal characters of Hamilton and of his coadjutors for strict integrity stand at the highest possible point. He and his fellow-secretaries served the public to their own financial cost. They went into office poor, and they came out poorer. It is humiliating to read of Timothy Pickering saying that he cannot go into society in Philadelphia, even upon the cheap and simple scale then prevalent, because his income would suffer him to make no return of the hospitalities he might receive. Hamilton was of a liberal turn, and would have liked to keep open house. During the intervals when he was at home, practising law and in the receipt of an income adequate to his wishes, the indications are numerous of the hospitable system upon which his household was conducted. But so long as he was in office, he, like his fellow-servants, received but niggardly wages, and was kept rigidly poor by the principles of strict republican simplicity and economy which prevailed.

It had not in those days become the custom for underpaid officials to eke out their meagre salaries by indirect and questionable resources. Immense clamor was raised about corruption, but it was of the vaguest kind, and so far as I can discover no charge of any fraudulent effort to enrich himself was ever brought against Hamilton save such as was embodied in the investigation conducted through the instrumentality of the notorious Giles, whose ignorance of accounts led him to suppose that there was a deficit in the treasury. When Jefferson and his comrades cried out corruption against Hamilton they meant, as often appeared, that his financial schemes had enabled speculative congressmen and others to make money, and that such persons were made subservient to him in pursuance of their own interests in the stock-market. It was insinuated that Hamilton played improperly upon this chord of influence, but never, I think, that he became himself mixed up in any even questionable schemes. Had he done so he must inevitably have grown rich. No man, since money was first invented, ever had better opportunities for amassing it than Hamilton had at the time of his first report on the public credit, when he recommended the measures of funding and assumption. Yet no mousing detractor ever found the semblance of a flaw in his conduct at this time.

It must be confessed that his opponents did not behave very handsomely by him in this respect. All the while that they unquestionably were fully convinced of his perfect integrity they seem to have considered the charge of dishonesty a perfectly fair weapon to use against him, — for in truth what is unfair in politics? Can any one undertake to establish the code of political ethics, or to lay down any rule of conduct which has not at some time been broken by some man of high repute, and capable of creating, by his conduct, a precedent which will generally be considered respectable? So the anti-federalists certainly assailed Hamilton with accusations of corruption so vaguely phrased as quite naturally to take the construction of charges of vulgar dishonesty, when the speakers themselves were perfectly satisfied of the contrary. When Hamilton resigned his secretaryship Madison wrote, " Hamilton will probably go to New York, with the word poverty for his label." The words put into the shape of a slur what should have been an honorable distinction. Madison probably saw this, and regretted the language which he had at first been led to use, for he subsequently eliminated the last words. A few days earlier Jones had written to Madison: " I am at this moment informed that Hamilton told H. Lee that he meant to retire and go to the bar, where he could make his £2,000 per annum; whereas in office he had spent what he had before, about £3,000 — except a house and lot — and that if he was now to die his family must depend on their grandfather for their support."

Of all Hamilton's opponents Jefferson, by his own showing, behaved most unhandsomely by Hamilton in the way of gratuitous calumny. Many occasions have already been mentioned when, in letters and conversations, he impeached Hamilton's character as an honorable man. In his famous letter to Washington, at the time of the quarrel about Freneau, he declared that he never could have " imagined that the man who has the shuffling of millions backwards and forwards from paper into money and money into paper, from Europe to America and America to Europe, the dealing out of treasury secrets among his friends in what time and manner he pleases, and who never slips an occasion of making friends with his means," would have founded a charge on the appointment of Freneau. This passage is an excellent specimen of Jefferson's favorite nostrum of subtle *letter-poison*, if the phrase may be used. The picture might be *literally* true of a perfectly honest man, but the choice of language and expression was such as to inculcate a strong prejudice and to create a sort of flavor of dishonesty. If Jefferson sincerely believed Hamilton's personal character to be bad, some persons might think him bound to make known his sentiments to the president, even though he could advance no proofs. In the absence of evidence his remarks could be only taken as the expression of his own opinion. But had he in fact a bad opinion of Hamilton's personal morals? It is by no means clear that he had. In 1824, long after Hamilton's death, Jefferson talked about him with Mr. Van Buren. There was no reason to suppose that the conversation would pass into history, and therefore there was no motive for any disingenuous utterance. Perhaps this is the only occasion of which there is any record when Hamilton's principal enemy in public, and pertinacious calumniator upon every private occasion, spoke his thoughts without having any immediate end in view. Concerning this interview Mr. Van Buren wrote as follows to Mr. John C. Hamilton:

" Whilst dissenting in the strongest terms from [Hamilton's] political views, he (Jefferson) expressed himself very decidedly in favor of the sincerity of his motives and of his frankness in regard to party matters and public affairs in general. These [remarks] were substantially repeated in a letter which I received from him a few weeks after my return, in the following terms: ' For Hamilton frankly avowed that he considered the British Constitution, with all the corruptions of its administration, as the most perfect model of government which had ever been devised by the wit of man ; professing, however, at the same time, that the spirit of this country was fundamentally republican, that it would be visionary to think of introducing monarchy here, and that therefore it was the duty of its administrators to conduct it on the principles their constituents had elected.' " [1]

When was it that Jefferson spoke the truth? Was it when he charged his living rival with being a political corruptionist ; or when, that rival being dead, he praised the " sincerity of his motives " and " his frankness in regard to party affairs and public matters in general " ? Was it when he charged Hamilton with treasonable designs to subvert the republic and erect a monarchy out of the ruins ; or when he admitted that Hamilton thought that " it would be visionary to think of introducing monarchy here," and that

---

[1] Hamilton's " History of the Republic of the United States," vol. vi., page 253.

it was "the duty of the administrators" of our government "to conduct it on the principles their constituents had elected"? One might say that Jefferson spoke more charitably after death had removed rivalry and softened resentment. Unfortunately, however, he never said any thing worse against the living Hamilton than those accusations and innuendoes which, long after Hamilton's death and in his own old age, he perpetuated in the "Ana." But the "Ana" were written and bequeathed to posterity for a purpose, — the important purpose of influencing history and guiding opinion. The chat with Van Buren was apparently a mere careless repetition of old reminiscences. The reader may put his faith in whichever he may choose; for, after all, the real sentiments entertained by Jefferson towards Hamilton are not of sufficient consequence to deserve the space which has been given to this discussion concerning them.

That Hamilton retired from public life under the pressure of financial necessity seems unquestionable. The social position of his wife and himself could not be properly maintained, nor could the numerous family which was growing up in their home be properly launched in the world, unless his income could be increased. Nor could the chance that by his death he might leave them dependent on the liberal bounty of General Schuyler be otherwise than seriously annoying to Hamilton, who had shown a great pride and independence in this respect from the earliest days of his married life. The letter of Jones to Madison apparently made full as good a financial showing for Hamilton as was possible. His intimate friend, Colonel Troup, says that what little property he had was sold before he resigned his office, and that when he resigned he was worth little if any thing more than his household furniture. His son says: "Eight hundred dollars in the three per cents, which he sold to pay his debts, was the amount of his fortune," — the fortune of the greatest financier of his age!

Had Hamilton been better able to afford it he would probably have remained in office. For he certainly appears to have had a strong liking for a public career and for the dignified tasks of State. The grand field and noble usefulness had a strong and honorable attraction for him. It was not an ignoble ambition which stimulated him, nor any desire for office or station. It would be difficult to name any other distinguished man who, having equal claims to become the presidential candidate of his party, never sought to bring himself into the line of promotion, or even to remain in that line when chance had given him a position in it. There is no part of Hamilton's career which does not fully justify the assertion that he was, not reluctantly but by nature, far removed from the passion for office or for any of the formal badges of distinction. On the other hand he was equally distant from the feeble and too common affectation of pretending to put from him that for which his fingers obviously itched. Jefferson thanked God and his destiny that he could spend the rest of his days planting clover; and almost, as it were, before the ink was dry he abandoned his clover and spent twelve consecutive years in the vice-presidency and presidency. Hamilton was as frank in these matters as in all else. Whenever he was sounded as to his willingness to accept office he always boldly said, that if in a post worthy of what he conceived to be his abilities he could be sufficiently useful to make it worth while for him to leave for it his private affairs he would certainly do so. He was not afraid to make the acknowledgment, lest in the event of his failure to obtain the position people should deride his disappointment.

In truth nearly all his life was public life. He began actually in boyhood, and short intervals of respite did he have during the remaining years which his chary fate allotted to him. He seemed always to live and move in a perfect glare of publicity. His comings and his goings, his every act and word, were noted. Few men in modern times have been subjected to such a scrutiny. His most private affairs were dragged before the public in an unprecedented manner. If he had a fault it was published abroad; if he committed a peccadillo it was proclaimed from the housetops. He was at one time so unfortunate as to be led into an intrigue with a woman possessing some personal attractions, but without education, and, as it proved afterward, having no generous traits to be set off against her want of chastity. She was, or pretended to be, married, and her ignoble husband used to extort money from Hamilton. His enemies got scent of the unpleasant tale, and at once tried to make it useful in their political campaign. Hints were darkly dropped of corruption of a singularly dishonorable character in the administration of the treasury. The consequence was that James Monroe, Muhlenberg, and Venable constituted themselves a sort of committee of investigation. By the time they had finished their task they were well ashamed of having entered upon it, apologized to Hamilton, and fully acquitted him of every charge affecting his public character. But the matter was brought up again a long while after,—not without giving rise to charges of gross carelessness, if not of a graver nature, against Monroe for having failed properly to guard against the records of this inquiry falling into untrustworthy and inimical hands. Such publicity was then given to it that Hamilton, feeling that his official integrity must be vindicated at whatever cost of mortification to himself and pain to those dearest to him, published a complete narrative of the whole transaction. The explanation was perfect; the generous ones among his enemies were heartily sorry for the occurrence ; the ignoble ones alone rejoiced at the temporary humiliation which he suffered. It is painful to relate that an episode, which even in the heat of party warfare the more high-spirited of Hamilton's enemies declined to use against him, has been found a tempting morsel by writers of the present day. Whoever wishes to read the tale at full length, with all the misspelled letters of the woman and other piquant details narrated in the spirited style of a low newspaper report of a modern scandal, can find it thus set down in Mr. Parton's " Life of Thomas Jefferson," in which chronicle it has been found necessary to devote an entire chapter to this topic.

This circumstance shows not inaccurately the keen scrutiny to which Hamilton was perpetually subjected. Those who are familiar with the private annals and social records of that generation know well that the fault which he committed was no uncommon one ; that he was no worse than his contemporaries. Very few of those great men whose public virtues adorned the earlier period of our national existence numbered a strict chastity among their private excellences, and some of the most revered among them fell into opposite extremes. But they were never brought up for public castigation; it was only Hamilton who had the misfortune to live in a glass house into every cranny of which the full noon-tide sunshine seemed to be ever pouring.

It was however far from being wholly due to hostility or malice that a sort of espionage was established over Hamilton; on the contrary the manner in which the people at large turned their eyes continually upon him was highly complimentary. Washington's grand figure is to be eliminated from any comparisons which may be made between the other distinguished men of that age, and after this elimination there was none left whose prestige was equal to Hamilton's. Nay, more even than Washington Hamilton attracted the popular gaze. For did not his most resolute opponents put the highest estimate upon his genius? His friends did not use such extravagant language as fell from his foes concerning his astonishing intellectual powers. This manner of speaking of him, added to the consideration of his extreme youth and the way in which the anti-federalists singled him out individually as their one object of assault to the neglect of all other members of the party, created an immense curiosity and admiration concerning him. The man whom those who hated loudly declared to be " a prodigy " was not likely to go unobserved. If another quotation from the same letter of Mr. Van Buren to Mr. John C. Hamilton may be pardoned, it will show that the unusual prominence of his position has not been exaggerated by partiality in this description : " Observing that, whilst speaking of the conduct of his own party, he (Jefferson) invariably said the Republicans did so and so, and that he on the other hand as uniformly described the course of the Federal party as that of your father, by saying Hamilton took this or that ground, I took the liberty of calling attention to this peculiarity. He smiled and remarked that he was aware that he had fallen into that habit, and attributed it to the great extent to which he had regarded your father as the master spirit of his party."

The anecdote lately narrated should not be allowed to give rise to any disagreeable inferences concerning Hamilton's domestic relations. A more tender and affectionate husband and father it would be difficult to name, or one who found such sentiments more warmly and faithfully reciprocated by his family. He was eminently fitted to inspire both love and loyalty. His correspondence with his wife evinces the delightful footing upon which they stood. The too eager filial spirit of his eldest son cost the young man his life. It is a touching story. The lad was only eighteen years of age, but of singular promise, especially endeared to his father by his brilliant talents and noble temper. A distinguished career could justly be anticipated for him ; he had recently graduated from Columbia College, and had on that occasion delivered an oration which had attracted much remark and praise. In the autumn of 1801, when party spirit was even more than usually high and bitter, a Fourth-of-July orator levelled some exceedingly severe and unjust censures at Hamilton. Philip Hamilton, already exasperated by the many calumnies to which his father was then being subjected, happened one evening in company with a friend to enter a box at the theatre, and found the obnoxious orator in close proximity. In loud tones the two young men ridiculed the oration. Their offended neighbor arose, and summoning the two into the lobby seized young Hamilton by the coat-collar, applied an insulting epithet to both and then left, remarking that he should expect to hear from them, and if he did not he should treat them both as disgraced persons.

The lads saw no way out of the unfortunate business' save by a challenge. Hamilton's friend, the older of the two, fought first, and four shots were exchanged without injury to either combatant. It was then thought by the gentleman who acted for Hamilton in the matter that he might save his principal from a duel, and in an interview with the offended party he used every effort to do so, representing that that person having been out once might well and honorably pardon a youth of eighteen naturally incensed in his father's cause. But the appeal was fruitless; nay, the insult was actually renewed. Philip Hamilton then sent his challenge, but being " averse in principle to the shedding of blood in private combat, anxious to repair his original fault as far as he was able without dishonor, and to stand acquitted in his own mind," he resolved to receive the fire of his antagonist, to discharge his own pistol in the air, and then through his second to inform his opponent of the motive of his action, and leave it to that gentleman to take such farther action as he should see fit. Upon the ground the young man behaved with calmness and intrepidity; indeed, from the moment of rashness which led to the offence, surely not unpardonable in a warm-hearted lad, to the instant when he fell mortally wounded at the first fire of his antagonist, his behavior was in every respect admirable. He acknowledged and regretted his error, and was ready to do all that a gentleman could to avoid the hideous consequences. The wound which he received caused him excessive pain and anguish, which he bore without flinching for a period of twenty hours, when at length death came to his relief. His father, hearing of the meeting before he heard of the result, hastened to summon his physician, but fainted upon the way. His grief and despair may be imagined; but it is useless to describe the painful scene of the death-bed and the long mourning afterward. It was the severest bereavement of Hamilton's life.

Such incessant labors as Hamilton pursued taxed his physical powers severely. He worked with ease and rapidity, and thus might have saved for himself some wholesome leisure had the amount of his undertakings been anywise reasonably limited. But this was not the case, and the completion of one task however expeditiously accomplished always found another at hand awaiting its turn for attention. We find him at one time in the summer writing that he is not well, and saying that of late years he has seldom passed through that season without illness. When worn out with excess of application, his habit was to seek rest and recreation in a journey upon horseback. He had that taste for country life so common with men whose destiny calls them to un-remitted labor in cities; and as soon after his return to professional practice as he felt able to do so he purchased an estate on the Heights of Haerlem, about nine miles from the city of New York. It is described as a place of great natural beauty, having a variety of deciduous and evergreen trees very effectively grouped and intermingled, masses of picturesque rock in one part enveloped in the wild native wood-land, smooth lawns by the house, the Hudson River close beside it, and a fine view to the eastward over the ocean. He called his grounds " The Grange," naming them after the residence of his father's family in Ayrshire; and here he began to construct a charm-ing country-seat, and in connection therewith to carry on farming to some extent. As he laughingly said, he had fallen back upon the customary solace of retired statesmen.

But there was no more disappointment lurking behind this remark than was easily overcome; he was thoroughly happy in the prospect opening before him, and looked forward with cheerful anticipation to the enjoyment of a more uninterrupted career of domestic pleasures than his busy life and public avo-cations had hitherto rendered possible. There is something very touching in his letters to his wife at this period, as they are now read with a knowledge of his real future. " I may yet live twenty years," he wrote, little imagining with what rapid strides his untimely fate was even then hastening toward him. Pathetic indeed now appears the elo-quence with which he often sketched the happiness which he expected to enjoy amid his family, pursuing congenial pleasures and labors not too exacting. There is the atmosphere of sincerity throughout these aspirations; they were not in the fashion of those epistles which politicians write to their friends, deprecating public office, and of which the expressions may be usefully disseminated in the event of failures and defeats. Hamilton was writing to his wife with a candor and a fervor indicative of the tenderness and affection of his nature. He had seven children living, and dearly did he love the young family. The picture of him as he romped with them, playing marbles, flying kites, joining in all their games as if he had been no older than themselves, gives a very amiable idea of the thoughtful, vigorous, and much persecuted statesman. He concerned himself much also with their education, and the cultivation of agreeable accomplishments. He himself was very fond of the ancient literature of the Greeks and Romans, and found time amid all his absorbing occupations to keep fresh his familiarity with his favorite authors.

By degrees he found himself floating out of the swift current of active political life, and so well satisfied was he to do so that he declared, not privately but publicly, that he would never again hold office except only in case of a " foreign or civil war." But the theory and science of government constituted a study too attractive to be abandoned by him, and he seems now to have been meditating a grand scheme. Upon a visit made to him at " The Grange " by Chancellor Kent, and of which that gentleman has left a very delightful sketch, Hamilton unfolded the plan of a work which he was contemplating, and which should embrace a "full investigation of the history and science of civil government, and the practical results of the various modifications of it upon the freedom and happiness of mankind. He wished to have the subject treated in reference to past experience, and upon the principles of Lord Bacon's inductive philosophy. His object was to see what safe and salutary conclusions might be drawn from an historical examination of the effects of the various institutions heretofore existing upon the freedom, the morals, the prosperity, the intelligence, the jurisprudence, and the happiness of the people." A task too extensive to be achieved by one man — even though that man was endowed with the laboring capacity of Hamilton — was expected to be accomplished by the assistance of others. But the great work was not destined to be so much as entered upon; not long after this conversation Aaron Burr intervened between the able projector and his grand design. It is painful to reflect upon what was thus lost. "I have very little doubt," says the chancellor, "that if General Hamilton had lived twenty years longer he would have rivalled Socrates or Bacon, or any of the sages of ancient or modern times, in researches after truth and in benevolence to mankind. The active and profound statesman, the learned and eloquent lawyer, would probably have disappeared in a great degree before the character of the sage philosopher, instructing mankind by his wisdom and elevating his country by his example."

CHAPTER IX.

THE DUEL.

THE jealousy and enmity which were nourished by Aaron Burr towards Alexander Hamilton were reputed by many persons to date very far back in the lives of the two men. It was said that Burr envied Hamilton the distinction of being appointed upon Washington's staff in the Revolutionary war, deeming that among the younger officers of the army he himself stood forth fully as conspicuous for his merits as did Hamilton. But be this notion true or false, certain it is that in good time Burr had what must have appeared to him ample cause for a vindictive animosity toward Hamilton. He could hardly be expected to recognize the fact that for the existence of this cause he was himself fundamentally responsible. He saw that Hamilton thwarted him in almost every one of his objects of ambition; he was not likely to reflect that Hamilton so thwarted him because of his own vicious character, and that therefore Hamilton was right, and he himself was in real truth the blameworthy party. He was conscious only of that relentless and successful opposition, and he keenly hated the man from whom it proceeded.

Both Hamilton and Washington early entertained an instinctive aversion to Burr. They distrusted him; they thought him not only a bad, but a very dangerous, man. People generally conceived him to be a selfish politician, having no strong principles which he would prefer to his own aggrandizement. But, as is often the case, many who cherished these sentiments concerning him did not dread him; were willing to see him advanced in the State; nay, themselves to aid in advancing him. But not so Hamilton and Washington; they seriously feared his designs, and were gravely alarmed at any increase in his power or prestige. It is hardly worth while now to seek to prove that this opinion concerning Burr was correct. Efforts enough have been made to rescue his memory from infamy, but they have been attended with no success. The death of Hamilton was but one item in the long list of his villanies; nor should the true relation of this incident to his general reputation be misunderstood. There are abundant other counts in the indictment against him; and as regards this particular one it may be said, that it was not because Hamilton fell in the duel that Burr was covered with an obloquy which has seldom pursued other duellists who have slain their antagonists: it was because he, of malice aforethought, forced the duel upon Hamilton, and did all in his power to take from his enemy any option as to the matter of exposing his life. It is not the single fact of Hamilton's death, but the innumerable facts of Burr's life, which inevitably draw after them his utter and irrevocable condemnation.

A study of Burr's character, so far as it can be

learned from any printed records, leads to the conclusion that his cardinal characteristic was an entire absence of the moral sense. He seems to have been born and to have lived without the sense of moral right and wrong, as he might have been born and have lived without the sense of smell or taste. The practices of society he adopted as a code made by mankind, and to be observed by each individual man partly from an inherent necessity of having some established code, partly from compulsion. He came to the game of life as he might have come to a game at cards; the set of rules in the one game he would obey just as he would the set of rules in the other. He would take his enemy's life in a duel for sufficient cause, just as with sufficient cause he would trump his partner's trick at whist. The one expedient was to be resorted to by a wise man, as the other by a good player, only in rare and extreme cases; but in such cases was strictly permissible. He would not poison his adversary as he would not revoke, simply because to do so would draw after it reproach and punishment for a breach of those arbitrary and artificial regulations established to control the conduct of the transaction in which he was engaged. There is nothing in Aaron Burr's public or private life to gainsay the accuracy of this view of his character, or to show that he recognized any higher reason for doing the actions which men had chosen to classify as right, or for avoiding the actions which men had chosen to classify as wrong, than the pure expediency of respecting the doctrines which prevailed in the society in which he moved. To him the classification appeared purely arbitrary and hu-

man, and might have been reversed had society un-
wisely so willed it.

Burr's enmities were always in perfect subjection
to his judgment. He had no overpowering fiery
wrath against Hamilton. It will hardly be questioned that if on the morning of the duel he had seen
it to be for his own advantage that the meeting
should not come off, he would have displayed no less
ingenuity in averting than he had previously shown
in promoting that event. But he was fully satisfied,
and with perfect reason, that Hamilton had not only
been chiefly instrumental in bringing about all his
past failures, but would continue in the same course
with regard to all his future schemes. Hamilton had
prevented him from being sent upon a foreign embassy in Mr. Adams' day. Hamilton had prevented
him from beating Mr. Jefferson in the famous tie-
struggle for the presidency. Never certainly did
man strive harder than did Hamilton upon that occasion, and if Burr wanted to find occasion for a duel
he might have learned of abundant sentences written
and words spoken by Hamilton in those days, which
would have afforded him infinitely better justification
than that with which he was finally satisfied. Had
he been instigated by anger he would have fought
then.

But Burr was not at that time ready to force a
duel upon Hamilton; for he was not at that time
assured in his own mind of the expediency of doing
so. How fully he was aware of the extent of Ham
ilton's exertions against him cannot be known, yet he
was certainly sufficiently aware both of their quantity and their quality to have made use of them

as a ground of quarrel had he seen fit. But he did not then see how fatal was the defeat which he was suffering by reason of this vigorous action of his life-long adversary. He did not care to risk his life when he still thought that he had a political future before him; nor was it until some considerable time had elapsed that he began to appreciate how very dubious that future was. When Jefferson, well seated in the presidential chair, and the monocrat of his party, set in motion the machinery for expelling Burr from the Democratic ranks, then Burr began to see in what an embarrassing position he stood. The chief Democrat cherished a revengeful hatred to him; the second Democrat, Madison, entertained a secret jealousy of him, for Burr obstinately insisted upon standing directly in the road of Madison's ambition. What hope then had Burr of achieving any great success by the aid of this now dominant party? Clearly none. But he had never been a strong partisan, never been regarded or relied upon as such. In whatever ranks he found himself he always kept up a friendly negotiation with all the other factions in the State. He stood among the Democrats, and ceaselessly cast many secret and amiable tokens towards the Federalists. Now that the chiefs of the Democrats sought to discredit him, it would have been an easy matter enough for him to go over to the other camp. But then the other camp was now a beaten minority, and was in tolerable subjection to his arch-enemy, Hamilton. To him contemplating the situation a very cheerless outlook supervened. Other indications were equally discouraging to Burr. In the political struggles in

New York into which he entered he found himself completely beaten by the combined forces acting under the Clintons and Livingstons. In all nominations to office his adherents were uniformly passed over. Even in the Manhattan Bank, for which he had fraudulently secured a charter under pretence of the enactment of a law for the better supplying of pure water to the city of New York, he found his influence on the wane, and he was finally actually ousted.

But he was not the man readily to retire worsted from a contest. His private affairs moreover had come to a desperate pass, and ruin could only be averted by some brilliant stroke of success which should restore his prestige and return to him his scattered followers. Early in 1804 therefore he was again in the field, this time seeking the governorship of New York. The Democratic majority at the last annual election had been so large that the Federalists could have no hope of carrying the State for any candidate of their own. Burr and his partisans therefore resolved that, whoever might be the regular Republican nominee, a "bolt" should be made and Burr should run independently. It was hoped that he might collect enough votes from the two parties to win the day. Nor did the project seem to be altogether devoid of a fair chance for success. Burr was a master of political intrigue; he had a kind of prætorian cohort of clever, active, devoted followers, who sought no other occupation than to do his bidding with equal ability and zeal. The city was the headquarters of his party, where they mustered in the largest numbers and made the most imposing show. Amid the gallant but disreputable band there was many an one who would gladly have perilled his life in the cause of his chieftain; and about this time political duels were of frequent occurrence, the personal adherents of Burr usually being the parties upon whom the moral if not always the technical responsibility lay. They were exciting days. Outside of the city many persons in the interior counties, of high standing and influence in the Republican ranks, declared for Burr.

A meeting of the Burrite members of the legislature was held at the Tontine Coffee-House in Albany, on February 18, 1804, at which he was nominated for governor. The precise number present at this meeting has never been ascertained; probably it was kept secret on purpose, because the attendance was extremely meagre. A caucus of Republican members had already been held and had nominated Chancellor Lansing; on this same February 18, however, he had declined. Two days later another caucus met and nominated Chief Justice Morgan Lewis, a selection which was far from being received with universal favor, and which was therefore favorable to Burr's prospects. Yet one hundred and four members of the legislature signed an address urging the election of Lewis, leaving only twenty-eight members to be divided in a proportion not now accurately known between Burr and the Federal party.

After the nomination of Chancellor Lansing, and before his refusal to stand as a candidate had been received, a meeting of prominent Federalists was held at a tavern in Albany. It was intended that the consultation should be secret; but two of Burr's emissaries found admission into a bed-chamber adjoining the room in which the gentlemen met, and there very coolly listened to all which passed. These eavesdroppers had the pleasure of hearing General Hamilton " address the meeting with his usual eloquence and point out the expediency of the Federal party voting for Chancellor Lansing in case they should have no candidate of their own. The principal part of his speech went to show that no reliance ought to be placed on Mr. Burr." This meeting took place two or three days before Burr was publicly nominated, but the tactics of that gentleman were evidently well known and discussed in advance. Hamilton did not succeed in carrying his point, since the bulk of the Federalist party made up their minds to vote for Burr. But, so nearly as could be estimated after the election, the number of Republicans who abandoned the regular nominee of their party in order to vote for Burr were fully replaced by the number of Federalists who voted for Lewis. The result therefore was that Burr was beaten by an ample majority.

The partisans of Burr among the Federalists sought to encounter Hamilton's opposition by attributing it to a " personal resentment towards Burr." The question is an important one as regards the true relationship between the two men. If Burr could have shown that Hamilton traduced him as a private individual he would have had a much better cause for conducting a personal vendetta against such an enemy than could be furnished by an avowed political opposition. The truth is that there is not a particle of evidence to show the existence of any *personal* feeling whatsoever upon Hamilton's part. All his strictures were directed against Burr as a public man. Burr's

private life offered abundant points of offence which
a virulent adversary might have fastened upon, but
which were never once approached by Hamilton. It
was only when Burr was an aspirant for political
office that Hamilton opposed him, and showed what
traits in his character seemed to justify opposition.
Of course such opposition could not always be openly
made in speeches at public meetings; it had often to
be expressed in conversation, in correspondence: but
it was never concealed, never cloaked beneath dissim-
ulation. Burr always knew, the public always knew,
precisely where Hamilton stood on all such occasions.
His sentiments were no secret. But towards Burr as
a man he often said that he had no enmity. He did
not praise him, but neither did he censure; he held
his peace, and remained on terms of civility and courtesy. Nay, it would seem that Burr used him and
Hamilton allowed himself to be used as a very active
friend. It was not long before the duel took place
that Burr appeared at Hamilton's country-house at a
singularly early hour in the morning, much agitated,
apparently almost ready in his despair to take his own
life. His errand actually was to beg Hamilton to aid
him in obtaining immediately a sum of ready money.
Hamilton, much concerned, bestirred himself energet-
ically among his friends and raised the amount, — no
less than ten thousand dollars, — which he at once
made over to the embarrassed and deeply indebted
politician. The tale has been doubted by certain of
Burr's defenders, but there seems to be abundant
proof of its perfect truth.

Yet in spite of the preservation of an external
appearance of amity, and even of such substantial

passages of friendship as the foregoing, Hamilton was
not without a shrewd appreciation of the true state
of Burr's feeling towards him. Knowing well how
often and how stubbornly he had stood in Burr's way,
and how unscrupulous that gentleman always was in
removing an obstacle, Hamilton recognized his danger, and once at least expressed a presentiment that
he might not improbably in time encounter death in
the course of this opposition.

At the time of this attempt upon Burr's part to
snatch the governorship from the dominant party,
there were more than usually strong reasons for opposing him. The course of Jefferson and his Republican coterie at the national capital had been viewed
with alarm and distrust at the East and North. With
much thoroughness and assiduity these skilful politicians had been shaping and training the southern
States into a powerful and consolidated party feder-
ation; and, what with admirable leadership and a
singular unanimity of feeling throughout that region,
it seemed but too likely that a permanent domination
of the middle and southern section might be achieved
over the northern and eastern parts of the Union. The
acquisition of Louisiana was considered as putting
this result almost beyond a doubt. Then the malcontents began to talk about a severance of the Union,
and to mutter among themselves that a northern empire must be cut off and established. It was feared
that these elements of secession would crystallize
around Burr as their chief, and that his governorship
of the State would expand into his presidency over
a new nation. I confess that I think the danger of
this result was much overrated. Many individuals
not devoid of note and influence had begun to talk

and write privately in this manner, and upon rare occasions the like sentiments found expression in the newspapers. But a great deal of smoke of this kind precedes the actual outburst of flames, nor were the symptoms as yet sufficient to show that the flames were near at hand. Hamilton, however, was gravely disturbed and anxious. Persons who had such designs naturally strove to sound him. As a great party leader, of signal ability and extensive influence, in a premature retirement from public life, his opinion and probable course in such a juncture were matters of great consequence. Thus it naturally happened that he had the subject brought so frequently and prominently before his eyes that it may have assumed an undue magnitude. But be this as it may — and it is impossible to obtain accurate knowledge in the matter — it is certain that Hamilton was seriously concerned at the spirit which he saw working around him. So often as opportunity offered he expressed his positive and vehement reprobation of all such projects. In the conference of the Federalists already alluded to, in urging the party to vote for Lansing rather than for Burr, he openly based his exhortations upon this ground. " Certain causes," said he, " are leading to an opinion that a dismemberment of the Union is expedient. It would probably suit Mr. Burr's views to promote this result, to be the chief of the northern portion ; and placed at the head of the State of New York no man would be more likely to succeed." Often did Hamilton at this period express his deep and stanch feeling in favor of preserving the menaced integrity of the Union. His heart was in it, as he frankly avowed ; and it was because he believed that Burr's heart was set upon the contrary project that he was so uncompromisingly opposed to Burr's success.

On April 12, 1804, Dr. Cooper wrote an electioneering letter from Albany, in which was this sentence: "General Hamilton, the patroon's brother-in-law, it is said, has come out decidedly against Burr. Indeed, when he was here he spoke of him as a dangerous man, and who ought not to be trusted." General Schuyler on seeing this at once wrote, in correction: "I think it proper to mention that, while Chancellor Lansing was considered a candidate, General Hamilton was in favor of supporting him; but that, after the nomination of Chief Justice Lewis, he declared to me that he would not interfere." Dr. Cooper reiterated his previous assertion, and farther said: "I could detail to you a still more despicable opinion which General Hamilton has expressed of Mr. Burr." Within a few days this correspondence was published in the newspapers at Albany.

Nearly two months later, when the election was over and Burr defeated, Hamilton received the following letter: —

NEW YORK, June 18, 1804.

SIR, — I send for your perusal a letter signed Charles D. Cooper, which, though apparently published some time ago, has but very recently come to my knowledge. Mr. Van Ness, who does me the favor to deliver this, will point out to you that clause of the letter to which I particularly request your attention.

You must perceive, sir, the necessity of a prompt, unqualified acknowledgment or denial of the use of an expression which would warrant the assertions of Dr. Cooper.

I have the honor to be your obedient servant,

A. BURR.

GENERAL HAMILTON.

Hamilton, after consultation with one of his friends, returned the following answer : —

New York, June 20, 1804.

Sir, — I have maturely reflected on the subject of your letter of the eighteenth inst., and the more I have reflected the more I have become convinced that I could not, without manifest impropriety, make the avowal or disavowal which you seem to think necessary. The clause pointed out by Mr. Van Ness is in these terms : " I could detail to you a still more despicable opinion which General Hamilton has expressed of Mr. Burr." To endeavor to discover the meaning of this declaration I was obliged to seek in the antecedent part of this letter for the opinion to which it referred, as having been already disclosed. I found it in these words : " General Hamilton and Judge Kent have declared in substance that they looked upon Mr. Burr to be a dangerous man, and one who ought not to be trusted with the reins of government."

The language of Dr. Cooper plainly implies that he considered this opinion of you, which he attributes to me, as a despicable one ; but he affirms that I have expressed some other more despicable, without mentioning to whom, when, or where. 'Tis evident that the phrase " still more despicable " admits of infinite shades, from very light to very dark. How am I to judge of the degree intended, or how shall I annex any precise idea to language so indefinite ?

Between gentlemen, " despicable " and " more despicable " are not worth the pains of distinction ; when therefore you do not interrogate me as to the opinion which is specifically ascribed to me, I must conclude that you view it as within the limits to which the animadversions of political opponents upon each other may justifiably extend ; and consequently as not warranting the idea of it which Dr. Cooper appears to entertain. If so, what precise inference could you draw as a guide for your conduct, were I to acknowledge that I had expressed an opinion of you " still more despicable " than the one which is particularized ? How could you be sure that even this opinion had exceeded the bounds which you yourself deem admissible between political opponents ?

But I forbear farther. comment on the embarrassment to which the requisition you have made naturally leads. The occasion forbids a more ample illustration, though nothing could be more easy than to pursue it.

Repeating that I cannot reconcile it with propriety to make the acknowledgment or denial you desire, I will add that I deem it inadmissible, on principle, to consent to be interrogated as to the justness of the inferences which may be drawn by others from whatever I may have said of a political opponent in the course of fifteen years' competition. If there were no other objection to it this is sufficient, that it would tend to expose my sincerity and delicacy to injurious imputations from every person who may at any time have conceived the import of my expressions differently from what I may then have intended or may afterwards recollect. I stand ready to avow or disavow promptly and explicitly any precise or definite opinion which I may be charged with having declared of any gentleman. More than this cannot fitly be expected from me; and especially it cannot be reasonably expected that I shall enter into an explanation upon a basis so vague as that which you have adopted. I trust, on more reflection, you will see the matter in the same light with me. If not, I can only regret the circumstance, and must abide the consequences.

The publication of Dr. Cooper was never seen by me till after the receipt of the letter.

I have the honor to be, &c.,

A. Hamilton.

Colonel Burr.

The course pursued in this letter was by no means satisfactory to the person to whom it was addressed. An argument might too clearly have shown Burr to be in the wrong. He accordingly declined to be led into discussion, and contented himself with a brief and peremptory reply, as follows:—

New York, June 21, 1804.

Sir,— Your letter of the 20th inst. has been this day received. Having considered it attentively, I regret to find in it nothing of that sincerity and delicacy which you profess to value.

Political opposition can never absolve gentlemen from the

necessity of a rigid adherence to the laws of honor and the rules of decorum. I neither claim such privilege nor indulge it in others.

The common sense of mankind affixes to the epithet adopted by Dr. Cooper the idea of dishonor. It has been publicly applied to me under the sanction of your name. The question is not whether he has understood the meaning of the word, or has used it according to syntax and with grammatical accuracy, but whether you have authorized this application, either directly or by uttering expressions derogatory to my honor. The time "when" is in your own knowledge, but no way material to me, as the calumny has now first been disclosed so as to become the subject of my notice, and as the effect is present and palpable.

Your letter has furnished me with new reasons for requiring a definite reply.

I have the honor to be, sir, your obedient servant,

A. BURR.

GENERAL HAMILTON.

This truculent missive was brought to Hamilton by Mr. William P. Van Ness, a gentleman who assisted Burr in the composition of his letters, and in many other ways shared the guilt of his principal throughout this transaction. To him Hamilton said that the letter was so rude and offensive that he could give no other answer to it save to say that Colonel Burr must take such steps as he might think proper. Van Ness hypocritically begged him to take time to consider, and offered to call for an answer later. Hamilton then visited his friend, Colonel Pendleton, narrated the course of events up to this point, and left with him a letter for Van Ness. The next day was Sunday, and Hamilton, passing it at his country-seat, received this note : —

JUNE 23, 1804.

SIR, — In the afternoon of yesterday I reported to Colonel Burr the result of my last interview with you, and appointed the evening to receive his farther instructions. Some private engagements, however, prevented me from calling on him till this morning. On my return to the city I found upon inquiry, both at your office and house, that you had returned to your residence in the country.

Lest an interview there might be less agreeable to you than elsewhere, I have taken the liberty of addressing you this note to inquire when and where it will be most convenient to you to receive a communication.

Your most obedient and very humble servant,

W. P. Van Ness.

General Hamilton.

He replied that if the communication was pressing he would receive it that day at " The Grange," otherwise he would receive it on Monday, at his house in the city.

Interviews meantime were held between Pendleton and Van Ness, in which the former said that if Burr would write a letter requesting to know whether in the conversation alluded to by Dr. Cooper any particular instance of dishonorable conduct had been imputed to him, or any impeachment of his private character had been made, General Hamilton would in return declare to the best of his recollection what had been said on that occasion. He farther stated what Hamilton's recollection was. He then handed to Van Ness this letter: —

New York, June 22, 1804.

Sir, — Your first letter, in a style too peremptory, made a demand in my opinion unprecedented and unwarrantable. My answer pointed out the embarrassment and gave you an opportunity to take a less exceptional course. You have not chosen to do it ; but by your last letter received this day, containing expressions indecorous and improper, you have increased the difficulties to explanation intrinsically incident to the nature of your application.

If by a "definite reply" you mean the direct avowal or disavowal required in your first letter, I have no other answer to give than that which has already been given. If you mean any thing different, admitting of greater latitude, it is requisite you should explain.

I have the honor to be, sir, your obedient servant,

ALEX. HAMILTON.

AARON BURR, ESQ.

Afterward Pendleton put in writing that, in reply to a letter "properly adapted to obtain" such information, Hamilton "would be able to answer consistently with his honor and the truth, in substance, that the conversation to which Dr. Cooper alluded turned wholly on political topics, and did not attribute to Colonel Burr any instance of dishonorable conduct, nor relate to his private character; and in relation to any other language or conversation of General Hamilton which Colonel Burr will specify, a prompt and frank avowal or denial will be given."

On the day following, Van Ness wrote to Colonel Pendleton asserting that Hamilton evinced no disposition to come to a satisfactory accommodation; that Burr had been sufficiently explicit, and could not confine his inquiry to particular times and places; that no denial or declaration would be satisfactory unless it should be "general, so as wholly to exclude the idea that rumors derogatory to Colonel Burr's honor have originated with General Hamilton, or have been fairly inferred from any thing he said." Colonel Pendleton replied that Hamilton could not possibly submit to "an inquisition into his most confidential conversations, as well as others, through the whole period of his acquaintance with Colonel Burr;" that he disavowed "an unwillingness to come to a satisfactory, provided it be an honorable, accommodation;" and that his difficulty lay in "the very indefinite ground which Colonel Burr had assumed, in which he was sorry to be able to discern nothing short of premeditated hostility." Van Ness replied at length, concluding with the statement that Burr felt "as a gentleman should feel when his honor is impeached or assailed," and was "determined to vindicate that honor at such hazard as the nature of the case demands." A formal challenge accompanied this reply.

Never surely was any person more artfully drawn against his will into a mortal contest than was Hamilton drawn into this one. With so much as he had to live for, — purposes of affection and of usefulness, noble objects of public ambition and private ends not less worthy, — he could not walk lightly and carelessly to encounter death in the very prime of his years, and with the prospect of so many grand achievements left yet to be performed by him. The elaborate correspondence shows how firmly he was resolved not to meet his adversary half way, not to quarrel unless the quarrel was absolutely forced upon him. His reputation was such that he was raised far above any considerations of alarm for his name as a man of courage. His bravery had been too often proved and was too well known to be questioned because he did not choose to rush into a needless fight with the recklessness which may be forgiven in a youngster, but in a mature man is simply revolting. Matters, however, had now reached such a pass that he felt that he could not refuse the challenge which had been sent without imperilling his usefulness. In the condition of public opinion at that time he would have been generally regarded as disgraced by such a course. He felt that this must be conclusive in the matter. He made one more declaration of his position, because it appeared to him " necessary not to be misunderstood," and directed his friend Pendleton to make the proper arrangements in his behalf.

" I should not think it right," he said, " in the midst of a circuit court to withdraw my services from those who may have confided important interests to me, and expose them to the embarrassment of seeking other counsel, who may not have time to be sufficiently instructed in their cases. I shall also want a little time to make some arrangements respecting my own affairs." It was accordingly agreed to await the close of the term of court, then distant a few days. During the interval the secret was well kept by the few who had become acquainted with it. Hamilton devoted himself assiduously to the causes of his clients ; Burr devoted himself with equal assiduity to practice with a pistol. He had not previously been skilful with this weapon, but he now set up a target in his garden and exercised himself for many hours daily. While matters stood thus, the anniversary dinner of the " Cincinnati " took place on July 4. Hamilton, who had been chosen to the distinguished position of president-general of the society, was obliged to preside. He exerted himself to appear even more than usually cheerful ; yet gentlemen thought afterwards that they had noticed an unwonted shade of tenderness in his manner toward the friends around him. He was urged to sing, and when the company would take no refusal he gave them the ballad of

" The Drum." Burr sat at his left hand, and was observed to be silent and gloomy, gazing with marked and fixed earnestness at Hamilton during this song.

The shadow of his fate had evidently fallen across Hamilton's soul. His gayety at the banquet was the result of his strong resolution not to cause remark by any unusual manner; his conspicuous position at the head of the feast rendered such conduct imperative. But at home and about his affairs a thousand little marks of peculiar affection were noticed. Colonel Smith, son-in-law of President Adams, who knew the dread secret, visited Hamilton during the period of suspense at " The Grange." After dinner Hamilton turned to him, and with deep feeling and a significant air, referring to the threats of secession then so rife in the eastern States, said : " You are going to Boston. You will see the principal men there. Tell them from *me*, as *my request*, for God's sake to cease these conversations and threatenings about a separation of the Union. It must hang together as long as it can be made to."

It was the melancholy foreboding of the result of the meeting which led Hamilton to prepare the following paper, in explanation and vindication of his course : —

On my expected interview with Colonel Burr I think it proper to make some remarks, explanatory of my conduct, motives, and views.

I was certainly desirous of avoiding this interview for the most cogent reasons : —

1. My religious and moral principles are strongly opposed to the practice of duelling, and it would ever give me pain to be obliged to shed the blood of a fellow-creature in a private combat forbidden by the laws.

2. My wife and children are extremely dear to me, and my life is of the utmost importance to them in various views.

3. I feel a sense of obligation towards my creditors, who, in case of accident to me, by the forced sale of my property may be in some degree sufferers. I do not think myself at liberty, as a man of probity, lightly to expose them to this hazard.

4. I am conscious of no ill-will to Colonel Burr, distinct from political opposition, which as I trust has proceeded from pure and upright motives.

Lastly, I shall hazard much and can possibly gain nothing by the issue of the interview.

But it was, as I conceive, impossible for me to avoid it. There were intrinsic difficulties in the thing, and artificial embarrassments from the manner of proceeding on the part of Colonel Burr.

Intrinsic, because it is not to be denied that my animadversions on the political principles, character, and views of Colonel Burr have been extremely severe ; and on different occasions I, in common with many others, have made very unfavorable criticisms on particular instances of the private conduct of this gentleman.

In proportion as these impressions were entertained with sincerity, and uttered with motives and for purposes which might appear to me commendable, would be . the difficulty (until they could be removed by evidence of their being erroneous) of explanation or apology. The disavowal required of me by Colonel Burr, in a general and indefinite form, was out of my power, if it had really been proper for me to submit to be so questioned ; but I was sincerely of opinion that this could not be, and in this opinion I was confirmed by that of a very moderate and judicious friend whom I consulted. Besides that, Colonel Burr appeared to me to assume, in the first instance, a tone unnecessarily peremptory and menacing, and in the second positively offensive. Yet I wished, as far as might be practicable, to leave a door open to accommodation. This, I think, will be inferred from the written communications made by me and by my directions, and would be confirmed by the conversations between Mr. Van Ness and myself, which arose out of the subject.

I am not sure whether, under all circumstances, I did not go farther in the attempt to accommodate than a punctilious delicacy will justify. If so, I hope the motives I have stated will excuse me.

It is not my design by what I have said to affix any odium on the conduct of Colonel Burr in this case. He doubtless has heard of animadversions of mine which bore very hard upon him, and it is probable that, as usual, they were accompanied with some falsehoods. He may have supposed himself under a necessity of acting as he has done. I hope the grounds of his proceeding have been such as ought to satisfy his own conscience.

I trust, at the same time, that the world will do me the justice to believe that I have not censured him on light grounds, nor from unworthy inducements. I certainly have had strong reasons for what I may have said, though it is possible that in some particulars I may have been influenced by misconstruction or misinformation. It is also my ardent wish that I may have been more mistaken than I think I have been, and that he by his future conduct may show himself worthy of all confidence and esteem, and prove an ornament and blessing to the country. As well because it is possible that I may have injured Colonel Burr — however convinced myself that my opinions and declarations have been well founded — as from my general principles and temper in relation to similar affairs, I have resolved, if our interview is conducted in the usual manner, and it pleases God to give me the opportunity, to reserve and throw away my first fire ; and I have thoughts even of reserving my second fire, and thus giving a double opportunity to Colonel Burr to pause and to reflect. It is not, however, my intention to enter into any explanations on the ground. Apology — from principle, I hope. rather than pride — is out of the question.

To those who, with me abhorring the practice of duelling, may think that I ought on no account to have added to the number of bad examples, I answer that my relative situation, as well in public as private, enforcing all the considerations which constitute what men of the world denominate honor, imposed on me, as I thought, a peculiar necessity not to decline the call. The ability to be in future useful, whether in resisting mischief or effecting good in those crises of our public affairs which seem likely to happen, would probably be inseparable from a conformity with public prejudice in this particular. A. H.

What a sad picture do these lines portray of a man endowed with so noble a spirit, so brilliant an intellect, feeling that, unless he should stand up and permit his enemy to shoot at him, the prejudices of the world would deprive him of all power for future usefulness! This was simply the true state of the case; for Hamilton declares his resolve not to fire at Burr, at least in the earlier stage of the duel. Should his adversary prove vindictive it must be supposed that he would in time, after an exchange of one or more shots, have felt justified in firing in self-defence. But at first he had fully determined not to do so, and he further communicated this intention to his second. He had no desire to wound or slay his antagonist. He had no quarrel with Burr, and could gain neither satisfaction nor advantage by injuring him. But out of deference to a·brutal rule of society he must expose himself unflinchingly to the deliberate fire of Burr's pistol! He must offer his life without the possibility of any even inadequate compensation for the sacrifice, because if he did not offer it he—a public man—would suffer fatally in public estimation!

As the hour approached he set his papers and affairs in such order as he could, and wrote his will. "Should it happen," said he, "that there is not enough for the payment of my debts, I entreat my dear children, if they or any of them should ever be able, to make up the deficiency. I without hesitation commit to their delicacy a wish which is dictated by my own. Though conscious that I have too far sacrificed the interests of my family to public avocations, and on this account have less claim to burden my children, yet I trust in their magnanimity to appreciate as they ought this my request." Had he taken such fees as most professional men around him were taking, these adjurations would have been needless. Some very tender words followed concerning his wife. He wrote her a letter of farewell; and, as if he could not bear to feel that the last word had been uttered, he soon afterward wrote another. The pathos, tenderness, affection, of these notes is indescribably touching. I confess that I do not like to copy these sacred words of parting, which seem to belong only to those two, — to him who wrote them, and her to whom they were addressed. Burr at the same time, a notorious libertine, was writing his farewell letter to Theodosia, begging her to be sure to burn all those letters from his female correspondents, which, if found, might do them injury.

The morning of July 11, 1804, dawned warm and bright. The place selected for the scene of the encounter was a little secluded ledge nestled beneath the heights of Weehawken, and not far above the level of the Hudson. It was the favorite spot for duels in those days, the same spot where Philip Hamilton had fallen about three years before. The parties came up the stream by boat from New York. Burr and his friends arrived first, by special arrangement made in order to avoid observation and interference. When Hamilton came he found Burr and Van Ness breaking the twigs and clearing the ground. None but the two principals and two seconds were present; the doctor and one or two other friends being kept at a little distance and out of sight, in order that they might not be eye-witnesses in the event of any legal proceedings supervening. The two combatants were then placed. Hamilton's second obtained by lot the choice of position, which advantage however he appears to have used with very little discretion. He not only placed Hamilton at the end of the ground least favorable in respect of light, but also where an abutting rock left a space not more than four and one-half feet wide for him to stand in, thus aiding the accuracy of Burr's aim.

Pendleton handed Hamilton his pistol, asking him whether he would have the hair-spring set. "Not this time," replied he, with a very quiet manner. "Are you ready?" said Pendleton to them. They replied that they were. Then, in a moment, he gave the word agreed upon: "Present!" Burr paused an instant to take a deliberate aim, and fired. Hamilton convulsively raised himself upon his toes, and fell forward upon his face; his pistol going off as he did so, and sending the ball whizzing high through the foliage of the surrounding trees.

At the noise of the pistol the doctor and two others hurried to the spot. Van Ness hastily opened an umbrella to cover Burr from their sight, and these two hurried to their boat. Col. Pendleton and Dr. Hosack raised Hamilton into a sitting posture; he had been struck in the right side. In feeble tones he could just articulate, " This is a mortal wound;" and then fell into a swoon. The doctor saw at once that these words were too true; he did not even expect that the victim would rally from his present collapse. But as they bore him tenderly to the river bank he opened his wandering eyes and said, " My vision is indistinct." A moment afterward he caught sight of the case of pistols; the one he had used was lying on the outside of the box. "Take care of that pistol," he said, "it is undischarged and still cocked; it may go off and do harm. Pendleton knows"— and he strove to turn his head toward his second, "that I did not intend to fire at him." He then bade them send for his wife. "Let the event," said he, "be gradually broken to her; but give her hopes."

To sketch the scene of that death-bed would be needlessly painful. Hamilton's sufferings were intense, nor could any anodynes serve to remove them. His wife and children were beside his couch. The agony he bore heroically, but the sight of those so dear to him was almost too much for endurance. Again and again he sought consolation both for his wife and himself in their religious belief. He was a sincere and earnest Christian. He had lately said of Christianity, in his firm, positive way: "I have studied it, and I can prove its truth as clearly as any proposition ever submitted to the mind of man." His thoughts and interests, amid all the exciting whirl of public and private affairs, had been often and fervently turned in this direction of late years. He now requested to have the communion administered to him. There was some difficulty apparently by reason of his never yet having been formally admitted to the church; but this obstacle was finally overcome, and greatly to his comfort he received the sacrament. He declared with the "utmost sincerity of heart" that he had "no ill-will against Colonel Burr." "I met him," he said, "with a fixed resolution to do him no harm. I forgive all that happened."

During the rest of that day and the night which followed Hamilton lingered in much suffering. The next day his pain abated, but he became gradually weaker, and died at two o'clock in the afternoon.

Though Hamilton was but a private gentleman when he died, and had expressed an intention of remaining so for the rest of his life, except only in the contingencies of foreign or civil war, yet the general outburst of grief was such as is seldom seen. It is rarely that the death of a great statesman seems to throw a nation into mourning, to destroy for the moment party lines, and to evoke the sorrow of political opponents as well as political friends. Something of this sort was seen by the present generation, when the death of President Lincoln struck horror to the hearts of all alike. Such also was the aspect of the country when Hamilton fell. Rancorous individuals enough there were among the Democrats to rejoice; but the mass of the people, whether Federal or Democratic in their predilections, grieved sincerely. The confidence which had been felt in him could be measured by the sense now manifested of the greatness of the loss; and it was obvious that multitudes who had opposed him in politics had, nevertheless, entertained a lurking feeling that in him, so long as he lived, the country had a powerful resource. It was the noblest possible tribute that could be paid to him, — this spectacle, not of his party, but of his countrymen in tears. While life yet lingered his fellow-citizens of New York crowded around the bulletin boards which announced from hour to hour his changing condition, and mingled rage and execrations with their grief and sobs. The city was not a safe place for Burr; he fled for his life, and his terrified myrmidons hastened to avail themselves of the protection of obscurity. `Never again could that blood-stained man redcem his blasted reputation bef)re mankind : so infinitely more fatal was that duel to the survivor than to the victim!

INDEX.